6D-2^{qo}

MIDNIGHT SUN

TOR BOOKS BY RAMSEY CAMPBELL

Ancient Images
Cold Print
Dark Companions
The Doll Who Ate His Mother
The Face that Must Die
Fine Frights (editor)
The Hungry Moon
Incarnate
The Influence
Midnight Sun
The Nameless
Obsession
The Parasite

RAMSEY CAMPBELL

MIDNIG

HT SUN

0204491264

TOR®

A TOM DOHERTY ASSOCIATES BOOK
NEW YORK

MIDNIGHT SUN

Copyright © 1991 by Ramsey Campbell

A Tor Book
Published by Tom Doherty Associates, Inc.
49 West 24th Street
New York, NY 10010

Book design by Judith Stagnitto

Library of Congress Cataloging-in-Publication Data

Campbell, Ramsey
    Midnight sun / Ramsey Campbell.
        p.   cm.
    "A Tom Doherty Associates Book."
    ISBN 0-312-85051-4
    I. Title.
    PR6053.A4855M5   1991
    823'.914—dc20   90-48784
                                                                  CIP

Printed in the United States of America
First edition: February 1991
0 9 8 7 6 5 4 3 2 1

For Chris and Lis, with love:
something to read by the fire

ACKNOWLEDGMENTS

As always I'm grateful to my wife Jenny (my first editor). This time I must also thank our children Tammy and Matty for appearing under assumed names in the book. I'm especially grateful to those writers who are keeping the tradition of visionary horror fiction alive—among them M. John Harrison, T.E.D. Klein, Fritz Leiber—and to the good folk of the Arthur Machen Society for the same reason. I mustn't forget my friends in publishing who saw the book into print: Peter Lavery, John Jarrold, Tom Doherty, Harriet McDougal, Julia Bunton, Anna Magee . . . and I've a special thank-you to Karl Edward Wagner for lending me the title.

CONTENTS

THE SEEDS

ONE

He was almost home before they noticed him, and by then he had crossed half of England. As the June day lumbered onwards, the railway carriages grew hotter and smokier and, like the stations where he had to change trains, more crowded. On the train out of Norwich he had to convince a motherly woman whose lap was hidden by a mewing wicker basket that he was being met at Peterborough. Having to wait for trains was the worst part; at Peterborough, and at Leeds almost five hours later, the stations were caves full of giants, any of whom might seize him. But once he was on the train out of Leeds to Stargrave, he thought he was safe. It never occurred to him that the closer he came to home, the more likely it was that someone would recognize him.

His breaths tasted of the musty carriage, his heart sounded loud as the train. He wished he could have bought something to eat, but the fare from Norwich had left him only a few pennies of his savings. He swallowed dryly and breathed hard until he no longer felt threatened by the early summer mugginess and the rocking of the train as it raced through the suburbs towards the Yorkshire moors. Each time it stopped, the bleak slopes beyond the houses seemed closer and steeper. Fewer people boarded at the stops than left the train, and by the time it reached the open moorland he had the carriage to himself.

The sky grew paler as the train climbed towards it. Slopes sleek with grass or bristling with gorse and heather bared limestone ridges above the track. Spiky drystone walls which put him in mind of the spines of dinosaurs separated fields crumbed with sheep. He felt as if the familiar landscape were welcoming him. That, and the exhaustion of so much travelling, allowed him to drowse, to forget why he was coming home.

When the train pulled into the small bare station before Stargrave, he blinked his eyes open. A headscarved woman in an unseasonable purplish overcoat, using a wheeled basket to nudge one child ahead of her while she dragged his twin brothers behind her, flustered onto the platform as the train gasped to a halt, and launched herself and her burdens towards the nearest door. Ben saw her face, which lit up red as she puffed on the perilously short cigarette stuck in the corner of her mouth, and he shrank back out of sight. She was a cleaner at the Stargrave school.

Perhaps she hadn't seen him. He slid down the seat as the last door of the carriage slammed open behind him. The three boys charged up the aisle, the twins pummelling and shoving each other while their little brother wailed at them to wait for him, and their mother seemed too busy following them to spare the solitary traveller more than a glance. "Stop that or I'll give you such a thump. Sit down on them seats, right there," she cried, and dumped herself across the aisle from Ben. "Here, I want you here."

She stubbed out her cigarette and immediately lit another as the train moved off. The gritstone houses of the village gave way to lonely slopes scattered with stones like eroded buildings, and Ben turned as much of himself as he could towards the window. He was afraid not just of being recognized but of losing control of the emotions he'd been choking down all day, saving them for when he reached his destination. "Sit still when you're told," the woman cried, and then he felt her lean across the aisle to peer at him. "On your own, love, are you?" she said.

He tried to pretend he hadn't heard her, but he couldn't help

2

turning further towards the window. "I'm talking to you, love," she said, raising her voice. "I know you, don't I? You shouldn't be out on your own."

The twins were whispering together. "Is it him?" one said.

"It's him, Mam, isn't it? The boy whose mam and dad and everyone got killed on the moors?"

Ben squeezed his eyes shut to keep his feelings down, and then she lowered herself beside him on the seat. "All right, son, no need to be frit," she murmured, so close that he felt the heat of her cigarette on his cheek. "I know you're the Sterling boy. Where are you coming from? They're wicked, them, whoever's meant to be looking after you, letting an eight-year-old wander about by himself."

The idea that he might get his aunt into trouble dismayed him. She was doing her best for him as she saw it. He sucked his lower lip between his teeth with a sound that made the twins giggle, and chewed the flesh inside it to quieten himself. "Don't mind us, Ben," the woman said. "You have a cry. You'll do yourself no good keeping that to yourself."

His eyelids couldn't squeeze any harder, and so he opened them. His surroundings were blurred, as if the storm of tears he was struggling to control was already falling. He felt as if she were stealing his grief and putting it on show. He wanted to lash out at her pudgy face that looked heavy with concern for him, at her nostrils where snot peeked out and withdrew every time she breathed, at her mottled double chin whose dividing crevice sprouted a wiry reddish hair. "You stay with us now," she said, "and we'll find someone to take care of you, poor lamb."

He might have told her he was travelling beyond Stargrave, but she never took much notice of anything children said. All he could do, he thought with a clarity which made him feel cold and hollow, was open the door and jump. At least then he should be with his family. His hand crept behind him and found the handle, and he felt the door shake. He had only to lean on the handle and fall backwards out of the train. He'd close his eyes when the door gave way. The rocking of the carriage threw his weight onto the handle, and he felt it turn downwards—and then the door rattled in its frame, and she grabbed his arm and hauled him along the seat. "Never play with train doors, son. You boys are all the same."

Even more than her interference, her classing him with her children made him want to weep with rage. He'd throw himself at the door as soon as she let go of him, he'd show her that she hadn't summed him up—but the delay had let him realize how falling from the train would feel, and he hadn't the courage. He was scarcely aware of her children except as a scabby sullen restlessness on the seat opposite, until she gripped his arm harder and flurried her free hand at them. "Don't go rummaging. We'll be getting off in a minute."

One of the twins was rooting in the basket, and her voice sent him digging deeper. "I want my sweets."

The youngest started wailing. "Not fair. They always have the green ones."

"Leave it," she yelled, and let go of Ben's arm. Potatoes spilled out of the basket as the youngest boy snatched the bag of sweets and pranced away with it. The train was slowing as it crossed the bridge over the road on the outskirts of Stargrave, and Sterling Forest came into view, a shadowy mass of green and silver above the terraced streets of gritstone cottages and houses the color of old parchment. The youngest boy had jumped on a seat at the end of the carriage and was brandishing the sweets above his head, and then the twins grabbed the bag so hard that it burst. The woman gathered up the potatoes and lurched along the aisle, shaking a finger like a yellowed sausage at Ben. "Don't you dare move."

He'd never disobeyed a grownup. He'd sneaked away from his aunt's house before dawn, leaving her a note which told her not to worry about him, and as he'd inched the front door open he had been terrified that she would waken and call him back. Now he felt crushed by dutifulness. The twins were laughing at the youngest, who was still clutching the torn neck of the bag, until he kicked one of them on the shin and poked the other in the eye. "Stop that before someone gets hurt," their mother screamed, flailing her arms at whomever she might strike. "None of you's having any sweets now, nor chocolates neither, and no chips. And I won't be buying you them toys I promised, and them new shoes can go back to the market . . ."

Suddenly Ben was filled with contempt for her, so intense that it frightened him. The train had reached the station. He lunged at the door and shoved the handle down. The door swung open, stone bruised his heels, and he was running faster than the train towards the end of the platform.

The slow old stationmaster, whose handlebar moustache was the colors of pipe smoke and nicotine, came out of the office to meet him. He glanced at Ben's ticket, and then past him so sharply that Ben had to look. The purplish woman was heaving at a window with one hand and laboring to open the door with the other, and shouting to the stationmaster to keep Ben there. Ben thought the whole of Stargrave must be able to hear, muffled though her voice was. "You'll have to wait," the stationmaster said.

He was between Ben and the passage out of the station. Ben's chest was aching with holding his breath by the time he realized that the stationmaster meant the woman. "You'd think she'd know how to open a door by now," the stationmaster said, and winked at Ben as he took the ticket from him.

Ben hurried out of the passage, hunching his shoulders for fear of a shout behind him. The bell of a shop door rang somewhere on his left, towards the bridge. To his right, in the square, market stalls were being dismantled, their skeletons clanging on the cobbles. Ahead of him the narrow side streets wandered towards the forest as if they were too tired to climb straight. When he heard the door of the railway carriage slam open and the woman yelling at her children to shut up, he dashed across Market Street, dodging a spillage of oil beside the deserted taxi stand, and up an alley between the backs of two side streets.

He didn't slow down until the station was out of sight, and then he trotted uphill between the high rough walls of backyards. Someone was hammering and being told "Mind the paintwork," someone was repeating a name to a squawking bird. A sports commentator was chattering so excitedly that the radio lost its grip on his voice, while in an upstairs bedroom a woman was saying "See if her old dress fits you."

5

Hearing the town around him and unaware of him made Ben feel as if he were on a secret mission—a mission which, as he approached his destination, was beginning to seem less than entirely clear to him.

A lorry chugged around The Crescent towards the builder's yard. Once it had passed the mouth of the alley, Ben sprinted across the road into the next stretch, which was steeper. A dried trickle of earth dislodged by rain snaked over the plump uneven flagstones. Two twists of the alley brought him in sight of Church Road, and he seemed to feel his heart shiver. He tiptoed quickly to the end of the alley and peered hard at both downhill curves of the road until he was convinced that there was nobody to stop him, and dashed across to the churchyard gate. He lifted the latch and opened the iron gate just wide enough to let himself slip through, and made himself take his time about closing it so that it wouldn't squeal again. "I'm visiting," he said, and then he had to turn and show his face.

Nobody was behind him after all. A few small marble angels perched on headstones, gazing at the sky. St. Christopher towered in the window beside the church porch, securing a boy on his shoulder with one massive stained-glass arm and holding hands with a little girl, a scene which looked as if it had been assembled from fragments of a dozen skies and sunsets. Ben glanced about the grid of paths which led away from the church, and picked his way through the graves to the white marble obelisk.

It was among the older graves, between a cracked stone urn and a dried-up blackened wreath. It stood almost as tall as the infrequent trees which made the graveyard seem a borderland between Sterling Forest and the town. The marble was so bright with sunshine that Ben had to narrow his eyes. As he read the inscriptions, interweaving his fingers in front of him, the miles of forest above the common beyond the hedge felt like a shadow encroaching on his vision. His father's and grandparents' names were carved on the shaft now, above the name of Edward Sterling and his dates from the previous century. Only Ben's mother was missing, because his aunt had had her sister buried in the family grave in Norwich.

He stared at the names as if they might tell him why he was here. After travelling so far, he felt as if he hadn't gone far enough. He gripped his fingers with his fingers until the flesh between them ached, as if the ache were a wordless prayer that might bring him guidance. At last he had to desist, and the pain faded slowly, leaving him feeling hollow and bereaved, unable to think of anything to do except gaze at his breath, which was misting the air in front of him.

He had been staring at it for some time before it occurred to him to wonder how his breath could be visible on such a hot day. By then he had wrapped his arms around himself to stop him shivering. Again he had the sense, much stronger than it had been at the gate, of being watched. He lifted his gaze and made himself peer through the mist of his breath towards the forest.

Something had entered the graveyard. Ben had to shade his eyes with one shaky hand, to block off some of the glare from the obelisk, before he could begin to distinguish what he was seeing. Between him and the hedge below the common, a patch of air as wide as several graves and taller than the obelisk was glittering with flecks bright as particles of a mirror. Beneath it a faint pale line glistened on the grass, and Ben saw that the particles were dancing leisurely towards him.

As the glittering passed beneath a tree, two leaves fell. He saw them turn white as they seesawed to the ground. He thought he drew several long breaths as he watched them fall, but he could no longer see his breath. His body seemed to be slowing down, becoming calm as marble, though he felt as if he were holding himself still against a threat of shivering panic. Yet his hands were moving, rising almost imperceptibly as if to greet whatever was coming to him. As they reached the level of his vision he saw that his fingers had begun to glitter with flakes of the ice in the air. A silence far more profound than the peace of the churchyard was reaching for him. He was distantly aware of pacing towards a gap in the hedge which led onto the common, following the dance of ice as it moved away. He felt that if he followed where it led, he might understand what the dance was suggesting.

A man was shouting, but Ben ignored him. He was sure he had time to reach the trees and hide. He felt as if the hushed dance might already be hiding him, for the dazzling crystals were lingering around him as if they wanted him to join in the dance. The vanishing patterns they made in the air, and their almost inaudible whispering which he was straining to hear, seemed to promise mysteries beyond imagining.

Then he was falling behind as the glittering passed through the hedge around the gap. A man's hand fastened on his shoulder, jerked with surprise, redoubled its grasp. "He's ice cold, poor little bugger," the man called, and Ben heard a woman—the purplish woman—emit a sympathetic groan. He saw a group of trees at the edge of the forest sparkle and grow dull, and then there was nothing to see beneath the trees except the greenish gloom. He felt abandoned and bewildered, and all he could do was shake.

TWO

The Stargrave police station was a cottage with a counter dividing the front room. A policewoman with large wrinkly hands took Ben into a smaller room next to the kitchen and brought him a glass of milk. "Straight from the cow, that. Drink it right up." The policeman who had found him in the graveyard questioned him with a slowness which Ben realized was meant to be kind but which he found patronizing. Did Ben know his own address? Had he come all this way by himself? Had he told anyone he was coming? Even if he'd left a note that told his aunt not to worry about him, didn't he think she would? "Suppose so," Ben muttered, feeling small and mean.

At least he wasn't shaking now, though his body felt so brittle that he thought a touch might set it off again. While the policeman went to a desk behind the counter to phone Ben's aunt, the policewoman held Ben's hand and told him about her daughter who wanted to be a train driver when she grew up. Before long the policeman called him. "Just tell your aunt how you are, will you?"

Ben could hear her voice demanding a response as he trudged to the phone; she sounded like a tiny version of herself buried in the desktop. He picked up the receiver in both hands and held it away from his face. "I'm here, Auntie."

"Thank God," she said, so tonelessly that he wasn't sure if she were telling him to do so. "Are they feeding you? Have you had nothing to eat all day?"

"I don't want anything," he said, and knew at once that honesty would do him no good. "I mean, I had something before."

"I'll be speaking to you when you're brought home. Put the policeman back on."

Ben dawdled back to his seat, feeling as if he had nowhere to go. "We'll look after him, don't you fret," the policeman was saying, and then his voice grew efficient and stiff. "Yes, ma'am, of course I know who the Sterlings were. . . . A sad loss to our town. . . . I'm sure we can, ma'am, and then I'll see to it that he's delivered safely to you. . . ."

By now Ben was squirming with embarrassment. Every time the policeman said "ma'am" he sounded like the children on the train. "I shouldn't like to specify a time just yet, ma'am. . . . He was in a bit of a state when we found him. . . ." Was that all? Could he really not have seen what Ben had seen in the graveyard, when he had been so close to him? "I believe the doctor's here now, ma'am," the policeman said.

The doctor was a dumpy rapid woman who smelled of mints, one of which rattled against her teeth as she shifted it into her hamsterish cheek. "What's his name?" she said as she peered into Ben's eyes and palmed his forehead, and he felt as if he weren't there, as if the dance in the graveyard had carried him off. "What's his story?" she said.

The policeman had managed to terminate the phone call. "He just wanted to come back to Stargrave and pay his respects, I reckon—it's only been a few months since. Is that about right, son? Nowt wrong where you're living now, is there?"

"My auntie's good to me," Ben said with a guilty vehemence which left him short of breath.

The doctor was holding Ben's wrist and gazing at her watch. "Remind me why you called me. He seems right enough now."

"He was shaking like a leaf when I got hold of him," the policeman said, and Ben remembered the leaves turning white. "Shivering with cold on a day like this. The other thing was, I thought I saw—they must have been insects flying around him just before I got to him."

"They weren't insects," Ben protested.

The doctor glanced at him as if she'd only just noticed him. "Ah. Ah. Ah," she said, and stared at his mouth until he realized he was meant to echo her. "Wider, wider," she urged, and eventually met his eyes. "What were you saying?" she said, poising her thermometer as if she would use it to cut him off as soon as she'd heard enough.

While she had been peering down his throat he'd decided to keep his secret. "I didn't see any insects."

"They were there, son, a real swarm of them. They flew off into the forest when they saw my uniform." To the doctor the policeman said "I just thought you'd better know."

She elbowed Ben's head onto one side and then the other so as to examine his neck. "Thinking of bites, were you? None here." She thrust the thermometer into Ben's mouth and tapped the linoleum with the heels of her scuffed boots until it was time to glance at the reading. "Nothing up with him. Too much travelling and running about on an empty stomach, that was all. I'd prescribe a big helping of bangers and mash."

She snapped her battered bag shut and marched out. "Will pie and chips with lots of gravy do?" the policewoman said to Ben.

"Yes." He was suddenly so exhausted that he found his encounter in the graveyard drifting away from him, becoming unreal—almost too exhausted to remember his manners. "Thank you," he added, and the policewoman patted his head.

When she brought him the food from the fish-and-chip shop he found he was ravenous but hardly able to raise his leaden arms. He remembered an unexpectedly hot day when he'd felt like this. His mother had sat him on her lap and fed him soup. He remembered how she'd kept ducking her head to kiss him on the temple and smiling at him as if to deny the glimmer of anxiety in her eyes. He'd felt so drowsy and protected, it had seemed he could stay like that forever. For a moment he wished the policewoman would see how tired he was and feed him.

But she was answering the phone. "The doctor's pronounced him fit for the road, ma'am. The sight of food's woken him up. . . . I'm sure you feed him well, ma'am. . . . Someone from the county force is on his way here to bring him back to you. . . ."

As Ben was dipping the last of his chips in the gravy the officer arrived, a lanky unsmiling man whose jaw seemed to take up at least a third of his long face and whose peaked cap made the boy think of a chauffeur. "Whenever you're ready," he said to Ben.

"Take your time. We don't want you being sick all over the car on top of everything else," the policewoman said.

She saw Ben out to the car and buttoned his collar for him, and said to the long-faced driver "Look after him. He's a good little chap who's had more bad luck than anyone deserves."

Ben was grateful to her, though he didn't mind that the driver seemed to regard him as a nuisance not worth talking to: silence and sitting passively might let him recapture what had happened in the graveyard. The car followed its own lengthening shadow onto the moors, and Ben felt as if he were leaving part of himself behind. When he glanced back at the forest, the sun hurt his eyes. He squeezed them shut and saw a shining blotch that grew as it darkened. He felt as if the sun had blotted out the memory he was unable to grasp. He put one hand over his eyes, trying to remember, but almost at once he was asleep.

He kept jerking awake. Whenever he did so, he felt as if the memory had dodged farther out of reach. He was beginning to think he'd lost it by not holding onto it. His blinks of consciousness showed him towns he couldn't name, a sky sliced open by a sunset, a road which appeared to lead to the edge of the world, an avenue of lamps like concrete dinosaurs whose heads turned orange in unison against a sky of dark blue glass. Once he was shaken awake by the driver so that he could be transferred to a car from another police force. Once he awoke under a bare black sky, where the glittering of stars in the void seemed for a moment to sum up everything he was unable to grasp, to be a secret message intended solely for him. Then the moment was past, and try as he might, he couldn't stay awake.

The next time he was aware of wakening, he realized that the car had halted. When he heaved his eyelids open, he saw he was outside his aunt's house. The small paired houses and neat gardens and parked cars were steeped in darkness which made even the streetlamps look befogged and which seemed to cling to him. He fumbled with the doorhandle and floundered out of the car.

A policeman who Ben couldn't recall having seen before was ringing the doorbell. Ben saw his aunt jump up beyond the front-room window and steady herself by grabbing her chair, in which she must have slept to wait for him. As he stumbled up the garden path, between shrubs tarred with night, she opened the front door. Her wiry black curls looked lopsided, her horn-rimmed spectacles were crooked, the trademark tag of her cardigan was poking over her collar. She stared dolefully at Ben and folded her arms. "Never do that again unless you want to kill me," she said.

THREE

At first Ben thought she was exaggerating. She thanked the policeman and watched to make sure he closed the gate behind him. "Up with you" was all she said to Ben for now, waving her hands as if she were wafting him upstairs. He used the banister to haul himself to the bathroom, where the lid of the toilet was disguised by white feathers, and was sleepily brushing his teeth when he found himself peering at his face in the mirror. Just now it seemed unreal as a mask, his metallic blue eyes underlined by tiredness, pale bitten lips precisely bisected by the shadow of his sharp nose on his thin face, silvery blond hair lolling in all directions above his large ears. He was still wondering what he felt the sight should tell him when his aunt bustled in to drag a comb through his hair. Even the scratching and yanking at his scalp was unable to rouse him. He staggered into his bedroom and buttoned his pajamas haphazardly, and crawled under the blanket, his eyes closing before his head located the pillow.

Midday sunshine and the rusty notes of a huge music box wakened him. He laid his forearm over his eyelids and enjoyed his unhurried return to consciousness, his feeling that it didn't matter how long it took him to recognize the sound as the call of an ice-cream van. It

14

receded gradually, dwindled, went out at last like a spark, and only then did he realize that he couldn't hear his aunt in the house.

He pushed himself out of bed so hard that his arms shivered, and clattered downstairs, hoping the noise would make her respond. She wasn't in the kitchen, where the stove and the metal sink gleamed as though she had just polished them; nor in the dining room, where black chairs stood straight-backed around the bare black table overlooked by framed browned photographs of old Norfolk seaside views; nor in the front room, where the radio sat on top of the revolving bookcase. Usually the radio put him in mind of an outsize toaster made of off-white plastic, but just now it seemed to crystallize the silence of the house; it made him think of a heart which had ceased beating. He was staring at it, afraid to move, when he heard a sound upstairs: a choked snore, suddenly cut off.

She must have slept as long as he had. He wasn't supposed to go in her room, but surely she wouldn't object if he made her a cup of tea. He took the kettle to the kitchen sink and listened to the clangor of water in it growing less hollow. He watched the kettle boil, grasped the handle as soon as the lid began to twitch, poured the water onto the tea he'd spooned into the pot, forcing himself to keep hold of the handle when the steam made his fingers flinch. Surely now she wouldn't be so cross with him. Placing one foot and then the other on each stair so as not to spill the brimming liquid, he bore the fragile cup on its saucer to her door and knocked timidly on a panel. When a longer knock brought no response, he set the cup and saucer down and inched the door open.

The room felt muggier than his, as if its contents—the quilt which hung down to the floor on both sides of the bed, the dwarf cushions bristling with hatpins on the dressing table, the fat-bottomed chair confronting itself in the mirror beyond the pins—had soaked up the heat. His aunt was huddled under the quilt, looking smaller than she ought to. Her face was grayish, pulled out of shape by her slack drooling mouth. He couldn't tell if she was breathing.

Then she snorted and closed her mouth, and her eyes wavered open. As soon as she saw Ben she sat up, wrapping the quilt around her

15

and wiping her chin furiously with the back of one hand. "I've brought you some tea, Auntie," he stammered.

By the time he reached the bed with it she had put on her bed jacket and spectacles. Her squashed curls were springing up, but she still looked grayer than she ought to. "Leave it on the little table," she said when he attempted to hand her the cup and saucer. "Go and be a good boy while I get up."

Perhaps she wasn't fully awake, but the blurring of her voice unnerved him. "Are you all right, Auntie?"

She placed one hand over her heart as if she were examining herself. "I hope I will be this time. But you must never upset me like you did yesterday, do you see?"

"I won't ever," Ben said, and retreated to his room. If she died he would be wholly alone, and where would he have to go? He set about tidying his room to take his mind off the possibility, lining up his Dinky toys on the windowsill, one model car for each Christmas since he was three years old. They made him think of frost at the windows, sparks flying up the chimney as the wrapping paper blazed.

He carried the bundles of his books down to the front room. When he untied the string from around them the books seemed to expand with relief, the Hans Andersens his father had given him and the boys' adventure annuals his aunt had. Best of all, because it was still mysterious, was Edward Sterling's last book, *Of the Midnight Sun*. He had only begun to leaf through it when his aunt came downstairs. "Don't put too many books in my bookcase or you'll be making it lean. We don't want people thinking we bought our furniture off a cart, do we?" she said, and frowned at the book in his hands. "What's that musty old thing? You don't want that. It might have germs."

Ben hugged it. "I do want it, Auntie. It's the book Great-granddad wrote. Granddad gave it to me and said I should keep trying to read it until it made sense."

"There's no sense in it, Ben. These books I gave you, they're the kind boys ought to read. There's nothing in that one except stories made up by people who had to have Edward Sterling write them down because they couldn't do it for themselves. Nasty fairy tales, like some of those Hans Andersens, only worse. They're from the same part of the world." She held out a hand which he noticed was shivering slightly. "Why don't you give me it to look after if it means so much to you? It can be a special kind of present to you when I think you're old enough."

"Can't it be in the bookcase where I can see it? It makes me think of Granddaddy."

His aunt was struggling with her emotions. "You'll have me thinking I shouldn't have wasted my money on buying you those books," she said, and blundered out of the room.

By dinnertime she seemed more in control of herself. They had meat and vegetable stew as usual, the meal which she often told him was what a growing boy needed. As usual, it tasted blander than it had smelled, as though the tastes had drifted away on the air. He mimed enjoying it, and after a few mouthfuls he said "I like you buying me books, Auntie. I do read them."

"Do you, truly? They weren't just my idea, you know. Your mother thought they would put your mind on the right track." She scooped a mush of vegetables onto her fork and looked up, balancing her cutlery on the edge of her plate. "Try to understand, Ben—this is hard for me too. It was one thing having you stay for a week every so often, but I never thought I'd be sharing my life with someone after I'd got used to living on my own, even with such a good boy as you. You mustn't think I'm complaining, but you'll give me time to get used to it, won't you? I know I can never replace your mother, but if there's anything within reason I can do to make you happier, don't be afraid to speak up."

"Please may I have one of the photographs you brought from the house?"

"Of course you may, Ben. Will you have one of you with your mother?"

Ben chewed another mouthful, but that didn't keep his question down. "Auntie, why didn't you like my dad and his family?"

She closed her eyes as if his gaze was hurting her. "I'm being silly, Ben, you're right. I'll find you a photograph of all of you."

"But why didn't you like them?"

"Perhaps I'll tell you when you're older."

He thought she was blaming them for his mother's death. If he persisted she mightn't give him the photograph. Later, while he was clearing the table, she went up to her room, and stayed there until he began to think she had decided to refuse. At last she brought him a photograph of himself as a baby in his mother's arms. "That's your christening. I got your mother to have you baptized."

His father was supporting Ben's mother, or perhaps he was leaning on her; he looked as if he wanted to mop his shiny forehead. The summer heat which had stretched wide the leaves of the trees in the churchyard of St. Christopher's had visibly enfeebled his grandparents. All the smiles, even his aunt's, were past their best, as if everyone had tired of waiting for the click of the camera. Ben gazed at the photograph, feeling as if he was somehow missing the point of it, until his aunt hugged him awkwardly, making him smell of her lavender water. "You can always talk to me about them if you need to," she said. "You ran away because I hadn't given you enough time to say good-bye, didn't you?"

The question sounded casual, but he sensed how on edge she was for his answer. "Yes, Auntie," he said, unable to decide how far he'd fallen short of telling the truth. "What do you think happened to them all? Nobody would tell me."

"Carelessness, Ben. That's all it could have been, up there in broad daylight in the middle of nowhere. You should never distract someone when they're driving." She enfolded his hands in her warm plump slightly wrinkled grasp. "Thank God you were staying with me that week. We can't bring any of them back, but we'll do our best for each other, won't we? Time for bed now. No arguments, you've school tomorrow. A fine guardian I'd be if I let you bend the rules."

When he was in bed he called down to her. She let him lie under the blanket while she knelt by the bed and intoned prayers for him to amen. Her praying for peace for his family stayed with him after she'd tucked the blanket tight as a bandage around him. Somehow the idea of eternal peace invoked a memory of being carried on his father's shoulders, feeling as though he could pull the stars down from the black ice which held them and from which they had seemed already to be falling, gleams turning slowly in the night air. It had been snowing, of course, but it was odd that his father had carried him into the forest on such a night, so deep into the forest that it had swallowed the lights of Stargrave. Where had his father meant to take him that Ben had been shivering with anticipation? Ben's mind seemed to shrink from the memory, and soon a jumble of thoughts like overlapping channels on a radio put him to sleep.

He awoke feeling full of the night at its darkest. A thought had wakened him—the thought that the dark, or something in it, had a message for him. He lay staring up, trying to recall what he'd failed to grasp. Surely this wasn't yet another of the mysteries which had to wait until he was old enough. That reminded him of Edward Sterling's last book, of Ben's grandfather telling him that in order to finish it Edward Sterling had ventured so far into the icy wastes under the midnight sun that he'd had to be brought back more dead than alive from a place without a name, and had died in Stargrave almost as soon as he'd finished the book. "What did he find?" Ben had wanted to know.

His grandfather had gazed hard at him, looking like himself reflected in a distorting mirror—withered, pale, his limbs stiffening into unfamiliar shapes—and Ben had wondered if Edward Sterling had looked like that too. "One day you'll know," his grandfather had said.

Ben gathered himself like a swimmer and slipped quickly out of bed. His aunt was snoring so loudly she must be fast asleep. Nevertheless he left the light above the stairs switched off as he tiptoed down to the front room. The house stood in the dimness between two streetlamps, and the houses opposite were unlit, but he was just able to distinguish Edward Sterling's book, its spine darker than those of its companions on the shelf. He closed his fingers around the spine, whose binding made him think of old skin, and squatted by the gap between the curtains.

The book fell open at the frontispiece, which showed a wizened old man sitting crosslegged and beating a drum with the palms of his hands. In the dimness his eyes resembled globes of black ice. Ben had often thought that he must have been one of the magicians who were supposed to beat drums for months to keep the midnight sun alight, but now the eyes unnerved him. He began to turn the pages, peering at the chunks of unrhymed verse which the book said was magic poetry but which he had never been able to follow. He supposed he would have to turn on the light when he found what he was looking for, though the stars tonight seemed almost bright enough to read by. Indeed, he was beginning to distinguish the separate lines of print on the pages. He felt as if illumination were reaching for him. He didn't know how long he crouched there, but he was sure he was about to be able to read the words and what they had to tell him when he heard his aunt wailing his name.

She ran downstairs clumsily, switching on lights. She must have found his bed empty while he'd been so engrossed in gazing at the book that he hadn't heard her get up. When she barged into the room, grabbing wildly at the light switch, he wobbled to his feet. "I couldn't sleep, Auntie. I only wanted . . ."

He wasn't sure how to continue, but she appeared not to be listening; she was staring gray-faced at the book in his hands as if it mattered more than anything he could say. He leaned it against the boys' adventure annuals on the shelf and headed for the door as she stepped aside like a wardress.

The guilt of having upset her again kept him awake almost until dawn; but when she wakened him for school she was smiling as if the day had disposed of the night. He felt better at once because she did. If his reading the book bothered her, he'd wait until she was out of the house.

But that evening, when he sneaked into the front room for a surreptitious glance at the picture of the shaman with the drum, he found the annuals were alone on the shelf. He ran into the kitchen, where his aunt was chopping vegetables. "Auntie, where's my book?"

She glanced at him with a casualness which didn't begin to fool him. "I couldn't have been thinking, Ben. A woman came collecting books for some charity, and I didn't like to let her go away empty-handed. Never mind, you've still got the photograph I gave you. It was only an old book."

FOUR

In the weeks that followed she tried to make it up to him. On Saturdays, shopping in Norwich, she kept showing him the oldest parts of the town, cobbled streets where muddles of houses seemed about to tumble downhill. On Sundays after church she often took him to the coast, where she played timid football with him on the stony beaches or walked with him along cliff paths whose seaward edges smoked with windblown sand. Once she took him to the highest point on the coast, a token hill a few hundred feet above the sea at Sheringham. He gazed at the grassy landscape which was almost as flat as the sea, and wished the day were already tomorrow, because he'd realized how he might track down a copy of the book. The father of one of the boys in his class at school was a bookseller.

The boy's name was Dominic, and Ben knew little more about him. He seemed not to have any close friends—certainly not Peter and Francis and Christopher, who let Ben join in their schoolyard games, such as they were. Peter and Francis punched each other several times daily and made faces at each other in the classroom to try to get their classmates hit for giggling. Christopher had saved

Ben from that on his very first day by faking a coughing fit to cover up Ben's fit of mirth, and the next day Francis had bitten a chocolate bar in two and given Ben the smaller piece, glistening with saliva. Ben had swallowed the offering, along with some nausea, and since then he supposed the four of them had been friends. All the same, he didn't mean to allow that to keep him away from Dominic.

On Monday his aunt walked him to school as usual, though in Stargrave he'd walked as far to school by himself. She said "Do your best" and patted his bottom—a gesture which she seemed to assume would embarrass him less than a kiss in front of his schoolmates—as he tried to dodge out of reach through the gates. The July sunlight capped his head with heat and glared from the tilted-open windows of the school as he waved to his aunt until she was out of sight and then strode across the crowded stone-flagged yard.

Dominic was standing close to the boys' entrance to the school, humming to himself with his hands in the pockets of his baggy shorts and gazing down past his clean scabless knees at his feet, which were tapping the rhythm of his tune, a jazzed-up hymn, as his socks sagged to the beat. His face looked as if it had just been rubbed with a rough towel; his broad short nose and wide mouth seemed squashed by his high forehead, above which sprouted coppery hair that made Ben think of exposed wire. Ben was suddenly aware that Peter and Francis and Christopher were watching, and he blurted out the only question he could summon up. "Is your name Dominic?"

Dominic watched his feet stop tapping. "Want to make something of it?"

"No, why should I?"

"Just thought you might have." Dominic bent to pull his socks up. "Nicidom, you could have made, or Nodicim. Modinic's my favorite, though. Sounds like something you have to drink when you're ill." He straightened up and stared past Ben as if he didn't like what he saw. "What do you want, then?"

"Your dad sells books, doesn't he?"

"And yours feeds worms."

Ben gasped and didn't know how to respond. "When we had to say in class what our parents did and Mr. Bolger let you off answering," Dominic continued, "I kept wondering what you'd have said."

Ben bit his lip and realized that though he was struggling to keep his feelings down, they weren't necessarily of grief. Without warning they spluttered out of him so violently he had to wipe his mouth. "I expect I'd have said they were under the sod."

Dominic made such a shocked face that Ben shrieked with laughter. It felt less painful this time, more of a relief. "What would Mr. Bolger have said," Dominic prompted gleefully.

"He'd have said," Ben responded, and deepened his voice: "'How dare you contaminate my classroom with such language, boooy?'"

Dominic laughed at that, or at least wagged his head open-mouthed to indicate mirth. "So what were you going to say about books? I've never seen any of your gang in our shop."

"I'm not in a gang," Ben said, and turned to look where Dominic was staring. Peter and the others had come up behind him, their faces puffy and threatening. "Were you skitting at us?" Peter demanded of Dominic.

"Just at a teacher," Ben said. "We're talking. It's private."

"Maybe you'd better go in the girls' bogs," Francis suggested, fluttering his hands.

"What do you want to talk to him for?" Christopher complained to Ben. "He thinks he's too good for everyone just because his father's a stupid shopkeeper."

"He's not stupid, he's a bookseller. You're stupid if you think he is. My great-granddad used to write books."

"We're sorry, your lordship," Peter hooted, bowing low.

"Your two lordships," Francis said, and repeated it more loudly as if to bully someone into appreciating his wit.

Christopher ducked his head as if he meant to butt Ben. "You watch who you're calling stupid."

"I am watching."

Christopher shoved him against the wall and then, as a teacher appeared in the boys' entrance, swaggered away with his cronies. "So what did your great-granddad write?" Dominic said.

"Books of old legends and stuff that hadn't been written down. I wanted you to ask your dad if one of them's still published. *Of the Midnight Sun* by Edward Sterling."

"Shall my dad get it for you if he can?"

"Better tell me how much first," Ben said as the teacher blew her whistle for everyone to line up, and covered his mouth in case she'd heard him talking after the whistle and would send him to Mr. O'Toole the headmaster.

As his class filed into the building, Ben's shoes his aunt had bought him for his new school making rodent sounds on the linoleum, he saw the headmaster waiting in the corridor, cocking his head which always made Ben think of a horse's grinning skull. He felt as if the heat and the smells of mopped floors and of the sickly green paint on the walls were writhing inside him as the class marched him to his doom. His ears were throbbing so hard that he barely heard what Mr. O'Toole said to him. "I should get those oiled if I were you, or you may be more than squeaking."

"Yes, sir," Ben stammered, feeling isolated and vulnerable and horribly ashamed of himself. He was only a few paces past the headmaster when Dominic's murmur behind him almost caused him to trip himself up. "Funny, *fun*-ny," Dominic said.

Ben felt breathlessly exhilarated, and terrified for him. He didn't dare turn round, but he flashed Dominic a grin as they filed along the row of folding seats in the assembly hall. When Mr. O'Toole thundered prayers at the hallful of children while the teachers glared prayerfully at them, Ben no longer felt alone. In the classroom he even raised his hand when Mr. Bolger asked questions, and found that his palms no longer started sweating.

He was glad that his aunt didn't ask why he was pleased with himself; she seemed content that he was. That night he could hardly sleep for waiting; it felt like Christmas Eve. Soon he might know who Edward Sterling had met on his last exploration and what they had revealed to him. But when he hurried into the schoolyard, not even waiting until his aunt was out of sight, Dominic showed him his empty hands. "My dad laughed."

"How do you mean?"

"He said to tell you he wished you had a copy of that book, because he'd have given you a year's pocket money for it. He rang up a friend of his who sells old books who said he's never seen a copy in his life. You're as likely to see one as snow in summer, my dad said."

FIVE

At least Ben had made a real friend at school, which was more than he ever had in Stargrave. His aunt let him stay at Dominic's house until she came home from her tax office job to collect him. She must be pleased that she no longer needed to work in her lunch hours and that he had someone else to keep him in Norwich. Dominic's parents welcomed Ben, but it took him a while to get used to them. Mrs. Milligan kept offering him food in no apparent order, perhaps because Mr. Milligan was constantly on the move even during mealtimes, picking up books from the sideboard, from chairs, from a dozen other perches in the small house crammed with dingy rooms, and strolling about like an actor at a rehearsal, reading aloud. "Just listen to this," he would say, raising his squat face and half-closing his eyes under their fierce reddish eyebrows as if he were smelling the pages rather than reading them, until Dominic's mother would lose patience with him and fly at him like a terrier, her short-legged body crouching to shove him towards the table, her square head lowered so that her chin appeared to engulf her stubby neck. "Their brains need feeding as well as their breadbaskets," he would protest mildly as his wife confiscated the book, growling "Don't be teaching them your manners."

The first time Ben visited Milligan's Bookshop he saw a portly man with a briefcase waddling away like an endangered penguin, almost tripping over cobblestones as Mr. Milligan harangued him. "Stop that man, he's living off immoral earnings. Where's a policeman? I'd like you to show him that page you didn't want me to read out loud," he shouted, and the salesman broke into a stumbling run. "Just a fellow with no respect for books or people," Mr. Milligan told Ben as he ushered him into the shop. "Read whatever you think you might like so long as your hands are clean."

That was how Ben spent much of the summer. He read all the fantasies and myths and legends he could find, partly because he knew his aunt wouldn't quite approve, and some of the science fiction Dominic liked, which led Ben to the astronomy books. The measurements of space and time, the photographs of far stars and of points of light which proved to be composed of thousands of stars, filled him with an awe which felt like the edge of a delicious panic. Sometimes he was glad when Mrs. Milligan rescued him from these thoughts by bringing him a bowl of cereal or a fried-egg sandwich from the house. Otherwise Mr. Milligan could be relied upon to provide some diversion, reading aloud to prospective customers or trying to dissuade people from ordering books he disapproved of or disentangling authors' names and titles from their memories, whenever Ben's thoughts threatened to grow too large and dark.

When he lay in bed at night, however, there was nothing to distract him, especially once he was back at school and it was growing dark by the time he went to bed. Soon there was an autumn chill in the air, and he felt as if the summer had failed to keep it away, just as the daylight couldn't hold back the nights. As the nights lengthened, it seemed to him that the dark grew larger. He didn't know why the increasing cold and darkness should make him apprehensive; he wasn't even sure if praying every night in front of the photograph of himself and his family helped. Each night the reflection of the sky in the dressing-table mirror beyond the photograph seemed darker. Once he thought he saw the sky go out, having failed to hold back the starry emptiness, and he prayed as hard as he could.

Each night he crept out of bed to pray after his aunt had tucked him up, and he didn't realize she'd heard him until she took him to Father Flynn. That Sunday was the day the clocks were put back so as to bring the night forwards an hour. Perhaps that was why the church service seemed so remote from him, the priest and his assistants performing their slow ritual motions while their prayers and the responses of the congregation fluttered under the arched ceiling like trapped birds. After the service he tried to sidle unnoticed out of the porch, but his aunt steered him in front of the priest. "Thank you for a lovely mass," she said.

"One tries to do one's best, Miss Tate." The priest bared his small even teeth in a smile which concealed his gums, and gave Ben's head a token pat. "I don't need to tell our young Ben that, do I?"

Ben had been afraid that the priest would see from his face that his attention had been wandering during the service, and now his panic started his thoughts chattering: a lovely mass of coconuts, a mass of pottage, a mess of a mass . . . "I want you to know I admire the way you've borne your cross," the priest was telling him.

"Actually, Father, that was what we wanted to talk to you about," Ben's aunt said. "The tragedy, that is."

Ben hadn't wanted to talk to him about anything. "My door is always open," the priest said.

His house must get cold in the winter, Ben thought, and struggled not to smirk—but nobody was looking at him. "I always have a pot of tea after mass, and like everything else in this life, it's better shared," the priest said.

The presbytery was at the end of a street in which twinned houses placed gardens between themselves and a row of discreet shops. An elderly housekeeper with beads big as acorns rattling around her stringy neck opened the door. "One more for the pot," the priest said breezily, "and I think there might be an order for a glass of milk."

One chair faced several in the front room, before a tiled fireplace in which a coal fire was crackling. Records were stacked beneath an old gramophone in one corner of the room. "You sit there," Ben's aunt said and nudged him into the chair directly opposite the priest's before sitting on the edge of the chair next to him. "I hoped you might be able to make things clearer to him, Father."

"I believe that's why I'm here. What about, now?"

"About, as we were saying, the tragedy. He isn't over it yet, not that you'd expect him to be. Only I've heard him praying for them as if his heart was about to break. God can't mean a child to feel like that, can he?"

"We mustn't presume to know what God means, Miss Tate. I was taught it may take us the whole of eternity even to begin to glimpse his meaning." The priest ducked his head towards Ben. "Perhaps our little soldier would like to tell us in his own words what he feels."

He was trying to make it sound like an adventure, but it didn't seem at all like one to Ben. "What about?" Ben said awkwardly.

"Why, how you've felt since God took your family to Him."

Ben managed to think of something he could put into words. "I keep wondering where they've gone."

"Well, Ben, I would have thought a good boy who goes to such a fine Catholic school would know."

"He means purgatory, Ben."

"You knew that, didn't you? And I'm sure you can tell us from your catechism what it means."

Ben parroted the answer. Perhaps his aunt sensed his mounting dismay, because she said "It's a hard thing for a little boy to grasp."

"Hard means durable, Miss Tate. Shall I tell you something that may surprise you, Ben? I expect you're feeling very much as I felt when I was just about your age. See my grandmother up there? I lost her when I was nine years old."

He was referring to a yellowed oval photograph on the mantelpiece, Ben saw as his thoughts began to chatter. "I couldn't understand why an old lady who'd never done anyone any harm had to wait to be let into Heaven," the priest said.

Whatever Ben had avoided thinking since the car crash, it wasn't this. "Do you think she's there yet?" he said.

His aunt made a shocked sound, but the priest smiled indulgently at him. "That isn't for us to know, is it? If we thought we did we might stop praying for them, and that's one of the jobs God gives us on earth, to pay Him our prayers so our loved ones can get to Heaven sooner."

Ben was beginning to panic because this meant so little to him. "But some dead people don't have anyone on earth to pray for them."

The priest flashed his teeth at Ben's aunt. "He's a bright boy. It's a good job you're bringing him up in the faith," he said, and to Ben: "That's why we pray for all the souls in purgatory, not just those who belong to us."

"That's better now, isn't it, Ben?" his aunt said as if he'd scraped his knee. "You know where your mother and everyone is now, and you know you're helping them."

Ben knew nothing of the kind. Mustn't there be more souls in purgatory than there were stars in the sky, since Mr. O'Toole had once told the assembled school that a single unconfessed sin could keep you in purgatory until the end of the world? If praying for all the dead people you'd never even met could help them, what was the point of singling out your own? If praying for them by name reduced their time in purgatory, how could that be anything but unfair to people who had nobody to pray for them by name? The whole setup struck him as so unreasonable as to be meaningless, and that terrified him.

The priest leaned towards him almost confidentially. "I think you're wondering what all this suffering is for, aren't you? Such a bright boy would. Now, Ben, whatever happens to us in this life and after it, however hard it may seem, don't you think it must be worth it if it leads us to see God?"

"I don't know."

"I mean, if we have to suffer so as to be worthy of it, mustn't being able to see God for all eternity be a reward beyond anything we can imagine?"

"I suppose so."

The priest sat back. "I think that may do for now, Miss Tate. There's a little chap with a few big new ideas to turn over in his mind. If they're too much for you, Ben, don't be afraid to ask questions. Now what's this I see coming for a good boy? I do believe it's a glass of milk."

Ben thanked the housekeeper politely and concentrated on drinking the milk. He had plenty of questions, but he was sure that the answers weren't here. The priest must be mistaken in his thinking; he'd said himself that he didn't know what God meant. But then was the church mistaken about death and what was waiting beyond it? Ben thought so, and he felt as if Father Flynn had separated him further from his family, had sent them further into the unknown dark.

That night Ben prayed for them more intensely than ever, under his breath so that his aunt wouldn't hear. He prayed in front of the photograph and then in bed until he fell asleep. He kept imagining them in purgatory, naked and writhing like insects thrown on red-hot coals, unable even to die. He gripped his praying hands together as if their aching would drive out the pain which clenched his whole body, and prayed so hard that he no longer knew what he was saying. When the vision faded, there was only the cold dark that felt like a promise of peace.

SIX

On Halloween night the streets smelled of mist and charred leaves. All day Ben had felt surrounded by signs too secret to interpret: the dance of decaying leaves in the air, the long shadows where the autumn chill lurked like winter biding its time, a sun which looked swollen with blood as the mist dragged it down beyond the unconvincing cutout shapes the houses had become. He was almost able to believe that the anticipation with which the growing nights affected him was only the excitement he could see on the faces of the children around him, but then why was it making him nervous?

The Milligans invited him and his aunt to spend the evening with them. After dinner Ben's aunt led him through the streets, gripping his arm harder whenever they met figures wearing masks or pointed hats. "They're just children dressed up," she kept muttering, unaware that he was nervous of them only in case they might jeer at his costume, a sheet which she had reluctantly lent him and which he had to bunch in his fist to prevent the skirt of it from tripping him up. At long last they reached their destination, where a grinning pumpkin flickered in the front-room window, and Mr. Milligan opened the door. "Why, here's a Roman senator," he shouted. "Hitch up your toga, Bennius, and come in."

Mrs. Milligan bustled out of the kitchen, carrying two aprons and an apple from which she took a loud bite. "He looks more like a little old pagan priest," she said and then, so forcefully that she spat bits of apple, "You don't really, Ben. You're the best ghost I've seen tonight. It makes me shiver just to look at you."

She gave him and Dominic an apron each so that they could duck for apples in a washing-up bowl placed on a bath towel in the front room. The water and the apple which Ben eventually snagged with his teeth tasted of soap and of the smell of the candles which illuminated the room. Afterwards Mrs. Milligan brought in sausages protruding from snowdrifts of mashed potato on large oval plates, followed by conical cakes meant to resemble snouts of rats, from which one had to pull the inedible whiskers. Ben's aunt kept glancing unhappily at the shadows of the sausages, flexing on the tablecloth like fingers threatening to shape a silhouette, and she wouldn't touch the snouty cakes. Mrs. Milligan cleared the table and came back into the room, her shadow billowing after her as though the dark of the hallway had sent part of itself to join them. "Time to tell some tales," Mr. Milligan said.

"Nothing unsuitable," Ben's aunt warned.

"Nothing to turn anyone's hair any whiter."

"Tell us about the man who found the whistle on the beach at Felixstowe," Dominic said.

The boys sat on either side of the fire, their backs against the fireplace, which felt to Ben as if the snatches the heat made at him kept being thwarted by the chill of the tiles. Mr. Milligan told them about a whistle that called a ghost which was dressed in a sheet, except that when it got between the man and the only door out of his bedroom he saw that nothing was wearing the sheet. Ben listened enthralled, feeling that he was sitting at the feet of giants with firelit faces, and watched their shadows merge and part and merge on the ceiling, a shifting center of deeper blackness drawing them together. When Mr. Milligan finished, having let the man escape from the room, Ben heard his aunt breathing hard with distaste. "It's just a story someone made up, boys. It didn't really happen," Mrs. Milligan said to placate her.

"That's mean. You didn't have to say that," Dominic complained.

"It sounds to me as if your mother did," Ben's aunt said.

"Do you know any stories, Beryl?" Mrs. Milligan suggested.

"If you mean about the supernatural, there are plenty in the Bible."

"It's Ben's turn now," Dominic said.

Ben wasn't sure if Dominic meant to aggravate the tension in the room, and he didn't care. He felt oddly excited, as if Mr. Milligan's storytelling had awakened a story in him. "I'll try," he said.

"We'll have to be going shortly," his aunt announced.

"You'd better have the storyteller's seat, Ben," Mr. Milligan said, and relinquished the lopsided armchair to him. Ben gazed into the flames and felt as if he were sitting by a campfire, as if the dark behind him were bigger than the world. A story which he had to speak in order to know it seemed to be gathering inside him, but he didn't know how to begin. Mr. Milligan brought a dining chair from the next room and sat on it beside the fire. "Try 'Once upon a time,' Ben."

"Once upon a time . . ." Ben said, and felt the phrase bring the story alive. "Once upon a time there was a boy who lived at the edge of the coldest place in the world. It was so cold that the ice there had never melted since there was ice in the world. The boy's father went out hunting every day while the boy and his mother tended all the fires that people had kept burning since before anyone could remember, because if even one fire should go out, the spirits that lived beyond the flames would come down the mountain where they lived in the ice and through the pass the fires were guarding and capture the rest of the world. The boy's father told him that his father's father almost let a fire go out when the father's father was a little boy, and he'd seen the spirits come walking. Their eyes were like ice that nothing could melt, and each of their breaths was like a blizzard, and their footsteps sounded like all the snow as far as you could see in every direction squeezing itself together. Just looking at them had made his own eyes begin to turn to ice. Only *his* father had grabbed a burning log from the next fire and driven the spirits back and thrown the log on the fire that was nearly out, and they'd never let a fire burn down that low again.

"Well, hearing about that frightened the boy the story is about, but he wished he could see one of the spirits just to know what they looked like. Only he couldn't see up the mountain for the mist and fires, and whenever his mother or his father caught him looking they would beat him. Then one day his mother told him she was going to have a baby and he would have to tend the fires by himself for as long as it took the baby to come, and she made him promise that he wouldn't let a single fire get low and wouldn't look beyond them for even a moment . . ."

Ben's aunt had begun to shift uneasily in her chair when he mentioned having a baby, but the story had taken over; Ben was as eager as the Milligans visibly were to discover how it came out. "The day his mother took to her bed the boy got up before dawn and put some of the wood that he and his father had brought from the forest on the fires, and then he stood with his back to them and only looked round to see if they needed feeding. He watched his shadow turn with the sun, and when it looked almost as long as a tree is tall he heard a voice behind him. It sounded like the ice cracking in the heat from the fire, which was a sound you always heard in that place, but he knew it was a voice because it was calling his name. So he ran to get more wood and throw it on the fires, and he didn't look at anything but them until his father came home from hunting. But he didn't tell his father what he'd heard, because he was afraid of being beaten for letting the spirits get so close.

"That night he kept getting up to make sure none of the fires were going out because his mother and father were sleeping so soundly from waiting for the baby to come. And the next day he was up before dawn to tend the fires. He made them so hot he had to stand twenty paces away and couldn't look at them for more than a breath at a time. So he watched his shadow turning east and growing longer than yesterday's as the sun began to go down, and then he heard someone calling his name beyond the fires in a voice like a stream turning into ice. So he ran to the forest for wood and threw it on the fires until they were so hot he had to stand thirty paces away, where he couldn't hear the voice. But he could feel the eyes of ice watching him over the flames.

"He might have told his father about that, because they frightened him more than the thought of being beaten, except that just as his father came home with a deer across his shoulders his mother started having the baby. She cried out all night, and in the morning it still hadn't come, so because they had enough meat for a week the father stayed with her and the boy had to tend the fires even though he'd had no sleep. So he made them so high he thought they must be able to melt the ice on the mountain, and then he watched his shadow turning and listened to his mother crying out, until his shadow looked like a giant that could swallow his father in one mouthful, because that was the shortest day of the year and the sun was lowest. And just when the sun touched the horizon he heard someone calling his name in a voice that sounded like a snowfall talking, and the fires were so hot and he was so tired that it hushed him to sleep.

"He didn't wake until he started shivering, and as soon as he did he knew that one of the fires had gone out. He ran to the forest to get some wood, but there was just one branch left from all the wood they'd cut, because he'd been building the fires so high. And when he ran back with it he saw that the fire wasn't just out, it was covered with frost as thick as a finger.

"So he ran to the hut to tell his mother and father, but he couldn't hear his mother crying out or his father singing to her, it was quiet as a snowdrift in there. And when he looked in he thought he saw two white bears that must have eaten his mother and father, but they were really his mother and father covered with frost that had caught them when they'd tried to run. The only living creature in the hut was a baby as white as a cloud. So the boy went to pick it up, but when it opened its eyes he saw they were made of ice. Then he was going to kill it with the branch, but it started to cry, and its breath was like a blizzard so fierce it cut his skin and froze his blood when he started to bleed, and the last thing he ever saw was the world turning white. So that's one story about what happens when the ice comes out of the dark. . . ."

Ben's voice trailed off. He felt light-headed with talking, and awkward now that he'd finished. The fire was almost out, he saw. Then Mr. Milligan came to himself with a start and shovelled coal from the scuttle onto the embers until the fire flared up. "That was a tour de force, Ben," he said. "If I were you I should write all that down and try sending it to a publisher."

Ben's aunt slapped her knees and pushed herself to her feet. "Come along, Ben. I've let you stay longer than you should have. I'll put the light on if I may. I like to see where I am."

The Milligans were still narrowing their eyes at the light when she brought Ben's coat from the hall and caught his arms in the sleeves. She said nothing further to him until the Milligans had closed the front door. "Where did you get that from?"

She meant the story. "Granddad told it to me," Ben said, which seemed as if it might be close to the truth.

"Well, I hope you'll forget it. You shouldn't be dabbling in such things at your age. You'll be giving yourself nightmares, and me as well. I'm sorry, but I'm going to have to ask your teacher what kind of books he thinks you should be reading."

"Mummy and Daddy wouldn't mind what I read."

"Don't you be so sure about your mother," she said, and more gently: "I can't look after you properly if you keep making me afraid for you, can I? You've been through enough without putting silly stories into your head. You can read them when you're older if you must, but I'm sure you'll have grown out of them by then."

She was wrong, Ben thought, in more ways than one, though he wasn't sure which. Even if she told him what to read, she couldn't reach the stories that were in his head. There were others which would tell themselves to him in their own time, he was sure. The mist was extinguishing the streetlamps around him, turning the distance into a dark mystery which he couldn't reach by walking. The sight and his thoughts made him feel breathlessly expectant. Perhaps he didn't need to find Edward Sterling's last book. Perhaps he had leafed through it so often that its burden was inside him, waiting to be understood.

SEVEN

On Guy Fawkes Night weeping willows of many colors appeared in the sky, blotting out the stars. Christmas was already in the shops, sprinkling the windows with imitation snow like a promise of the real thing. Christmas had come early to the school too, bringing little goodwill but multiplying the questions which the children had to answer instantly if they weren't to be shouted at or worse. It would be Ben's first Christmas without his family, and he felt as if his grief had been waiting for him to realize. Some nights as he prayed in front of the photograph, his lips were quivering so much he couldn't even whisper.

In the weeks before Christmas his aunt did her best to console him. During the first weekend in December she hung the decorations, wavering on top of a stepladder while Ben clutched the legs. For the first time in her life she bought a Christmas tree, a Norway spruce no taller than Ben. It lent the house a chilly scent of pine and sprinkled the carpet with needles as the trees from Sterling Forest had done in the Stargrave house, but it wasn't the same—Ben wasn't sure how. Nor were the Father Christmases she paid for him to visit in the department stores, a fat man who sneezed as often as he chortled and a thinner whose beard was too big for him, quite able to invoke the anticipation he'd begun to feel around this time of year in Stargrave, though both of them patted him on the head and murmured noncommittally in the manner of their species when he asked to be brought an astronomical telescope. He knew they were dressed up as someone who didn't exist, but that wasn't the difference; he would have known that last Christmas.

Soon Mr. O'Toole set about preparing the school for the festivities. When they opened their presents and ate their Christmas dinner, he yelled, they should be thinking of the child God sent to earth to suffer because people were so sinful that nothing less could make up for their sins. He dabbed spittle from his lips with a large stiff handkerchief and glared red-eyed around the assembly hall. "Have you no souls?" he demanded, his voice rising almost to a shriek. "File past that crib, the lot of you, and think of Christ's blessed mother having to see her only son whipped and crowned with thorns and nailed to a cross to die with vinegar to drink. I'll see a few tears before this assembly's over, or I'll know how to get them."

The crib was the size and approximately the shape of a rabbit hutch. The cradle in the straw was surrounded by three identical sheep from a toy farmyard, two plaster shepherds and a Virgin Mary whose hair a trace of dust was graying. A star cut out of silver paper hung above the scene, one of its points drooping. The cradle and the swaddled baby it contained were too big for their entourage, and Dominic had claimed to Ben that if you picked the baby up it would cry *ma-ma*. When Dominic shuffled alongside the crib now, however, he emitted a loud sniff. "Use your handkerchief, boy," the headmaster snarled, low enough to suggest grudging approval of Dominic's performance. There were just three girls in front of Ben, sniffing almost in unison, and suddenly Ben knew that he would be the first child to fail to weep, unable to respond to the crib whose incongruities seemed to have been arranged as a test of faith. It wasn't just those that troubled him, it was the sight of the headmaster glaring across the crib. If what the crib represented were real, how could it need someone like Mr. O'Toole to terrorize people into believing in it? How could it bear to have anyone act that way on its behalf? The questions frightened him even more than the headmaster did, and so he began, rather to his own bewilderment, to weep as he came abreast of the crib.

At first he thought he was weeping only for his family and from knowing he would never again spend Christmas with them. He remembered the snap of crackers as the family formed a chain with them around the laden table and pulled them all at once, his grandfather saying "To the season" as everyone raised a glass of wine, the long evenings when the boy would sit on his mother's lap by the fire while she and his grandmother sang carols that seemed somehow to embody the time of year, the icy sparkling of the vast night over Stargrave, the wind rushing down from the moors and through the forest and fluttering softly at the windows—and then he found himself observing himself. Perhaps this was the only way he could deal with the confusion of his thoughts. He felt as if he were looking down on the crib and the headmaster and himself from somewhere too high for his emotions to reach. This new clarity seemed to unlock his mind, and with disconcerting vividness he remembered learning to walk, his father and grandfather dancing out of reach and leading him deeper into the forest, their faces proud and a little nervous. The family had looked like that when he'd begun to realize that Father Christmas was a myth, but had there been a secret for him to realize in the forest? A sudden panic which he didn't want to understand jarred him back to full awareness of the crib, and for a moment it seemed to be the source of his panic rather than any kind of a reassurance.

During the last few days of that school term he felt as if whatever he had almost glimpsed was lurking at the edge of his thoughts. The days were growing colder, not with the clinging chill of mist but with a relentlessness which made him feel like frozen bones imperfectly insulated by flesh as he walked between his aunt's house and the school. He tried to distract himself with schoolwork and with the token party which Mr. O'Toole conceded to the school, apparently at the request of the teachers, on the last day of term, but the schoolwork seemed as much of a game as the party. Wearing a paper hat and consuming sandwiches and lemonade and playing battleships with Dominic in squared exercise books all felt like putting off the inevitable, and he was afraid to know what it was.

"Enjoy your Christmas," their teacher said when the final bell rang, "but don't eat so much you won't fit behind your desks." Some of the children gave him Christmas cards, and Ben wished he had thought to bring one, not least so that he could linger in the classroom. But his aunt was waiting at the gates. Taking deep breaths and pinching his coat collar shut, Ben sent himself out of the school.

There was no mist. The first star hung low in the sky as if it had crystallized out of the deep blue. The star was so bright, and the unblemished sky so glassy, that he felt as if the blue were about to shatter and let the starry night appear. The roofs of buildings and the bare branches of trees looked as though they had been outlined with a razor, and to Ben that seemed a sign that everything was about to grow still clearer. Buildings and trees were absolutely motionless against the sky, which appeared to solidify as it darkened, holding fast the luminous peaks of roofs, the sunlit tips of branches. As he walked home the glowing branches turned gray, and he remembered this was the shortest day of the year.

When his aunt opened the front door, a draft followed her in. Ben heard pine needles scattering on the carpet, and fetched the brush and dustpan from beneath the kitchen sink. As he cleared up the needles he saw his reflection in a silvery globe on the tree, his head swelling as he shuffled closer on his knees, until he thought he looked like a tadpole held by ice. His grandfather had had to be begged to decorate the trees they brought into the house from Sterling Forest; he'd seemed to believe that the trees, or whatever they signified, were enough.

His aunt gave him sausages and Christmas pudding for dinner, and found a carol concert on the radio to accompany the meal. Afterwards, while she put away the dishes, she sang along with the last carols as if she hoped Ben would. However, when he told her well before his bedtime that he was going up to his room she only said "I'm here if you need me."

He didn't switch on the light above the stairs as he climbed towards the stars he could see beyond his bedroom. From his window he gazed at the stars, which barely pierced the blackness in whose depths galaxies floated like snowflakes. The blackness was no more than a hint of the limitless dark in which the world was less than a speck of dust. He imagined seeing a star move as the Christmas story said it had. The idea disturbed him, and he didn't think he wanted to know why. He switched on his bedroom light and knelt in front of the photograph.

But praying was no use: the words meant nothing to him. Had the headmaster robbed them of meaning, or had it been Father Flynn? Even the photograph unnerved Ben—not so much the frozen smiles of the women as something about the eyes of his father and grandfather and even his own eyes. He turned off the light so as not to see the eyes, and returned to the window.

A star blinked, and then another. For a moment he was sure he was about to see one move. Downstairs his aunt had tuned the radio to a comedy show to which he often listened with her. He thought she was turning the volume higher in case that would tempt him to join her, but the signature tune might as well have been trying to reach him from another world, because he'd understood at last how reassuring the sight of a moving star would be: it would mean that however dark and cold and empty it appeared to be, infinity *cared*.

He felt as if he were falling off the world. The endless dark seemed to be reaching for him with its swarm of stars, with light which felt as bleak as the space between them and which might be older than the world. He thought he could feel how the light was travelling towards him, unthinkably swift and yet slower than snowflakes when set against the expanse of time. All at once he was sure the headmaster was right to suggest that the truth which the crib made appealing was far more terrible and awesome. He realized he was shivering uncontrollably when he shoved himself away from the window, towards the light switch. But the dark and the stars were in the mirror too, and so was he, beside the photograph. The dark was gazing back at him out of his own eyes.

The sight paralyzed him. He thought of the eyes of the old man with the drum in Edward Sterling's book, but he sensed that something far older—so old that the fleeting thought of it stopped his breath—was watching him. He didn't know how long he crouched in front of the mirror, unaware of resting his weight on his knuckles on the dressing table. As he leaned inadvertently closer his breath whitened the mirror, which sparkled as if the stars around the silhouette of his head were settling on the glass. He felt as if he himself were only an illusion that would flicker for an instant in the vast darkness, as if he were gazing through himself deep into the dark. He was afraid to move, but if he didn't he would see what was watching him out of the lightless depths.

Someone was calling his name. The voice was too distant to reach him, but it was distracting him. It was his aunt who was calling him, standing at the foot of the stairs and raising her voice to be heard over the music at the end of the comedy show. She must be wondering why he had stayed so long in his room, though as far as he was concerned no time at all had passed. When he didn't answer, she would come to find him.

She would find him in the dark, gazing entranced at himself, and it would kill her. His running away to Stargrave almost had, and he was sure that she would find the sight of him as he was now at least as dismaying. The thought made him squirm with concern for her, scraping his knuckles on the rough wood. The inane music finished its scurrying, and she heard her start up the stairs, calling anxiously to him.

A surge of panic stiffened his arms and flung him away from the mirror. He gulped a breath and flailed at the light switch. "I'm here, Auntie," he stammered. "I was only resting." Then, terrified of what she might be able to see, he forced himself to turn to the mirror.

There was nothing to see but his own face and the photograph, nothing in his eyes except bewilderment and fading panic, nothing secretive about the faces in the photograph. Whatever had made him see what he'd seen, surely it had gone back into the dark. "I'm coming now, Auntie," he called, managing to keep his voice steady. When he heard her stop and eventually descend the stairs, he let out a shaky

43

breath. He went downstairs as soon as he was able to conceal his nervousness, vowing that Christmas would mean everything to him that it meant to her. He mustn't ever see anything like that again, please God, for her sake.

EIGHT

Mabel Broadbent was locking her shop on Christmas Eve when the newsagent's daughter ran up, looking so crestfallen that Mabel asked what she'd wanted to buy. "Only some blue thread," Anita said as if the smallness of her purchase were an open sesame. "I nearly finished sewing something that said Happy Christmas to my mam."

Mabel had to take pity on her. She reopened the shop long enough to sort out a reel of the blue which matched the sample Anita had wound around her forefinger, and told her to bring the money after Christmas; the day's takings were already banked. The little girl stuffed the reel into her pocket and stood on tiptoe to give Mabel a clumsy kiss that smelled of chocolate. "Have a lovely Christmas, Miss Broadbent," she gabbled.

"I've just started, love. You have one too," Mabel said as the child dashed across the square and up the hill. By the time she had locked the shop, she was alone. Without the market stalls which sprouted weekly around the eroded stone cross, the town square sounded hollow. Wrapping her scarf more snugly about her neck and burrowing her hands into her gloves, Mabel gave the unlit shop a last appraisal—she would change the display of balls of wool and knitting patterns on New Year's Eve as usual—before strolling home.

The sun had sunk beyond the moors. Above Stargrave and the gloomy mass of Sterling Forest, a jade sky exhibited the carving of the jagged gritstone ridge. On Market Street, the main road through the square, most of the shops scattered among terraces of cottages on the northward stretch and clustering on both sides of the half mile which paralleled the railway line were shut until next week. Outside the station, the estate agent and his wife were loading armfuls of last-minute purchases into the larger of the taxis as the next-to-last train before the holidays chugged north. Mabel stopped at the newsagent's for a carton of du Maurier cigarettes and sipped a glass of the sherry he offered all his customers on Christmas Eve, and then she braved the night again while the alcohol was keeping off the chill.

The newsagent's was the last shop on the main road. Further on were a few whitewashed cottages with rough brick porches, the walls of their large gardens decorated with extravagant rocks brought down from the moors. Across the railway line acres of heather divided the town from the farms, one of which was showing a lit window like a fallen star. Mabel's was the last cottage before the railway bridge, but not the last building. Above it, at the end of several hundred yards of bare track which met the main road beside her garden, was the Sterling house.

A car was approaching from the town as Mabel reached her gate. Mabel waited with her hand on the latch for the headlamps to illuminate the unlit house. She didn't like to think that any children might have ventured into it, though surely they would have better things to do on this night of all nights. The car swung around the curve out of the town, raising its headlight beams as the streetlamps gave out. The light streamed across a cottage garden and found the Sterling house.

Both the house and the forest above it seemed to step forwards. For a few seconds the house and a glinting mass of trees were the brightest things in Stargrave. She had always thought that the tall gray three-story house with its steep roof and overbearing crown of disproportionately large chimneys looked as if it had been separated from a Victorian terrace—as if it needed something to complete it—but now she had the disconcerting impression that the light had caught the building in the act of sharing a secret with the forest. It must be because all the curtains were drawn that it looked secretive, she thought, but she couldn't help remembering Ben Sterling and how she had failed to intervene on his behalf. The shadows of the grotesque stones which squatted on the wall surrounding the unkempt garden danced across the outside of the building as the car sped towards the bridge, and darkness rushed into the space occupied by the house. Suppressing a shiver, Mabel hurried along her path.

As she unlocked the door her cottage greeted her with scents of the wild flowers she'd twined around the oval mirror in the hall and through the uprights of the dresser in the front room. She turned on the caged electric fire in the sitting room, where the rugs looked like perfectly circular islands of snow on the green carpet. She picked up the handbag-sized radio from beside her armchair, where an Agatha Christie novel was keeping her place, and tuned the set to the Home Service as she marched into the kitchen to deal with the dripping tap.

Though she screwed the tap shut as hard as she could, the plop of water on stone went on and, just as she kept thinking it had stopped, on. She would have to ask someone at Elgin's yard to deal with it when the holidays were over. While she waited for her casserole to heat up, she listened to a voice plummy as a pudding reading Dickens and worked on the mince pies, shaping the pastry cases and spooning in the fruit before fitting the pastry lids and ventilating them with a fork. There should be enough for everyone who came to visit during the next few days—Edna Dainty from the post office and Charlie who worked on the railway, Hattie Soulsby and her husband, whose efforts to have children Mabel prayed for every night, the retired teachers who lived next door to Mabel, not to mention all the customers who always brought her presents. She had put the first trays of pies in the oven and was ladling herself a second helping from the casserole, basking in her sense of a job well done, when a wind rushed down past the Sterling house, so cold it penetrated the warmth of the kitchen and so fierce it made the window creak.

It sounded as if a tree were outside the cottage. Mabel held onto the edge of the thick stone sink and peered out of the window. All she could see was her lawn dotted with wormcasts and bordered by earth in which her flowers were hibernating, and the night leaning on her restless privet hedge. She finished her meal as "A Christmas Carol" came to an end, and then she switched the radio off, despite the dripping of the tap, and lit a cigarette. She waited for the mince pies and gazed towards the lightless Sterling house, and at once her memories began to race.

She had never resented the Sterlings, as many of the townsfolk had. In her childhood she'd found them somewhat unnerving; whenever their large dusty black car which made her think of a hearse crept past the garden the sight of them had given her a shiver even on the hottest days, the men with their thin sharp faces and startlingly pale hair, the women who seemed to be growing to resemble them. Once Mabel grew up, however, she'd decided they were just decayed gentlefolk. If they had spent Edward Sterling's legacy on planting the forest in accordance with his last wish, as a memorial to him around the grove where he had died, what was wrong with that? Most of the townsfolk seemed to disapprove of them for having acquired so much money without working, but now both men taught philosophy in Leeds. Considering Stargrave's attitude to them, it was hardly surprising if the family were aloof. Their lives were no business of Mabel's—or so she had thought until Ben Sterling's grandmother had begun to patronize her shop.

Charlotte had seemed to sum up the seedy grandeur of the Sterlings. That February day she had been wearing an ankle-length black coat of corduroy so thick that her arms had looked twice as plump as her frail wrists. She'd unwound several lengths of a black scarf from around her head and let it flap from her shoulders as she'd stalked up to the counter. Her gray hair had been restrained by heavy combs above a long pinched face of tissue-paper skin. "Some spools of green thread, the most expensive, *if* you please," she'd told Mabel with regal politeness. "Are these all? In a stout bag, thank you. Please don't trouble," she'd added when Mabel had reached for her change, a few pence. She'd flung the scarf around her ears and had swept out, leaving Mabel too amused to be furious.

Some weeks later Charlotte had come back. "Have you replenished your stock? I should have made myself clearer. I shall need a regular supply of your finest green thread. Meanwhile, please show me your white."

"You must enjoy sewing."

"So it appears," Charlotte had responded curtly. This time, however, she had accepted her change, which was a start. As she had continued to visit the shop she'd unbent very gradually, letting slip a compliment about Mabel's dress one day, another time remarking that a shopkeeper such as Mabel must see all manner of people to talk to. Thus encouraged, Mabel had eventually asked "What are you sewing with all this thread?"

Charlotte had stared so hard at her that meeting her gaze had made Mabel's eyes sting. At last the old woman had said "When it's finished I'd like you to see."

Mabel shivered and went to the oven to pull out the trays of mince pies. She slid in the last tray and stood close to the oven, hugging herself. Translucent flames of frost were spreading imperceptibly up the window. She hurried upstairs to put on a heavier cardigan before sitting with her back to the kitchen window and the dripping tap. She wouldn't be driven out of her kitchen, but while she was remembering the Sterlings she preferred not to face their dark house and darker woods.

A little more than a year ago, Charlotte had brought in her sewing, producing it from a worn black handbag large enough to contain the cash register. It had proved to be an embroidered message, GOD IS GOOD, in a heavy wooden frame. "It's for Ben, my grandson," Charlotte had announced with a kind of grim pride.

The message had been surrounded by elaborate patterns which looked as if Charlotte had been trying to fix the meaning of the words forever. To Mabel the patterning had seemed obsessive almost to the point of compulsion, the symmetry somehow discomforting. "Look at all the care you've taken," she'd said. "You must think a lot of your grandson. Are you pleased with how he's growing up?"

As Charlotte had stared at her, Mabel had thought she'd presumed too much—and then Charlotte had gripped the edge of the counter and leaned so close that Mabel had smelled medicine on her breath. "His mother is," the old woman had whispered, "but not her sister."

It was clear which of them she agreed with. Before Mabel could think what to ask next, Charlotte had shoved herself away from the counter, sucking in her breath so hard that her lips had turned white. A moment later the shop door had opened to admit both of the Sterling men, pale nostrils flaring as they thrust their sharp faces forwards almost doglike, white eyebrows raised in identical expressions of mild reproof. "We were wondering where you'd wandered off to, Mother," the younger man had said.

"Come along now, Charlotte. You're always saying you don't like the cold. Let's get you back to bed. You'll be losing your sewing if you start taking it out of the house, and it's been doing you so much good."

As each man took hold of one of her arms, Charlotte had given Mabel a look which stopped just short of an appeal. The memory made her shiver and glance towards the window as if her thoughts might be overheard. There was nothing to see except the frost climbing the glass, the cold of the night rendered visible. She turned away and moved closer to the oven.

Perhaps Charlotte had been as confused and senile as the men had made her seem. Perhaps her own condition had been what she was afraid of, and her public image her defense against it. Mabel had dismissed the notion that the men had been putting on a show for her, but she'd wondered what sort of Christmas the little boy would have. Whenever the black car passed her cottage she'd watched for him, sitting bright-eyed and alert beside the driver, and she couldn't help thinking he looked starved of an ordinary childhood, though mustn't children always regard their own childhood as the norm? She'd considered inviting the Sterlings to her house over Christmas, and once she'd started up the track, but had felt so cold in the shadow of the forest that she'd turned back. Later that day she had been shocked to see the two men and the little boy disappearing into the pathless forest when it was almost dark. She'd watched for them to reappear, but she must have missed them. Surely they couldn't have been in there until after midnight, when she had gone to bed.

Early in January Charlotte had returned to the shop. She'd looked withered, exhausted, barely capable of supporting the weight of her overcoat. She'd stood at the counter, flicking her fingers irritably at locks of gray hair which wouldn't be contained by her scarf, until Mabel had said "Did your grandson like his present?"

The old lady had gripped the counter as if she might fall. "It isn't finished," she'd said.

Presumably she'd meant her embroidery, but why should that have caused her voice to shake? Mabel never knew, because at that moment she'd seen Ben's mother hurrying across the square. She'd thought of warning Charlotte, and then it had been too late. The old lady had started nervously as Ben's mother opened the door. "There you are, Charlotte. Carl and his father were worried about you."

Her face had looked fattened by Christmas and dull with suppressing emotion, with doing her duty as she saw it, and Mabel had instinctively disliked her. "You know where I am if you need to talk," Mabel had wanted to tell the old lady—but mightn't that have brought her to Mabel's house as, perhaps, she grew more senile? In retrospect, too late, that seemed unlikely. Holding her head high, Charlotte had stalked out of the shop so abruptly that Ben's mother had had to trot to keep up with her. Mabel had never seen Charlotte to speak to again, but surely that was no reason for Mabel to feel guilty about the car crash.

Nobody knew for certain what had caused it, even if the only witness had seen the Sterlings arguing as their car had passed hers—even if the witness had thought she'd seen the people in the back seat, Ben's mother and grandfather, trying to calm down an old woman. Perhaps Charlotte had finally lost her temper at the way they treated her, but could that have been enough to cause the crash on a moorland road where you could see for miles? It must have been. Surely there was no need to wonder if Charlotte had deliberately caused the accident to put a stop to something she'd imagined, or to save Ben from his family.

Mabel told herself that she had been reading her own anxiety about the little boy into Charlotte's behavior, and huddled closer to the

51

oven. Perhaps she wouldn't think about the Sterlings any more until she could discuss her thoughts with someone; just now they were making her feel vulnerable. Had she caught a chill? Though she would be disappointed if she had to forgo midnight mass, she thought she might be well advised to take a glass of brandy up to bed once the last tray of pies was out of the oven. At least the tap had finally stopped dripping, but it would require some effort for her to wait for the pies if she kept on shivering like this. Could she have left the front door open? No, the cold was coming from the direction of the window, for her back felt like ice. The casement must have opened somehow. She staggered to her feet, her legs trembling, and waved her hands to try and clear away the sudden mist of her breath.

The window was closed tight. It was closed, even though an icicle was hanging from the tap. At first she didn't understand what else she was seeing. Even when she held her breath until her head swam, the window still looked pale and blurred. She flapped her hands at the air as best she could—they were beginning to feel stiff and unfamiliar— and then she realized that the pallor wasn't in the air, it was on the window itself. Ice was spreading across the entire window, so swiftly she could see the translucent tendrils growing.

She couldn't move. Her legs felt withered and unstrung, barely capable of supporting her. An intricate circular pattern of ice was spreading from the center of the window as if a focus of intense cold were approaching the glass. It was like a mask, Mabel thought with a terrible clarity: a mask for a head that must be wider than she dared imagine, the head of a presence so cold that its advance was causing the ice to form—a presence, she knew suddenly, whose attention her thoughts had drawn to her. She sensed its hugeness in the dark outside her cottage. Please make it go away, please let her be preserved from seeing what it looked like behind its mask of ice, she vowed before God to stop thinking if that would make it go away . . .

And then she had a thought which would have made her clench her fists if she had been able to move them. If her thinking of Ben Sterling had brought this out of the night to her, what might it want of him? She could feel the arctic cold settling over her like sleep made tangible, but she mustn't let go: someone had to keep the little boy away from whatever was waiting for him. Then the ice on the window spread onto the wall like marble coming elaborately to life, and she felt that happening inside her too. As she fell helplessly towards the stove, her thoughts were extinguished like a match.

THINGS
OVERHEARD

Understand me, when I talk of purity. I don't mean a little matter,

but my purity—the purity I have in mind—is distinguished and

aloof . . . metaphysical, of the stars . . . of the big spaces. . . .

—David Lindsay, *Devil's Tor*

NINE

The children were expecting London to be an adventure, and it proved to be one. Ellen was congratulating herself on having navigated the Volkswagen into the West End despite the lunchtime traffic when they were confronted by a sign which said Oxford Street was closed to private cars. Now Ellen saw why it was surrounded by so many one-way arrows on the map. The car tailgating Ben's blared its horn at him for braking, and a businessman crossing in front of him brandished two fingers at him as if he had sounded the horn. "That's a bad example," ten-year-old Margaret advised her brother.

"I expect he was wishing us success," Ben said. "V for victory. I don't mean to change the subject, but where do I go now?"

The map appeared to have turned into a mass of arrows which collided and dodged away like a diagram of turbulence. "Across and next right," Ellen said, since that seemed to be the only way to go.

The route took them past the British Museum. "That's where they have lots of old weapons, isn't it, Dad?" seven-year-old Johnny said. "Could we go and see them if there's time?"

"I don't suppose they'd have an old tank we could use to make our way to where we're going," Ben wondered, showing his teeth at a NO ENTRY sign.

"Only if there's time," Johnny said rather plaintively. "We aren't going to be late, are we? Won't they publish your book if we're late?"

"I'm sure they will, sweetie," Ellen said, turning to smile at his thin pale eager face, almost a miniature of his father's except for his hair, which was black like hers. "Be a little quiet now until we get there."

Shaftesbury Avenue led them across Cambridge Circus, beyond which Ben raced the oncoming traffic into a side street, beating a double-decker bus to the intersection so narrowly that Johnny cheered while Margaret screamed and Ellen held her breath. Traffic wardens and women wearing fishnet stockings prowled a labyrinth of streets made even narrower by illegally parked cars, some immobilized by wheel clamps. Whenever a gap opened in the traffic there seemed to be a taxi poised to dart into it. Ben drummed the wheel as if he were about to fling up his hands, and then he bumped the car over the curb into a one-way street. "A miracle. A space."

Most of the parking meters in the street had bags over their heads, but the one at the end was working. He steered the car into the space and jumped out, and was reaching in his pocket when he read the sign on the meter. "*How* much for ten minutes? At this rate we'll just about have time to walk to the end of the street and back. My curse on whoever's responsible. May their noses turn into sausages and be eaten by dogs, may their toes grow so long they have to tie them in knots to walk . . ."

Anxiety and mirth and dismay because she'd brought no money were chasing one another over Margaret's long delicate oval face. "What comes after noses and toes?"

"Don't ask, or something might be after yours," Ellen said, searching her own purse. "Oh dear, the milkman took all my change."

"Shall I ask that lady in the doorway if she can change your notes, Mummy?" Johnny suggested.

"I think she might misinterpret your intentions, Johnny," Ben said, squeezing Ellen's knee and winking at her as he climbed into the car. "Let's blunder onwards. I see now, this is like a kind of life-size board game where the object is to avoid Oxford Street. I only hope this isn't an illegal move."

He backed to the intersection and was veering left when Margaret said "What's the name of your and Mummy's publishers?"

"Any other time I'd enjoy repeating it. Ember, a subsidiary of Firebrand Books."

"We just saw it."

"Across the road you just came out of," Johnny gabbled, and Margaret added "Where a lady's jumping up and down and waving."

Ellen looked back. On the far side of the crossroads a young woman was pointing at their car and gesturing with her other hand as she tried to cross the intersection. "She's telling us to go left twice and come back," Ellen guessed.

"You don't think her idea of fun could be misdirecting strangers."

When they managed to return to the crossroads, the young woman was still there. She ran to the car as it turned right. She was wearing a moss-green suit, green tights and dark green shoes, and struck Ellen as altogether pixielike, even her smile which was disproportionately wide for her small triangular face. "I didn't think there could be many families with children cruising through Soho. If I'd known you were coming by car I'd have given you better directions."

"We thought driving would be cheaper than training it," Ben said.

"Let me show you our car park and then we'll eat. You kids must be starving." She jogged beside the car as it coasted down the ramp beneath the Firebrand building. "I'm Kerys Thorn, as if you didn't know," she said when the Sterlings piled out of the vehicle. "It's really ace to meet you two at last after so much talking on the phone. How does Italian food for lunch sound? Slurp, slurp if it's spaghetti, would you say, kids?"

Johnny giggled. "Sounds like him eating most things," Margaret said.

"You should hear me eating Chinese soup, Margaret," Kerys said.

"My name's really Margery."

"Do your mum and dad know?"

"We're kept informed of changes," Ellen said, and gave Margaret a kiss when the girl frowned at her.

Kerys led the Sterlings into the dull January daylight and through a confusion of streets to the restaurant, racing Johnny to it when they reached the block where it stood. A fat waiter who looked ready to burst into song ushered the party to their table as soon as he saw Kerys and brought them a bottle of Krug. "Here's to a best-seller. Success and long lives to us all," she proposed, and nudged Johnny when he made a face at the taste of his token glassful while Margaret demurely sipped hers. "We have to drink this stuff because we're grownups," she told him and helped him read the menu, which was half as tall as he was. When he remarked loudly on the prices before Ellen could hush him, Kerys nudged him again. "Ember's paying. You have whatever your mum and dad say you can have," she murmured in his ear, and Ellen found herself growing increasingly fond of her.

Once the waiter had taken their orders, Kerys produced a notepad from her handbag. "Kids, I'm going to ask your brilliant parents about themselves so I can tell our publicity department what to say about them, but if you've any extra ideas, just shout. Who do I start with? Do you write the books around Ellen's pictures, Ben? What was it you said, Ellen, about each taking half the year?"

"Ben writes the book in the autumn and winter, and then I illustrate it in the spring and summer when the light's better and the children are at school."

"Was Ben already writing when you met?"

"Not until years after we were married. I managed to persuade him to write down some of the stories he used to tell the children, and you took some persuading, didn't you, Ben?"

"Some."

"Don't worry, Ben, we'll let you talk," Kerys assured him. "We'll want everyone to hear from both of you when we send you touring to promote your book. We'd have done that with your other books if I'd been with Ember then."

"We may have to go separately if it's when the children are at school," Ellen said.

"The one of you who stays at home could be the inspiration behind the other one. The media should go for that." Kerys sat back as their meal arrived and the waiter departed, blowing a kiss in appreciation of their choices. "I mean, if it's true. Do you think you'd be a writer if you hadn't met Ellen, Ben?"

"I don't think I'd be much of anything."

"Let me ask you the question I always like to ask writers. Where would you say your stories come from?"

Ben raised a portion of veal Marsala to his lips, then laid it down on his plate. "I'm not sure I ought to know. It works best if I just let the story tell itself to me. I think writers can be too conscious of their technique or what they're trying to say or who they're influenced by. I suppose I must be influenced by everything I've read, particularly when I was a child."

"I'd say your stories read like nobody except yourself. Who did you—"

"I've never understood this thing about writers trying to find their own voice. It seems to me that if you've got one you're more likely to develop it when you're not straining to hear it yourself. I just try to tell the story as if you were listening to me tell it. I interrupted you."

"I'm glad you did," Kerys told him, and Ellen sensed she was relieved that his enthusiasm had overcome the self-consciousness he always experienced with strangers. "Don't let your food get cold. I was only going to ask what you used to read."

"Anything that helped keep my imagination alive." Ben chewed the forkful as if he were tasting his memories. "Children's fantasies, ghost stories. Science fiction one summer. And when I was a bit older, all the books I could get hold of that were supposed to get you sent to Hell for reading them, or so my aunt who brought me up believes. Don't think I'm getting at Auntie Beryl, though, you two. Too much imagination scares some people, that's all."

"Not you kids, I can tell. Which is your favorite Sterling book?"

"The new one," they both said.

"*The Boy Who Caught the Snowflakes?* Mine too. What do you think we should tell children about it to make them want to read it?"

"About when he wishes he can't feel the cold," Margaret said, "and then the snowflake lands on his hand and he sees it not melting."

"And his second wish is the world should never be cold again, and the cold all goes inside him."

"Tell them about how the icecaps start melting and the seas begin to flood the land and all sorts of birds and other creatures start to die out. That was sad."

"But it's all right at the end, because he uses his third wish to put the cold back in the world."

"And you have to show them some of Mummy's pictures," Margaret told Kerys. "I like the one where the boy's standing in the snow and the two snowflakes are sort of perching on his hands like birds."

"That's superb. I thought we might use it on the cover."

"You remember I told you I've worked in advertising," Ellen said. "I was wondering if you'd want me to make suggestions about that side of things."

"You bet. I'll introduce you to our publicity person and you can sort her out," Kerys promised. "But I just saw some little eyes looking at the sweet trolley when they thought nobody was noticing."

Almost an hour later she ushered the family back to the Firebrand offices, where they were introduced to so many people who wished the book success, and shook so many hands, that Ellen promptly forgot all the names. She was left with a sense of general goodwill which more or less compensated for their being unable to track down the publicity director. "You can meet her next time you're down," Kerys told her, and led them through the children's book department to her office, grabbing an armful of books each for Margaret and Johnny on the way. She cleared a space amid the precarious piles of typescripts and memos and books on her desk while her assistant brought milk for the children and coffee for the adults, extra strong for Ben. When the drinks arrived Kerys raised hers in a last toast. "Here's to making this the year of the Sterlings," she said.

TEN

Twilight and traffic were gathering on the motorway out of London. Long before the car reached Cambridge, Johnny was asleep. He was still her baby, Ellen thought as she glanced at his dreaming face in the light from an oncoming vehicle, even if he'd reached the age at which her telling him so annoyed him. Once they were past Cambridge she and Margaret and Ben took turns to spot strange place names: Stow cum Quy, Snailwell, Puddledock, Trowse Newton . . . By now they were on the outskirts of Norwich and following the ring road to their suburb while Margaret widened her eyes as if she were inserting invisible props under the lids and protested that she wasn't tired. "Then you're the only one," Ben said, beginning to snore loudly as he steered the car off the ring road. "Ouch, Margery. Don't kick."

"If you're not tired," Ellen told her, "you can finish clearing away the books and games you and Johnny left in the front room."

"Johnny has to help."

"He clears up when you're at dancing class. Don't sulk, or we'll think you aren't old enough to go to the market again with your friends."

"Mummy . . ." Margaret protested, and left it at that, though when her father parked the car outside the house she peered suspiciously at her brother in case the movement made him betray that he wasn't

63

really asleep. Convinced that he was, she relented and attempted to carry him into the house as she had when they were younger, but had to settle for helping him stumble along, which woke him up. "You can go to bed if you're tired," she said.

"I'm hungry," he mumbled.

Margaret's tone had been so saintly that Ellen gave her an amused loving hug. "You're always hungry, Johnny. Tidy away your things while Margery and I make you something to eat," she said as she unlocked the house.

The front door swept a gathering of envelopes and leaflets off the doormat. Johnny pounced on them, handing his mother the leaflets, which advertised a knife grinder and a newspaper bingo game and a charity which recycled Christmas cards, and sorted the envelopes in case there was one for him. "Just bills," he complained.

"Better give them to Bill, then," his father said. "On second thoughts, give them to me. Bill may be worse off than we are."

"Aren't we well off?" Margaret said.

"We are so long as we have one another, don't you think? And I don't think we'll have to leave either of you at the bank as security just yet." He swung his fist playfully past Johnny's chin to snatch the solemn look from the boy's face. "I get the feeling we're on our way to bigger things, don't you think, Ellen?"

"I hope so," Ellen said and headed for the kitchen, where she added a few vegetables to the soup in the stockpot while Margaret made sandwiches on the table. From the front room they heard the whir of Johnny's model car which recoiled from obstacles. "Put that away now," Ellen called.

"We've put away everything else," Ben responded.

Margaret sighed loudly. "Boys," she said like someone several times her age.

"Maybe if your father hadn't stayed that way inside himself he wouldn't write our books."

Margaret carried the trayful of sandwiches and plates into the front room while her mother followed with the soup. Because this was the largest room in the house it functioned as dining room and sitting room and the children's playroom, while the smaller room beside the

64

kitchen was where Ellen and Ben worked. Johnny dropped his car in the box of toys in the corner cupboard and ran to the table to slurp his soup, gazing past her at her charcoal study of Lakeland fells. "When are we going to the mountains?" he said between quick mouthfuls. "You said we could one year."

"Maybe this year. Your father and I often used to have walking holidays, but then Margaret was born, and by the time she was old enough to keep up with us you'd come along."

"I like walking," Johnny protested. "I walked all those miles round and round the school field for the starving children."

"It's a good job you didn't see the food you bought them," Margaret said, "or you'd have gobbled it all up."

"We'll have to make sure you don't get too far ahead of us, Johnny," Ben intervened. "We don't want you running off the edge of everything. I thought I'd done that once, and your mother had to save me. That was how we met."

"Tell us the story," Margaret pleaded.

"How old were you?" Johnny said.

"More than three times your age, so don't even dream of doing what I did. And your mother was even younger than she is now," Ben said, ducking as Ellen aimed a punch at him. "I'd gone up to Ambleside with my aunt for a week, and I did most of the ambling while she went on coach trips with a retired couple she'd got talking to at the hotel. So the day before we were due to leave for home I decided I was going to walk along the ridges all the way to the next lake, and I almost didn't come back.

"Maybe it was being up so high there was nothing to get in the way of my seeing, or maybe it was the air up there, which is so clear you can taste how clear it is, but suddenly it was as though a light had been switched on inside everything around me. All the rocks and the grass and the heather looked as if they were made out of the same brightness as the sky and the clouds. That's what I was trying to capture in our first book, where the whole world seems to take a step forwards and greet our hero with its shapes and colors and the rest of it, which shows you how far short I fell of putting what I experienced into words."

"I liked that bit," Margaret said, and Johnny nodded hard.

"I remember you did. I wouldn't have left it in otherwise. You two and Mummy are the only readers I try to please, you know. Anyway, that day I got so drunk on what I was seeing that at first I didn't realize I wouldn't be at the hotel in time for dinner if I went back along the top—not that I cared about keeping body and soul together, but I didn't want my aunt to get herself into a state. So I did one of the worst things you can do in the mountains: I followed what looked like a shortcut down. And an hour later I couldn't go back up and couldn't see how to go down."

"Why couldn't you climb back up?" Margaret wanted to know.

"Because I'd slid down a shale slope. Climbing that stuff is like trying to climb a pile of slates. It looked fine from above, just a narrow path between two walls with lots of tiles sticking out to hold onto, but when I lost my footing halfway down all the tiles I grabbed came away in my hand. So I slid maybe two hundred yards on my bottom towards what looked like a sheer drop, and when I managed to stop myself by digging in my heels and elbows I couldn't have been more than fifty yards from the edge."

"You shouldn't have gone down that way," Johnny said like a rescuer.

"My thoughts exactly. Only the other routes had looked a lot more dangerous, and when I'd started down it seemed as if there ought to be an easy way over that edge. You had to be as close as I was then to see that the last fifty yards were even steeper and more treacherous than the path I'd just fallen down. And the only way I'd have been able to see if there was a path beyond the edge would have been to scramble down so far that it would have taken a host of angels to carry me back to safety if there turned out to be no path. So I panicked. I started snivelling and praying to whoever might be listening, and when that didn't get me anywhere I told myself I'd have to climb up the shale. I told myself I'd be all right so long as I planned every move before I made it and only moved one limb at a time. So I started inching myself upwards on my back to get to somewhere I'd feel safe to turn onto my front. And as soon as I moved, half the shale I was lying on slid out from under me.

"I can still remember how it sounded as it slid over the edge—like bones rattling. I remember what frightened me most was how long I might be falling. I was clenching my fists so hard I felt as if I was holding two handfuls of rock, only they were my nails, and digging my elbows and the back of my head into the shale so hard they ached for days. And just about the moment I realized I hadn't slipped after all, I heard a voice."

"It was Mummy," Johnny cried.

"I told you I needed an angel to save me. Though I have to admit that what she was saying wasn't exactly angelic."

"Words to the effect of 'Is some silly sod trying to start a landslide up there?'" Ellen recalled.

"To which my response was to ask if she could see a way down for me, though I had to shout so loud because of the wind I was afraid that was enough to start me sliding. She told me there was an easy climb down on my left, in the angle of the overhang, she said. And I thought she must mean my right, because all I could see to my left was shale that looked practically vertical. We almost got into an argument about which left she meant, and I'd have asked her to climb just high enough to show me which way she was coming, but I suppose that was more than my masculine pride was worth. So all I could do was trust her and crab myself down on my back to where she said I'd be safe. And I was nearly at the edge when I slipped and felt myself going head first towards the drop."

"But you were saved," Johnny insisted.

"Yes, because your mother had realized I might need help and she was coming up as I went sliding. She caught my shoulders and held me up while I managed to get one leg round and stand on the first step, and after that it was just like walking down a staircase onto a ledge as wide as this room. Mind you, I didn't take in much of that until my arms and legs stopped shaking. We sat on the ledge and chatted for a few minutes and discovered we were both on holiday from Norfolk. Then she asked me if I'd like her to walk down with me in case I got into any more difficulties. And of course I said no, being a man."

Ellen remembered him striding unsteadily but determinedly away down the uneven path. Sometimes Johnny reminded her of what had seemed at the time to be her last sight of his father. Once Ben had stumbled, flailing his arms, at a point where she'd needed to take care on her way up. She'd started after him, both anxious for him and glad when it had seemed he'd given her an excuse to follow him, until she had seen him regain his balance. She'd watched him out of sight before sighing and returning to her study of the fells, only to discover that frustration had interposed itself between her and the view she was trying to sketch. She'd pushed her pad into her rucksack and made her way down to the hostel, wishing that she had suggested to whatever his name was that they should meet in Norfolk, blaming herself for not having suggested it, surprised at herself for expecting that of him so soon after his mishap on the shale, snorting at herself for having missed her chance.

"You mightn't ever have met again," Margaret said accusingly to her father.

"Then you wouldn't be here to tell me off. Believe me, all the way down I was berating myself for being so eager to show off, and trying to think of a reason to go back. But you'll have to wait for the next installment. You've school in the morning and it's time for baths and bed."

Later, as Ellen lay naked under the duvet with him, he said "After you saved my life that day, did you see me nearly miss my footing on the way down?"

"I couldn't have seen you any clearer if I'd had a telescope."

"I was sneaking a look at you, that was why I slipped. For years I used to dream of how you looked, all by yourself with your pad and pencil and the mountains. And sometimes I'd dream of you appearing like the good fairy of the mountain when I thought the shale had finished me off."

Ellen rolled onto her side and laid one leg over his. "I'm a bit more substantial than a fairy, you'll have noticed."

"Rather. I was remembering how you looked in jeans, you realize. Pretty tight, they were," he said, running a finger along the inside of her thigh. "That was another reason I hoped when Milligans got the poster for the exhibition that it would turn out to be yours. But I was only hoping to carry off the artist, not the art."

"I couldn't have let you pay for that picture when I saw how much it meant to you."

"Remember how your boyfriend tried to convince you that justified raising the price?"

"And went off in a huff when I told him it was the picture I'd been working on when you and I first met." She closed one hand gently around Ben's penis. "Hugh wasn't such a bad sort really. He was there when I needed him at art school, to tell me I mustn't be shy of promoting my work. And he put in a word with a friend of his father's which got me into Noble's, even though I was going out with you by then. He couldn't have foreseen the trouble I'd have there. I think he always wanted me to do more with my talent than he thought he could do with his."

Ben slipped one arm beneath her shoulders as his penis began to push her fist open. "No need for either of us to feel the way he did, as I hope Kerys and the rest of them at Ember managed to persuade you," he said, and kissed her breasts.

"I wouldn't paint those pictures if you didn't make me see them."

"I wouldn't write the books if I didn't have your pictures of them to look forward to."

"You know that's not true," she said, though she liked the idea. As she felt her nipples swelling, she took hold of his chin and raised his head so that she could look into his eyes. "Do you think this one could really be *the* book?"

"The book," he intoned like a footman announcing royalty, and then grew serious. "I think if Kerys has her way we're going to be in every bookshop in the country."

"Only the country?"

"And the towns, and the airports, and that hotel in Grasmere where the paperbacks in the revolving bookstand looked as if the dust was holding them together."

"We never did go back there after we were married to flash our certificate at the manager. I still think he rang the fire alarm that night to catch me coming out of your room. And I'm sure that old lady sent her poodles down to trip him up, because she tipped me a look that was as good as a wink." Ellen gave Ben a long deep kiss, feeling his tongue rough on hers, and opened her thighs around his. "It would be grand if the book does soar, wouldn't it? The children would be so pleased."

"So would the bank manager."

"He'll have no reason to complain once I get back into advertising. And listen, I truly don't mind working in it for a while, so stop worrying. Wherever I go, I'll come back the same."

"That's all I'll ever want," Ben said, and eased himself into her. She hugged him and slowed down his rhythm with hers, waves of warmth growing in her before the flood. Afterwards she laid her head on his chest, breathing in the smell of the two of them, before drifting off to sleep. Sometimes she liked this kind of sex best of all, the kind which was so gentle and familiar it felt like stability made flesh. If their books raised their life to new heights, it mustn't leave this behind. "Not too far," she murmured drowsily to Ben's sleeping face.

ELEVEN

The night before her interview at Ballyhoo Unlimited, Ellen leafed through her portfolio and was impressed by hardly anything. She had already preferred her illustrations for Ben's books, but now she saw that it wasn't just a matter of her having developed her skills: nearly all the work in the portfolio was dated. Admittedly some of the assignments—a teenage fashion store, a chain of discos which had been meant to light up the winters of half a dozen Norfolk towns but which had winked out before Johnny was born—would inevitably have dated, but why should she expect the agency to take that into consideration? She quite liked the work she'd done on the campaign to advertise the houseboat holiday firm, but that wouldn't be enough. She pulled out all the material which seemed stale to her and gazed wistfully at her depleted portfolio, and came to a decision. "I'm going to show them Broads Best."

Ben glanced up from copying changes of address from last year's Christmas cards. "I should hope so. It's your work."

"It isn't quite that simple."

"Then it should be, and if anyone can make it so, you can. And if you ever bump into Sid Peacock you can tell him from me to insert himself up himself and twist."

"I can't imagine ever seeing him again," Ellen said on her way to the back room. Beside the desk in front of the large window which in daytime gave the room all the light it could hold, one shelf of the deep bookcase contained a few copies of each of the two Sterling books, Ben's battered electric typewriter, pots of Ellen's brushes bunched like withered blossoms waiting for the spring to return their color to them. A pile of folders of her work occupied the bottom shelf. She extracted the Broads Best folder and took it to the desk, where she rested her elbows on either side of it without opening it. She was suddenly afraid that it would prove to be less inspired than she remembered it to be.

It hadn't seemed inspired only to her, judging by Sid Peacock's behavior. He was the head of what he liked to call his department of Noble Publicity—an office in which he'd worked with Ellen and an older man called Nathan, who was gay and who openly loathed him. Sid, who was three years older than Ellen, had borne his wide tanned face and Oxford accent like presents he was offering the world, and smelled of aftershaves with savage names. Whenever the agency bosses had assigned him a campaign he would call a brainstorming session, draining Ellen and Nathan of their ideas and usually preferring his own. Three years of this and no promotion had begun to frustrate Ellen, but there had been no other opening for her in Norwich. Then the agency had acquired the Broads account and she had lost her innocence.

Broads was the oldest brewery in Norfolk, and its directors had wanted to give it a new image. Everyone at the agency had been delighted to have the account—at least, until Broads had turned down all the proposed campaigns. The directors didn't like spacemen drinking their ale in free-fall, they didn't care for anything involving computers, they especially disliked the idea of associating their product with pop stars or film stars, either current or nostalgically revived. After several rejections Sid had stormed into the office. "It's like talking to mummies. Why the hell did they bother coming to us if they think they know more than we do about what's up-to-date?" And Ellen had begun to wonder if the agency was missing the point—if they couldn't make the future of the brewery by delving into its past.

72

She'd thought she remembered something she'd once heard about the ale, and over the weekend she had tracked it down in a history of Norfolk.

"Something you may not know about Broads Best," she'd scribbled on her pad, and then "Ten things you may not know . . ." On Monday Sid hadn't seemed particularly impressed but told her to come back to him if she managed to develop the idea. On her way home on Friday she'd seen a jigsaw in a toyshop window and had realized how the campaign could work, and she'd been so eager to show him that she'd arranged to meet him in the office on Saturday morning. She'd let him hug her to express his enthusiasm for her idea, but when he'd tried to give her breasts a clammy squeeze she'd poked him in the stomach. "Let me see your work when it's finished," he'd said like a spinsterish schoolmaster, flinching out of reach.

Her growing anger at her memories of him made her open the folder on the desk. The designs still looked as impressive to her as they must have looked to Sid. THIS MAN ONCE SAID IT WAS ENGLAND'S PROUDEST ALE was the first thing people might not have known about Broads Best, printed above a tenth of the picture which the other nine slogans gradually assembled, her portrait of Henry VIII with a tankard in his hand. But when she'd taken it to Sid he'd grimaced at it. "I used to think it would be clever to advertise tartar control with a toothbrush getting rid of Genghis Khan. Too clever by half," he'd said, and she had felt so disappointed and vulnerable that she didn't wonder why he told her, as if he were doing an undeserved favor, that he would show her idea to their boss.

She ought to have realized what Sid was up to. Nathan would undoubtedly have warned her, but he'd been on holiday in Marrakesh that week. A few days later, when the junior partner had congratulated her on helping Sid visualize his idea for the Broads Best campaign, she had been too stunned to argue, and by the time her rage had been clamoring to be articulated it would have seemed too like an afterthought, a lie. Besides, she had seen enough of the partners to be pretty sure that they would have regarded the Saturday incident as negligible and would probably have dismissed her accusation as an attempt at revenge. Worst of all, Sid's self-righteous look had made it clear that he would have treated her more fairly if she had given in to him.

She'd let herself believe that the whole sordid incident had become irrelevant once Sid Peacock had moved to an agency in London and she had become pregnant with Margaret, but now she saw that she ought to have laid claim to her work for later use. Perhaps she still could, she thought as she took the folder to show Ben. "Would you hire me?"

"You bet I would, and so would anyone with any sense."

"Yes, but you're married to me."

"Anyone with any sense would be," he said, and made a face at having contradicted himself. "As soon as my aunt's home and can sit with the children, we'll go out for dinner. We'll have plenty to celebrate."

In the morning Ellen walked the children to school, Johnny racing ahead to each intersection and glancing back for her to tell him he could cross, Margaret holding her hand and chattering about fashions, records, changing schools next year, a classmate who was rumored to have been off school with her first period . . . The children were plenty to celebrate, Ellen thought, and so long as the family was happy, what else mattered? Sometimes she worried that they wouldn't grow up normally with a writer for a father and an artist for a mother, but they kept reminding her that it seemed unlikely. At the school gates they each gave her a fleeting kiss and ran off to join their friends, and she walked home to prepare dinner before heading for the interview.

Ben had left her the Volkswagen with a note on the driver's seat: IF YOU'RE HALF AS PROUD OF YOURSELF AS I AM OF YOU YOU'LL SLAY THEM. She smiled at that and drove into Norwich, and had time to stroll from the car park, arriving at the long new building of yellowish stone near the cathedral less than five minutes before she was due there.

A lift which smelled perfumed and which hummed to itself on one note eased her up to the third floor. Past an accountant's office where women were typing what headphones told them and another door which looked as if whatever name its pane had once displayed had been frosted over, she found the reception area of Ballyhoo Unlimited beyond glass doors as wide as the room. Fat blue settees dwarfed by posters almost big enough for billboards faced each other across a floor padded with blue carpet. The two men waiting on the settees glanced at Ellen and then resumed their nonchalant expressions as the receptionist behind the desk between them greeted her, raising her face as if her eyes and her cherry-red smile were fixed. "Mrs. Sterling? You're first in," she said.

Ellen smiled apologetically at the men as she sat down. Her companion on the settee, a man who was approaching middle age and who wore a spotted bow tie and a tweed jacket slightly too large for him, was staring at his stubby fingers as if they might somehow count against him. The other man, who couldn't have been more than thirty, was gripping his portfolio with his bony knees and folded hands as though he were either praying or restraining himself. Ellen listened to the awkward silence and the sounds it amplified, the creak of the tweedy man's new shoes as he flexed his toes nervously, a faint heartbeat which was the younger man's left heel drumming on the carpet, the receptionist proclaiming "Ballyhoo Unlimited" to callers in exactly the tone of a game show hostess enthusing about a prize. Presumably that constant repetition was inaudible wherever Ellen would be working, if she got the job. "That would be our Mr. Rutter," the receptionist was saying now. "He's in London unexpectedly. Can our Mr. Hipkiss help you? What was it concerning? I'm going to ask you to hold for a moment . . ." Ellen was still waiting for her to do so when she resumed: "I'm afraid Mr. Fuge and Mr. Peacock are in a meeting. I'll tell Mr. Hipkiss you rang just as soon as he's free."

She switched off the call and ducked her head as if challenging her audience to prove that her blond hair was dyed, and Ellen had to begin her question twice before the receptionist would look up. "Who did you say . . . who did you say were in a meeting?"

"The partners except for Mr. Rutter. They'll be ready for you any moment now," the receptionist said with a briskness that suggested faint reproof.

"Mr. Fuge and Mr. . . . ."

"Peacock. He used to work locally, then he went away until Mr. Rutter tempted him back. Why, do you know him?"

Ellen was taking a deep breath when the switchboard buzzed and addressed the receptionist in a small sharp voice. "They want you now," the receptionist said. "I'll take you in."

Ellen stood up. She could walk straight out of the building and leave Sid Peacock wondering—but she wouldn't let him off that easily; she wanted to see how he would conduct himself. She followed the receptionist down an inner corridor, past a large office where several men in shirtsleeves were working at drawing boards, to a conference room.

Two men were seated midway along the extensive heavy table, which took up much of the room. One of them, a ruddy man whose waistcoat buttons appeared to be in danger of snapping their threads, came to meet Ellen. "Mrs. Sterling," he said in a voice thick as a cigar. "Sorry we kept you waiting. I'm Gordon Fuge, and this is Sidney Peacock."

So he was *Sidney* now, Ellen thought, growing tense as Peacock put aside the papers he was scanning and extended a hand to her. His wide face looked worn, his tan was turning purplish with veins. When she gave his hand a single hard shake he peered at her as if confused by her brusqueness and then let his gaze drift over her breasts. "Pleased to meet you," he said.

For as long as it took her to sit down she thought he was pretending not to know her. He watched her sit as though that was included in the appraisal to which she was submitting herself. "Well, Mrs. Sterling, can you sell yourself to us?"

Ellen stared at him until he glanced away, at the papers in front of him. She was enjoying his apparent discomfiture when he said "Don't be afraid to repeat whatever you said in your letter. I haven't had a chance to read it. I'm sitting in for Max Rutter at short notice."

Unexpectedly and infuriatingly, she couldn't help feeling offended. How dare he forget her after the trouble he'd caused her? He deserved the shock he was going to suffer when he recognized the work in her portfolio. "Where would you like me to start?" she said with a sweetness she could almost taste.

"Give us some idea of your experience."

Both he and his colleague were gazing expectantly at her portfolio. She was about to pass it across the table and sit back to watch Sid Peacock's face when Fuge said "What brought you into this game?"

"Advertising? At art college they were always telling us it was the place to aim for. And it paid decent money, which came in handy when I got married."

"That's what I like to hear."

Ellen counted three slowly and silently. "What do you like to hear, Mr. Peacock?"

"A designer who doesn't try and impress us with how much of an artist she is."

"Oh, I'm only sublime when I'm working on a book."

"Mrs. Sterling illustrates her husband's books," Fuge explained.

"Should I have heard of him?"

"That depends on the kind of company he'd find himself in," Ellen said.

"They're children's books, Sidney."

"Won't mean anything to me, then. It was my wife who wanted kids, so she gets to deal with anything connected with the little treasures. If you and your lord and master produce books instead of children, Mrs. Sterling, I reckon you've the right idea."

"We've produced both."

"So let's see what you've got to offer us," Peacock said.

Ellen handed him the portfolio. She didn't feel as detached as she had expected; she was uncomfortably aware of her heartbeat and of her suddenly dry mouth. Peacock turned over the first sheets, making a sound in his throat as if he were clearing the way for a comment he then decided not to utter, and she remembered how he would do that when he was milking her and Nathan of ideas. She started, heart thumping, when Fuge said "Your letter didn't mention where you've worked."

"No—" Ellen swallowed so as to be able to speak up. "Noble Publicity."

"You were there for a while, weren't you, Sidney?"

"I learned the basics there, yes." Peacock frowned at Ellen and continued leafing through her work. "When were you there, Mrs. Sterling?"

Ellen paused enough to let him turn over two more sheets. "When you were."

He didn't look up. He had just uncovered the first of the Broads Best sheets, and she saw the studiedly neutral expression drain from his face. His partner glanced at the picture to see why Peacock was lingering over it, and gave a surprised laugh. "Why, weren't you involved in that campaign, Sidney? Don't tell me you never met the artist. What are the two of you up to, eh? What's our Sidney been promising you, Mrs. Sterling?"

"I'm sure Mr. Peacock knows I expect nothing from him," Ellen said, feeling her cheeks redden, gazing at Peacock to force him to look at her.

But he only spoke to her. "This is embarrassing. I'm sorry I didn't know you at first, Mrs. Sterling. A lot of lunches have flowed under the bridge in what must it be, nearly eleven years?" To his partner he murmured "I'll bet if all the folk you've worked with in your life walked in here right now there'd be a few you couldn't put a name to."

"Just the same, I think I'd be insulted if I were Mrs. Sterling."

Peacock met her gaze then. If he dared to say he was sure she wasn't, Ellen thought, she wouldn't be responsible for her reply. "If I may say so, Mrs. Sterling, I think having children has turned you into quite a handsome lady. I hope you'll accept that as my excuse for not recognizing you to begin with."

"It's thoughtful of you to say so."

"And I hope you'll agree with me that we can both be proud of the Broads Best campaign."

"Ever hopeful, aren't you, Sidney? Not as crude as you used to be, or at least not in front of witnesses. I don't mean to exclude you from the conversation, Mr. Fuge. Let me explain . . ." But now that the moment had come, taking her revenge seemed petty and demeaning, not worth the risk of regretting it later. All she said was, "I won't argue with you."

"Take a look at these, Gordon," he said, and passed his colleague the portfolio. "So have you been keeping your hand in since you left Noble's, Mrs. Sterling?"

He was going through the motions of interviewing her, she thought, in case his colleague suspected that something was wrong. She responded automatically, wanting only to be finished with the pretense and outside in the open air. "Thank you for your time, Mrs. Sterling," he said as Fuge closed the portfolio and folded his hands over his stomach as if he'd just enjoyed a meal. Peacock slid the portfolio across to her and stood up when she did. As Fuge heaved himself to his feet and told her it had been a pleasure, Peacock met her eyes, not quite expressionlessly. "We still have to interview the other candidates," he said.

Ellen was out of the building before his implication caught up with her. Throughout the interview she had been assuming she had already lost the job, but his expression at the end had said that he knew he owed her a favor. Given the context, it could only mean that he intended to hire her. Her instinct was to march straight back and tell him what he could do with the job, but then where would she go? *Could* she bear to work with him again even if she was certain he would keep his hands off her? She made her way through the crowds, which felt both oppressive and distant, to the car. Until she had the chance to discuss the situation with Ben, the best she could offer herself was a good strong cup of tea.

By the time she was halfway home she was savoring how the first sip would taste. She came off the ring road and steered the car into her street, and the taste grew sour in her mouth. There was a police car outside the house, and a uniformed officer was ringing the bell.

She parked awkwardly behind the police vehicle and ran up her path, her pulse accelerating. "What's the matter? Can I help you?"

The policeman turned, his face so carefully unemotional that she missed a breath. "Is this where Mr. Benjamin Sterling lives?" he said.

TWELVE

That morning Ben awoke feeling that his life was about to change. The impression resembled a trace of some dream he couldn't quite recall. The children raced up past him to the bathroom, while he descended as if he were counting the stairs. Ellen snatched his plate of breakfast out of the oven and pulled off her threadbare oven glove to blow on her fingers, and he thought that his sense of imminent change must relate to her interview. He gave her a long hug to make up for almost forgetting and to wish her luck, and kissed her fingers. "You be careful of yourself."

He was finishing breakfast when she took the children off to school. Oddly, once he was alone his impression felt stronger, though still as indefinable. As he brushed his teeth he found himself gazing into his eyes in the bathroom mirror, until he wondered what on earth he was expecting to see. He let out a sigh which blurred his reflection, and hurried downstairs to leave a note for Ellen in the car.

The day wasn't as cold as the gray sky seemed to promise. By the time he reached Milligans, having run for the bus and been hemmed in by commuters fat with winter coats, he felt as if his expectancy had been sweated out of him. Dominic was changing the window display, taking books to the door and blowing fake snow off the tops of the

80

pages. "Good riddance. Next Christmas this will be one shop that turns away this kind of rubbish," he said, patches of his squashed face flaring almost as red as his wiry hair. "Books that nobody would buy for themselves, which these television personalities wouldn't put their names to if they weren't sure that everyone knows they don't really write this trash."

The tinsel flakes glittered in the slanting sunlight as they fell into the gutter, and Ben felt a memory gleam and darken, so swiftly that he hadn't time to glimpse it. "Don't look so dubious," Dominic said, widening his eyes until his high forehead was a mass of ridges. "You're an evangelist compared with these soulless swine. Here, help me cast them out of the window."

When a clock above the roofs began to chime nine, Dominic turned the placard hanging on the door to announce that the shop was open. "We're on our own this week, old pal. Fiona's mumsy says she isn't well. If you want my opinion it's how they bring them up these days, all fashion and fast food and flabbiness. People would be queueing up for my father to open the shop when you and I were at school, but that was when schools taught you how to read and made you sweat."

"They'll be back once they've got over their Christmas spending."

Dominic began to prowl the shop in search of books he could grab off the shelves. "I came into the business because I thought books still helped educate people, but the last thing the public wants these days is to be made to feel it can improve itself. At least it sounds as if there's some point to this new book of yours, giving children a hint of the mess we've made of the climate."

Magic is the point, Ben wanted to retort—the magic of imagination, of language which awakens dreams, of rediscovering the child in oneself and seeing through its eyes—but that would only provoke another monologue from Dominic. "Here's to more winters like we used to have," he said, which seemed safe, and set about packaging books for return to the wholesaler.

Once customers began to appear, Dominic cheered up. Two students exchanged book tokens for textbooks, and then a slow fat man with a clownishly red nose came in, emitting a loud sniff every few seconds as he peered at the spines of books. While he was paying for a thesaurus, painstakingly writing a check before tearing it up and sniffing nine times in the course of making a fair copy, a grandmother went to the children's section to choose a present. Ben watched her approach his and Ellen's last book, pass it by without examining it, rest her hand on it as she retraced her steps, pull it off the shelf and read the blurb, hold it in her hand as she scanned the shelves again, touch an Enid Blyton and take that to the counter, filling its space on the shelf with the Sterlings' book. "Never mind," Dominic said afterwards. "We sold one of your books last week."

Soon Dominic's mother arrived with two bowls and spoons and a panful of porridge. "You boys have this to keep you warm," she said, trying to bustle despite her arthritic limping. "The doctor's been, Dominic. Your father has to go for a stroll every day, and when that doesn't tire him he'll be able to come back to the shop. Just now and then, but you know how happy that'll make him."

"God willing, mother. Leave the pan and I'll bring it home with me."

Dominic watched her out of sight and carried out the pan to empty it into a waste bin once the street was relatively deserted, grimacing at Ben as he did so. Ben often wondered when he'd begun to turn into this staid intolerant man, middle-aged before his time—but wasn't he disliking Dominic's version of those aspects of himself he would rather not acknowledge? He went back to the mechanical task of certifying books unsalable before consigning them to their fate, and had achieved a kind of drowsy trance as he worked when Dominic roused him. "Isn't that your wife?"

Dominic was unpacking a carton of books. For a moment Ben thought he'd misidentified the artist responsible for the cover of the book he was holding, and then he saw that Dominic was gazing past it through the window. Ellen was on the far side of the street, waiting to cross over. She must be eager to tell him about the interview; she was still wearing her gray suit and white blouse and her grandmother's brooch at her throat. He made for the door, waving his clasped hands above his head, but as she dodged between two vans he let his hands drop. Whatever her news was, he could see from her face that she wished she didn't have to tell him.

Her oval face was rounder since she'd had the children. She still wore her black hair long despite the traces of gray which had started to appear. Sometimes at rest her face seemed almost plain, but never when her feelings reached her large blue eyes and wide mouth. Now the dullness of her eyes dismayed him. He closed the door behind him and went quickly to her. "Never mind, love. It's their loss."

"What do you mean?" She looked momentarily shocked by him. "Oh, the interview. I'm not sure about that, I need time to think. But listen, Ben—"

He grabbed her by the elbows and pulled her out of the path of a van which was reversing onto the pavement. Not the children, he thought, feeling as though ice were massing in his stomach. "I'm listening," he said.

"Shall we go somewhere there aren't so many people?"

"Tell me here, for Christ's sake."

"Your aunt died last night, Ben."

"Aunt Beryl?" he said stupidly, knowing that she was the only aunt he had. "Who says so?"

"The police heard this morning, and one of them has just been to the house." She led Ben into the shop, stroking his hand with both of hers. "He said there are no suspicious circumstances, but they'd like you to call in at the station when you're able."

"Happy new year, Ellen," Dominic said, and saw her expression. "Sorry, er, I—"

"We've just learned that my aunt's dead," Ben told him.

Dominic touched his own forehead, navel, left shoulder, right shoulder. "May she rest in peace. She was a fine woman, a great loss to us all. Would you like time off? I can manage on my own if I have to."

"Thanks, Dominic. I'll go and see the police, at any rate. Maybe I'll be back this afternoon."

His grief began to reach him as he followed Ellen to the car. He'd felt relieved when his aunt had gone to stay with friends for Christmas and the new year—relieved that the family was spared the usual two days of sustaining polite conversation and being determinedly convivial. She'd seen the Christmas cards the children had painted for her, he thought, but they wouldn't be making her any more birthday cards.

He'd never thanked her for bringing him up, and now it was too late. He gulped and clenched his fists and managed not to weep until he was sitting in the car, where Ellen put her arm around him. Eventually he mumbled "Let's find out what there is to know."

He blew his stuffed nose as she eased the car into the traffic. "Did the police say how it happened?"

"I don't think she could have suffered much, Ben. Apparently she had hypothermia."

"How could she have? What did her friends think they were up to?"

"She wasn't with her friends. She was in the town where you were born."

"Stargrave? What would she have been doing there?"

"I never thought to ask."

His eyes were aching, his mouth tasted of grief, his incomprehension felt like a storm which wouldn't break. He hurried into the police station while Ellen parked the car. A policeman who looked incongruously like a doorman was at the inquiry desk. "Can I help you?"

"I'm Ben Sterling. You had a report that my aunt died up north. I wonder if you know what she was doing there."

If he found it strange that this was Ben's primary concern, he kept his opinion to himself. He tramped away into an office where typewriters were clacking. By the time he reappeared with a sheaf of papers in his hand, Ellen had joined Ben and was squeezing his arm. "Your aunt is the lady who was found in a place called Stargrave?"

"She must be, but I don't understand why she was there."

"I believe the police there have established that she was visiting her house."

Ben felt dizzy, and grasped the edge of the counter. "What house?"

The policeman scrutinized the topmost paper. "The house she's apparently been letting for a good many years. If you'd like to follow me," he said.

THIRTEEN

The day after the funeral, Margaret asked "Dad, how many houses do we own now?"

They were walking along a path at the edge of a cliff, where their Sunday drive had ended up. The gray sky was broken only by the shining of a cloud like a sliver of mirror above the sea. Wide slow waves floated down from the horizon to part at the corroded breakwaters protruding from a beach overlooked by hotels which were closed for the winter. Margaret's question took Ben by surprise, interrupting a reverie which he was immediately unable to remember. "Just the one we live in, Margery," Ellen said.

"But Dad said his Auntie Beryl wanted us to have everything of hers."

"Soon," Ben told her. "Unless my long-lost brother Shackleton Sterling who was sent abroad before he was out of his cradle and who's been exploring the unexplored regions of the world ever since he was a teenager turns up."

"You haven't really got a brother," Johnny pleaded.

"I've just got Mummy and you two and whoever's taking shape inside my head."

"If there's all those people, it's a good job we'll have lots of houses."

"Only three, Margery," Ellen said, "and I shouldn't think we'll be keeping all of them."

"Will we keep the one in the mountains where Daddy came from? Can we go and see that house?"

"Yes, Daddy, can we?" Margaret cried. "I'd love to see that house."

"I suppose we could."

A wind sharp as salt brought sand hissing through the grass at the edge of the cliff. "Get a move on or we'll be too cold to see anything," Ellen said.

Ben lagged behind on the way back to the car. So, he thought again, his aunt had overcome her dislike of the Sterlings enough not only to accept the legacy of their house but also to have an estate agent in Stargrave collect rents from tenants for her ever since. She must have kept her ownership a secret from him because she'd been afraid the knowledge would revive some aspect of his childhood which she had tried to suppress, but couldn't she have told him once he had grown up? Then he would have been able to visit Stargrave on her behalf, and she wouldn't have died alone up there, having apparently fallen and injured herself on her way back from the house to the hotel. Why couldn't she have followed the main road instead of wandering along the common alongside the forest, too far above the town for anyone to notice her in time? "Silly old woman," he muttered, and had to fight back tears before following the family away from the sea.

Later, when the children were in bed, Ellen said "As long as you're going to look at your old home, shall we all go?"

"It's quite a way to drive."

"We could make a weekend of it. Unless you'd rather we weren't there, of course."

At once he felt selfish. It might be their only chance to see Stargrave, and he could always go for a solitary walk while his memories surfaced. "Let's see if there's room at the inn."

The hotel receptionist sounded delighted to be asked and to reserve two rooms for Saturday. "We can have a bit of a dirty weekend when the children are asleep," Ellen said, and matched his grin. "We can practice now if you like."

86

Afterwards, as he pulled the duvet over them and rested his head on her breast, she whispered "Tell me a secret."

"I don't think I have any from you."

"Then tell me what you remember best about growing up in Stargrave."

"Waiting," he said at once. "Feeling as if I was always waiting for something like Christmas, only it never quite came."

"Poor little boy."

"I don't mean I was disappointed. I mean those years of my childhood seemed like the start of an adventure. Everything around me felt like a preamble to some event I couldn't put a name to."

"That sounds like childhood right enough."

"I suppose that must have been all it was," Ben said, but he felt as if she'd reduced the reality to a cliché which prevented him from remembering. "Anyway, I lost it once I moved away from Stargrave. I still experience something like it now and then, sometimes when I'm writing."

"Not when you're with me?"

"Of course," Ben said, kissing away her wistfulness. "I'm having it now."

He was certainly experiencing a sense of imminence which put him in mind of the first hint of light above the horizon before dawn. When he awoke next morning it was still there, and it stayed with him during the week. By Friday evening he was as expectant as the children were. That night he dreamed of standing on a mountain where the ice grew beneath him and raised him towards the stars.

In the morning, however, the prospect of breakfast on the motorway was barely capable of rousing the children. Margaret had gone dutifully to bed but had then been unable to sleep, Johnny had had to be harangued up the stairs, and now they were having to rise before dawn. For the next half hour the family stumbled in and out of the bathroom, bumping sleepily into one another as they vied for space. They straggled out to the car, into a heavy darkness which seemed to cling like grime to Ben, making him feel unable to waken fully. He trudged back to the kitchen and splashed his eyes with handfuls of cold water until he felt alert enough to drive.

Their route led them away from the dawn. An hour later, as he drove through darkness which felt as if it had accumulated the weight of the long night, the children began to stir. Margaret played with her mother at relishing place names aloud—"Swineshead, Stragglethorpe, Coddington, Clumber Park"—while the sight of villages awakening as milk floats groaned through the streets was enough of a treat for Johnny. As the road swung northwest towards the motorway, Ben saw the leafless tips of trees at the edge of a wood turn golden with the dawn. The sight seemed so like a promise that he felt enlivened at once.

Before the car reached the westbound motorway, peaks appeared in the distance, gleaming with snow. By now the children were insisting they were famished. He stopped at the first motorway service area, though if he had been alone he would have driven to Stargrave without a break. "Finish your drinks in the car," he said as soon as they'd done eating, and waited for them outside the toilets like a stereotype of a father-to-be outside a delivery room.

Half an hour later he came off the motorway through Leeds too soon. What had appeared to be the most direct route to Stargrave led him through streets teeming with Saturday shoppers so contemptuous of vehicles that he had to restrain himself from leaning on the horn. At last the crowds were left behind, and the road found a river to follow. As he trod on the accelerator, he felt the heat of the city fall behind as if he were emerging from a suffocating room into the open air.

The terraces of houses which flanked the road out of Leeds gathered themselves into a few small towns, and then they petered out. The moorland road sloped upwards between drystone walls, frozen explosions of stone miles long, bordering fields and tracts of gorse and heather from which protruded squarish lichened rocks like ruined houses which the moor was swallowing. The road climbed gradually for half an hour towards limestone ridges bare except for a crust of snow gleaming beneath the glassy sun. The smoke of lonely farmhouses vanished into a thin sky which held neither clouds nor birds. Winds cold as frozen snow set the gorse and heather shivering. Every time the car sped over a ridge, Ben expected to see Stargrave ahead. He must be assuming that it wasn't as far across the moors as it had seemed to him as a child, and his expectancy was making him nervous, until he started talking to distract himself. "When I wasn't much more than your age, Johnny, I came all this way by myself."

The boy gasped in admiration. "Why?"

"You know Daddy's parents died when he was young," Ellen said. "His Auntie Beryl took him to live with her before he'd had a chance to say good-bye properly, and so he came back."

Ben opened his mouth and closed it again. He felt as if she'd stolen his memory and rendered it banal. He was trying to recall what had really been in his mind the last time he'd returned to Stargrave when Margaret rebuked him. "You shouldn't tell Johnny things like that or you'll have him wanting to do it too."

"You wouldn't run away and leave us, would you, Johnny?" Ellen said.

Just shut up for a moment, Ben was close to shouting, let me think—and then the road swung around a curve enclosed by spiky walls and climbed into the open, and he saw the railway bridge ahead. The line had been disused for years; a mass of sullenly green weeds led away from both ends of the parapet and vanished among standing shapes of limestone which the years since his departure seemed to have rendered even more grotesque, more nearly meaningful. His foot wavered on the accelerator, because he felt suddenly cold. He gripped the wheel and sent the car racing under the low dark arch.

The road curved upwards beside the overgrown railway, and the moors above Stargrave came into view, dominated by limestone crags which made Ben think of icebergs. Ellen gave a sigh of pleasure at the view, but he found he was holding his breath. The car reached the crest of the slope, and Sterling Forest and the Sterling house both rose to meet him.

The shared movement made them seem part of a single entity, as if the tall gray steep-roofed house were posted as a sentry for the forest wider than the town. The forest was a darkness hovering above Stargrave, its tens of thousands of trees rooted in shadow under their canopy of somber green. Before he could grasp these impressions, they were driven out of his mind by the sight of a For Sale board outside the Sterling house.

At the junction of the main road and the rough track which led to the house, he stopped the car beside a bungalow he didn't recognize and stared bewildered at the sign. "Can't we go in?" Margaret said.

He was unexpectedly daunted by the idea of visiting the house while it was occupied by people he didn't know. Realizing that they were his tenants, or would be once his aunt's will had gone through probate, aggravated his nervousness. At least one of the tenants was at home; someone had just appeared at the window of a room on the middle floor—Ben's old room. The vague pale face at his window made him feel ousted. "I haven't got the key," he said, and drove into the town.

At first it looked as he remembered it, the chunky buildings huddled beneath the moor, Church Road leading up from the main road to the church above the station and down again to the market square, The Crescent describing a small curve below Church Road, the narrow crooked side streets climbing across them from Market Street. The view infected him with nostalgia, even when he passed a torn poster for a concert in Leeds by a band called Piss In The Sink, until he was confronted by the names of several of the shops: Country Taste Pizza Parlour, Video Universe, Brats Boutique, The Food Trough . . . Presumably some of these were meant to appeal to tourists; the railway station had been turned into an information center for climbers and ramblers, flanked by a record store called The Bop Shop and a furniture maker's by the name of Suites and Sawer. "Half a wit is even worse than none," he growled, and headed for the Station Hotel.

It was a thickset three-story building which occupied one side of the square. In the darkly panelled lobby, beneath the stalactites of a chandelier, a woman was poring over a ledger, ticking off amounts with a stub of pencil as chewed as a dog's rubber bone. "Mr. and Mrs. Sterling and the kiddies," she said in a Yorkshire accent as broad as she was. "Write yourselves down and I'll show you up."

Since the vintage lift was out of order, she led them up the wide staircase, emitting a wheeze as each stair gave a creak. "Keep your hand in your pocket, lad," she said as Ben made to tip her. The children switched on their television and bounced on their beds while he lay down for a few minutes to relax. "How does it feel to be home?" Ellen said from the bathroom.

"I don't know yet," he said, and swung his legs off the plump, slightly shabby counterpane as soon as she managed to turn off the rickety taps. "I'd better head for the estate agent's. They may not be open this afternoon."

"Come on, you two, we're going out again."

"Can we have lunch at the pizza restaurant?" Johnny begged.

"If we can't find somewhere even more like paradise," Ben said.

Tovey's agency was on the northward stretch of Market Street. A photograph of the Sterling house gleamed and dulled on a rotating pillar in the window. A portly young man with a scrubbed smile and eyebrows like an inverted Mexican moustache came to meet him and shook hands with him. "Henry Tovey. How can I help you?"

"I'm Beryl Tate's nephew. I see you're selling her house."

"We do have that for sale. Please allow me to express my condolences, by the way. I only met the lady once, but she was always a pleasure to do business with."

"Have you had any offers for the house?" Ellen said.

"Not yet, but business is always slack at this time of year. Normally we might not have put the property on the market so soon after your tragedy, but Miss Tate had been most insistent that it should be advertised as soon as possible."

So Ben's aunt had come to Stargrave in order to get rid of the house. "What do her tenants think about the sale, do you know?" Ellen said.

"Most of them had already moved away. We assumed that was why Miss Tate decided to sell."

"I was wondering if we could have a look around the house," Ben said.

"By all means. Would you happen to have some identification so that I can keep our records up to date?" Tovey glanced at the photocopy of the will Ben had brought with him. "Ordinarily we'd show people over the property, but I'm sure that isn't necessary in your case. You may as well hold onto the key."

"You don't think whoever's in the house will mind if we just go in?"

"Put your mind at rest, Mr. Sterling." Tovey held the door open for them and said "Your aunt's last tenant moved out once he got wind of your aunt's intention to sell. There's nobody at all in the house now."

FOURTEEN

To keep Johnny happy they lunched at the pizza parlor. A large-boned woman whose plastic apron swarmed with pigs in bibs stood over the display of slabs of dough, slapping the top of the counter in time with a pop song so tinny that the relentless percussion sounded like an uncontrollable sneeze. Once she'd brought a trayful of generous helpings of pizza to the table, an unsteady disc draped in gingham, she pretended not to notice the Sterlings. So did the other diners—a birthday party of several children and a man with a paper hat balanced on his head, an old couple taking turns to order their Alsatian to lie down, a woman who kept underlining phrases in a newspaper and who stirred her tea vigorously every time she was about to sip it—but Ben was sure they were wondering what had brought the newcomers to town, which made him realize that he didn't quite know himself. He dawdled over his pizza until Margaret said "Shall we go and see the house now?"

"No hurry. I'd like to walk off all that driving first." When she made a face he said "And you'd better walk off that pizza before you start looking like the wrong kind of doe."

In the space of a couple of seconds her face crumpled, grew furious at having done so in public, warned Johnny not to laugh. "Daddy said you might, not that you do," Ellen comforted her. "I'd like to see some of the moors, wouldn't you? It may not be a walking day tomorrow."

Ben's instinct had been for a stroll in the forest, but he didn't want to cause any more conflict. In the street he apologized to Margaret, but she snatched her hand away. Once they were past the increasingly scattered houses where the northward stretch of Market Street became Richmond Road, however, she let him help her over the stile in the gritstone wall onto the nearest moorland path.

As soon as he set foot on the path he felt as if he could walk for days. The frozen grass was springy as wire; here and there the path crackled underfoot. A sprinkling of frost highlighted the traceries of heather, and tiny crystal globes on the gorse beside the path sparkled where the failing sunlight touched them. A mile above him on the slope, against vegetation luminous as an afterglow, every grotesque outline of the limestone crags stood out lucidly. Overhead the deep blue sky looked frozen solid by the night which was massing beneath the horizon; it made him think of blue ice spreading across the sky and forcing the sun down. A solitary bird hovered above the western ridge above him, emitting a high thin cry, and the whole of the landscape seemed to share the piercing clarity of the sound.

Johnny ran ahead in search of puddles to trample and splinter, and Ellen strode after him. Margaret ventured a few paces and turned, looking rather daunted by so much loneliness. "Quick, Daddy, or we'll be left behind."

He felt as if she'd come between him and his perception of the landscape, of a meaning which he might have grasped. When he and Margaret caught up with the others by the crag, Johnny's teeth had begun to chatter. "It's lovely up here, but I think we'd better start back now," Ellen said.

"You three go back. I'll be down soon."

"I shouldn't stay up here by yourself. It'll be dark before you know it, and you need to see the path."

He stayed where he was and watched her lead the children down the path, into a twilight which appeared to grow darker in some exact but obscure relationship with the shrinking of the three of them. When Ellen sent him a look of mingled appeal and reproach, he trudged after them, and found that he felt as if he were walking further into the open. The fields and moors beyond the railway line stretched to the horizon, but it wasn't just the view; the openness he felt himself approaching was larger than that. He must be anticipating the night beyond the horizon, the night which was the edge of boundless darkness, yet for a moment it felt as though the edge of that darkness was much closer, massing above Stargrave. The mass was Sterling Forest, of course, and the night which came earlier beneath the trees than to the rest of the landscape, as if the tips of the pines were drawing the night down to earth.

Before he reached the stile, the forest was above him. Though the nearest trees were several hundred yards away he felt as if the shadow of the forest had fallen across him, an icy exhilarating shadow which helped him see the first star in the eastern sky, a bright steady star like a sign of the clarity he was aching to grasp. But Ellen was poking her head over the stile and making faces at him. "You look as if you're about to take root," she said.

As he followed her into Stargrave the streetlamps lit up. Beyond the chains of yellow light like an inverted double necklace, the silhouette of the Sterling house was reaching for the star. Ben was gazing towards it when Johnny said "Are we going there now?"

"I've already said, no hurry. We'll have plenty of time tomorrow."

"Remember Daddy hasn't been here since he was about your age," Ellen said. "It may feel strange to him."

"Let's go to that playground I saw," Margaret suggested.

As she and Johnny raced towards the square, Ben murmured to Ellen "Strange in what way? Tell me later."

The playground was on the highest curve of Church Road, between the church and the school. Two streetlamps stood guard outside it, but it was deserted. The streets staggered lamps and lamplit patches of terraced houses down to the railway; the church and the school were ponderous blocks of dimness relieved by the glint of streetlamps on the edges of bricks and in windows. None of this made Ben feel more than impersonally nostalgic; any childhood memories it conjured up were too faraway and minor to be worth recapturing. He moved closer to Ellen, who was jogging on the spot while the children pushed themselves on the swings, the shadows of the chains reaching for the forest as the children competed, each swing taking them higher into the dark. "Strange in what way?"

"I thought you might be remembering so much all at once that you needed time to adjust. You didn't seem to want to go to the house yet."

So she hadn't seen the face at his old bedroom window. Now that he was sure, he felt unexpectedly sad. "I haven't remembered anything worth telling you," he said, and squeezed her hand.

As the family walked back to the hotel Ben felt as if he weren't quite with them—as if he were already on the way to where he meant to go. During dinner he told Margaret and Ellen how pretty they looked, helped Johnny cut up his steak and unobtrusively picked up scraps of food the boy dropped on the carpet, kept the conversation light and flowing. A couple in evening dress, the only other diners in the panelled dining room which occupied one side of the ground floor, glanced with increasing approval at them. When the Sterlings rose to leave, the woman beckoned Ellen over. "Your family's a credit to you," she said.

Once the children were out of the bathroom, Ben told them the story of his next book, about the little boy who had to keep the fire alight to imprison the ice spirits. Tonight it seemed so clear to him that if he'd been at home he would have started writing it at once. He scribbled a few notes while Ellen tucked the children into their beds, and when she rejoined him he was ready. "You look tired," he said. "You don't mind if I go for a stroll, do you?"

"Don't wake me if I'm asleep when you come back. You aren't thinking of going on the moors so late."

"Of course not." He kissed her and held onto her, his reluctance to let go surprising him. He must feel guilty that he was concealing his intentions from her so easily. He gave her a last kiss and went quickly out of the room, out of the hotel, towards the Sterling house.

FIFTEEN

Market Street was deserted. In many of the houses, televisions flickered like will-o'-the-wisps. The temperature had dropped further while he was in the hotel. The cold and the solitary sounds of his footsteps excited him, made him feel almost childlike, out by himself on a night near Christmas. Beyond the streetlamp which stood outside the newsagent's at the edge of Stargrave, the glinting tarmac led past a few cottages. They seemed to sink into the night as the Sterling house came into view, a shape like a monolith crowned with stone and stars. All the windows were unlit, indistinguishable from the bricks, and the house seemed darker than the night to him, as dark as the forest which loomed at its back.

A floodlight on the wall of the new bungalow on the main road whitened the hedge and the garden around the bungalow and lit up the end of the rough track. A friend of his grandmother's had lived where the bungalow stood; he wondered why her house had needed rebuilding. He picked his way past it along the track, over chunks of road and their elongated shadows, which looked as deep as the ruts frozen into the earth.

A frosty wind came down through the forest to meet him. He heard its long slow breath like the sound of a wave on an invisible beach and saw the forest stirring wakefully, a dim movement which appeared to spread to the outline of the house. The forest creaked like a great door. His breaths glimmered in front of him, ghosts leading him towards the house, and their appearance made him feel close to recovering a memory. That sense of imminence, and the need to walk carefully on the uneven track, preoccupied him until he was nearly at the gate. As soon as he looked up at the building, however, the sight drove everything else out of his mind. The face was still at the window.

Or was it a face? As he gazed up, clouds like rags of the moon which was rising beyond the forest streamed between the stars above the top-heavy roof, and the house seemed to topple towards him. Surely the pale shape must be a mark on the glass; no face could be so perfectly circular, and besides, it was in exactly the same place where he had seen it earlier. He gazed at it until the crescent moon and its globe of blackness were clear of the crags, and the darkness of the house appeared to solidify around the shape at the window. With a start like awakening from a trance, he stepped into the shadow of the house and opened the rusty gate in the chest-high stone wall.

He couldn't really be feeling the shadow, but he felt suddenly colder. He ventured along the cracked path bordered by weedy flowerbeds and stood on the doorstep between the secretively narrow window of the cloakroom and the unwashed bay window beneath a lintel the color of lead. The front door used to seem like the entrance to a giant's domain, and it was still several heads taller than he was. Paint fell from it, exposing the oak, while he groped for the keyhole. As he jiggled the key into the lock he smelled the old wood and heard flakes of paint whispering down. He twisted the key back and forth, but it failed to engage the mechanism. He gave the door an angry shove, and it swung inwards as though it had been opened from within.

All he could see beyond the doorway was darkness so deep that it appeared to have no end. Dropping the key into his pocket, he waited for his eyesight to catch up with the dark. He felt more childlike than ever, as if he'd risen in the middle of the night to see the house transformed, and almost unable to breathe for the pulse in his throat. Eventually he began to distinguish hints of outlines: a thick banister which began in midair several paces ahead of him and which slanted upwards to vanish in the gloom, the edges of two ajar doors and their frames to his right. He would have seen more if the kitchen door were open at the far end of the hall, but he'd retrieved enough of a sense of the layout to step forwards, reaching for the brass light switch outside the cloakroom. It resisted momentarily, then clicked down, its lever skewing almost imperceptibly leftwards in its housing. All this was as he remembered, but the light above the hall stayed dark.

He could just see the bulb, a hovering bulge of dimness. He paced forwards over the worn carpet and pushed the first door wide open. Beyond it was a shadeless bulb above a barren room twenty feet square. He groped around the doorframe and found the chilly switch, but it had no effect on the bulb. The electricity must be turned off. He couldn't recall where the main switch was, and it might be dangerous to search for it without a flashlight. Sighing, he stepped away from the room, and the front door slammed shut.

"All right, if that's what you want," he said. It had been the wind, of course—he thought he heard the forest creaking faintly beyond the kitchen door—but it felt as if the house had told him to stay. He held onto an upright of the banisters while his heart slowed down, and gazed at the patterns of light on the floor of the room, long oblique glowing slabs so indistinct that he wasn't sure he was seeing them. The promise of light enticed him into the room.

The echoes of his footsteps made the room sound considerably larger than it was. If it hadn't been for the circle of plaster from which the light bulb hung, plaster carved into a pattern which looked elaborate even in the dark and which put him in mind of snow frozen halfway to melting, he could have imagined that the ceiling was tall as the trees in the forest. By the time he was beneath the pattern he felt as if he'd taken as many paces to cross the room as he would have when he was a child. That impression, and the view of the lights of Stargrave beyond the window to his right, sent a shiver through him, so violent that it made him feel he was shaking off a burden. "My God," he whispered.

He wasn't seeing Stargrave, just the lights. The view of the town seemed no more than a symbol, a key to unlock his memory. At about this time of year the room had been full of lights, crystal blossoms shining in the tree the Sterlings brought out of the forest, and the sight of Stargrave made him feel that everything the room had seen was still present around him in the dark. He could almost hear his grandfather's voice, telling wintry tales which had seemed to invoke the dance of snow on the crags, the winds that roamed the forest and the moors under the stars. Those tales had been taken from Edward Sterling's books, Ben thought, and he'd told some of them in his own books; they'd become so much a part of him that he hadn't realized where they came from. Now he felt as if he'd missed the point of them—he felt as if something in the dark were close to making itself clear to him. Suddenly too nervous to stand still, he retreated to the hall.

It seemed less dark, or more familiar. He strode to the kitchen door and pushed it open. Cupboards packed with darkness hung open on the walls; outlines of a sink and a cooker glinted in the light of the bony scythe above the forest. Helping in the kitchen had been an adventure, especially near Christmas: he'd been allowed to pierce the fowl with a giant fork, and his grandfather had promised to teach him how to decorate the solstice cake, which the old man had iced with designs so intricate that gazing at them had made Ben dizzy. How could he have forgotten that? For a moment he was sure that if he looked around him he would see the design gleaming somewhere in the dark. He swung away from the moonlight and shoved the dining room door open.

The large room was denuded of furniture, but he could imagine that the huge round oak table was still there in the darkness—could imagine that his family was waiting there for him to join their circle, to pull their Christmas crackers all at once to signal the beginning of the dance which his grandfather led three times each way around the table. At the end of the meal his grandfather would cut the cake and present Ben with the first slice, saying "Put some winter inside you." Ben gave a loud uneasy laugh at himself for having forgotten so much. When the room laughed with him, he made for the hall.

This time he noticed a door under the stairs. Of course, the cupboard contained the fuse board and the main switch. He could turn on the lights, but now he chose not to; his memories would guide him through the house, and he thought it was partly because he couldn't see the rooms in detail that his memories of them were so vivid. The memories were beginning to seem important only as a means to an end, but what end? He had yet to determine what he'd seen at the window of his old room.

As he climbed the stairs, keeping hold of the frosty banister, he felt as if the darkness of the stairwell were rising above him. He imagined himself climbing a slope beneath the night sky with only the dim ghost of his breath for company. He hauled himself onto the landing and found he was reluctant to let go of the banister. "Grow up," he shouted, but his voice sounded lost in the dark. He flung himself away from the banister and shouldered open the door of his old bedroom.

It was bare except for a carpet and a tattered lampshade tilted rakishly over the lightbulb. From the landing, he could see the sky above the moors beyond the railway. Could those stars be the very ones he'd watched between the curtains as he'd lain in bed in this room, stars like promises of dreams too enormous to imagine while he was awake? But something was confusing his view. His eyes focused on the window. What he'd seen earlier was still there: a circular mark on the upper sash, a mark which resembled a patch of ice more than double the size of his head.

He hadn't realized it was so large. He must have perceived it as smaller because at first sight he'd taken it to be a face. He was tiptoeing across the room, holding his breath. The closer he approached, the more like ice it looked—cracked ice, in which thousands of delicate lines composed an abstract mandala so nearly regular that it took his breath away. What could have caused such a flaw in the glass? He gripped the windowsill and craned to touch the mark. Just as his fingertips brushed the edge of it, he saw that the lines went all the way through the pane. The next moment the entire cracked patch collapsed.

Most of the shards fell outwards, jangling among the weeds under the window, as he dodged back. He was left staring at an almost perfectly circular hole in the glass and feeling like a destructive child who couldn't be trusted to behave himself alone in the house. He went in search of some material with which to plug the hole. At the far end of the landing, on the bathroom floor beside the pale dim open coffin of the bath, he found a mat so disreputable that he shuddered as he snatched it up, though in fact there were no insects underneath. He stuffed it into the hole in the pane and wiped his hands on his coat, feeling as if he'd robbed the house of the magic it had offered him.

The next bare room had been his grandparents' bedroom. He remembered hearing his grandmother wheezing in the bed to which she had been increasingly confined in the months before the car crash. She had apparently been sewing a present for him, but he had never seen it. "Shouldn't have been such a perfectionist," he muttered sadly as he climbed the stairs.

The first room on the top landing had been his parents' room. Its barrenness made him feel close to tears, especially as he remembered how his mother would come down to him when he cried out with whatever dreams the stars above the moor had given him. His aunt had slept in the adjacent room when she was visiting, and next to that one was the attic. This had been his favorite room, full of broken toys so old they were fascinating, crippled furniture, incomplete books whose pages crumbled at the edges when he'd tried to read them. Now it looked pillaged; four dents in the carpet beneath a skylight obscured by night and grime showed that it had recently been used as a bedroom. Nevertheless he went in, because it seemed to be the brightest room in the house.

It must be, for him to have distinguished the marks in the carpet. He wouldn't have expected the room to be so visible under such a thin moon. As he crossed to the dormer window, pines the color of the moon appeared to rise to meet him. He was at the window before he realized that the moon was out of sight above the house; it was the forest that was shining.

Had frost gathered on the trees while he was exploring the house? Surely it took more than moonlight to turn the forest so pale that the trees resembled great feathers of ice. As he gazed wide-eyed at the spectacle, the forest seemed to brighten gradually, and he thought the room did so. There was movement among the trees near the edge of the forest, an approaching glow. He fumbled at the catches of the window and pushed its two wings open. The chill of the night gathered on him as he saw what was out there. Snowflakes luminous with moonlight were dancing beneath the trees.

How could it be snowing there and not above the forest? Indeed, it appeared to be snowing only in an area about as wide as the house. He strained forwards, trying to understand the sight, scarcely aware of the steep slope of the roof below him. It seemed to him that the silent luminous dance was constantly about to form a pattern in the air—that if he could only distinguish the pattern, unimaginable revelations might follow. He'd almost seen it once before, he remembered at last, when he had run away to Stargrave, but this time there was nobody to prevent him from following it into the woods.

He didn't know how long he gazed entranced from the window before a shiver roused him. He closed the window and ran downstairs, the echoes of his footsteps racing ahead. He dragged the front door closed behind him and shook it to ensure it was fastened, and was hurrying around the outside of the garden when a clock chimed in a nearby cottage.

Ben listened to the microscopic sound and shook his head, bewildered. It couldn't really be two o'clock. He bared his wristwatch and peered at its face until he had to believe it. Somehow he'd spent over four hours in the house. What might Ellen be imagining had happened to him? Dismayed for her, he nevertheless went up the track past the house to a point from which he could see Sterling Forest. The trees and the shadows beneath them were quite still, and there was no sign of snow in the air.

He felt profoundly disappointed, but he had to admit that he was also experiencing some relief. If expectancy was what he valued, hadn't he preserved it by allowing the mystery to stay mysterious? Now that his trance was broken, the depths of the forest seemed more ominous than alluring; even the trees were no longer so luminous. All the same, as he made for the floodlit end of the track, he stopped and closed his eyes to let the dazzle fade from them, and turned for a last look. He hadn't opened his eyes when he realized what his trance had caused him to forget. Whatever had cracked the window, it wasn't just a flaw in the glass. He'd seen it appear there as he had arrived in Stargrave, and that was why he had mistaken the appearance for a face.

His eyes snapped open, perhaps not quite swiftly enough. For a moment he was sure that he was being watched; he thought he might have glimpsed the watcher withdrawing into the dark, but where? His impression of the glimpse seemed to expand as he glanced from the house to the forest to the sky. Nothing moved except the flickering of the stars. Surely all he'd seen was the blind Cyclopean eye of the plugged window, he told himself as he retreated to the main road—but he felt as if he were descending from a height and losing all sense of what he had in fact experienced.

Once he came in sight of the market square, all he felt was embarrassment at having to rouse someone to let him into the hotel. A porter whose left eye seemed unable to waken trudged to the doors in response to the night bell. "Sterling from room six," Ben explained awkwardly. "Has anyone been wondering where I am?"

The man gave him a suspicious look, the more concentrated for being monocular. "If they have, they've not told me."

Ben thanked him and sneaked upstairs. Ellen was asleep in the middle of the double bed, one arm stretched out as if she'd reached for him. He was both touched by the sight and grateful that she wouldn't want him to explain his absence. When he slipped in beside her, she shivered and mumbled a drowsy protest and retreated to her side of the bed. He lay awake trying to fix in his mind his experiences at the house, but the harder he tried, the more elusive they seemed. He wasn't aware of falling asleep. If he dreamed, his dreams were too large to remember.

The children wakened him, bouncing on the bed and clamoring for breakfast. "And then can we go to the house?" Margaret pleaded.

"We'll see," Ben said, no longer sure how much of the night he had dreamed. At breakfast he gulped several cups of coffee and then agreed to visit the house.

Families were strolling up the eccentric streets to church. As he reached the beginning of the track to the Sterling house, Ben had the fleeting impression that the churchgoers had taken the wrong route. Of course he would, he thought, as a lapsed believer. The house looked shabby and abandoned, its isolation emphasized by the gloomy forest and pale sullen sky. "What happened to the window?" Margaret wanted to know.

"Someone must have broken it," Ben said nervously.

"It was like that yesterday," Ellen said. "I thought there was something wrong with it. That's what I saw, whatever it's mended with."

Ben felt guiltily secretive, but what could he say? Only "Stay with your mother and me" as he unlocked the front door. As soon as he stepped over the threshold he was sure that he didn't need to be uneasy on their behalf; it was just an old house where he used to live, a house empty of everything but daylight. He thought this disappoint-ment might have been what he was afraid of, why he'd been loath to agree to visit the house, even though it hadn't felt quite like that kind of fear.

Once he'd gone through the motions of exploring all the floors he let the children run shouting through the rooms. "It's going to need some money spent on it," Ellen said, but otherwise kept quiet, presumably out of respect for his memories. When the children were tired of playing he led the family back to the hotel and checked out, wishing he could stay another night and go back to the house after dark. He drove out of Stargrave, trying to think of an excuse to return soon. As the car raced under the bridge he saw darkness fill the driving mirror, swallowing his last sight of the house. The car sped onto the moor, and he saw Johnny nudge Margaret, who leaned forwards to meet her father's eyes in the mirror. "Daddy, could we come and live here?" she said.

SIXTEEN

Ellen had fallen in love with the landscape around Stargrave. She thought she mightn't see it again, given the way Ben's homecoming appeared to have disheartened him. She was sorry they hadn't taken time to explore the moors, but he had grown so taciturn since they'd visited the house that she hadn't liked to suggest lingering. The sooner they were home and the children were in bed, the sooner she might be able to help him talk out his feelings. Retreating into himself so as to write was part of his job, but she didn't see how brooding over his memories could benefit him.

The car sped past the house and gathered speed towards the bridge, and she saw Ben look for the house in the mirror. When she stroked his knee, he didn't seem to notice. Feeling snubbed, she moved her hand to her lap as the car passed under the bridge. She was telling herself not to be silly when Margaret said "Daddy, could we come and live here?"

Ben stared at the oncoming road, and his face and voice grew blank. "Who knows."

Johnny began to jump up and down in his seat belt. "Could we? Could we?"

"Calm down now, Johnny," Ellen said. "Don't you two like where we live any more?"

"I do," Johnny said, sounding abashed.

"Well, so do I," Margaret said angrily.

Ellen decided it was time to close the subject. "Quiet now. Let Daddy concentrate on driving."

At the hotel she'd offered to drive, but now it looked as if driving might beneficially occupy his mind. Half an hour later, when the moorland road straightened out as it descended into the first of the villages outside Leeds, he broke the silence with one of the nonsense verses he used to invent for the children on family walks:

"Come quaff the mugs and fill the jugs

And baste the goose with lotion.

Haraldahyde has sunk inside

The coracle of potion . . ."

"Say another one," Johnny requested as traffic built up dangerously ahead. When the way was clear Ben intoned:

"There are wombats in the kitchen

And tapirs on the stairs.

The large old chest of drawers supports

A family of bears . . ."

The sight of the sun sinking over Lincolnshire prompted

"Red sky at night,

Fish won't bite.

Red sky in the morning,

Frogs are spawning."

"No they aren't," Margaret said sleepily.

"Frogs are yawning, rather. Don't you, or we won't be able to eat out on our way home."

By the time the car crossed the Norfolk border, both Margaret and Johnny were asleep. Ben glanced in the mirror as headlights rushing by on the winding road illuminated their faces, and confided to Ellen:

"The rich man often dines on quail,

The poor man picks at scrod.

But the hungry man consumes their turds
And says 'Thanks be to God!'"

"That's terrible," she said with a grin. "I take it you're feeling better now we're nearly home."

"Got to grow up sometime. Maybe I should think about writing a book for adults."

He hadn't really answered her, but this wasn't the time or the place to insist. When he began to look out for restaurants she said "Let the kids sleep and we'll eat in Norwich."

It was only when she awoke to find Ben placing a hot bundle in her lap that she realized she had nodded off. The car was parked outside a fish-and-chip shop where several youths with their hair in tarry spikes were gesticulating at the Chinese family behind the counter. The smell of food in newspaper roused the children, who stretched as if their bodies were gaping to be fed. Once they were home and taken care of, Ellen hastened them up to the bathroom and into bed.

Ben seemed more exhausted than the day's journey would normally have made him. "Sweet dreams," Ellen said as she wriggled under the duvet and slipped her arm around him, but he was already in his own dark. The next she knew, a shape like thin gray breath was dancing above her: steam from a mug of coffee on the bedside table. The children were kissing her awake. "I'll walk them to school and go on to Milligans," Ben said behind them.

When she heard them in the street, Johnny emitting sounds of a rocket launch while Margaret chattered to her father about books, she propped herself up in bed, feeling luxurious. She stayed in bed until she heard the postman pushing letters into the house. As she went downstairs she could see that they weren't bills; the envelopes didn't have that dingy thickset bullying look. She examined them as she took them to the desk in the back room. Two of the long white envelopes were from Ember Books, the other was from Ballyhoo Unlimited. "Say what you like," she told the latter, forcing a laugh at her tenseness as she thrust a finger under the flap and pulled the single sheet out of the envelope.

Dear Mrs Sterling,

Thank you for submitting yourself for interview with regards to a position with our agency. Both Gordon Fuge and myself were impressed by your presentation and the main reservation expressed by our senior partner Max Rutter concerns whether after twelve years absence from the business you would have lost the aggressive qualities our clients look for in our campaigns. We have therefore decided to offer you a trial contract for twelve months to run from 15 February at the advertised rates. Max Rutter has asked me to mention that the contract makes no provision for maternity leave. May I say how much I personally look forward to working with someone as mature as yourself. Please let us know at your earliest convenience if these terms are satisfactory.

Yours sincerely
Sidney Peacock

Ellen read the letter and stared open-mouthed at it and then flung it into the air. When it landed face up on the desk she read it again. She couldn't tell how much of the letter was intended to be slyly insulting or even what Peacock thought of her, and it infuriated her that she was wondering. She was tempted to drop it in the wastebasket, but she wanted Ben to read it first, if only for a laugh. She opened one of the Ember envelopes instead.

Dear Mr and Mrs Sterling,

I am eleven years old. First I want to say how much I enjoyed your book "The Boy Who Fell Up The Mountain". All my friends did except one who said there could not be a mountain so high you would fall into the sky instead of down. I told her there probably is on the moon

and anyway it says on your book it is a fantasy, which is
the kind I like best.

When I grow up I want to be an artist like Mrs Sterling.
Do you think I may have a chance if I work hard at my
pictures? Do you have to have an agent if you want them
to be published? I am enclosing some of them for you to
look at so you can say what you think of them. I hope you
will not mind writing and saying.

Yours admiringly,
Melanie Tilliger.

Behind the sheet of paper were three more, small enough not to
have needed folding to fit into the envelope. They were scenes from
the book. In one the boy was more than halfway up the mountain,
because his staff which had started out taller than he was had been
worn to the length of a walking stick. In the second he was among the
birds, so high that they were white with frost, and in the last one he
must have reached his destination, the height where he was able to
hover for just the duration of a heartbeat, the one point from which
you could see the meaning of the world, before the winds cast him
down and he awoke at the foot of the mountain with nothing to show
that he hadn't been dreaming except his worn staff. "When he tried to
tell the people of his village what he knew, they called him mad and
drove him into the forest . . . All this was many years ago, but
perhaps he is still wandering the world, looking for someone who will
listen to him," Ellen quoted to herself, laying the pictures side by side
on the sunlit desk. They were colorful and imaginative and meticu-
lously detailed, and they seemed worth dozens of favorable reviews,
not that the book had attracted so many. She was thinking how to
reply as she opened the third envelope.

Hi Sterlings!

Hope some or all of you will be in town again soon so I
can buy you lunch. Meanwhile maybe you should treat

yourselves to an answering machine—I've been trying to call you for a few days. Ellen, if you've got any ideas for the *Boy Who Caught the Snowflakes* promo, could you let me have whatever you want me to see? Ben, if you can tell me what your next book will be about I'll make an offer for the next two. We don't want you getting away from Ember just when you're about to be mega!

Kiss the kids for me and tell them lots of stories.

Love,
Kerys

"Phew," Ellen said. She prepared dinner, feeling rather dazed, straying back now and then to the desk to reread the letters, and then she made herself sit down and write an encouraging response to Melanie Tilliger before she set about sketching ideas to send Kerys. An hour later the ideas were breeding, and she hadn't had time to sketch them all when she had to dash out to collect the children from school.

Johnny was even more impressed by her receiving fan mail than by the books themselves, and Margaret asked if she could write her own letter to the girl. "Do something sensible while I finish off some work," Ellen told them.

They tried, bless them. Johnny watched television with the sound turned low while Margaret wrote to Melanie Tilliger. When he tired of cartoons in which the characters lacked the energy to move their faces and their bodies simultaneously, Johnny read for a while and then wandered into the kitchen, wanting to draw. Soon Ellen had to sort out a squabble over pencils, after which the children began to accuse each other of increasingly heinous peccadilloes. She was ordering a few minutes' peace as Ben came home.

He seemed oddly amused by the uproar. "Shush, now," he said to the children, and "Well" to each of the letters. When he left it at that, Ellen demanded "Are you going to let me into the secret?"

"Tell you when you're older," he said, and gave her a kiss in case she thumped him. "When the rest of us are in bed," he added for only Ellen to hear.

She hustled him into the front room as soon as the children were tucked up. "So?"

"I was thinking that we'll have so many rooms we might want to use a few more of them."

"Go on."

"Well, if we lived here and used my aunt's house for an office, we'd have all the peace we needed for working."

"That's silly and moreover it's wasteful."

"I suppose it is when we've another house that's the size of them both put together. We could sell this one or my aunt's and let the other in case we wanted to come back."

"You've been thinking this over."

"Do you blame me?"

"Of course not. I'm glad you feel that way. I wasn't sure how going home had affected you."

"It isn't only me. The children were asking me again this morning if we could."

"I wonder if they realize how much change would be involved, leaving their school and all their friends."

"They insist they don't mind. They seem to think it would be an adventure."

"What sort of job could you find up there? I didn't notice many opportunities on offer."

"I was wondering if it isn't time for us to take the chance we've been working for."

"Write and paint full-time, you mean."

"That's still what you want, isn't it? Otherwise you won't hear another word from me about anything I've said. It's been a few years since that anniversary when we raised our glasses to the day when we could devote our lives to being the people we really are."

She knew how much it meant to him—even more than it meant to her. His proposal seemed to solve so many problems that she was instinctively suspicious of it. "Give me time to consider," she said, and was touched by the way he immediately went to the desk to work on their next book: he reminded her of a child finding himself a task to distract himself from some almost uncontainable eagerness. After an hour or so he reappeared. "I'm just going out to get some night air."

He closed the front door gently behind him, letting in a cold wind which rustled papers on the desk. She listened to his footsteps being carried away by the wind, and felt as if her indecision were making him restless. When he returned, his eyes glittering with chill, she told him, "I want to go up to Stargrave first for another look."

SEVENTEEN

Two days later Ellen drove to Stargrave, out of a dawn like a great fire of Norwich. Whenever she reached a clear stretch of motorway she found herself composing responses to Sid Peacock. *Dear Mr. Peacock, While I appreciate your invitation to be aggressive I think you might prefer me not to be . . . Dear Sidney, Given your skillful choice of words I don't think you really need my assistance . . . Dear Sid, Thank you for making it clear in your letter that you're as gallant as ever . . . Dear Peacock, Up your tail . . .* She mustn't start thinking as though everything were resolved, she told herself. She was going to Stargrave to see what needed to be done to the house.

Once she was past the villages beyond Leeds, she tried not to enjoy the landscape too much. As the road soared up through a multitude of clumps of moist bright grass under a piebald sky, the car started a moorhen out of the heather. The flight of the bird drew her gaze to the first crags, dark masses of gnarled stone which neither the weather nor the vegetation could overcome and which made her feel as if the landscape were baring its soul to her. She drove for half an hour without meeting another vehicle, and was quite glad when she saw the railway bridge ahead. Feeling solitary was fine, except that she had the family to think of.

"Having a rest from the family?" the receptionist at the Station Hotel said, and showed Ellen to a small room at the front of the building. The lift was still out of order. "Better than a three-mile hike, this place," the receptionist panted as she unlocked Ellen's room.

Ellen freshened up after the drive and headed for the estate agent's, where Henry Tovey exhibited his scrubbed smile for her. "Still no offers?" she said.

"Some folk from out of town said they'd be letting us know. You'll have noticed that in general our local homeowners prefer more compact properties. But I'll guarantee that Elgin's can make it more attractive."

She and Ben had asked him to recommend a builder, and now he took her to the yard. It was diagonally opposite the school, between the two loops, Church Road and The Crescent. As Tovey opened the wicket in the wooden gate, a woman surrounded by children imploring "Mrs. Venable" gave Ellen a smile as she crossed Church Road to the schoolyard, where she all but vanished in a larger crowd of children. Of course, Mrs. Venable and her husband had been the only other diners at the hotel when the Sterlings had stayed there. "She's the headmistress," Tovey said as he let Ellen through the gate.

A bulky man in overalls and a black wool cap slammed the bonnet of the only van in the cobbled yard and came to greet them, wiping his hands on a rag which he stuffed in his pocket. His wide ruddy face and swaying gait made her think of a sailor who'd lost the sea. "Stan Elgin," he said and shook her hand fastidiously, using one large finger and thumb. "I'll look after her, Henry. I've put a sheet in the van."

He'd spread what appeared to be a lacy tablecloth over the passenger seat. "I was thinking I could show you some of the work we've done for folk," he told her. "See that or your house first, whichever you like."

"Let's go to the house."

"You're the boss."

He drove out of a lower gate onto The Crescent, where a curve of houses pulled in their gardens and turned into shops. As Market Street brought the van in sight of the bungalow at the end of the track to the Sterling house, he pointed without letting go of the wheel. "I helped my dad build that."

"It looks very snug."

"Old Mrs. Broadbent used to live where that is now. Your husband might remember her. She had the sewing shop when he went away." The builder swung the van onto the track and said "Her house burnt down that Christmas. She had a stroke or summat like. Fell against the stove while it was on and must have cracked the pipe."

"At Christmas," Ellen mourned, her voice shaking with the jouncing of the van. As he parked the van beside the house, on a weedy patch of earth frozen hard as concrete, she said "You'd think my husband's family would have had this road improved."

"Reckon they weren't as well off as folk thought, and they never had much time for visitors."

Ellen climbed down from the van, thinking how lonely the house might have felt to a child. The forest and its miles of secret shadows seemed more present than the town. All at once she was determined to rescue the house from its own loneliness. She unlocked the front door and was met by her breath in the long shabby hall. "One thing this house could use is some heating," she declared.

"We can put that in for you." The builder followed her in and set about stamping on floors, rolling back carpets and poking floorboards with a screwdriver, opening and closing doors, peering at ceilings, tapping on walls or laying his palm on them as though feeling for a heartbeat. Every so often he scribbled on a pad in handwriting which looked as if it were struggling against a high wind. At the top of the house he hoisted himself through the attic window, elbows on the slates, to scrutinize the roof. "We'll need to get the ladders to the other side, but it's a rock of a place, this house," he said. "Damp course and your heating and a replacement for that broken window and a good strong coat of paint outside are most of what it needs. I can drop the estimates into the Station tomorrow morning if you're happy when you've seen some of our work."

"That would be ideal," Ellen said, gazing from the window he'd vacated. From up here the presence of the forest was even more overwhelming—because she could see more trees, she told herself. "Does anyone walk in the woods?"

"You won't see many. There's no paths, and if you aren't careful you'll think you've found one. It's not a place to walk on your own, but there's been a few who have."

"What happened to them?"

"Got lost and couldn't find their way out before dark. Had to stay there overnight and froze to death." He shook his head slowly and turned towards the stairs. "Unless you reckon they strayed in there after dark."

"What would have made them do that?"

"Just what I say," he responded as if she'd expressed more skepticism than in fact she had. "But to hear some of my dad's generation talk you'd think the forest was to blame, not these folk who go gallivanting when anyone with any sense wouldn't put their nose out of doors if they could help it. They're born that way if you ask me. If they aren't getting themselves stuck on the crags because they think they're Edmund Hillary, they're trying to prove they've more ice in their veins than the rest of us when it comes to the weather."

"Are the winters very cold here?"

"Mostly they're like it is now. It's when the rest of the country freezes you need to watch out. Maybe the cold drove those folk crazy," he said as if the explanation had just occurred to him, "and that's why they wandered up there after dark."

When she'd locked the front door he drove her to a cottage which backed onto the railway. Mrs. Radcliffe, who alternately coughed and smoked a cigarette, was even prouder of her new conservatory that overlooked the lower moors than the builder, who was trying to conceal that he was. "If you want your windows doing, you know where to come. Heights no object, my old man always says," she told Ellen as she saw her to the garden gate.

The next stop was a terraced house halfway up Hill Lane, a narrow street which led from the station to Church Road as if it was in no particular hurry to get there. The house was owned by the Wests, who greeted Ellen as warmly as they greeted the builder. By the time they had shown her Stan Elgin's work—a gritstone fireplace, built-in bookshelves, sliding doors between two downstairs rooms—she'd

learned that Terry drove the Stargrave mobile library and Kate helped
run a playgroup. On the gritstone mantelpiece she noticed a
photograph of a boy and girl slightly older than Margaret and Johnny.
"Are they at secondary school?"

"Since last September," Terry said.

"Here in town?"

"There isn't one," Kate said. "It's a bus ride over the top every
morning for Stefan and Ramona, most of an hour each way to
Richmond. Smooth enough for them to do their homework en route,
and we think the school's pretty recommendable. Why, have you got
some candidates?"

"One who's ten."

"If you need any help with settling in, just let us know. Nothing
worse than moving somewhere you don't know anyone."

The final stop on Ellen's guided tour was a cottage on The
Crescent, where the curve was so steep that the doorstep was
wedge-shaped. The owner, Hattie Soulsby, was a compact wrinkled
woman of about sixty, dressed in half a dozen bright colors, who
served Ellen and the builder tea from a clay teapot as large as a football
before showing them through the house, nudging Stan Elgin and
saying "That's his" every time they encountered some of his work—
new ceilings, a fitted kitchen, central heating which felt like a
welcome. In the front room she perched on a chair and said to Ellen,
"Hubby at work today?"

"Yes, in a bookshop."

"He writes books too, doesn't he?"

"We collaborate on them."

"You must be the girl of his dreams," Hattie said, and sat forwards. "I
only meant to say I hoped you weren't here on your own because your
hubby felt he might be unwelcome."

"Should he?"

"Not any more if I know Stargrave folk. When he ran away to come
back here, half my friends would have adopted him if they could have,
so he could stay where he felt at home."

"How did people feel before that?"

Hattie looked uncomfortable. "You know how folk can be about

118

things they don't understand. I think his family would have had no trouble fitting in if folk had just forgotten about that old explorer."

"Edward Sterling? What about him?"

"The state of him when they had to bring him back to England. My gran said it was in all the papers."

"I'm sorry to seem ignorant, but what state was that?"

Hattie raised her eyebrows, and Stan Elgin came to the rescue. "They found him naked as a baby in the ice and snow. The cold makes folk strip off sometimes, only that's usually when they're about to die of it. All his exploring must have toughened him up."

"I never knew that was how they found him," Ellen said.

"Well, there you are," Hattie said. "Shows it can't bother your hubby or he'd have told you about it. And you can tell him from me that nobody worth knowing cares."

"What was his family like?"

"They brought your hubby up by their own lights. I don't know of any harm that did him." Hattie seemed to find the question a little unfair, but she went on: "I'd have liked to see him play more, mind you, but then you'd expect me to say that, seeing as Kate and me run the playgroup. The old feller quite likes me having children I can send home, as long as him and me can't have any of our own."

Ellen complimented her and the builder on the house, and walked back to the hotel through streets suddenly full of children, chattering and playing and fighting. She lay on her bed for half an hour, catching up on the rest she hadn't had time for when she'd arrived in Stargrave, and then she called home. The phone only rang. She had a bath and went down for dinner, hoping there might be someone to talk to in the dining room. A young woman who worked in the cottage-sized bank on one corner of the square was being treated to a birthday dinner by half a dozen of her colleagues, who shouted across the room to Ellen and popped streamers in her general direction. Ellen raised her glass to them and joined in the chorus of "Happy birthday, dear Mona." Once she'd had a piece of birthday cake to go with her giant thimbleful of coffee, she returned to her room.

This time Ben answered the phone. "I'm just emptying Margery out of the bath so they can have a story."

"Don't make it too long, will you? Johnny really should be asleep by now. Don't forget to put out their clothes for the morning. What did they have for dinner?"

"A Big Mac each," he said, which explained why she hadn't been able to reach them earlier. "How are you finding my place?"

"It's stood up well, the builder says. He seems reliable to me."

"I wish I were there right now."

"With me, I hope."

"With all of us."

"Maybe we will be," she almost said, but there were questions she wanted to ask him when they were face to face. Before she could respond he said "Here's Johnny to speak to you, and a wet Margery."

She told Johnny to brush his teeth properly and Margaret to put her hair in a ponytail for school, and sent Ben a good-bye kiss. "Don't get too lonely in bed," she told him.

She felt exhausted by the long day. When she was ready for bed, she went to the window for a last sight of the town. Above Market Street the lamps rose towards the church, but it seemed to her as if the forest were drawing them towards itself. There was a faint glow in the air above the forest. It was mist, she thought, made to glow by the scrap of moon in the bare sky. Was it shifting? As she gazed at it, she couldn't even distinguish where the treetops ended and the vague luminosity began. If she gazed much longer she would be convinced that the dim glow and the forest were merging into some new vast shape. She closed the curtains and rubbed her eyes hard, and climbed shivering into bed. Mustn't Ben be responsible for Sterling Forest now? Surely it wouldn't cost much to mark paths through it. If the family came here to live—*if* they did, she repeated to herself as though the idea were an impatient child—then the least they could do for the town would be to make sure there were walks in the woods.

EIGHTEEN

An envelope from Elgin's was waiting on the breakfast table. The estimate was so low that at first Ellen thought she was misreading it; it wasn't much more than a tenth of the amount which the sale of one of their Norwich houses should realize. It only meant they could afford to improve the Sterling house, she told herself, but she wanted to see what the secondary school was like. She called the number Kate West had given her, and the school secretary told her she was welcome to look around. She packed her case and checked out of the hotel.

As the car passed between the first crags, Stargrave vanished. For a couple of miles she was surrounded by crags like arcs of several concentric stone circles too large to be seen as a whole, or like fragments of something whose original shape could only be guessed at after centuries of weathering. They made her feel as if the landscape had tried to form itself into a pattern above the forest. Fifteen minutes out of Stargrave the crags dwindled into a mile-wide border composed of hundreds of crumbled rocks, beyond which the moors spread like a tartan of heather and limestone and grass pinned with stony sheep. Apart from the sheep and the cry of a curlew, the only sign of life was a glinting dot ahead. It proved to be a green double-decker bus coming back from Richmond and now bound for Leeds. The driver waved to her, the bus shook the Volkswagen with its tailwind, and then she lost sight of it until the gleam of its windows in the mirror caught her attention. As the bus disappeared over the horizon towards Stargrave, she heard the shriek of a bird overhead, so lofty that it sounded thinned by the air. For no reason she could grasp, she imagined the bus toppling over the edge into a gulf dark and deep as a night sky. "Save your imagination," she told herself, and shrugged off a sudden chill.

Richmond was a huddle of brown brick and slate which reminded her of a great nest of moorland birds. She drove down into the busy streets, heading for an obelisk balancing a stone globe on its snout, and parked near the school. As she crossed the deserted yard, she heard an orchestra more or less agreeing on a key. A lanky schoolgirl in a skimpy uniform who was relaying a message from classroom to classroom directed her to the headmistress, an ample quiet-voiced woman who gave Ellen coffee and quizzed her about Margaret and Johnny before showing her around the school. The pupils seemed bright and happy, and Ellen was impressed by what she saw of the teaching and its results. "If you're thinking of enrolling your daughter," the headmistress said, "I'd ask you to let us know soon."

Ellen could no longer see a reason to procrastinate. "I'd like to put her name down," she said, and immediately felt liberated from her doubts.

She could always cancel the enrollment if she changed her mind, she thought as she drove south through the Vale of York, but why should she? Hours later she drove out of an ashen sunset into Norwich and was greeted by the lighting of the lamps as she turned along her street. The sound of her car door brought the children running along the path. "Are we going to live there?" Margaret cried, and Johnny echoed "Are we?"

"Let me into the house at least. Hasn't anyone a kiss for me?"

Johnny trotted into the house with her case, and Ellen followed with Margaret clutching her hand and chattering about her day at school as if she couldn't bear the silence that was letting her question linger. "I wouldn't mind a cup of tea," Ellen called, dropping herself onto the front-room couch.

"We heard your tongue hanging out ten minutes ago, didn't we, kids?" Ben responded from the kitchen. Soon he paced in with a brimming cup in each hand, and gave her a kiss so prolonged she was afraid the cup he'd given her would spill. "Did you drive straight home today?"

Ellen would have liked to relax before the excitement began, but you shouldn't have children, she thought, if you wanted to relax. "I had a look at the secondary school."

Margaret jumped and widened her eyes as if her whole body were performing a double take. "Was it good? Will I like it?"

"Now, Margery, I haven't said we're going there."

Margaret clenched her fists and her face, and slumped into a chair. "Oh, *Mummy* . . ."

Ellen took pity on her. "How do you feel now, Ben?"

"About Stargrave? The way I said I did before you went."

She handed him the builder's estimate and saw that he was pleasantly surprised. "Listen, you two," she said, "I want to be sure you realize what it would be like to live there, not just to visit. Think how much smaller than Norwich it is. Think of all the places you wouldn't be able to go—"

That was as far as she got before the children leapt up and danced around the room and then flung themselves on her and hugged her. "When are we moving?" Margaret cried.

"Not for months at least." When the children let go of her and grabbed each other's hands to dance in a ring, she turned to Ben. "Well, that seems to be decided."

"It was time we moved up in the world."

He seemed contented, but she wished he would express himself more directly. Later, too exhausted by her driving to do more than lie next to him in bed, she said drowsily "Do you know how they found Edward Sterling?"

"Deep in a forest that hadn't even grown yet."

"I don't mean when he died, I mean when he had to come back to England."

"Somewhere under the midnight sun where only the mad and the English would go."

123

"What do you think he was looking for?"

"Someone who could tell him the oldest story in the world, maybe," Ben said, and smiled dismissively. "I don't really know. I always thought of him more as a legend than a relative. He was a folklorist, and from what I remember of the book he was writing when he died he'd been researching the lore and legends of the midnight sun. As far as I can remember, the book doesn't say what he found at the end."

"Did you know they found him with no clothes on?"

"I didn't, but maybe I should have guessed. The way I heard it from my granddad, he could hardly wait to be thawed out before he fathered him. Edward must have been a randy old cove for the cold to have affected him that way. Who told you the story?"

"The builder. I think most of Stargrave knew."

"Probably everyone but me."

"Didn't any of your friends at school ever mention it?"

"I didn't let outsiders get that close to me. A family trait, I suppose it was."

"Do you think it bothered your family that so many people knew?"

"About old Edward? I should think it must have. They weren't *that* strange."

"Would that be why they kept people at a distance?"

"That and not wanting to mix with the herd." He dug his elbow into the pillow and propped himself above her. "What are you getting at? What's the mystery?"

"I was just wondering—if they felt like that about Stargrave, what kept them there?"

She was suddenly afraid she'd probed too deeply or too clumsily into his memories, because a cold glint appeared in his eyes. "What do you really want? Have you had second thoughts? Are you trying to put me off going back?"

"Of course not, Ben."

"Because if you've any doubts, then we'll just have to stay where we are."

"I do want us to move. I'm sure the people there will make us feel at home. I just wanted to be certain that you do."

"Then stop worrying." He stroked her cheek so gently that at first

124

she didn't realize he was wiping away a tear. "I didn't want to say before," he said, "and I can't tell you why I feel this because I don't know myself, but I feel as if it'll make a new man of me."

"Can't I keep the one I married?"

"Wait until you test the new improved model," he said with a wink, and traced her spine with one finger to give her a delicious shiver. When his hand settled on her bottom she nestled against him, and almost at once she was asleep.

The event of the week was an offer from Kerys Thorn—twenty thousand pounds as an advance against royalties for their next two books, to which Ember would buy world rights. "It's meant to show how much faith we have in your books," Kerys assured the Sterlings when they called her, Ben holding the receiver between his face and Ellen's. "We'll be acting as your agent, since you haven't got one. Let me send you a contract and if there's anything in it you don't like, give me a call."

"Sounds fine," Ellen mouthed, and Ben said "Sounds fine."

The contract arrived three weeks later, and Kerys sounded quite relieved that they were asking for changes. "You keep the media rights by all means and double your number of complimentary copies. I'm here to keep you happy if I can."

By then Ellen had written an icily polite letter thanking Sid Peacock for his consideration and hoping that he would be pleased to learn she had received a better offer. She had also returned to Stargrave to see how work on the house was progressing, since Dominic Milligan had asked Ben to avoid taking days off. The newly plastered walls downstairs and the floors stripped of their worn carpets made her footsteps sound as though she were walking through a series of vaults. She heard Elgin's men shifting like large birds on the roof, and once she thought she heard a voice from somewhere even higher. It must have been one of the workmen on the roof, but for a moment she thought it was calling her by name. Perhaps that was why it reminded her indefinably of Ben, though the shrill voice had sounded nothing like his.

Stan Elgin offered to redecorate the house for her. Choosing carpets and wallpaper and paints in Stargrave made her feel she was already part of the town. Next day in Norwich she learned that a married couple, both teachers, had made a bid for her home. The pattern of her life and the family's was falling into place, but she couldn't help feeling wistful on behalf of the house where the children had always lived. She wondered if Ben shared her melancholy; he seemed so preoccupied that she decided not to ask.

Soon she felt happier. An elderly couple signed a lease for Ben's aunt's house, and Dominic Milligan interviewed a young woman who he thought would be perfect for the shop. She hadn't started work there when it was time for a last check of the Sterling house.

It seemed transformed. The exterior had been painted red as autumn, except for the woodwork, which was bright yellow. Ellen switched on the central heating and strolled through the house, smelling the newness. The only addition about which she felt even slightly dubious was the wallpaper in the corridors and over the stairs, patterned with pines so dark you had to gaze at them to make sure they were green, but she would learn to live with it. "Here's to you, Stan Elgin," she said aloud, and thought she heard an echo more or less repeating her last word, though it didn't sound like her voice. On second thoughts, it must have been a voice calling someone from above the house.

The teachers had obtained a mortgage and wanted to move into the Norwich house in six weeks. Preparing for the move took the Sterlings as long: wrapping in newspaper anything which might be fragile, packing cartons until they were piled nearly to the ceiling in the rooms their contents had occupied, Ben having to lift them down again to write on each carton which room in the Stargrave house it was bound for, Ellen trying to persuade the children that they had outgrown at least a few of their toys and books . . . In the midst of all this Ben managed to complete the text of their new book, which he finished rewriting and sent off to Kerys the day before they would leave Norwich.

The morning was bright and cold, the sort of spring day which feels poised to revert to winter. Johnny insisted on helping the removal men load their huge van, and then stood panting to watch his breath appear. "We're leaving our breath behind," he said. Margaret gazed at the daffodils blossoming beside the garden path and ran into the house to hide her tears, and Ellen let her stay in there until it was time to check that nothing had been overlooked. Once Ben had strode through the rooms as if he could hardly wait to leave, Ellen dabbed at the girl's eyes and coaxed her downstairs from her denuded room. "It's been a good little house, but the new people will look after it. Just you wait until you see how snug we're going to be, though. It's like being in a cocoon," she said.

THE GROWTH

Daddy's pattern, heart and brain,

Sprinkle with the golden rain

For the rising of the Star.

—Algernon Blackwood,

The Starlight Express

NINETEEN

Ben dreamed of being surrounded by ice under a featureless sky. On every side of him a flat blank whiteness radiated to a perfectly circular horizon. Either the ice or something in it was aware of him. He was gazing into the ice on which he stood when it began to shine with a light colder and more pale than moonlight as whatever was beneath him rose towards him, and he awoke in the dark.

He didn't cry out, but he turned to Ellen, his mouth opening before he made out that she was asleep. All at once he had so much to tell, but he was suddenly glad that he would have to keep it to himself, at least for now. He eased himself away from her and tiptoed out of the bedroom.

It was on the top floor of the house, above the children's bedrooms. Next to it was the guest room and beyond it the workroom which used to be the attic. He stood in the dark, listening to all the breathing in the house, feeling enlivened by the chill which had settled into the core of the house as it waited for the central heating to switch on, and then he inched the workroom door open.

As soon as he was in the room he saw the forest. The twilight before the October dawn must already have reached it, because as he made for the desk at the window he was able to distinguish ranks of trees, patterns developing from the dark. He sat at the desk and gazed into the forest and let thoughts manifest themselves to him.

If the anticipation he had begun to experience couldn't be put into words, the insight which had wakened it could be. He felt as if he were growing up at last. As a child he'd half-believed that Edward Sterling had discovered a ritual which kept the midnight sun alight, and even as an adult he'd found the idea imaginatively appealing, but now he saw that it was nonsense: no human action could affect the sun. Edward Sterling might have witnessed such a ritual, but it made no sense to deduce that he had then set off to discover its source. If he had found anything significant in the unpopulated frozen wastes, it could only have been the reason for the ceremony—the reason why people were afraid the midnight sun might fail.

If only Edward Sterling had written down what he had found! But the last word he'd written had apparently been his last wish. Once he had been fit enough to travel after being brought home to England, he and his wife Catriona had journeyed north. Stargrave had apparently been intended only as an overnight stop. Perhaps the late December cold had affected his mind, because he'd risen in the night and headed for the moors, shedding his clothes as he walked. In the morning his naked corpse had been found in the center of a grove of ancient oaks. His limbs had been flung wide as if he'd been trying to embrace the night or had been crushed by it; his eyes had been wide and pale as ice, and he might have been smiling or gritting his teeth. He'd broken his nails in the process of scratching two words in the earth in front of him: "trees grow." The way Ben's grandfather had told the story one night just before Christmas, those who found the corpse had had to snap the strings of frozen blood which bound the fingers to the marbly earth.

Could it ever have been so cold in Stargrave? Ben had never previously wondered who had told his grandfather the story—one or another of the searchers or perhaps Catriona—and now it was too late to inquire. He was inclined to wonder if Edward Sterling's message had been merely a delirious reference to the grove in which he'd lain. Catriona had taken it as a plea, and by the time Ben's grandfather was born she had used much of her legacy to buy the house and to plant the forest which over the decades had hidden the grove from the world.

Ben gazed out of the window while feeble sunlight ventured down the crags and was seized by the forest. When he heard the children beginning to stir on the floor below, he sneaked back to bed. Their sounds made him feel somehow less awake than he had been while musing at the desk, and he continued to feel that way as Ellen wakened drowsily and snuggled against him, as Margaret and Johnny made the house sound full of children, as the family took turns in the bathroom to get ready for a walk before Sunday lunch.

A small sun like a coin whose features had been seared away by heat hung low in a sky suffused with blue. Autumn had extinguished the brightest colors of the moors beyond the railway, and not only the vegetation but also the houses of Stargrave appeared to be seeking to merge chameleonlike with the ancient limestone. As Ben opened the new gate in the garden wall, a wind like the first stirring of winter set trees dancing and brought him the scent of pines. The whisper of the forest made him feel as if he and the trees were about to share a secret. Then a dog barked, and he sighed and turned to look.

It was Mrs. Dainty's Doberman. Edna Dainty was the Stargrave postmistress, a dumpy muscular woman whose red hair was growing white. She came stumbling up the track, leaning backwards and heaving at Goliath's leash. "Don't pull, don't pull."

"Ideal day for a run, Mrs. Dainty," Ben said over the wall.

"Golly," she cried, and the dog halted, panting. "You've put your nail on the head there," she agreed.

"Are you for the woods?"

"Too blowy up on top for me today. It's an ill wind," she added in case that had some relevance, and almost fell on her face as the dog surged forwards. "Excuse me for shaking my legs, but you know old dogs."

"Can't be taught?"

She peered at him, obviously suspecting a verbal trap, and then lurched away, dragged by the dog. Her voice dwindled up the track, crying "Golly, don't pull."

Ben held the gate open for the family. "If they're going to be in the woods I'm heading for the moors."

Johnny looked disappointed, and said to Ellen, "When can we mark some more paths in the woods?"

"Better ask your father. He's the pathfinder."

"No more this year, Johnny, I shouldn't think."

"We've only made titchy paths," Margaret protested.

"We've plenty of summers ahead of us, Peggy. And don't you want to keep some of the forest for just the family to walk in?"

"Besides," Ellen told the children, "you won't have time to make another path if you want to be in the Christmas play, and go to Young Dalesfolk with Stefan and Ramona every Thursday, and all the way to Richmond every Friday for the swimming club, and help me keep our garden tidy . . ."

"And play with all your other new friends," Ben added as he led the way to the main road. Their talk of the woods was aggravating his own frustration, but he'd had enough of Mrs. Dainty and her apparently inexhaustible supply of misheard clichés for one day. "They're just words," he said under his breath as he ushered the children across the road to face any oncoming traffic.

They hadn't met any by the time they reached the newsagent's. All summer Stargrave had been packed with tourists, driving up from Leeds to tramp the moors or basing themselves in the hotel or the dozens of houses which offered bed and breakfast for the season. Now just three climbers, two in bright orange and one in a blue which rivalled the sky, were visible above the town, moving so slowly they looked frozen to the crags.

Most of Stargrave was indoors. Passing a row of houses, Ben saw successive images of a space battle on their televisions, as if he were reading a comic strip. The clank of swings thrown over their metal frames drifted down from near the school. One of Johnny's school-mates ran home from a newsagent's, a Sunday paper flapping in his hand. The tourist information center in the converted railway station was still open; Sally Quick, whose name always sounded to him like advice and who had exhibited Ellen's paintings all summer in the information center, waved at the Sterlings through the window.

Beyond the deserted square and the estate agent's, old Mr. Westminster was rooting weeds out of his front garden, chortling vindictively whenever a weed lost its grip on the soil. He was often to be seen driving his rusty Austin through Stargrave, shouting "Baa, baa" at anyone who crossed the street in front of him. "Rub my back, somebody," he greeted the Sterlings, then emitted a hum which was half a groan as he stooped to fork the earth.

"Race you to the top," Margaret told Johnny as soon as they were over the stile. They chased along the grassy path towards the crags, on which the blue and orange insects appeared scarcely to have moved. A wind set the moor trembling, the gorse and heather and countless tufts of grass interspersed with mounds of moss and lichen, and as Ben heard the wind enter the forest all the somber colors of the moor seemed to leap up. Ellen clutched his hand as if she were sharing what he saw. "I really think that getting married and having the children and coming here to live may be the best things we've ever done," she said.

"Good. I'm glad," Ben responded, feeling as if she'd interrupted a thought he was about to have.

"Don't you agree?"

"I can't imagine living anywhere else." In case he hadn't matched her enthusiasm he added "Or with anyone else."

"I should hope not. That part of your imagination's all mine." She cupped her hands to her mouth. "Be careful where you climb," she shouted to the children, but the wind flung her voice back at her. "Don't climb until I'm there," she shouted, and ran up the path.

As Ben watched her take their hands and lead them towards the sky, three figures growing smaller in the midst of the luminous moor, he experienced a rush of love and satisfaction on their behalf. The children had never been happier at school, and both Johnny's handwriting and Margaret's spelling had improved. Ellen's latest paintings showed a new toughness mixed with her old sensitivity, and she'd joined Sally Quick's moorland rescue team. As for himself, he was beginning to feel as though the whole of his life between running away from his aunt's and finally returning to Stargrave had been no more than a prolonged interlude, most of which he had to make an effort to remember. The only problem was that he couldn't write.

At first he'd assumed that the excitement of coming home was distracting him. As soon as the air had begun to smell of autumn he'd taken himself to the desk every morning and kept himself there until he'd written at least a paragraph, but he felt as if the story wouldn't come alive. He was nervous of telling it to the children in case the act drained it of whatever energy it had. He was beginning to wonder if having signed a contract in advance were making him afraid that he couldn't deliver, but he thought more than that was involved. As he sat at the desk each morning and gazed into the forest, he felt as though an inspiration or a vision larger than he could imagine was hovering just out of reach.

"Climb with us, Daddy," Johnny was calling, and Ben relinquished his thoughts with a sigh. By the time he arrived at the children's favorite crag, which Margaret had immediately compared to a giant loaf nibbled by giant mice, the family was halfway to the top. The wind tugged at her clothes as she followed her mother up the zigzag path worn into the rock, and Ben clambered after her in case she needed help.

Johnny danced on the flat summit and chanted "I'm the king of the castle" while the others hauled themselves over the edge to join him. Having wavered upright, Ben planted his feet well apart before he surveyed the view. All he could see were another few distant slopes and isolated farmhouses. Even if the view had anything extra to offer, his anxiety in case the children strayed too close to the edge was distracting him.

From the foot of the crag they walked across the moor to the common between the forest and the town. A faint path which Mrs. Venable forbade her pupils to use on the way to and from school led through the grass above the schoolyard and churchyard and back gardens of Church Road. As the road curved downhill, half a mile of allotments took the place of gardens beside the path, and ended near the track which led past the Sterling house.

As the Sterlings reached the track, Mrs. Dainty stumbled out of the woods onto the further stretch of path, mopping her forehead with her free hand. "Thank the heavens it was you I kept hearing, and you stayed there long enough for me to find you."

"We've only just got here, Mrs. Dainty," Ellen said.

"If I was hearing some other lost soul whispering in there, may the dear Lord see them out before it's dark. The dog only had me off the path as far as you are from the church, and I thought we were gone forever."

"There you are," Margaret said to her parents. "We need to make some more paths."

"I wouldn't ache my head with that if I were you, lass," Mrs. Dainty said. "There won't be many besides me walking in there till spring. There's not many can take the chill."

"Thank you, Mrs. Dainty."

Ben didn't think she heard him as the dog yanked her away, but Ellen heard. "What were you thanking her for?"

"Showing me where I can be alone to work out my story."

"I expect all you need is not to feel under pressure. I won't need to start painting for six months. You do whatever your feelings say you have to, but don't get lost in there."

"How could I?" Ben said, and waited until she turned away before following her and the children to the house. He heard the forest creak and whisper behind him, and shook his head at himself. Finding his way into the book had to be his only reason to spend time in there. It wouldn't help him in his task to feel that he was using the book as an excuse to be alone in the woods.

TWENTY

The cold wakened him before dawn. He couldn't tell whether it was the night which was cold or only himself. When he put one arm around Ellen, she shivered in her sleep. Though he didn't feel the need to shiver, the cold was making him restless. He padded into the workroom and watched the stars flickering above the forest, and wondered how many of the crystal sparks were ghosts of dead stars, their light kept alive by the gulf the starlight had to cross. Just now, when the night was darkest, the mass of trees looked like a distillation of the space between the stars. He would have switched on the desklamp if he'd thought of so much as a phrase, but his nervous exhilaration seemed for the moment to have nothing to do with writing. He watched until the forest began to glimmer and then to glow faintly as the stars went out. It was the dawn, but it looked to him as though the starlight were settling into the forest, impregnating the silvery branches.

The click of the central heating reverberated through the pipes and brought him back to himself. Soon the family would be about, and he didn't want the bother of explaining why he had been sitting naked at the desk; he hadn't even realized until now that he was. By the time he'd bathed and dressed himself, the family was still asleep. He brought Ellen a cup of tea, and sang softly in the children's ears to rouse them.

He was brushing his teeth after breakfast, gazing into his eyes as if they could tell him a secret, when he heard Ellen losing patience with the children. "Try and get a move on instead of arguing. You know I need to be quick on Mondays."

She taught an art class at a college outside Leeds twice a week. A niece of Sally Quick's was a student there and had persuaded Ellen to take the class. "I'll walk them to school," Ben told Ellen as he went downstairs. "I need to get away from the desk."

"Any joy this morning?"

"Nothing on paper to show for it. It's in here," he said, tapping his forehead. "I just need to give it room to breathe."

"If you go in the woods, will you stay where we've marked?"

"If it keeps you happy," he said, feeling guilty as he saw how prepared she was to believe him. There was no point in troubling her when he knew what he was doing. He wanted to make sure nobody distracted him from his imagination, that was all.

When he opened the front door the October cold settled on him. The flowers in the garden were dusted with frost, the cobwebs on the spiky wall had turned into webs of spun glass. He felt entranced by the clarity of his surroundings, the cold made visible. When he reached the newsagent's and a newsboy with an empty shoulder bag dodged into the shop, the furnace blast from the heater above the door almost shocked Ben into the roadway. Johnny was being a steam engine while Margaret strolled with two of her friends and pretended that her father wasn't there. As the horde of schoolchildren converged on the school, they seemed to him to be drawn towards the forest. The sight made him think of some fairy tale, perhaps one he had yet to tell.

At the school gates Margaret said good-bye with a kiss and a regal wave, and Johnny managed a hasty peck once he was sure that none of his friends would see. Ben watched as the two of them became part of the crowd in the schoolyard. He felt unexpectedly vulnerable, childlike. He wandered down Hill Lane to the main road, and was past the newsagent's again before he wondered why he hadn't made straight for the forest instead of heading for the end of the marked paths nearest the house. What reason could he have for putting off an exploration of the woods? He'd already explored the lower reaches of the forest with the help of Ellen and the children, after all.

Though the borough council was technically responsible for its maintenance, the terms of the original bequest meant that the Sterlings owned the forest. During the summer, at Ellen's suggestion, they'd begun to identify walks and paint arrows on the trees. Green arrows marked a path which curved from above the Sterling house to the edge of the woods nearest the stile on the moorland road, blue arrows led deeper into the forest and then returned across the green path to emerge onto the common above the church. Stan Elgin had erected marker posts along the paths, and the council was apparently proposing to gravel the paths if it ever had sufficient funds. "They'd rather argue about money than spend it," Ben told himself as he strode past the house.

When the track reached the common beside the allotments it vanished. Only his shadow was there to lead him across the frosty grass to the start of the blue-arrowed path, where the earth showed black through a threadbare embroidery of moss. He halted there and stood listening. All he could hear was the silence of the trees, ranks of Norway spruce radiating away from him like centuries of Christmases until they met the pines which composed most of the forest. As he set out along the path, he found he was instinctively trying to make no noise.

The silence closed around him like water, icy and gloomily green. He had taken only a few steps when he felt he was deep in the forest; the trees cut off all the sounds of the town. Soon the trees were towering over him, their spires of green branches perched high on mottled scaly trunks as tall as the spire of St. Christopher's. While he'd been leading the family along the paths they'd marked, the forest had often seemed a refuge from the summer heat, a reservoir of wintry shadow, as though the trees had immobilized the seasons. Now he found they had trapped a chill which felt as if it might never recede. It made him breathless, and he walked faster, almost in a trance, until the sight of a marker post ahead told him that he was about to leave the path.

The arrow carved and painted on the waist-high post indicated that the path wound sharply to the right, and Ben wondered why he'd sent the path in that direction. He mustn't have wanted it to lead any deeper into the forest. Several hundred yards ahead the Norway spruce gave way to pines, and he felt as if he was about to cross a threshold, not necessarily one that was visible to him. He went to the post and held onto it, trying to decide whether he'd wanted to save the depths of the woods for himself or to protect Ellen and the children from them. Perhaps it had been the latter, because suddenly he felt reluctant to leave the path.

As his left hand clamped his right on top of the post, he was reminded of a game he and his mother used to play, piling their hands alternately on top of one another, faster and faster, towards some goal which he had always thought they'd failed to reach because of laughing. Infuriated by the childishness of the gesture, he shoved himself away from the post and off the path, onto a carpet of fallen needles which silenced his footsteps. He was heading for the center of the forest, as far as he could tell. He wouldn't look back until he was certain that the path was out of sight. It was his forest more than anyone else's, and he felt as if it were poised to watch over him.

The pines multiplied around him with every step he took. He followed his shadow over mounds of decaying needles towards what appeared to be the edge of an infinity of pines, an edge which constantly renewed itself. Fallen needles surrounded him, green needles scattered on old gold and bronze and shards of ivory where frost had settled, and they made him feel as if the forest contained a pattern he was soon to distinguish. He looked over his shoulder at last and saw only pines leading away; he didn't know how long ago he'd left the spruce plantation behind. He was still walking as if he were under a compulsion to walk, and the next moment he lost his footing on a slippery root beneath the needles. He fell to his knees, his hands sinking into prickly decay, and was about to heave himself to his feet when it was borne in on him that his would be the only movement in the entire forest.

He crouched there, hands on thighs, too awed to stir. The countless slender pines and the lattice of their shadows surrounded him with a calm which suggested to him that the very air had turned to ice. The avenues of bare trunks rose to a ceiling of gloomy green high as a cathedral roof, and he felt as if he were kneeling in a vast natural shrine to a stillness of which his surroundings were merely an omen. What might he find at the center of such a stillness? Just as he wondered that, he heard a sound behind him.

It began above him, rattling through foliage, and came scuttling down a trunk. Ben gave a cry and twisted around, kicking up a heavy shower of needles. He was in time to see an object small and brown as a sparrow drop from the leaning trunk and land among the roots. For a moment, bewildered by the sound which had responded to his cry, he thought the object was a spider. It was a pinecone, and he told himself that the sound had been the echo of his own voice; if it had been anyone else's, he would surely have been aware of its owner by now. All the same, he wished that he hadn't been making so much noise himself that he'd obscured the sound which, as he strained to recall it, seemed like a whisper coming from several directions. "He could imagine that it had been the sound of the forest calling to him," he muttered, as if making his impression more like a story would distance it from him.

A shiver sent him wavering to his feet. He stared about, trying to determine which way he'd been facing when he had looked over his shoulder, and then he saw that the forest itself was showing him: most of the shadows were pointing that way. His own shadow had joined them as he rose, and he went quickly after it, as though he could outrun it if he went fast enough.

There was another idea for a story. He must remember to write it down once he was home, and carry a notebook in future. That should help him focus his imagination, which seemed just now to be escaping his control. He was beginning to think that all the shadows around him and ahead of him were indicating the route he should follow, and that too many of the fallen needles were. Surely none of this need trouble him, because he could see open sky beyond the farthest trees. It had to be the edge of the forest, and he was bound to admit he felt a little relieved. He would welcome a few natural sounds once he was in

142

the open. Until he was out of the forest, however, he would rather not hear anything beyond his breathing and his muffled footfalls which sounded like heartbeats in the earth.

He would have expected the patch of open sky to grow more quickly as he strode forwards. Even when he jogged towards it, it stayed frustratingly localized. The soft ground muffled his footfalls so completely that he felt as if the silence were intensifying, swallowing any sounds he made. Then he faltered. That wasn't the edge of the forest ahead; it was a glade deep in the forest. He knew that because he had already been there.

He remembered being taken to the glade on a day so cold his mother and grandmother huddled close to the fire in the house. Had the place looked then as it looked now? The pines around it glittered as though ice were crystallizing faintly on their bark, and the grass at its center resembled an explosion of frost yards wide. His memories were slipping away, because he'd realized what he must have been too young to realize then. This was the place where Edward Sterling had died.

Ben stepped between two pines and halted at the edge of the grass, wondering how he knew. This might not be the only glade in the forest, after all. But Edward Sterling had been found in a grove of oak trees, and there were the remains of oaks among the pines which encircled the glade. Ben walked to the middle of the open space and gazed around him.

The glade was circular, about thirty yards in diameter. Within this, roughly equidistant from the center, were four dead oak trees. He assumed that the pines had stolen their light and their nourishment, because the oaks were withered, little more than a scattering of twisted limbs around collapsed trunks. They reminded him of huge dead spiders. He stood on the grass which yielded stiffly underfoot like a frozen pond about to give way, and tried to see what else he should be noticing. Whatever it was, he felt as if it were waiting for him to notice.

He peered through the veils of his breath at the trees radiating from the edge of the glade, and thought he saw. Could the glade really be as perfectly circular as it appeared to be? He positioned himself as close to the exact center of the glade as he could judge, then paced to the perimeter, placing the heel of each foot against the toe of its follower.

Forty-six paces brought him to the edge. A foot was a foot long, he thought, but now he had forgotten precisely where he'd started from. He took forty-six paces back and dropped a pound coin on the patch of frosty grass, then he continued in a straight line to the far side of the glade. Forty-six paces again. He'd managed to locate the center by instinct, and he felt as if he had unlocked an unsuspected aspect of himself.

He went back to the coin and paced along a diameter at right angles to the first. Forty-six paces brought him level with the pines. He grunted with surprise, retreated to the coin and set out along the other half of the diameter. The toecap of his right shoe reached the edge just as he counted forty-six, and he couldn't help shivering with excitement or nervousness or the growing chill. No glade could be that regular, he told himself, and he meant to prove it. Until he'd walked a line across the glade which didn't measure ninety-two paces, or even a radius which wasn't precisely half that length, he wouldn't let anything distract him.

He didn't know how long he spent at the task, no longer looking at his feet as he mouthed the count rather than break the silence, trusting his instincts to find the diameters which bisected the angles between those he'd already paced, as if such obsessive precision would lead sooner to an irregular measurement. Here was one—the distance from the center to an oak. He turned away from the snarl of whitened branches, towards the marker coin, which was so frosted it resembled a tiny moon. The oaks deformed the glade, he thought, and that would have to do; how much longer did he propose to trot back and forth like a puppet? If he didn't head for the moors soon he might be in the forest when darkness fell. Just walk to each of the other three oaks, he murmured, just to be tidy. At least, he thought he'd spoken, almost too low to be audible. Certainly a soft voice had.

It was his unsureness which broke his trance enough for him to realize that something around him had changed. At once he was afraid to look away from the icy moon of the coin, and afraid not to. A shiver which seemed to begin underfoot before shooting through his body raised his head for him.

At first he thought it might be only his awareness which had changed, because he saw immediately that the avenues of trees radiating from the glade were absolutely regular, not just the placing of the trees but the shapes of their trunks and their high spreads of branches, as if some force emanating from the glade had aligned them like iron filings around a magnet. Then he saw how nearly similar to one another the shapes of the dead oaks were, as though what had killed them had shaped them. He sensed there was another pattern which he was afraid to identify. He stared at the glittering trees, at the shadows which had turned on their axes and were reaching towards him from the side of the glade opposite that from which he'd entered, and then he looked down.

"God," he whispered. The pattern was around him on the grass, a many-armed star of frost as wide as the glade. The outlines of the slender arms were awesomely intricate and yet symmetrical in every detail. He turned dizzily, feeling in danger of losing his balance, and saw that the star wasn't quite symmetrical: it lacked the three arms which would have pointed to the oaks he had failed to approach. The star showed where he had walked, as if a vast cold presence had paced behind him.

As soon as he thought that, he sensed it behind him or above him, waiting for him to be unable not to look. He couldn't move, but how would that help him? A snowflake settled on his trembling hand and lay between the tendons, a perfectly symmetrical snowflake like a feathery wafer of glass. He stared helplessly at it and saw that it wasn't melting but growing. Perhaps that was a sign of life—of the kind of life which the miles of forest hid.

Ben's trembling freed him from his paralysis. He staggered across the glade, slipping wildly on the frozen grass, and fled into the woods, trying not to see how even the ferns among the trees formed a regular pattern. He caught sight of a spider plucking at its web among the ferns in front of him, a spider striped like a tiger, and for a moment even that seemed welcome; at least it was a living creature. But the woods darkened around him as their denizen came after him. The ferns turned to marble as frost raced over them, and snowflakes whirled around him, bejewelling the trees. The spider paled and writhed into a shape which no living creature should form, and before Ben could suck in a breath after the cry that the sight wrenched from him, it was a crystal of flesh, the center of a mandala of frost and web. Then the forest grew dark as a starless night, and something like an incarnation of that darkness, far larger than the glade, seized him.

TWENTY-ONE

When Ellen arrived at the college that morning she learned that the model for her art class had called in sick. "She's off with a bug," the college secretary said. Nobody else was available, and so Ellen introduced her students to the drawing of still lifes, improvising a theme from random objects in the classroom—an apple, a bunch of keys strung on a safety pin, a handbag, a headscarf, a copy of *The Boy Who Let the Fire Go Out* which one young mother had brought for Ellen to autograph. Ellen encouraged them to look for the details which made each object unique at the moment of looking—the lopsidedness of the apple, the irregular mark which gave its crest the appearance of a miniature yellow beret with a frayed brown stalk, the hint of a bruise on its bright green cheek . . . You couldn't capture how the handbag smelled of unlit cigarettes and a dry perfume which tickled the nostrils, but that was reality for you: there was always more to any aspect of it than you could reproduce, and that was what made it real. She strolled up and down between the desks occupied by her eighteen students and talked about selecting the details which brought the subject alive for you. Here and there controversies were flaring, a pensioner who never let her bag out of her reach insisting that the objects Ellen had chosen were too ordinary to be called a still life, a

Pakistani chef maintaining that one had to master all the skills of draftsmanship before one could produce anything original, a claim which provoked support and disagreement and which vanished into a larger argument. Despite all this, everyone had a picture to show by lunchtime. Ellen was struck by the care quite a few of the students had taken in drawing the book, the ways the pages of the propped volume leaned, the random pattern of the text, the light and shadow of her illustration on the left-hand page; she wished Ben could be there to see. "Keep looking," she told her class as they straggled out of the room.

She was driving away from Leeds when the sky ahead began to darken. By the time she reached the last village, the horizon beyond which Stargrave lay was ominously black. She hoped Ben was on his way home if the weather was about to turn nasty. A small cold sun illuminated the moors, so that the slopes shone unnaturally bright against the strip of darkness. The vegetation seemed deadened, as metallic as the sheen of the exposed rock.

Could the height of the moors above Stargrave affect the atmospheric conditions? The blackness appeared to be poised over the town. She felt as if she ought to have found out more about the climate before the family had decided to move from Norwich. She hadn't listened to the car radio since their move, and now she had to assume that the geography interfered with the reception: she could raise nothing but a silence so total she would have thought she had fallen deaf if she hadn't been hearing the sounds of the car.

When she came in sight of the railway bridge, the sky was impenetrably black. She could imagine the sky having given way like ice, leaving a great hole above the town for outer space to show through. It was only a mass of clouds, she told herself firmly, and drove under the arch.

The dark closed over her like icy water so deep that no light could reach it, and she gripped the wheel harder in order not to shiver. For a moment she was nervous of how much darker it might be on the far side of the bridge than it was on the moors. Of course that was nonsense: when she drove up the slope beyond the bridge she saw the houses glaring almost silver; only the forest looked as if it welcomed the blackness overhead. She swung the car onto the track to the house, hoping that Ben would be there.

When she opened the front door she was greeted by a hint of central heating. "Ben," she called, stooping to pick up an envelope from the doormat, but even when she shouted up the stairs there was no response. She switched on the heating and gazed from the kitchen window at the deserted track. She tore off a length of kitchen roll to mop the rings of blackcurrant juice which the children had left like an Olympic emblem on the working surface next to the washing machine. She filled the percolator and turned it on, and then she opened the letter.

It was a form letter from Kerys at Ember. Apart from "Dear Ben and Ellen," only the signature and the lines beneath it were handwritten, and so Ellen read the postscript first. "Someone else who's gone to a better place is our publicity director, but the new bod Mark Matthews comes recommended. Give him a call to introduce yourselves or ask Alice to next time you're down. Remind them how good you are. Only wish I could've been around for your success. Heaps of good luck."

The letter itself announced that because of "a personnel rationalization exercise" at Firebrand and Ember, Kerys would be leaving at the end of the month, to be replaced by Alice Carroll, the new children's fiction editor "with several years experience in juveniles." Ellen stared out of the window, willing Ben to appear on the track so that she could stop worrying about him, but staring only seemed to make the sky and the forest grow darker. The contents of the letter felt like a dull ache in her mind, an ache she couldn't begin to deal with until she saw Ben. There had been no sign of him when it was time to fetch the children from school. She propped the envelope against the telephone on the fourth stair up and hurried out.

The sun was beyond the forest now. In the streets people were shaking their heads at the sky, blowing on their hands or burying them in their armpits. "Always dark before the silver lining," Mrs. Dainty called after the greengrocer as he dashed out of her post office and back into his shop next door, trailing a strip of stamps from one hand and pinching his shirt collar shut above his muddy apron with the other. Two young men from Elgin's were perched on the exposed timbers of the roof of a house near the school, fitting new slates, and she found their shouts to each other oddly reassuring. As she hurried uphill, the sky and the forest and the darkening town felt like aspects of a single darkness.

The sight which met her when she neared the school made her forget the gloom. Ben was leading Margaret and Johnny out of the schoolyard, and his eyes were glittering. "Wait until you hear my story," he said.

TWENTY-TWO

He seemed to be in no hurry to tell her, even when the children eased themselves out of his grasp and ran ahead. He seemed as exhilarated by the blackness of the sky and the possibility of its heralding snow as the children were. When Ellen cried "You're freezing" and rubbed his hands and then his cheeks, he gave her a vague smile. He was so cold that holding his hand made her shiver, but he was here, and what else mattered? She hurried him after the children, back to the warmth of the house.

The white envelope was still propped against the white telephone, both of them glimmering as Ellen closed the front door. Ben picked up the envelope and blinked at it, and eventually said "Good news?"

"Not the best. You'll see better if you put the light on," Ellen said, and headed for the front room to sort out an argument over first choice of television channel. "Let Johnny have the control now, Peg. The programs you like best are on later."

In the hall Ben was fumbling to unzip his quilted anorak and waving away the heat with his free hand. While she waited patiently he blinked again at the envelope, threw off his anorak, took out the letter. Since he hadn't switched on the hall light, she did so as he peered at the letter. "Well," he said.

"Well?"

"Well, Mark Matthews sounds like two kinds of saint, and can you imagine a better name than Alice Carroll for a children's fiction editor?"

"You don't think it's serious, then."

"Only one way to find out," he said slowly, and unplugged the phone to carry it up to their workroom. "Let's see what Kerys has to say for herself."

When Ellen followed, having told the children not to interrupt them, he was standing at the window of the unlit workroom. The darkness made the forest appear to have closed around the house; as she went into the room the window was full of a mass of black foliage which might almost have been printed on the glass. She switched on the light and crossed the floor to him, and the view of the forest regained some perspective, though it still looked as though the premature night were forming patterns on the hillside. "Will you make the call or shall I?" she said.

He plugged in the phone and dialled, then handed her the receiver. "I'll be your prompter if I think of anything to say."

She wouldn't have minded deciding for herself when she was ready to talk. She was moving to sit on the chair at the desk when a receptionist's voice announced "Firebrand Books."

"Kerys Thorn, please."

"I'll put you through to her secretary."

The receptionist had barely paused, but Ellen had noticed. "I think something may be up," she whispered to Ben, who knelt by her and brought his face alongside hers. Momentarily she felt as if he was kneeling before the dark forest. "Hello, can I help?" Kerys' secretary said.

"It's Gail, isn't it? This is Ellen Sterling."

"Who did you want to speak to?"

"Would you believe Kerys?"

"She isn't here now. Alice Carroll is if you want a word with her."

"I think I should."

Ben was hearing both sides of the conversation as far as she could tell. He'd leaned his face closer to hers and was gazing at the forest. She had never seen trees so still. She felt as if the stillness had invaded the telephone receiver, which was emitting none of the usual restless electrical sounds. When a new voice spoke, it seemed such a violation of the silence that she jumped. "Who is this?" the woman's voice said.

Her emphasis on the first word was light but unmistakable. "Ben and Ellen Sterling," Ellen said.

"Of course, the husband-and-wife team," Alice Carroll said briskly. "What can I do for you?"

"We were wondering what happened to Kerys."

"We decided I should take over now so that Ember can move forward."

Ellen wondered if "we" included Kerys. "When are you next in town?" Alice Carroll wanted to know. "We should meet and talk about directions you might take."

"From whom?"

"Not that kind of direction," Alice Carroll said with a token laugh. "Avenues for exploration. Ideas in keeping with Ember's new image."

"Our books aren't, you mean."

"I liked your snowflake book. I think that could point you the way you might want to go."

"Which is?"

"Developing the ecological theme which you were hinting at there. I felt you could have foregrounded that more, made your concern about it plainer. No need to be afraid of alienating your readers, if that was your problem. Today's children want relevance."

"You think so?"

"I wouldn't be here if I didn't. Have you talked to your readers lately?"

"Some of them."

"Let's hope we can make contact with many more. You've the talent. All it should take is an awareness of their needs," Alice Carroll said more briskly than ever. "We'll be putting out the book you delivered to Kerys Thorn, of course, assuming that you don't have second thoughts, but I really think we should get together for a drink and a chat before you start work on your next. How's your diary looking?"

"Kerys said we'd be wanted in London to help promote *The Boy Who Caught the Snowflakes*."

"That's up to Publicity. I'll have you put through to them and then you can let me know your plans."

The line went dead, which presumably meant she was having the call transferred. Ellen sat up, massaging her arms, which had stiffened with tension, but Ben stayed as he was. "Can you hear?" she said.

"What?" He seemed startled by her question until he glanced at her. "Yes, don't worry. You're doing fine."

She wondered fleetingly if he'd thought she was asking about something other than the conversation, but what else could he have heard? "Publicity," a voice said. "Cynth speaking."

"Could I have a word with Mark Matthews?"

"What's it concerning, please?"

"*The Boy Who Caught the Snowflakes.* This is Ellen Sterling."

"Who do you review for?"

"Not for anyone. I'm the artist."

"You'll want the art department, then. Hold on."

As Ellen drew breath to protest, Ben jerked his head towards the mouthpiece, so roughly that his cheekbone bruised her cheek. "This is Ben and Ellen Sterling. We wrote and illustrated the book. We want you to connect us with Mark Matthews while you've still got a job. Regard this call as a valuable lesson. One day you may be grateful."

"Don't take it all out on the poor girl," Ellen murmured as he withdrew from the mouthpiece. He blinked at her as if he didn't understand why she was rubbing her cheek, then gave it an apologetic kiss. She was turning her mouth to his when another voice separated them. "Mrs. Sterling?"

"I'm here."

"Mark Matthews. Sorry if Cynth got it wrong. She's new here, like me. How can I help you?"

"We were wondering about publicity for our new book."

"Let me just find the publication date." She heard pages turning, and then he said cheerfully "End of November. One of our Christmas books. I'm sure it will sell itself."

Though he wasn't infuriating her as Alice Carroll had, Ellen still felt vulnerable, unsure how important she and Ben and their books were. "Can't we give it a push?" she said.

"What do you feel singles it out from the rest of the season's books?"

"The advertising, I hope."

"Spoken like a true writer. We're holding over most of our advertising budget to relaunch Ember next year. I'm sure we'll have point-of-sale advertising for your next book."

"Aren't we supposed to be helping to promote this one?"

"Will you be free around the publication date?"

"One or both of us."

"I'll make sure our reps and the press know." He cleared his throat. "Sorry if I seem at all vague. I'll be in touch nearer publication, scout's honor."

His pleasantness seemed to have left her no honest response. She handed Ben the receiver in case he had anything to add, but he let it drop onto the cradle. "It sounds to me as if they're going to leave us on our own out there," she said.

"They must know how good we are."

"Are we really, though?"

"Believe it," Ben said, his eyes glittering fiercely. "If they don't know yet, they will when they hear my story. I'd like to see Alice Carroll turn this one into her kind of ideological sermon. The unimaginative always want to reduce imagination to a level they can cope with."

"Are you going to tell me the story?"

He turned back to the window. True night had fallen; it had seemed to spread out from the forest and across the landscape. "I need to spend more time on it," he said. "I don't want to write it until I've got it clear."

"Don't tell me if you aren't ready to."

"No, I want you to hear. Telling it to you and the children may help me see what I'm conjuring up." He gazed ahead of him as if the dark might show it to him, and said "Suppose that in the coldest places on earth the spirits of the ice age are still there in the snow and ice, waiting to rise again."

"Not much chance of that, the way the climate's going."

"It isn't the climate that keeps them dormant, it's the sun."

"I expect it would."

"The midnight sun, I mean. It shines so many nights each year that they can never build up enough power to leave the ice."

"So how do they, if they do?"

"They do, I promise you. I'm not quite sure how, but I know I've something in here," he said, tapping his forehead. "If I can just bring it out into the open . . ."

"I know you will. It sounds a wonderful idea. Do you think it might be best to save it until we've done our second book for Alice Carroll? Then we could make sure it goes somewhere it'll be appreciated. Or you could write it and then do something else for her. Your walk in the woods was productive, anyway," she added to cheer him up.

"It's started something. I only wish it would be a bit quicker taking shape."

"Had you just come out of the woods when I met you? How far did you walk?"

"I can't remember." He frowned as if she had distracted him unnecessarily. "I really don't know. I must have been too deep in my story. What does it matter? I came back."

"That's all that matters," she assured him. She gave him a long hug and stood up. "I'd better feed the starving before they realize they are."

She wasn't sure if he heard her. When she reached the door he had shifted onto the chair and was crouched over the desk, his face close to the window. "Turn the light off," he muttered, and she did so, hoping that would help him bring his tale alive. She'd sensed how much it meant to him, and she thought his passion for the idea meant it could be their best book.

When dinner was ready, she sent Margaret to fetch him. The girl ran downstairs almost at once, looking unhappy and refusing to say why. Soon Ben appeared, narrowing his eyes at the light, opening them determinedly wide and smiling. "Sorry if I made you jump, Peg. I didn't realize you were there until you touched me. I must have been far away."

During the meal he retold the story which had been Margaret's favorite when she was little, about the boy lost in the mountains who had to venture to the very edge of what appeared to be a sheer drop in order to be rescued by a girl who turned into a cloud once he was safe, and then he told an ideologically corrected version in which the girl proved to be a member of the local mountain rescue team and lectured the boy on do's and don'ts for climbers. The children laughed so much that Johnny choked and had to be thumped on the back, and Ellen stuck out her tongue at the new version. "Looks as if there are still children whose minds haven't been sewn up by Alice Carroll and her kind," Ben said.

He gave in to pleas for a repeat of the original version once Johnny was in bed. Margaret sat on the end of the mattress where Johnny's feet didn't reach. As soon as the story was over she got into her own bed. Ellen went to bed early too, taking refuge from the chill which seemed to seep into the house whenever the central heating pump clicked off. Ben was in the workroom, and hadn't emerged when she fell asleep.

In the night a shiver wakened her. She clasped Ben's waist with one arm and pressed herself against his back to warm him up. There was movement at the window, a soft irregular patting on the glass. A white shape which looked tall as the gap between the curtains was dancing in the darkness, fluttering against the window like a bird or a moth. The children would be pleased in the morning, she thought drowsily. For a few seconds the sounds on the panes seemed to grow absolutely regular, in a rhythm too complicated to follow. She was trying to define it when it lulled her to sleep.

TWENTY-THREE

Ellen's sleep was so profound and dreamless it felt like an absence of self. When the children's cries roused her, she struggled back to consciousness, feeling as if the stillness had accumulated on her, a weight whose impalpability made it all the more difficult to throw off. It filled the room, more than the room. She forced her eyelids wide and shoved herself clumsily into a sitting position, dislodging her pillow, which struck the carpet with a soft thud. How much had she overslept for the room to be as bright as this? She frowned at the clock, which was insisting that the alarm wasn't due for another ten minutes, as the children came racing upstairs. They both knocked on the bedroom door, inched it open, piled into the room. "It's snowed," Johnny shouted.

"It always will," Ben said.

Ellen hadn't realized he was awake; she wasn't sure even now that he was. He lay on his back with his eyes shut, his face as expressionless as his murmur had been. She put her finger to her lips and slipped quietly from under the duvet. Tiptoeing to the curtains, she looked through the gap.

The world had turned white. Beneath a blue sky which seemed

almost as bright as the sun, snow that reduced the moors and fields to their merest outlines sloped to the horizon, to the newly risen mountains which were clouds. Sheets of snow were folded over all the roofs of Stargrave. A few cars encrusted with white were proceeding slowly along the main road towards the bridge. A bird of prey hovered above the moors, its wings shining as if they or the sky around them were being transformed into crystal. It swooped to a small animal which dashed across the snow, seized it in its claws and wheeled away across the dazzling moors as the children wriggled under Ellen's arms to see the view. "Can we get dressed and go out?" Margaret whispered.

Ellen steered them out of the room. Though Ben's eyes were closed, she sensed he was awake; she thought he might be trying to shape his tale. "All right, but don't get too cold and wet. I'll call you when there's something hot to put inside you."

While she was making breakfast, having closed the kitchen blinds to shut out the glare of the swollen forest, she heard the slam of the workroom door. When she'd fed the children and brushed the melting snow out of their hair and ensured that they didn't spend too little time in the bathroom, she sent Johnny to tell his father that breakfast was in the oven. Johnny knocked on the workroom door and gabbled the message and raced downstairs, out of the house.

Once they were off the main road, the middle of which was already a mass of slush, Ellen let Margaret and Johnny run ahead, collecting snow from garden walls and shying it at each other. The streets were full of children doing so, as though a custard pie fight had taken over the town. She left the two of them, pink-faced in anoraks, at the school gates and tramped carefully downhill. Despite all the sounds— the creak of compressed snow underfoot, the scrape of spades on paths, the revving of car engines, shouts of greeting and speculations about the weather—the town seemed laden with silence which massed around her as she trudged beyond the newsagent's and along the edge of the rough track to the forest. Over the muffled squeak of her footsteps, she heard the phone ringing at the top of the house.

It continued to ring while she slithered towards the front door. Why hadn't Ben answered it? As she unlocked the door, the ringing ceased.

She stamped her boots clean of snow and stepped into the house, and heard the workroom door open. "Ellen? Call for you," Ben shouted down. "Sally Quick."

He must have been elsewhere in the house when the phone began to ring, though he was blinking as if he'd just come back to himself. "Don't forget your breakfast," she said, and he wandered downstairs as she picked up the receiver. "Hi, Sally."

"Fancy a trip to the moors?"

"Do you mean what I think you mean?"

"I've just had a call from Richmond. Someone who's supposed to have come over here yesterday for a walk and a clamber has been reported missing by his family. He didn't bother to let us know what he was doing," Sally added with a sigh. "Four of us should be enough to be going on with if we start from High Ridge and work our way down either side in twos."

"I'll meet you as soon as I've got my togs on, shall I?"

"Lucy's coming in on her day off. She'll be here in five minutes, and then I'll pick you up."

Ellen had pulled on her waterproofs and was lacing up her boots when she heard the Landrover approaching up the track. She zipped up the pocket in which she'd put her compass, in case the weather grew opaque, and went to find Ben. He'd opened the blinds and was dawdling over his breakfast, staring out of the kitchen window at the woods, whose burden of snow made the tree trunks look as black as the depths of the forest. "Someone's missing on the moors," she told him. "If I'm not back in time you'll be here to collect the children, won't you?"

"I'll be here."

She kissed him on the forehead. "You'd better be, for me."

Sally was turning the Landrover. Ellen ran through the churned slush and hoisted herself into the passenger seat as Sally set the wipers squealing back and forth on the windscreen before she drove down the track. She was a muscular redhead with a wide face which always looked humorous because of her lopsided mouth. "Did I interrupt anything?" she said.

"Don't worry."

"You wouldn't tell me if I had, would you? My niece says you're one of the stars of the college. Just you make sure you appreciate yourself."

She swung the vehicle onto the road in a flurry of slush and drove alongside the railway line, all traces of which had been erased by snow. An older Landrover was waiting outside the tourist information center. Les Barns, who sold climbing equipment in the center, was behind the wheel, and Frank from the butcher's was next to him. The walkie-talkie on Sally's lap cleared its throat as she drove up. "Men and their toys," she murmured to Ellen as Les said "Testing, testing."

"Head for the heights," Sally told him.

As she drove onto the moor the houses seemed to sink into the snow. She had reached the lowest crags when the green Stargrave bus appeared in the distance. The walkie-talkie spluttered. "Bus coming," Les announced.

"Thank you, Les. We had noticed."

When the meandering road eventually brought the bus and her Landrover face to face, Sally flashed her headlights. The driver slid his window open and leaned out of the cab, a frown supplementing the wrinkles on his weathered forehead. "There's a car abandoned just over the ridge."

"Did you happen to notice the number, Tom?"

"I did." He dug in his breast pocket and produced a tattered notepad no bigger than the palm of his hand. Licking his thumb, he leafed through the pad as though he were dealing cards. "There you are, you little bugger," he muttered at last, and read Sally the registration number. "Any help to you?"

"I'm afraid so. Thanks, Tom."

The phone harrumphed, but Sally ignored it while she made for the ridge and parked where the road was widest. Moors which looked to Ellen more than ever like a picture waiting for its details to be added surrounded the vehicle, sloping back to the crags above Stargrave and ahead more gently towards Richmond. A few hundred yards ahead a white mound stood beside the road, only its shape and the number plate which the bus driver must have scraped clear showing that it was a car. The other Landrover pulled up behind Sally's, and the walkie-talkie said "Is that our man's car?"

Sally stepped onto the road and waited for the men to do so. "It's his all right. We'd better look inside."

"You'd think Tom would have," Frank complained.

"He mustn't have wanted to deny you the pleasure," Sally said, so innocently that Ellen had to suppress a nervous giggle as she followed her along a rut the bus had crushed in the snow. Usually the murmur of the motorway in the distance beyond the horizon would be faintly audible, but now the only sounds were the breathing and the flattened footfalls of the search party. Frank marched up to the car and thumped on the roof to break the crust of snow, then he dragged off one of his gloves and cleared the windscreen, his nails squealing on the glass, his face as morose as it was every weekday at the butcher's. He leaned on the windscreen and squinted through it. "Nothing in here but a mucky old map."

Sally shaded her eyes and surveyed the moor, then used her binoculars. "This isn't going to be easy."

"Do we know what he was wearing?" Ellen said.

"Orange all over."

That made Ellen feel there was something she ought to have noticed on the way to the ridge. "Can I use your binoculars?"

"Have them. Maybe an artist's eye will help."

At first Ellen could see only snow, brought dazzlingly closer. She moved from rut to snowy rut to change her view, and then she halted, one foot skidding. "There."

The lenses planed the crags into shapes like slices of icebergs. Almost at the top of the crag closest to the unseen forest, a patch of snow was tinged faintly but unmistakably orange. She passed the binoculars to Sally, who admitted "It could be. We'll drive down while the men start searching here."

She turned the Landrover, crunching the ribs of snow between the ruts. It seemed to Ellen that the cold intensified as the vehicle headed for Stargrave, but perhaps that was partly her reaction to the patch of orange, whose shape was beginning to suggest the outlines of a body huddled against the rock. Sally parked by the stile above the town and raised the binoculars towards the crag, then she used the walkie-talkie. "I think we've found him where Ellen was looking."

Ellen followed her over the slippery stile in the gritstone wall. The women were trudging up the obscured path when Les Barns' Landrover screeched to a halt alongside the wall. He and Frank vaulted with inventive clumsiness over the stile and ran splashily along the path. "You girls can wait here if you like," Les shouted.

"Don't be daft," Sally said.

Ellen wouldn't have minded dawdling. The air was undoubtedly colder than it had been on the ridge. Perhaps that had something to do with the shadows of the crags, shadows whose blackness on the snow appeared to shine, but she felt threatened by an uncontrollable fit of shivering. She sent herself ahead of the rest of the party, through the shadows to the foot of the crag.

It looked like a massive ancient monument preserved in ice, and the orange blotch made her think uneasily of human sacrifice. She moved into the sunlight, moved again as the shadow of the crag inched towards her while Les and Frank fetched climbing gear from their Landrover. How long had the man been up there, near the top of the winding path which weather and climbers had worn in the limestone? She had to assume that he'd been trapped there by yesterday's premature darkness and had lost his nerve. Surely nothing could have made him scramble up the path after dark.

Les strode up to the crag, brandishing a spade, as Frank toiled up from the stile with the equipment. "Let's see about clearing a way up," Les said.

As soon as he dug the spade into the snow on the limestone path, Ellen began shivering. Each scrape of metal on rock seemed to vibrate her gritted teeth. She was trying to brace herself when Sally cried out and pulled her away. The spade had undermined all the snow which was clinging to that side of the crag.

A jagged diagonal fissure which reminded Ellen of an eggshell cracking streaked up from the stretch of path Les had scraped clear. In a couple of seconds the fissure stretched to the top of the crag, and the snow under the line began to slip. The next moment the snow above it lost its hold on the rock. To Ellen it looked so much like a collapsing wall of marble that its sounds, a soft rush followed by a wide lingering thud, seemed unnaturally muffled. A veil of white spray filled the air between the searchers and the crag. The veil sank to the mound of fallen snow which had engulfed the first yards of the path up the limestone, and the searchers stayed where they were; they all seemed to be waiting for someone else to venture forwards or even to speak. Ellen felt choked by her heartbeat, able to take only short harsh thin breaths. At last Sally spoke in a high panicky voice, as if any words were preferable to the silence. "Oh, bless him," she wailed.

The man high on the side of the crag appeared to have died while trying to shelter. He was huddled into a niche at a bend in the path, pressing his spine against the rock. His arms were outstretched as if to fend something off—the snow, Ellen told herself. It was his face which made her turn away: his lips were drawn back as if he was grinning in terror, his eyes in his whitened face appeared to be the color of snow. Rigor mortis might have given him that expression, she thought, and perhaps snow had lodged on his closed eyes. She risked one more glance. Rigor mortis must have affected his posture on the crag. He looked as if the cold which had killed him had rearranged his body, posed it against the limestone in an almost perfectly symmetrical shape.

TWENTY-FOUR

For over a week the death was the talk of Stargrave. Children dared one another to sneak up the moorland path to the crag, until Mrs. Venable had to warn the school not to do so. Most of the townsfolk seemed to agree with Stan Elgin that the man's death confirmed how unprepared too many city people were when they visited the moors, though anyone who said so to Ellen made it clear that didn't include her. Indeed, as she passed the church hall one morning on her way back from walking Johnny and Margaret to school, Hattie Soulsby called her in to tell her what the town thought of her. "We heard you were a shining example to Sally and her merry men."

"It's news to me."

"Why, Sally says you stood your ground while she was near wetting herself and the rest of the team nearly brought the deader sliding straight down on your heads."

Ellen hadn't considered herself to have behaved particularly admirably. She'd walked arm in arm with Sally to the Landrover, and they'd fetched two of Elgin's men to help Frank and Les bring the corpse down the rock. Ellen had been grateful to be spared a closer view of it, but now she wished she'd had the courage to examine the face, the better to deny the rumor which the children had brought home from school that not only the man's hair but also his eyes had been white with terror. It had just been snow, she'd told them firmly, but she couldn't help being disturbed by the strangeness of the rumor.

At least now she had the inquest to back her up. Sally had called her last night with the news that the verdict was death by exposure—"as if it could have been anything else." As Ellen watched the playgroup's toddlers stamping their tiny colorful boots and being released from their fat overalls, she found the sight more reassuring than the verdict had been. "Thanks for helping," she told Hattie and Kate, feeling relieved and somewhat guilty because of it. It seemed almost unreasonable of life to return to normal so soon after the death on the crag.

Of course life hadn't done so as far as the children were concerned. The streets leading down to the main road were ski slopes, the schoolyard had become a skating rink. Occasionally the snow began to thaw, but overnight it always froze anew, preserving that day's chaos of footprints and spiking gutters and garden walls with icicles for Johnny and his friends to use for sword fights. Margaret and Johnny had staked their claim on the stretch of snow between the house and the common, and together with their friends they'd crowded the area with families of snow figures. Every morning Ellen would glance out of the kitchen window to see how the shifts of temperature had reshaped the dozens of figures beyond the garden wall.

As October turned into November, more snow fell. It drifted through the lamplight on Halloween and feathered the children's masks as the family picked their way through the streets to spend the evening with the Wests. Stefan addressed a hanging apple with baboon sounds to make Johnny giggle and then accidentally hit himself on the nose with it, to ironic cries of sympathy from his sister and Margaret. Ramona spent minutes trying not to splash her party dress while she ducked for apples in a bowl, then plunged her face into the water with a drowned impatient squeak. Meanwhile the adults talked and drank, though Ben was quieter than usual. On the way home he gazed silently at the light snowfall, a pale dance which grew more massive in the distance where it merged with the restless dark. He was often taciturn while he was working on a book, but rarely as withdrawn as this. Perhaps, Ellen thought, his soul wasn't really in the book he was writing for Alice Carroll, though he was spending a great deal of time at the desk.

On Guy Fawkes Night he refused to be moved from it. "Won't you come down for the fireworks?" Ellen tried to coax him. "The children would like you to."

He crouched over the page of his writing, more than half of which was crossed out. "Tell them I can see from here. Better, though you needn't say that."

Ellen went downstairs cursing Alice Carroll. As Terry West let off the fireworks, she saw Ben at the window. Every time a firework blazed, his eyes lit up; he reminded her of a little boy who'd been banished to his room. The explosions of the rockets brought the glazed forest and the snow figures crowding towards the house, and turned the workroom window into bursts of radiance which seemed to emanate from Ben's face. As the last rocket fell back to earth she felt the kiss of snow on her cheeks. Because Ben's was the only lit window in the house, the snow appeared to be homing in on him, whitening the pane and his face.

He hadn't left his desk when Kate and Terry took their children home. Ellen got Margaret and Johnny to bed, and called into the workroom that she was for bed herself. "Not long now," Ben responded distantly, but he hadn't joined her by the time she fell asleep.

When she awoke, feeling isolated by stillness, the sun was up. Ben must surely have come to bed at some point, but now he was in the workroom. It was time she persuaded him not to work so hard, she thought as she saw the children to school. She picked her way home over frozen slush furred with last night's snow, tiptoed upstairs, eased the workroom door open and looked in.

Ben was at the desk, his head raised towards the dazzling forest, resting the palms of his hands on either side of the handwritten book. For a moment she thought she glimpsed movement in the forest. Perhaps snow had fallen from one or more of the trees, though the stirring had seemed much larger; perhaps his breath had made the view waver and immediately settle back into stillness. She was halfway across the room when a floorboard creaked beneath her feet. He turned to her, a dazed expression on his face. "Now I'm ready," he said.

As she went to stand beside him she saw that he'd written THE END at the foot of a paragraph and had followed the words with an exclamation mark in which an elaborate star took the place of a full stop. "I'm glad," she said and hugged him, rubbing his shoulders and arms to warm him up. She hadn't rid him of the chill, which was enough to make her shiver, when the phone rang.

TWENTY-FIVE

"And they all lived happily ever after," Ben wrote, and sat staring at the
words, his pen hovering above them like a bird of prey. They seemed
to mean nothing except that the story was over, and he could see that
there were too many of them. The pen swooped to cross out "all" and
"ever after," and was hesitating above "happily" when he shrugged and
moved his hand away from the page, the blunt end of the pen rapping
the desk. They were only words, only a way of releasing him from the
task of manufacturing a tale for Alice Carroll. He wondered why he
didn't feel released from the preoccupation which seemed to have
walled up his senses ever since he'd learned of her attitude to his work.

He made another change and smiled, or thought he did. "And they
lived happily for a while." That ought to be realistic enough for her,
and he wouldn't pretend that it didn't ring true to him. He wrote THE
END and let out a long breath. Now there was nothing to keep him
from the story with which he'd emerged from the forest, the story of
the presence which had been imprisoned by the midnight sun.

He was inking an ironically large exclamation mark after the capitals
when the thought of the forest drew his attention to the window. The
shapes which the snow had made of the trees seemed like a
promise—of what? Perhaps a resolution of the story which his solitary

walk in the forest had suggested to him and which was all he could remember of the walk. It wasn't the first time he had become so engrossed in his imagination that he'd lost all awareness of his surroundings, and he wondered why in this case it should make him nervous. What was called for, he decided—both to revive his ideas about the midnight sun and to show him where he'd got to in the forest—was another walk. He capped the pen and laid his hands on the desk to raise himself. Now I'm ready, he thought, and the thought was like a soundless voice which rendered time meaningless. He didn't know how long he had been poised at the desk when he heard someone enter the room.

He turned and saw Ellen. Though he couldn't imagine who else he might have expected to see, the sight of her was somehow disappointing. Guilt made him speak the only words he could find in his head, though he wasn't sure what they referred to: "Now I'm ready."

"I'm glad," Ellen said, and set about rubbing his shoulders and arms, presumably to rid him of the tension she assumed had been involved in finishing the book. When the phone rang he grabbed it, feeling like a wrestler released from a hold by the bell. "Who's this?"

"Mark Matthews at Ember. Am I taking you away from anything? Shall I call you back?"

From what? Ben thought. He gazed at the forest as if it might tell him what Ellen and the publicist had interrupted, and couldn't think why he was doing so. "It doesn't matter," he said.

"Would you like to hear what we've set up?"

Ben thought of the setting up of an image, an idol. "Go on," he mumbled.

"We've appearances for you in Leeds and Norwich."

Ben was tempted to hand Ellen the phone while he tried to grasp his unmanageable thoughts. "Appearances?"

"Yes, at bookshops. Signing your books. Are you sure it's convenient to talk just now?"

Momentarily Ben thought this referred to Ellen's presence, then he realized that the hint of reproach in the publicist's voice was directed at him. "I said so. When would they be, these appearances?"

"Leeds is a week today and Norwich the Friday after."

Ellen was smiling, and with an effort Ben appreciated why. "We'll both be available to sign the books in Leeds," he said.

"I'll let the bookshop know. Will lunchtimes suit you?"

"Whenever."

Mark Matthews promised to put the details in a letter, and Ben was lowering the receiver towards the cradle when Ellen stopped him. "Anything in London?"

"Anything in London, my wife wants to know."

"A syndicated interview the day before Norwich. You can do it over lunch on us."

"Couldn't the interviewer come up here and see us."

"Howard Bellamy never goes out of town except for the absolute top names, but his interviews do. I read a piece of his in the in-flight magazine on the way back from Frankfurt this year."

Ellen bent her head closer to the receiver, and Ben handed it to her at once. "The only problem is that we can't both be there," she said. "Even if our children were invited, they'll be at school."

"Having kids is a career decision, Mrs. Sterling," the publicist said, adding swiftly "Let's hope one day Howard Bellamy will come to you. Meanwhile, I'm sure I can fix you up with some of your local press, assuming you want them."

"They'll be welcome." Ellen kissed Ben on the forehead, apparently so that he wouldn't resent her next words. "I hope you didn't think my husband was rude or not interested. He'd just finished a new book when you rang."

"That's what we like to hear. Tell him we're all delighted. He deserves a break by the sound of it. I hope this little tour of ours will be some fun for him."

"It better had be," Ellen said, so vehemently that Ben might have felt uncomfortable if his vision hadn't been full of the bright stillness ahead of him. Even if they didn't know what they were talking about, he thought, perhaps they had hit on the truth. Perhaps some time away on his own would allow whatever was building up within him, so intensely that its presence seemed to underlie the entire transformed landscape, to make itself clear to him.

TWENTY-SIX

During the next week the thaw made progress. On some days the uphill streets turned into streams of melted slush in which children stamped while the gutter of Market Street became a miniature torrent. Those days were punctuated by the thud of snow slipping from roofs and the shrieks of children who'd stood underneath. Once the sun sank beyond the forest, however, the afternoons grew chill, and in the mornings the garden walls would be lichened with frost, the bedraggled plants seeded with it. Snow lingered on the moors and crags, but close to the road the paths were marshy. The only place from which the snow seemed hardly to have shifted was the forest, a situation which suggested that the paths in there would be relatively firm underfoot. Edna Dainty had had enough of being dragged through mud and slush, and so she decided to take the dog into the forest for its Thursday walk.

Thursday was early closing day. At one o'clock the post office was so crowded she had to struggle between the customers, all eight of them, in order to lock the door against latecomers. "The postal authorities should find you somewhere ampler," old Mr. Brice said, placing one hand on his heart as he let her by and unfolding the other as if he were presenting her with the door.

"They wouldn't have the nerve to cram us in here if this was Leeds or Richmond," Mrs. Tozer said, and went back to counting her pension out loud.

Mr. Waters, who always glowered at Edna's dog, looked up from peering suspiciously at the soles of his shoes. "It was just the same when I was down the mines. You could spend your whole life shouting and the bosses wouldn't hear."

"Out of sight, never mind," Edna said, sidling back to the glassed-in counter. Alfie was off with a cold, and Cath tended to grow flustered when she was faced with a queue. Edna doled out pensions and commiserated with the recipients, not all of whom seemed to welcome her homilies, and persuaded Mr. Waters to wrap a parcel full of presents for his grandchildren more securely. Mr. Brice insisted on letting all the women in the queue precede him, bowing low to them and fingering his military moustache, though when he reached the counter he wanted only to stamp a postcard to his niece in Edinburgh. Edna managed to usher him out of the shop as he suggested at length that he should draft a petition protesting about the inadequacy of the premises for all her customers to sign. She closed the door and leaned against it and then mimed running so as to hasten Cath. "Let's be off with you while the going's good."

Once Cath had gone, trailing perfume which always smelled strongest when she was flustered, Edna let the blinds down and tidied the shop, smoothing out information pamphlets crumpled by toddlers and replacing them in the rack above the chained ballpoint, collecting bits of perforated margin, some of which stuck to her fingers as she flicked them at the wastebin. She checked Cath's ledger entries, counted the money in the drawer, boxed the money and locked the cashbox in the safe. As she let herself out of the shop, the minute hand of the clock behind the counter had almost finished its halting climb towards two o'clock.

Her cottage was three minutes' walk away up Church Road opposite the post office. Before she came in sight of the house, Goliath started barking, having recognized her footsteps now that the pavement was clear of snow. He was at the front window, his paws on the sill and his nose pressed against the glass, and next door Miss Bowser was imitating his stance. "He's just having his day," Edna called, and when Miss Bowser turned haughtily away: "Speech is free in this country, even for dogs."

Before she unlocked the front door she began shouting "Down" to prevent the Doberman from knocking her over as he came bounding to greet her. When she slapped his glossy black flank, he gave a yelp of pleasure and dashed into the front room to dig the remains of his latest rubber bone out from beneath the sofa. It and the armchairs had obviously taken turns to bear his weight; one of the chairs looked positively drunken. "Bad boy, what happens to bad boys?" she cried, but took pity on him as soon as he started fawning. "If folk don't like sitting where you've sat, they can take their bottoms somewhere else."

The dog ran into the kitchen and dropped the bone into his basket so as to fetch his leash, turning so fast that he sprawled on the linoleum as if it had suddenly iced up. "Wait there. Sit. Stay," she said, but she was in her bedroom when he raced upstairs and lolled his tongue at her in the dressing-table mirror. She poked a few whitening strands of her red hair under her balaclava and made a wry face at herself. "That'll do for the world."

Goliath's first jerk on the leash dragged her off the doorstep and onto the pavement, slamming the door as she went. The battle for supremacy continued all the way to the edge of Stargrave, Edna yanking at the leash whenever he seemed disposed to linger. Once they were past the newsagent's she let the dog squat by the roadside, then ignored him so successfully that she almost lost her balance when he lurched towards the track which led to the woods.

As she stumbled onto the muddy track she thought she saw movement at the Sterling house, perhaps among the crowd of snow figures beyond the house and its long diagonal shadow which lay across the track. No, the Sterlings were being celebrities in Leeds and had taken their children with them. She didn't begrudge them their popularity, even if they'd gained it just by writing and drawing a few books. She was rather glad that Ben Sterling was away, because whenever she encountered him she felt he was lying in wait for her to commit some verbal blunder. "We've had enough of folk who want to tell us how to speak, haven't we, Golly?" she said.

Her husband Charlie had wanted to. When he'd taken early retirement after the railway through Stargrave had been closed down, he hadn't seemed to want much else. He would sit on the sofa with one leg up, his slipper dangling from his toes, and read yesterday's paper, which he begged from Miss Bowser even though he knew that embarrassed Edna. Before long the only domestic activity capable of enlivening him had been correcting Edna's speech. "It's *wood* you can't see for trees, not *woods*," she remembered him saying. "Not out of the *wood* yet, not *woods*." He'd been so busy listening for phrases he could pounce on that he had ceased to hear the sense of anything she'd said to him. Soon she'd had enough of being nervous of opening her mouth, and so she'd invented a response: she'd misquoted every phrase she could get wrong. Almost a year of turning purple and spluttering and thumping the furniture must have taken its toll, because one summer day he'd announced that he was moving to a railway workers' retirement home. Apart from the divorce papers, which she'd signed so zealously that the pen nib broke, and a yearly Christmas card which she tore up without opening the envelope, she'd heard no more of him. If she found it difficult to break the habit of saying her phrases wrong, that wasn't her tough luck. What the world needed was more variety, not less.

As she walked through the shadow of the Sterling house, she shivered. The shadows of the crowd of snow figures lay across her path like a spillage of water frozen black. The sunlight made those heads which had any features left appear to watch her sidelong as she passed, made blank white heads seem to turn soundlessly towards her. She ignored them and stalked up the track to the edge of the woods.

Spiny branches which reminded her of fishbones were beginning to gleam through the snow on the spruce trees. Here and there rays of sunlight solidified by mist touched up the colors of fallen needles. The forest was weighed down by frozen snow and stalactites of ice, a weight which seemed to trap the silence. Goliath halted abruptly, dragging his mistress to a standstill at the entrance to the paths. "Don't do that, you'll have me falling," Edna complained. "What can you hear?"

The dog was poised to run, ears cocked, left front paw raised. She wrapped the leash twice around her hand while she strained to hear, but even when she pulled the balaclava away from one ear the silence of the woods seemed absolute. "It was just an old bird," she said loudly. "Don't you dare run."

Goliath looked cowed as soon as she opened her mouth, and more so once she raised her voice. She had to tug at the leash before he would trot beside her onto the path. "We'll go the green way," she said.

That was the shorter of the walks, and apparently the more popular: when the paths diverged, most of the few footprints stayed on it. The path was muddier than she'd expected, but at least the footprints made the forest seem more inhabited, not that loneliness need bother her when she had Goliath with her. "Let's put our feet forward," she told the dog as she marched along the edge of the path.

He wasn't pulling ahead today. Soon she began to grow impatient with having to urge him onwards. The path would bring them out of the forest in less than an hour, well before dusk, but they hadn't reached the halfway point when she caught herself wishing there were a shortcut. Goliath had started to unnerve her by hesitating for no reason she could see and pricking up his ears, though to Edna the silence seemed more intense than ever, so much so that she had to restrain herself from tugging the balaclava away from her ears.

The further she progressed into the forest, the fewer the shafts of sunlight became. The mottled tree trunks gleamed darkly under their burden of snow, the weight and stillness of which felt like a snowstorm gathering overhead. If any part of it should give way and break the stillness, she was afraid she would make a fool of herself, though by now it felt too cold for any of the snow to shift. She considered turning back, but what on earth for? She ought to be ashamed of herself. "We're nearly on our way out," she said.

She felt compelled to raise her voice to relieve the oppressive stillness; but apart from causing Goliath to flinch, she succeeded only in emphasizing it. Never mind, the path at the limit of her vision was beginning to curve away from the depths of the forest. She halted so as to wrap the leash more securely around her hand, because her voice seemed to have made Goliath more nervous. "I wasn't shouting at you,

Golly. I don't know what I was shouting at," she said—and then she saw it hadn't been her voice which had disturbed him.

As she finished speaking and loosened her grip on the leash in order to adjust her glove, the dog turned his head and stared past her. His gray lips peeled back from his teeth, and he began to snarl and shiver. The next moment he bolted, snatching the leash out of her hand, and fled into the woods.

"Golly, come back," she cried in a voice so small she could hardly believe she had spoken out loud. As much as anything, it was the utter stillness behind her which made her terrified to look. The dog vanished among the trees, and she turned her head, though her neck was trembling.

At first she could see nothing to fear, which meant that everything around her seemed poised to reveal that it was. She was surrounded by the forest and its countless scaly legs, its green bones showing through the marble flesh. She felt as though the stillness were an elaborate pretence. The muddy path, the only sign of life, looked like an intrusion, a trail leading straight to her. The thought seemed to focus her terror; something else was wrong with the path, and she dared not see what it was. "Golly," she screamed, and heard the dog bark.

"Wait," she cried, and ran towards the sound, skidding on fallen needles. Clouds of her breath, and the flicker of sunlight and shadow, interfered with her vision as she ran. When Goliath barked again she saw him through the trees about a hundred yards ahead. "Stay," she shouted hoarsely, stretching out her gloved hand, so desperate for reassurance that she could feel the leash in her grasp.

He almost did as he was told. She was within a few yards of him when he bolted. This time he halted in sight of her, but only just. "Bad boy, stay," she screamed, and stumbled after him, flapping her hands to fend off the trees which were growing closer and more numerous and cutting off the sunlight with their vault of snow and ice. Surely he would wait for her this time; as he stared back towards her, he looked cowed enough. As she lunged for the leash he fled again and halted, sides heaving, at the limit of her vision ahead.

"It isn't a game," she wailed, and immediately realized that he didn't think it was. He must know where he was going—surely he was leading her out of the forest—but why couldn't he wait for her to catch hold of the leash? Perhaps he was afraid, in which case please let it be only of her. She lurched after him, too winded to shout, terrified to look anywhere but straight ahead.

She lost count of the times he waited until she was almost within reach. Soon she had no voice, and her lungs were laboring. In the midst of the silence which clung to her ears, the voice of her mind was incessantly repeating "Can't see the woods for the trees." It felt like an act of defiance, a last assertion of herself, an attempt to blot out some awareness which was capable of paralyzing her. She was keeping her attention on Goliath, but she thought that the shapes of the trees above her, or the frozen snow which hung from them, had at some point begun to seem unnatural—so regular that she was afraid to look.

Now Goliath bolted before she was within twenty yards of him. She floundered after him, trying to call to him, but her mouth only gaped as though she were drowning. Then she gasped feebly, the nearest she could come to a sigh of relief. He'd halted almost at the upper edge of the forest; above the trees beyond him she could see hints of crags and moorland. Surely she'd imagined the symmetry of the forest; the trees between her and the dog appeared ordinary enough. Once she was out of the forest she would be able to look back.

It seemed that the Doberman was too exhausted to run any further, or else he was waiting for her now that he'd shown her the way out. Except for his panting, each breath etching his ribs, he was standing quite still, his head slightly cocked towards her. "Good dog. Good dog," she managed to croak as she stumbled up to him. She stooped, her back aching like a bad tooth, and coiled the leash around her hand.

She almost lost her grip on it, because she had begun to shiver violently. She could hardly see for her own white breath. "Go on, Golly," she said in a painful dried-up whisper, and then she saw he was shivering too. He was so cold that his black pelt was turning white.

In that moment, as he rolled his eyes and stared beyond her, she realized what she had avoided seeing on the path. All the muddy footprints leading to her had begun to freeze, frost sparkling on them as whatever had caused the dog to bolt had advanced through the forest. Goliath bared his teeth and emitted a snarl which sounded like his shivering made audible, and fled toward the moors, dragging Edna with him.

She tried to hold on and keep up with him—the alternative was too terrible to contemplate. But the world was turning blinding white, or her eyes were, and her face felt as though it were being fitted with a succession of masks of ice. She ran blindly, clinging to the leash, struggling to draw enough breath to tell Goliath to slow down until she could see. Then she fell sprawling, and being dragged over the pine needles was so painful that her hand lost its grip on the leash. She heard the dog scrambling out of the forest, and then the silence came for her. Ice closed around her body, and she felt as if she were already dead and stiff. She had no words to fend off her sense of the presence which stooped to her, a presence so cold and vast and hungry that her blind awareness of it stopped her breath.

TWENTY-SEVEN

Ben seemed determined to be at his best in Leeds. The family hadn't been in the bookshop two minutes before he had charmed the staff, complimenting them on the window display for *The Boy Who Caught the Snowflakes*, one copy of which looked crystalline with silvery glitter. After that the generously chinned proprietress and her two assistants, both of whom were uniformed in overalls like hers which made them resemble fractions of her, couldn't do enough for the Sterlings, inquiring anxiously whether the chairs at the table where they were to sit were comfortable enough, bringing them and Johnny and Margaret drinks, making sure that everyone who set foot in the shop knew there was a book signing, even a diminutive pink-eyed man who was trying to be unobtrusive while straining on tiptoe to reach the erotica. As customers began to approach the table, Ben brightened further. "Is this for you? You look young enough to me," he told a grandmother who wanted the book inscribed to her grandson for Christmas. He talked to customers about the kinds of book their children liked or, if they were children, about the adventures which were snow and the lengthening nights. "They're our mum and dad, you know," Johnny informed anyone who came near him. Three of Ellen's students turned up to buy a copy each of the book, but it was undoubtedly Ben's show, and she felt happy for him.

The last people in the queue were a reporter and photographer from a local newspaper. The reporter wanted only to check that they lived locally enough to be of some parochial significance. "Let's have your brats in the picture to add a bit of interest," the photographer said, and Ben hugged the family so hard that Ellen gasped. When the photographer said "That'll do" Ben continued to hold on for several seconds, as if he were afraid to let go.

Afterwards they walked through the premature Advent of the city streets. Though Johnny was beginning to entertain doubts about Father Christmas, he wanted to visit his avatar. Ben and Ellen took the children into a department store and waited outside the grotto, whose evergreen plastic entrance was emitting scrawny carols, while Johnny queued and Margaret went off to look at clothes by herself, feeling grown up. "What do you think?" Ellen asked Ben. "Have we started off well?"

He was looking bemused by the thin singing which seemed to hover in the air. "Are you pleased?" he said.

"I thought we did rather well for beginners."

"If you're pleased, then I am."

"More to the point, the bookshop and the public were, particularly with you."

"The world's ready for me, you think? Wherever I go there'll be children around me? Ben Sterling, magnet of imagination, Pied Piper of the collective unconscious. Myths restored while you wait, tales retold which you'd forgotten you knew, dreams dreamed on your behalf while you sit closer to your fire . . ."

He was gazing across the cosmetics counter, at his reflection framed in an oval of seasonal glitter, and Ellen felt as if he were scarcely aware of her—as if, perhaps, he were taking refuge in the kind of almost automatic response which he'd produced for the customers at the bookshop. "Just do the best you can on your walkabout next week," she said, "and then it'll practically be Christmas."

"I can't take any responsibility for that."

"Not even for making our first Christmas in Stargrave special? I mean to, for all of us."

"I'm sure this year will be special."

Johnny came out of the grotto just then, wearing his grin which meant he had a tale to tell his parents, and he reminded her so much of his father that her love for both of them seized her deep inside herself. Ben grinned like that sometimes, like a little boy with a secret to share, and she hoped he always would. He was still the person she'd fallen in love with, and she mustn't let herself feel lonely if sometimes that person had to go into hiding inside him. "What was so funny?" she said.

"Father Christmas kept sniffing," Johnny giggled, "and the boy in front of me asked if he was sniffing the glue that kept his beard on."

"That's how you can tell he wasn't real," Ben said. "A real Father Christmas wouldn't need chemicals to give him visions. He'd spend the year dreaming of flying over the snow and ice under the stars, dreams like snowstorms that take all year to gather until the days are shortest and it's time for him to rise."

"That could be a book," Ellen suggested.

"What could?" Margaret said, emerging from among the teenage fashions.

"I've already told it once," her father said.

Disappointment and rejection and a shaky resolve not to show her emotions in public flickered across Margaret's face until Ellen came to the rescue. "If your father keeps telling it he may lose the urge to write it," she explained. "It was just the idea that Father Christmas spends nearly all year dreaming of when he'll wake up."

The idea stayed in her mind as she drove out of Leeds. The snow on the moors had all but melted, renewing the colors of the vegetation, shades of moist green which put her in mind of spring. Having at least two books to complete made her feel secure. If by any chance Ben proved not to be inspired by the idea he'd thrown out, she might have a go at writing it herself.

By the time they reached Stargrave, the first stars were glinting above the bridge. The miles of Sterling Forest were composed of night and ice, and seemed somehow to dwarf the lights of the town. The heat of the house welcomed the family, fending off the chill and effacing their breath. After dinner they played Monopoly, using a battered old set of the game, its banknotes crumpled from years of figuring in shops the children pretended to run, one tiny plastic hotel permanently crippled by being chewed and almost swallowed by two-year-old Johnny. Before the game was over, Margaret and Johnny were trying not to shiver. They were overtired, Ellen thought as she hurried them to bed, though perhaps the house was also chilly with a cold which seemed to settle on it from above. Only Ben was unaffected by the chill, unless that was why he grew randy once the children were out of the way. She pulled the duvet over his shoulders as he slid bulging into her, then she rubbed his body hard, trying to keep the chill at bay. When he subsided she held onto him. That didn't seem to keep the chill outside their bed, but soon she was so drowsy that it didn't bother her. She drifted into sleep which felt soft as snow, only to be wakened by a small voice in the dark.

It was Johnny. He was standing by the bed, huddling against the edge of the mattress. When she reached for his hand she discovered that he was shivering. "What's the matter, Johnny?"

"It wants to come in."

He sounded more asleep than awake, yet close to tears. Ellen let go of his hand in order to slip out of bed and fumble her way into her dressing gown, then steered him out of the room. "You've been dreaming," she murmured. "Let's get you back to bed."

He halted abruptly, and her hipbone struck the banister. For a moment she thought she would fall into the gaping darkness of the stairwell. "I heard it," he insisted.

She switched on the landing light and squatted in front of him to scrutinize his bleary rumpled stubborn face. "What do you think you heard?"

"The dog," he wailed as if she were affecting not to have heard it. "It's cold. It can't get in."

"If there's a dog its owner will hear it. We don't want you catching cold as well." She went down three stairs and led him after her, but he had taken only a few reluctant steps when he stiffened. "It's there," he said with a kind of unhappy triumph.

Ellen had already heard it—a distant howling somewhere above the house. It was worse than mournful; it was so distorted that it sounded like the cry of some new creature which was lost in the dark. "Whoever owns it must have heard it by now, Johnny. Snuggle back into bed."

He wouldn't close his eyes until she promised to stay with him while he tried to go to sleep. She sat on the end of his bed, hugging herself, willing slumber to take him before the howling rose any higher; it was turning into a thin hoarse shriek. When at last he fell reluctantly asleep she tiptoed up to the workroom. Of course she couldn't see the animal. The prospect from the window lingered in her mind as she sought sleep: the sight of the forest gleaming like an immense skeleton while the black sky blinked and the unseen creature howled as if the lonely dark had found a voice.

In the morning there was no sound above the house. Johnny seemed to have slept off his concern for the dog until Ellen drove past a knot of sorrowful townsfolk outside the post office. "It wasn't Golly, was it?" he pleaded.

"If it was, someone must have taken care of him."

Ellen parked near Tovey's and walked back to the market, where she left the children at Stargrave's nearest equivalent to a bookshop—everything exchangeable and mostly second-hand with a dozen or so new shrinkwrapped bestsellers—while she tracked down the news. Gossip blocked the aisles between displays of wide-eyed fish, of shoes like so many pricked-up ears, of Christmas cards and decorations and cheap toys which the season had caused to flourish. Beside the home brew stall Stan Elgin was saying to old Mr. Westminster "She'd no business having such a big bugger, she could never keep him under control."

"He near dragged her under my wheels once, as if the streets weren't already full of sheep on two legs looking for a shortcut to heaven."

"What's happened?" Ellen said.

"Edna Dainty took a fall in your woods and froze to death."

Ellen shook her head sadly. "Where did they find her?" she asked, disliking herself for hoping it wasn't too close to the house.

"Up near the moors," Stan Elgin said reassuringly. "It looks as if her dog dragged her off the path."

"But that's at least a mile. What could have made it run so far?"

Mr. Westminster gave a bubbling cough and spat behind the stall. "Like as not trying to escape a woman's prattling."

"If you ask me," Stan Elgin said, "he was after something. Those dogs were bred to hunt. Deep down we're all still what we were before we were born."

"I wouldn't ask except my little boy will want to know, but what happened to the dog?"

"They stuck a needle in him and carted him off to Richmond," Mr. Westminster said with relish.

"He'll be taken care of," Stan Elgin said.

Ellen wasn't sure if he was saying that for Johnny's sake or hers. When she passed on the message, Johnny cheered up at once, and Margaret was tactful enough not to express her dubiousness except in a momentary frown. As she bought next week's provisions, Ellen couldn't help wondering if anyone held her responsible for Edna Dainty's death. She hadn't known the woman well enough to mourn her except as an eccentric who had been part of the town, but the notion that Ellen might have revived some dislike of the Sterlings by doing her best to make the townsfolk welcome in the forest nearly reduced her to tears.

"Whatever they think," Ben said that night, "they'd better keep their hands off. They've no right to touch a single tree."

"I shouldn't think they would."

"Better be sure," he said, and must have realized that he seemed to be angry with her. "Mrs. Dainty didn't need us to lead her into the woods, she'd have gone where she wanted to go. At least now the place will be a bit quieter."

Perhaps nobody except herself blamed Ellen. "Nobody worth knowing," Kate West and Hattie Soulsby responded almost in chorus when she confided to them that she felt as if someone might do so. They wouldn't let her go until they were convinced she believed them—until she managed to conceal the anxiety which still hovered over her like the shadow of the forest, which every day brought closer to the house.

Ben must have sensed her unease. On Wednesday evening he said suddenly "Would you rather I didn't go?"

Was she secretly nervous because he was going away for two nights when he'd never left her and the children alone before? "Don't even think of it," she said. "You've got to tell the world that the Sterlings are coming for Christmas."

Since he would leave before dawn, he was in bed before her. She found him asleep on his back, his fingers interwoven on the duvet. He looked as if he were meditating, his face almost symmetrical with calm. She climbed in beside him, burrowing her face into the angle between his neck and shoulder, telling herself that she wouldn't be nervous if he weren't going away so soon after Mrs. Dainty's death, which was no reason for nervousness. She slept, and wakened to find herself alone in bed. She felt as if it she might have been roused by a good-bye kiss, though surely Ben's lips couldn't have left her forehead so cold. She padded to the window and saw that the car had gone. Perhaps that was its light beyond the moor, where lingering snow made the horizon glimmer, or was that a low star? The more she squinted at it, the less certain she became that the light was there or ever had been. "Go carefully," she murmured, wishing she had been awake to tell Ben so, and retreated into bed, where the chill kept her awake until dawn.

TWENTY-EIGHT

At first Ben thought he knew what was wrong with him: he was setting off for London before he was fully awake. He'd risen before he had planned to, having wakened from a dream which had seemed too large for his sleep to contain but which he'd forgotten on the instant of waking. He'd crept through the sleeping house for coffee and a shower, only to fail to realize until he was towelling himself that he'd forgotten to turn on the hot tap. At least the cold shower ought to help him wake up, but no wonder Ellen and the children had shivered when he'd planted kisses on their foreheads. He'd found himself wishing that he didn't have to leave them, a wish which was momentarily so intense it felt like fear. It would do them no good if he cancelled his appointments, and perhaps the appointments were the source of his nervousness, which if it was true was ridiculous. He grabbed his overnight bag from the foot of the stairs and let himself out, hoping that the open air would clear his head.

It was just after four o'clock. The darkness seemed to be congealing icily about him. Behind the house the crowd of white still figures stood like a vanguard of the forest, the pale mass like an earthbound cloud which had yet to release its storm. When he climbed into the

Volkswagen and switched on the headlamps, their beams looked as though the weight of the darkness were about to extinguish them. He released the handbrake and let the vehicle coast down the track so as not to waken the family, and started the engine when he came to the road. He drove under the bridge and onto the moor.

Chunks of the night flowered as the headlamp beams slid over them, patches of snow seemed to expand as the light found them. After most of an hour the glare of Leeds put out the stars. He drove through the empty streets, whose lamps made his eyes ache, and down to the motorway, where lorries bigger than he'd ever seen in daylight roared through the dark. From the sky the lights racing up and down the spine of England must look like nervous energy rendered visible, he thought, and then the need to concentrate on the traffic brought him down to earth.

By the time the sun wounded the horizon to his left, he felt as if the car were driving him. Certainly some compulsion was—not his appointments in London and Norwich. Perhaps his next tale was demanding to be told, which would explain why these two days seemed to be in his way. As daylight brought traffic swarming onto the motorway he was able to lose himself in driving, and once he reached the outskirts of London he found plenty to distract him: learner drivers leading slow processions along streets narrowed by parked lorries which dwarfed the shops they were stocking; pedestrians forced into the roadway by scaffolding and demolition; holes in the road planted with workmen in various stages of growth, no more than talkative heads protruding from one trench, men from the waist up sprouting from another. He lost his way at a diversion in Cricklewood because of a burst water main, and it took him the best part of two hours to reach Soho, where he parked beneath the Firebrand building and emitted a yell of relief.

Despite the delay, he was almost an hour early for his first meeting. He walked through Soho, where there seemed to be fewer sex shops than in January but more handwritten notices beside doorways, to look for *The Boy Who Caught the Snowflakes* in the bookshops on Charing Cross Road. He braced himself as he marched into Foyle's, but he wasn't prepared for the sight which greeted him. Every shop which sold children's books had his and Ellen's on display, and two of them had both *The Boy Who Caught the Snowflakes* and their other titles in the window.

He gazed at the second window display as lunchtime crowds hurried by. In Foyle's he'd wanted someone to buy the book while he was watching: he'd felt like a child, eager for his work to be appreciated. Now he wished Ellen and the children were here to see. Their delight would surely have communicated itself to him, but each time he was confronted by another group of Sterling books the spectacle seemed to have less to do with him, as if the books were products of a phase of his life which he'd left behind. He mustn't lose his enthusiasm now, when he needed it for the press interview. The thought sent him striding back to Firebrand Books.

Among the books displayed in a rack opposite the easy chairs in the reception area he found a copy of *The Boy Who Caught the Snowflakes*. While he was waiting for Mark Matthews he speed-read the book, and was on the last page when a voice remarked, "If even the author's reading it it must be good."

This was Mark Matthews, a tall man in his thirties, already balding. His long face appeared to be trying to smile with as many features as possible. "We can hustle now if you like," he said, "if you feel like getting a drink in before Howard Bellamy wants to talk."

"You think that will loosen my tongue, do you?"

"We have ways of making you talk," the publicist said, and relinquishing his fake German accent, "But the way I hear it, you don't need any."

Ben hoped there wouldn't be much of this. When Matthews said "Italian all right for you?" Ben thought momentarily that he was proposing to don another accent. "Whatever pleases Bellamy," Ben said.

It proved to be the restaurant where Kerys Thorn had lunched the Sterlings, and the interviewer was already waiting, perched on a bar stool just inside the window and feeding himself olives with one pudgy hand between sips of the cocktail in the other. He continued to survey the faces of the passersby until Mark Matthews cleared his throat, and then he swung round on the groaning stool and raised his handlebar eyebrows. "Howard Bellamy, Ben Sterling," the publicist said.

Bellamy gave Ben's hand a loose shake and retrieved his cocktail from the bar. "Wife following?"

"Someone had to stay home with the children."

"Thought I'd rather have the pretty half, did you?" Bellamy said to the publicist, and to Ben: "Shame, though. She could have made me a sketch to send out with my pieces. Let's put something in our tummies while you're being grilled."

"It sounds as if you're going to make a meal of me."

"Do you know, I think I'm going to like this man," Bellamy said, descending from the stool gracefully as a seal and tugging his velvet waistcoat over his paunch. "You'll be easy," he told Ben. "We'll have fun."

The interview was certainly fluent and slick. Once Bellamy had posed his tape recorder beside the bowl of parmesan, Ben forgot it and discoursed on all the subjects which Bellamy raised or which his own responses led to: childhood as a visionary state, the stifling of imagination by pressures to conform, imagination as the soul of man, the undying essences of myths and fairy tales, the need to let them tell themselves, the possibility that only children could hear them clearly and rediscover the meaning they must have had when they were told round the fire under an unknown sky in the midst of an unknown dark which perhaps had been the real storyteller, borrowing a human voice to tell its tales . . . Bellamy nodded and smiled and managed to look eager for more while he swallowed an extravagant amount of spaghetti. He didn't switch off the recorder until coffee had followed several bottles of wine. "That'll more than do," he said. "Unless you've anything else in your head that you particularly want to let loose on the world."

The termination of the interview took Ben off guard; he'd reached a stage where he was scarcely aware of talking. "I was just thinking how many people I've known who sound like adjectives or adverbs. Dainty, Quick, and now you. Not overweight, just comfortably bellamy."

Bellamy took his time about smiling at that, but once he did his smile looked set for a while. "I predict we'll be seeing you up high before long. I'll be bending my efforts towards it," he said, and wrote his address inside one of the restaurant's matchbooks. "Drop me a line if you think of anything you forgot to say."

As Ben and Mark Matthews walked back to Ember the publicist said "I'll want to use you a lot more next year. We mustn't let all that charm and eloquence go to waste."

"Maybe I should save some for my new editor."

"Maybe."

Without warning Ben felt as if the part of him which talked about writing and which had carried him through the interview had deserted him, exposing him to his impatience with the delay of the next two days. He was afraid he might be rude to Alice Carroll, and then so angry with being afraid that he felt like being yet ruder. But when he saw that she looked even smaller behind Kerys' desk than Kerys had, his anger didn't seem worth sustaining. "He was perfect for Bellamy," the publicist told her. "I've been there when Howard took against someone he was interviewing. Not a pretty sight, I can tell you."

Ben had to admit to himself that Alice Carroll was: the dabs of pink on her marbly cheeks emphasized her delicate bones, her blond hair cascaded to her waist out of a hairband shaped like a snake. She gave his hand two shakes and said "Anything you can do to maximize sales."

Ben assumed she was talking to Mark Matthews as well, which made him feel only half-acknowledged. "I'd like to have our photographer take you before you leave, Ben," the publicist said.

"What about Ellen?"

"Send us one."

"We can take him now," Alice Carroll said, and glanced at Ben. "If you don't mind, of course."

"I'll live."

She acknowledged his response with a terse smile and raised her faint eyebrows at the publicist until he retreated. "Coffee," she said to Ben as if she were advising him to sober up.

While they awaited the coffee she talked to him about the book she referred to as *Snowflakes*. She was pleased with the sales of *Snowflakes*, and sounded surprised as well. There was talk of submitting *Snowflakes* for a children's book award. Perhaps it was because her phone kept interrupting that he didn't find her comments as heartening as she presumably meant him to. Soon the photographer let himself into her glass-and-plywood booth. "Hold my calls," Alice Carroll told her secretary who brought the coffee, and nodded to the photographer to start whenever he was ready. To Ben she said, "You're waiting to hear what I thought of your latest submission."

"Of course," he said graciously.

"I thought you were trying too hard."

The electronic shutter of the camera emitted a sound like a stifled exclamation. The photographer was shooting. Let him, Ben thought furiously; he wouldn't catch Ben unawares, as Alice Carroll had. He was so anxious not to betray she had that his tongue stumbled. "To do, to do what?"

"To produce what you think the market wants."

"Wasn't that what you asked for?"

"True, but my authors don't normally take me so literally. I have to see the finished product before I can judge it, obviously, and in this case I'd say it shows you aren't as good at carrying out instructions as you think you are."

Repeated swiftly several times, the noise of the camera shutter sounded like imperfectly suppressed mirth. "So what are you saying?" Ben said in a tone intended to seem receptive but aloof.

"What I just said." She sat forwards on her high revolving chair, and Ben imagined spinning it until she vanished beneath the desktop. "If you're asking me what you should do," she said, "I'd say you ought to wag a few less fingers at your readers. Address their concerns but let your story make your points for you. People don't like to be preached at, children least of all."

"Nor do I," Ben retorted—not out loud, but he wondered if the snicker of the shutter meant that the camera had caught him thinking it. "And you might try injecting more imagination into the rewrite," Alice Carroll said, "since that's what you're good at and it seems to sell. Enough?"

Her last word was meant for the photographer, but Ben was

tempted to respond. As the photographer went out she said to Ben "I hope you didn't mind him taking you while we were talking. I think it makes for a livelier image. We've enough shots of you trying to look like an author."

"So to return to what you were saying . . ."

"I meant everything I said, of course."

Had Ben thought or hoped otherwise? "Simple as that," he said, and stood up.

"I'll walk you to the lifts." She held the door of her booth open while he struggled into his coat, which felt like his anger made heavy and hotter and even more frustrating, then she led him along the aisle between the unpartitioned desks. Someone held open a lift for Ben, but she waved it away. "Have your children read this book?" she said.

"Not yet."

"Don't you usually let them?"

"There hasn't been time."

"Maybe you should turn them loose on it and see if they're of my mind." When he didn't speak, she pressed the button between the lifts. "There wasn't any call to rush the book, you know," she said. "I appreciate your doing your best to please me, but I didn't need to see it so soon. If I were you I'd relax over Christmas and see how the story stands up in the new year."

"Thanks for making yourself clear," Ben said, and watched the doors of the lift close over her face. His rage seemed to have crystallized into a single thought: she was going to wish she hadn't been so smug about the new year. He wasn't quite sure what he meant by it, and its lack of definition aggravated his nervousness. When the lift touched bottom he hurried across the car park, where the chill was some relief, and drove the Volkswagen up the ramp.

Before he was out of the one-way maze he found that his instincts were leading him north. "Not yet," he muttered, and blundered more or less eastwards until he saw a sign for Cambridge. By the time he reached the motorway it was a stream of light and fumes. He came off it at Stump Cross and headed for Six Mile Bottom, a name which had given Johnny a fit of the giggles. The memory made Ben feel unexpectedly lonely in the midst of the flat landscape where headlamps passed like comets drawn by their tails into the dark. He'd call home once he arrived at Dominic's, he promised himself.

Most of the shops were closed when he drove into Norwich. As he parked beneath the only tree in the narrow side street, a gaunt metallic shape which he remembered bearing cherry blossoms, Dominic's father hopped off the Milligans' front doorstep and trotted over, leaning on a gnarled stick. "Here he is. Put the kettle on," he shouted, and to Ben in the same tone: "Let's have your bag."

Dominic hurried out of the house. "Hello, Ben. I'll take it, Father. We don't want you overexerting yourself."

"It isn't worth arguing over," Ben said, and carried his overnight bag into the hall, where Dominic's mother met him. "That's right, Ben, don't let them boss you about. What can I offer you after your travels? There's tea or coffee, and a snack to keep you going until dinnertime."

"I'm not hungry just now," he said, anxious to bypass her disordered cuisine as far as he decently could. "I hope Dominic told you I'm taking you all out to dinner."

The rooms with which the house was crammed were even smaller than he remembered, but brighter. The interior had been repainted— yellow in the hall and up the stairs, blue walls and one green in each of the rooms—until the house seemed almost to be turning into a cartoon of itself. It was no longer scattered with books, though there was a tottering pile of them beside the front-room chair into which Dominic's father subsided; Ben saw that he was doing his best to be tidy in his old age. "I read your new book," the old man told him. "It took me back to that time you told us a story. I said then you ought to see about finding a publisher."

"So you did," Ben said, and retreated to the spare bedroom. He'd forgotten the incident until now; what else might he have forgotten? He dropped his bag on the bed, which was surrounded by bookcases occupying all the space between the furniture against the walls, and went downstairs. "Would it be all right if I were to phone Ellen?"

"I should jolly well think it would," Mrs. Milligan declared, drawing the heavy curtain over the front door to keep out drafts, and shut all the doors to the hall as she returned to the kitchen. "You'll want some privacy while you're talking to your ladylove."

Margaret answered the phone. "Is that Ramona?"

"Not unless her voice has broken."

"Oh, it's you. Did you sign lots of books?"

"Maybe tomorrow."

"Mummy says did you drink lots of drinks. I'll get her."

He listened for her footsteps hurrying away or her calling to Ellen, but the silence was so total he began to wonder if he'd been cut off. He was suddenly aware of the expanse of night which separated them under the infinite dark. Ellen's voice made him start nervously. "What timing," she said. "I was taking dinner out of the oven."

"I just wanted to say hello."

"Hello. Were we a success? How did Alice Carroll turn out to be?"

"Unenthusiastic. She's decided she likes me better the way I was."

"She can keep her hands off. Or are you talking about the new book?"

"She thought it was all message and no magic."

"Shall I look at it again and see what I think?"

"It's your book."

"It'll keep me company when the children are in bed. Must go now before dinner gets cold. Drive carefully on Saturday but don't be too late, will you? I love you." The silence closed in so immediately that he thought she'd gone, but as he murmured "I love you" he heard her last words to him. "It's colder when you're not here," she said.

TWENTY-NINE

"It's colder when you're not here," Ellen said, and kissed the chilly mouthpiece. "Here you are, Johnny, if you want to say hello."

The boy ran out of the dining room, brandishing a handful of the cutlery he was placing on the table, and she took the dessert spoons from him to distribute them herself. She was touched and amused by how carefully he'd set the table; he'd already placed the knives and forks, and the settings on the round table were exactly equidistant, or as near to it as her eyes could judge. Children and their rituals, she thought, smiling. She closed the heavy floor-length curtains, shutting out the lights of Stargrave. "Hurry up with those plates, Peg," she called.

By the time Margaret had brought the plates and Ellen had ladled beef in red wine out of the casserole, Johnny was saying good-bye to his father. "Daddy says it hasn't snowed much there," he told them as he wriggled onto his chair. "When are we going to have more snow?"

"Johnny would like it to snow in his room," Margaret said.

"I would not," Johnny said indignantly, then admitted "Actually, I wouldn't mind."

"You'd feel it kiss you to sleep."

"That'd be good."

"It would feel like the heaviest blanket in the world," Ellen put in. "It'd be so cold you wouldn't know you were."

"You'd be able to have snowmen around your bed," Johnny said. "If you woke up in the night you'd see them all there."

Ellen was unable to find that idea appealing; indeed, it made her shiver. After dinner, as she carried casserole and plates into the kitchen, she noticed snow in the air beyond the window, motes dancing in a wind which hissed down from the forest. "You've made it snow, Johnny," she was about to call, but the thinness of the snow would only disappoint him. Besides, she found the sight of the faint icy auras sparkling around the snow figures oddly disturbing. She let the blind down and lifted the apple pie out of the oven, and felt grateful for its warmth.

Johnny saw off more than half the pie. Feeding him was like feeding a black hole, she often told him. The children were helping her at the sink when she said "Would you like me to read you the new book?"

"Yes please," Johnny cried, but Margaret hesitated. "Won't Daddy mind?" she said.

"I'm sure he'd want to hear what you think of it," Ellen said, and fetched the typescript from the workroom. Snow, or the imminence of it, whispered at the windows of the darkened rooms. As she crossed to the desk, a wind so large and cold it felt like a breath of the forest came to meet her at the window. Despite the wind, the trees appeared to be quite still. She thought the forest resembled an immense insect, its body hidden under a glimmering carapace and supported by countless thousands of legs. For a moment she imagined it moving all at once, but how would it move or change? "Just you stay where you are," she told it with a nervous giggle at herself.

The children snuggled against her legs while she sat on the front-room sofa and read *The Lady of the Heights* aloud. Ben had joked about writing a version Alice Carroll would find acceptable, but it seemed to Ellen that he'd forgotten he had been joking; the more she read, the more the book read like a handbook for young climbers, a collection of do's and mostly don'ts rather thinly disguised as fiction. As for the spirit who saved climbers lost on the heights, she never quite came to life, and each reappearance of her made Ellen feel sadder.

"And they lived happily for a while," she read at last, the spirit having fallen in love with a mortal and set up house with him where they could keep an eye on inexperienced climbers. She let the last page fall face down beside her on the sofa. "Is that the end?" Johnny said.

"Shouldn't it be?"

"S'pose so," Johnny said, clearly dissatisfied.

"So what did you think of the rest of it?"

"Good," Johnny said, so automatically that he contradicted himself.

"I don't think it'll mean as much to anyone but us," Margaret said.

That seemed so perceptive it stayed in Ellen's mind after she had put the children to bed. Rather than feel cold and lonely at the workroom desk, she took the typescript to the dining table and read through it again. Before long she found herself visualizing the lady of the heights: eyes gray and bright as sunlit slate, pale skin smooth as untrodden snow, a long dress which looked intricately woven out of heather but which didn't hinder her barefoot climbing. She thought of sketching the images, but scribbled them down instead for Ben to consider, together with a few ideas for bringing the character alive in prose. That done, she felt ready for bed.

She bolted the front door and locked the mortise lock, though none of that seemed necessary in Stargrave, and checked the downstairs windows and the back door. As she switched off the kitchen light she heard a thin whisper of snow beyond the blind. When she glanced out of Johnny's window, however, the air above the moors was clear. She gave the sleeping children each a kiss and brushed back Margaret's hair from her forehead, which was frowning at a dream.

It took her a while to get warm under the duvet, and by then she was almost asleep. Perhaps that was why her dreams were cold, though they hardly seemed like hers at all. The only familiar image, which they kept repeating like a refrain, was Sterling Forest, crouching beneath its white shell. Beyond it and around it was icy blackness. If she didn't go into the forest she would have to venture under the bridge or into the unlit town, but she was afraid to move in any direction until she had determined where the whispering was coming from, or what the vast thin voice was saying from its throat which might be as wide as the sky—so afraid that she started awake.

That wasn't the kind of dream to waken from alone in the dark. Nevertheless she relaxed almost at once, because Ben was home. She hoped he wouldn't leave the front door open long; an icy draft was reaching all the way up to her. She was awaiting the slam of the front door when she wakened enough to realize that he couldn't have let himself into the house. Both the front and back doors were bolted on the inside.

She had just imagined he was there because she needed comforting, she told herself. She was all right now, the dream had gone away. But so had the last of her sleepiness, yet the impression which had greeted her as she awoke was growing. She was sure that she and the children were no longer alone in the house.

The thought of the sleeping children jerked her out of bed. She grabbed her dressing gown from the duvet, where she'd spread it for extra warmth. She dug her fists into the sleeves and tied it around her as she padded shivering to the door. She closed one hand around the doorknob, which felt like a sculpted lump of ice, and snatched the door open. A white blur the size of her head rose out of the dark in front of her face.

It was her breath. The landing was so much colder than her room that she couldn't help flinching. The cold seemed to bring the darkness alive below her, a solid icy mass waiting for her to touch it unawares. She'd left the bedroom light turned off, but now she fumbled for the switch on the landing wall and pressed it, holding her breath to keep down the cry she was suddenly afraid she would have good cause to utter.

The stairs were deserted. The children's doors were ajar as she had left them, but she could hear no sound from either room. By craning over the banister she saw that the front door was still bolted. Surely the house couldn't be so cold unless a window or an outer door was open. Her mind was frantically cataloguing the contents of the workroom, but she could think of nothing in there that would be any use to her as a weapon. She darted back into her room and seized an empty wooden coat hanger from the wardrobe, and ran on tiptoe down the stairs.

She was shivering so much she had to hold the coat hanger away from the wall and the banisters. Even her heartbeats felt shivery. "Don't you touch my children," she hissed through her chattering teeth. She reached the middle landing and stared into the dark of Margaret's room.

Margaret was in bed. As Ellen made out her shape the girl shifted beneath the duvet, her hair spilling over the edge of the mattress. Ellen tiptoed to the adjoining room and peered around the door. That must be Johnny under his duvet, however oddly flat it looked. She took a nervous step forwards and saw that the shape was a faint shadow on the duvet. Johnny wasn't there.

She sucked in a breath which felt like a shudder, and made herself step into the room, praying that the sight meant what she thought it did, afraid to switch on the light until she knew. But yes, it *was* Johnny's shadow on the bed. He was leaning out of the open window, his head and arms reaching for the dark.

He must be sleepwalking; otherwise, why didn't he move when she spoke to him? "You'll catch your death, Johnny," she said, and put one arm around his waist to pull him back while she closed the window, beyond which she glimpsed a hint of snow, eddying around the corner of the house towards the forest. Under the pajama jacket his body was dismayingly cold. She carried him to his bed, trying to persuade herself that she'd felt him begin to shiver but knowing that the shiver had been her own. She deposited him gently on the bed and then, before she made for the light switch, she dared to look directly at him. Whatever she had been trying not to admit she was afraid to see, it wasn't this. His hands and face appeared to be glittering dimly like ice.

She ran to the switch. The light dazzled her. As she blinked, the traces of crystal melted from his hands and face, leaving his stiff features looking as though they had just been washed. Then his mouth twitched unhappily and, thank God, his eyes flickered open momentarily. "Where's Daddy?" he mumbled. "When's he coming home?"

"Soon, Johnny, soon. Let's get you warm." She sat him on the edge of the bed and set about rubbing him from head to foot with a warm towel from the bathroom. "You gave me such a fright," she murmured. "We'll have to ask Mr. Elgin to put a lock on your window if you're going to start sleepwalking."

He seemed not to have heard anything she'd said. His mouth twitched again as though it was stiff. "When's Daddy coming home?"

"We'll see him on Saturday." She pressed her mouth against his to warm his lips. "Why do you keep asking? What were you dreaming?"

"Wanted to know."

"Of course you did. I understand. He's never been away from us like this before. Don't fret, he'll be back."

The boy shook his head impatiently and let out a loud breath. "Wanted to know."

The breath sounded so like an unspoken word that Ellen blurted "Who did, Johnny? Someone in your dream?"

His face crumpled as if he wasn't sure how the memory affected him. "The big white," he said.

She thought of an enormous butterfly, and wondered why the vague image caused her to shiver. "It's gone now. You were dreaming."

She finished warming him at last, and dabbed away drops of moisture which lingered in his hair. When she laid him on his side on the mattress and covered him with the duvet, he was almost asleep. She fixed the catch of the window as immovably as she could. "No more roaming, Johnny," she murmured, kissing his forehead, and left his bedroom door open. As she tiptoed to her own room she glanced at the front door, and couldn't avoid wishing it had already let Ben into the house. "Come back soon," she whispered, hugging herself.

THIRTY

Ben awoke convinced that he ought to be on his way home. He was halfway out of bed before he remembered that he had yet to sign books at the shop. He listened to the world awakening around him, a bird shrilling at the dawn from a branch of the cherry tree outside the window, one of Dominic's parents plodding downstairs and back up, and leafed through books chosen at random from the several bookcases in the room. He wasn't reading, only occupying himself in order to avoid getting in anyone's way so early, and that gave him time to think.

Last night he'd fallen asleep thinking of the Milligans, having gone to bed before them to sleep off his long day. He'd heard Dominic's mother reading to her husband, whose eyes had grown too weak for him to read for more than a few minutes at a time. Whenever anything she read revived a memory for either of them she would stop so that they could share it aloud. Ben had been touched by this, but he'd thought it should mean more to him. Now, as he blew the dust off a faded book whose author he had never heard of, he wondered if it had reminded him of how he'd realized yesterday that his own books were lacking.

As he'd read through *The Boy Who Caught the Snowflakes*, not a line of it had inspired him in the way imagining the story had. Ellen's illustrations were truer to his inspiration than the writing was, and more genuine in themselves. He was sure that they were the source of the appeal of all the books.

Once he'd met the publicist, the day had become too demanding for Ben to reflect on any of this, but now he didn't find it as dispiriting as he might have. He'd done his best with the books, and now they were separate from him. They were really Ellen's books—Howard Bellamy had virtually told him so on meeting him—but that was a reason for him to feel prouder than ever of her. The trouble was, it also made today's session at the bookshop seem even more irrelevant to his real task.

Perhaps once the bookshop was out of the way his task would become clear to him. Last night, drifting off to sleep surrounded by old books, he'd thought it had to do with Edward Sterling. He'd realized that while he had been searching for his own books in Charing Cross Road he hadn't even considered trying to track down Edward Sterling's last book. He no longer needed it, he understood that much—because being denied it as a child had caused him to retell its stories, having forgotten where he'd found them. Whatever remained to him to tell or to perform, he felt instinctively that it had been with him since before he could remember.

The knock on his door and Dominic's announcement that the bathroom was free came as something of a relief. Ben took his time bathing and shaving, though his thoughts had given way to nervous anticipation, and then ventured down to Mrs. Milligan's inescapable breakfast. "That's it, you tuck in," she said, dumping more bacon on his plate as soon as he'd made room. "You've a big day ahead."

"We've been telling all our customers for weeks how you were coming back to us," her husband said.

"The second coming of Ben Sterling," Mrs. Milligan suggested with a wry grimace at her own wickedness.

"Mother," Dominic reproved her, and turned to Ben. "What will you do until this afternoon?"

"Eat, by the look of it," Ben refrained from saying. "I'll revisit some of my old haunts," he said.

Outside, where all the parked cars had gone blind overnight with frost, he decided to visit the houses where he used to live. His aunt's hadn't changed much, though there were dolls in the windows and more stray twigs poking out of the shrubs in the garden than she would have allowed to grow, but it seemed small and unfamiliar. When he strolled to his and Ellen's first house it looked shrunken too, and secretive with net curtains. He was glad Ellen wasn't there to see it, although the sight of it only confirmed the impression which had been developing in him, he didn't know for how long, that the whole of his life in Norwich had been no more than an interruption.

After a pub lunch which he would have been unable to describe as soon as he was out of the pub, he strolled for a while through the historic part of Norwich, old uneven streets which no longer seemed ancient enough to satisfy him, and then headed for the bookshop. A photograph of Ellen and himself was enshrined in the window by their books. Mr. Milligan opened the door and applauded him, to the bemusement of the customers. "Here's our celebrity," he announced, so enthusiastically that Ben had to feel pleased for him.

During the next hour the shop sold over forty of the Sterlings' books. Whenever a child brought him one to autograph, Ben wished that Ellen were there to see—that they were meeting her rather than him. As he kept up a stream of conversation, he felt as if he were talking for her. The last child was led away from the cash desk, clutching a copy of *The Boy Who Caught the Snowflakes* and being told that it mustn't be unwrapped until Christmas, just as Mrs. Milligan bore a cake into the shop. The skullcap of white icing was inscribed WELL DONE, BEN in pink so fierce it looked inedible. "That's fantastic, Mrs. Milligan," he said. "I wish the children could have had some. Do you mind if I let Ellen know how we did?"

"You keep asking," she chided him, though behind her Dominic looked as if he would have liked to be asked.

She cut the cake as he dialled and tried to indicate to her that he would be happy with not quite so generous a slice. He listened to the ringing of the distant phone and eventually replaced the receiver. "No luck?" Dominic said.

"Ellen must be on her way to the school. I'll try again later. This is

204

really kind of you," he told Dominic's mother as he bit through the white icing to the sponge beneath.

"We'll save some for you to take home to the family if you like."

"That's kinder still. I'll tell them when I speak to them," Ben said and took refuge in the staffroom, hoping that a few minutes by himself would calm his nerves. Surely it was the last of the energy he'd used to entertain his audience which was making him feel as if he should be rushing onwards. One or more of the Milligans kept coming to find him, and he chattered to them, hardly aware of what he was saying. He accepted coffee, and then a refill of the mug, by which time it was four o'clock. Ellen would be home, the children weren't due to go anywhere. He went smiling to the phone, and listened to the ringing until his smile grew so stiff he had to let it fade. As the hands of the clocks in the jeweller's across the street crawled silently towards five o'clock Ben tried the Stargrave number several times, and each time the ringing seemed more distant in the midst of the silence and the growing dark. At last he could stand it no longer. "I'm sure there's nothing wrong," he lied, "but I think I'll head back."

THIRTY-ONE

It was almost six o'clock before he left for Stargrave. Dominic's mother followed him to the Milligans' house, trotting as fast as was safe for the plateful of cake she was bearing. He would have taken it from her to hurry her up, except that then she might have realized that he was more anxious than he was trying to appear. At least he had time to call home again while she searched for a container in which to pack the remains of the cake. But the phone in the Sterling house only rang and rang far away in the dark.

Mrs. Milligan was securing the carton of cake with a festive bow when the rest of the family came home, Mr. Milligan enthusing about Ben's performance at the shop. He wouldn't let Ben go until Ben had inscribed a copy of each Sterling book to the Milligans. "You'll have a coffee at least before you set off, won't you, Ben?" Mrs. Milligan pleaded while he was struggling to think of a different inscription for each book, and he seemed to have no words left with which to explain a refusal. "We don't want the cold getting to you on your way home," she said.

While he sipped the scalding coffee as rapidly as he could, she began to wonder aloud why Ellen wasn't answering. "Maybe she was out shopping, buying something special for the prodigal. Try her again if you like," she said, and when he had: "Maybe she's stopped to gossip. You know how we women are."

"We all of us talk too much and say too little," Mr. Milligan said.

His wife took that as a rebuke. She turned her back to him and cleared away the dinner plate and cutlery she'd set for Ben. Ben gulped the last gritty inch of coffee, grabbed his bag from beside his chair and stood up. "Thanks for having me. Next year you may see how grateful I am to all of you," he said, thinking of the book he planned to dedicate to them, but for an instant his plan seemed lost in a darkness which lay ahead.

Dominic carried the boxed cake out of the house and placed it on the passenger seat while Ben threw his bag onto the rear seat. Beyond the lit hall Ben saw Dominic's parents settling their disagreement before they came out arm in arm. "Give our love to your family," Mrs. Milligan told him.

"Godspeed," Dominic said.

"So long as he doesn't exceed the speed limit," his father said, and was rewarded with a helpless grin from Dominic. As Ben swung the car away he saw the three of them beneath the leafless tree, standing so close together they appeared to be supporting one another. The sight stayed with him as he drove out of the lit streets.

The road wandered for hours before it reached the A1. It gave him no chance to think, but it couldn't stop him feeling. Whenever the headlights showed him a place name which the family had enjoyed on their journeys to Stargrave—Swineshead, Stragglethorpe, Coddington, Clumber Park—he felt increasingly nervous. Not long after eight o'clock he had to stop for petrol near a pay telephone, shielded to some extent from the uproar of the motorway by a plastic hood which, in the glare of the lamps above the forecourt, looked like a giant helmet carved from ice. He dialled and poised the coin, which was chill even though it had come from his trousers pocket, and listened to the feeble pulse of the phone bell. Suddenly there was a lull on the motorway, and he heard the ringing isolated by a vast silence. All at once he could no longer fend off thoughts he had been afraid to think. He was hardly conscious of digging the edge of the mouthpiece into his lips while he tried to make up his mind what to do: ring someone in Stargrave, invent a story which would send them looking for Ellen and the children? He didn't know where the family might be or what to say to have them searched for: his imagination seemed to be out of his reach and fleeing towards Stargrave. He flung the receiver into its cradle and ran to the car.

Most of the vehicles on the motorway were lorries, which left the outer lane clear. He shouldn't be staying in it, he shouldn't be driving at over ninety miles an hour; suppose the police stopped him? He felt as if he were trying to leave his thoughts behind. He knew why last night he had fallen asleep thinking of the Milligans growing old together, and why the sight of Dominic and his family had followed him as he'd driven away. He remembered hugging Ellen and the children in the Leeds bookshop, hugging them more fiercely than he had been able to explain to himself. Subconsciously he must have been afraid then, or even earlier—perhaps the October day he'd watched Ellen leading the children across the moor. Had the intensity of his emotions been preparing him for the day when he would lose them? The impression of loss felt like a wound at the center of him, and yet at the same time it seemed infinitesimal beneath the endless dark.

At last the westbound motorway appeared, a curve of white and yellow lights racing above a curve of red—a luminous blade hovering above the gash it had opened from horizon to horizon. He followed the raw stream to Leeds and drove as fast as he dared through streets which felt somehow lifeless despite crowds of people, many of them dressed as if there weren't frost on the ground, outside pubs and clubs. Whenever he passed a phone box he had to restrain himself from braking.

Darkness began to interrupt the outlying streets, and then it overcame them. Patches of snow gleamed like exposed bone on the moors; cold glints hovered in the headlight beams. When at last the bridge rose overhead, a faint gray outline around darkness yawning like a fallen jaw, one word struggled past his stiff lips: "Please . . ." The bridge squeezed the headlamp beams bright and released them, and he saw Sterling Forest beneath the crags which gnawed the sky. The forest appeared to be borrowing the glow of the town, like the second-hand light of a moon. Against the forest the Sterling house was dark.

Ellen and the children could be at home; it was almost eleven o'clock, late enough for them all to be asleep. As he swung the car onto the rough track, the jerking of the headlight beams sent shadows of misshapen stones capering over the front of the house and made the snow figures behind it appear to greet him with a grotesque dance. He parked clumsily beside the garden wall and ran to the front door, keys jangling in his hand. He turned the mortise key and then the Yale, and shouldered the door open.

Silence met him—total silence. Only a muffled echo of his shouts responded to him. He trudged through all the rooms, starting on the ground floor. The children weren't in their beds, but couldn't the family be on the top floor, the three of them in his and Ellen's bed? Certainly he felt as if he weren't entirely alone in the dark, as if he were climbing towards some form of life. When he pushed his and Ellen's bedroom door open, however, their bed was flat as an altar. He turned to the workroom, knowing Ellen and the children had no reason to be in there, hating the trick his unwillingness to give up hope was playing on him: it was making him feel that he was awaited beyond the door. He clenched his fist on the doorknob, twisted it, held onto it as the door swung inwards. He stepped into the room, and Sterling Forest came to meet him.

It seemed to fill the window even when he'd crossed to the desk. Perhaps it was by contrast with the darkness of the house that the miles of shrouded forest appeared to shine from within like a cloud, but the illumination meant more to him. The forest was where he had been heading as he climbed the stairs—because, he thought, it must be where Ellen and the children were.

He didn't question how he knew. His sense of needing to be in the forest was overwhelming; it felt so like a call that he could almost hear their voices. It sent him downstairs and out of the house, pausing only to lock the door before he sprinted up the track.

When he reached the trees he ran along the blue-arrowed path until it began to curve away from the depths of the forest, and then he left it and continued running. A white blur which he assumed to be mist hovered just above the laden trees, blotting out most of the sky, but his vision was improving. The slender tree trunks and the massive pattern of fallen needles gleamed as if they were tapping the light of the stars overhead. He felt he could run unerringly until he arrived at his destination. But he faltered suddenly, for he'd heard Ellen's voice, unquestionably her voice. It was far away behind him.

He staggered to a halt, grabbing a tree trunk which felt like a ruined pillar, scaly and chill. As his ears throbbed with the breath he was holding, he heard Margaret and Johnny protesting about something, and then Ellen quietening them. A minute or so later he heard another sound, tiny with distance but unmistakable: the slam of the front door. The family had been out somewhere, and now they had come home.

They were safe. The thought seemed to unlock his mind. All his fears fell away except one which was too large to define, so large that it felt as much like exhilaration as fear. Perhaps his anxiety for Ellen and the children had been nothing but a means of attracting him back to Stargrave. He was still hearing the miniature sound of the front door; it made him think of having crossed a threshold. He'd done so once before, here beyond the marked paths, but the experience had been more than his memory could cope with. Now he was as ready for it as he ever would be, he promised himself.

He pushed himself away from the slippery tree trunk and strode into the forest. He was walking through a vast silent starlit cathedral which had built itself. It was nearly complete now; its elaborate decoration of snow and icicles was taking shape. It had been planted for Edward Sterling, not just to commemorate him but to conceal where he had died, to protect the site from the world.

Ben felt as if he were using something larger than his own mind to think with, something large as the terror which was robbing him of breath and at the same time opening his mind wide. The pattern was fitting together at last. Edward Sterling's death had been only the beginning. The forest concealed what his death had liberated—what had accompanied him beyond the restraint of the midnight sun.

Perhaps it had been waiting for as long as there was ice there, waiting for someone it could ride beyond the light. Perhaps that hadn't been Edward Sterling who had come back, but only a shell of him compelled to walk and talk. It must have been the source of the strength which had driven him north again in search of somewhere it could hide, but his body had failed before it reached anywhere secret enough. The forest had hidden it while its power grew during the long nights, and now it was awakening.

Ben had tried to tell himself a garbled version of this without consciously realizing it had any basis in truth, but there was no avoiding that awareness here, surrounded as he was by signs of the truth. The icicles which hung like frozen starlight from the branches high above him all pointed deeper into the forest, in defiance of gravity. They were pointing to the unseen glade, as if whatever the forest hid was transforming it into a shrine of ice.

His terror had passed beyond awe into a kind of breathless calm. He was scarcely aware of walking or of how long he had been doing so since he'd left Ellen and the children behind. He must be near the glade, because the ice which sprouted from the trees was becoming more elaborate, forming shapes he couldn't find words for. It looked as though the trees were undergoing an identical mutation, revealing forms of which the foliage and slender trunks were merely skeletons. Though they were absolutely motionless, he sensed that their stillness was an omen of growth. Besides, all was not motionless in the forest. He could see pale movement beyond the trees ahead.

The movement was so large that he would have turned tail if he had had any control over his gait—but the compulsion which had brought him to the forest was in charge of his limbs now, and all he could do was scurry forwards. The trees parted ahead of him and closed in silently behind him. For a few steps he managed to believe that he was seeing a snowfall ahead, even though the flakes were falling only in the glade; but although the movement was within the glade, he sensed that it was nevertheless awesomely vast. As soon as he realized that, he was unable to avoid knowing that whatever he was seeing was aware of him. A shiver which felt like terror and anticipation and his body somehow preparing itself passed through him, sending him to the edge of the trees at a helpless stumbling run.

Perhaps he was seeing only ice and snow, or perhaps his mind was unable to cope with the reality after all. Certainly, thick snow was dancing just within the glade, though it appeared to be rising triumphantly from the ground rather than falling from the sky, which it blotted out. Within the snow, or forming from it, or both, something else had taken shape. He thought of a spider whose squatting body almost filled the glade and whose restless limbs were far too numerous, or a gigantic head obscured by tendrils of white hair or of its own white flesh, tendrils between which its many eyes were watching him. He could see that it was perfectly symmetrical; it must have eyes on every side to see the world into which it was emerging. All this was only a hint of its nature, he thought numbly. It was using the snow to hint at itself.

Because the snow obscured the sky as well as the far side of the glade, he couldn't judge how tall the shape was, but that wasn't at all reassuring; it made him feel that in some sense it went on forever. He had to look up, because pale tendrils were hovering above him, and he was afraid they were reaching for him. But they were only playing in the air around their body—playing with shapes which they were forming and reforming, letting them grow recognizable and then turning them perfectly symmetrical. They were human faces, he saw: masks composed of snow, except that to judge by their expressions and their desperate trapped fluttering as the tendrils toyed with them, some human consciousness was associated with them. The one above him, which appeared to be trying to scream as its halves were rendered identical, was Edna Dainty's face.

To Ben the sight was a promise of more wonders, of greater transformations. All that he was seeing was another metaphor, he realized, and even that was proving too much for him. His mind was going to forget again in order to preserve itself. He felt tears or snowflakes on his cheeks. He gazed at the appearance in the glade and its juggling of frozen souls for as long as he could bear, then turned shakily away. At best his experience would resemble a half-remembered dream before he was out of the forest, and tomorrow there would be so little left of it that he would mistake the remnants for another story waiting to be told. As he thought that, he heard its voice behind him.

It wasn't a sound he would ordinarily have called a voice: a whisper of snow, audible because it was both immense and isolated by stillness—the whisper of patterns forming and elaborating. Nevertheless his instincts were able to decode its message. He could contrive a tale about the midnight sun if he liked, to keep his imagination alive and under control, to let his mind grow toward the presence in the forest. He wouldn't have long to wait now. His shivering carried him away from the glade in a kind of helpless festive dance. All the stories he had told were scarcely even hints of the story he would soon be living.

THIRTY-TWO

As Ellen and the children turned along the track they saw the parked car. "Daddy's home," Johnny shouted, and ran towards the house.

Ellen wondered if one night at the Milligans' had been enough for Ben or if he had just been homesick. "Don't ring the bell, Johnny. He's probably asleep."

The boy dodged around the house and hid among the snow figures. "Mummy, he's going to chuck snow at us. It'll be hard. *Mummy*," Margaret protested, wailing with tiredness.

"Come out now, Johnny. I let you stay up late so you could finish your game on Stefan and Ramona's computer. I thought you were old enough to behave."

When she advanced towards him he leapt up among the figures, and Margaret screamed. "I said not to wake Daddy," Ellen said, thinking as she spoke that Ben might not be asleep yet: the windscreen of the car was clear of frost, and so it couldn't have been parked for long. She glanced past it, at the oddly symmetrical luminous cloud which had been hovering above the forest ever since they'd started home from Kate's. Somehow she couldn't judge how large or how distant the cloud was. She unlocked the front door and switched on the hall light. "Straight into the bathroom, now," she murmured.

"Can't we just peep at Daddy?" Margaret pleaded.

"Very quietly, then. Quiet as snow."

Sometimes the children took Ellen's instructions too literally out of contrariness, but now they seemed to be trying to do as they were told; by the time they reached the top of the house she couldn't hear them. From the foot of the stairs she watched Margaret ease open the bedroom door and then the door of the unlit workroom. "He isn't here," Margaret called to her.

Margaret must be too tired to realize that meant there was no need for quiet; Ellen could barely hear her voice. "Faces and teeth, then," Ellen said. "I'll be up to tuck you both in in ten minutes."

While they were in the bathroom she looked into the downstairs rooms in case Ben had been so exhausted by his journey that he'd fallen asleep in one of them, but they were deserted. She filled the percolator and switched it on before shooing Johnny up to his room, having checked that he'd washed his face and brushed his teeth. "Where's Daddy?" he repeated.

"He must have gone to look for us. The quicker you go to sleep now, the less time you'll have to wait to see him."

She was making Ben sound like Father Christmas, but she didn't want Johnny worrying about him and giving himself anxious dreams. She kissed Johnny as the pillow swelled around his cheeks; she stuffed the edges of the duvet under the mattress and made sure his bedroom window was securely fastened, then went into Margaret's room. "I'll come and tell you if I hear Johnny in the night," Margaret whispered.

"I shouldn't think he'll walk again. He never has before. Anyway, I'm going to wait up for your father."

"Can't I?"

"You go to sleep. You'll see him in the morning," Ellen said, and stopped Margaret's flagging protests with a kiss. She left the bedroom doors ajar and returned to the bubbling percolator.

The coffee took away a little of the chill which was penetrating the kitchen window and the blind, but Ellen felt as if something huge and cold were massing just beyond the glass. She pulled the blind cord and sent the strips of plastic rattling upwards. There was nothing to see except the frozen garden and the pack of rudimentary figures at the edge of the glow from the kitchen. She let the blind down and retreated to the living room.

The suite she'd brought from Norwich and the easy chairs she'd bought in Stargrave were old friends by now, all part of the room. She curled up on the sofa and sipped her coffee while she gazed at her pictures and the children's hanging on the walls, the velvet curtains shutting out the night, the gray stone mantelpiece which she would fill with Christmas cards. She tried to imagine how the house had felt before it had become hers and the rest of the family's, but she could call up nothing but an impression of empty darkness.

She finished her coffee and sat listening for footsteps on the track. Surely Ben wouldn't be long now; he'd had time to walk around Stargrave and back. She listened until her intentness made the silence seem to be settling against the windows and she had to resist an urge to break the silence. It evoked the night and the crowd of still figures behind the house, and for no reason she could identify, a phrase began to repeat itself in her brain: faces and teeth, faces and teeth.

When she found herself remembering the grin of the climber who'd frozen to death on the crag, she reached for the remote control and summoned up the channels on the television. Nothing looked like sufficiently good company, not even a Cary Grant film that she watched for a few minutes. She was keeping the sound low in order to listen for Ben, and once she realized that the black-and-white film was set mostly at night she felt as though it were helping darkness and silence to gather. She switched it off and closed her eyes.

She wasn't intending to fall asleep; she meant only to quiet her thoughts. Sleep came almost at once, a soft weight which settled on her eyelids and her mind. She didn't know how long she dozed before the cold wakened her. A door or a window must be open, and she was about to force herself fully awake in case Johnny was sleepwalking when she heard the front door closing quietly. It was Ben. He was home.

She ought to go to him or at least call a greeting to him. But he seemed to have brought sleep into the house with him, a drift of heavy enveloping somnolence. She no longer knew how much she was dreaming. She felt Ben come into the room and tower over her as if the winter night had added to his stature, but her eyelids were too ponderous to open. Now he was slipping one arm beneath her shoulders and the other behind her knees. He was carrying her upstairs, lowering her onto the bed, raising her legs out of the flower of her skirt, undressing her. The touch of his hands sent shivers through her, and she wanted him. But when he eased himself into her, his penis felt like ice.

She must be dreaming, otherwise surely that would have shocked her awake—though if she was dreaming, how was she able to rationalize the situation that way? She clenched herself around his icicle of a penis, trying to impart some warmth to it as her body responded drowsily to him. When he came and then shrank, she felt as if the icicle were melting inside her. The sensation was so dreamlike that she fell asleep almost at once.

The next time she wakened, the room was dark. She was lying on her side, facing away from the middle of the bed, her empty arms reaching out beneath the duvet. How much had she dreamed? She turned over and found Ben lying beside her. That was all that mattered. She pressed her face against his neck and drew the quilt over his shoulder, and was asleep.

The children's cries roused her. She was alone in bed. Brightness pressed against her eyelids, making them flinch: daylight between the curtains. As she shielded her eyes with one hand and levered herself out of bed with the other, she heard the children again. They were cheering.

They and Ben were in the living room, watching television. A long-range weather forecast was just ending, and Ben's eyes seemed even brighter than the children's. "Mummy," Johnny cried as his father continued to gaze ahead with an odd smile of which he seemed to be hardly aware, "there's going to be snow everywhere for Christmas."

THIRTY-THREE

Of course Johnny knew he might have to wait. The weatherman had said that when the snow came it would start in the far north and mightn't be here for weeks. All the same, that meant the weatherman didn't know exactly when it would start, and surely it couldn't do any harm if Johnny just looked at the sky now and then to see if the clouds were here yet. Before long he was doing so partly to irritate Margaret, once he saw that it would make her turn her eyes up and pull her suffering face. She was really as excited as he was, only she was trying to seem grown up. But being grown up didn't mean that you had to act as if you were bored all the time, because Johnny could tell how much his father was looking forward to the snow.

Sometimes Daddy seemed to lock himself away inside himself, especially when he was writing a book, though Johnny's mother never behaved like that when she was painting. At these times Johnny always felt that his father was storing up secrets, getting ready to present them to the family and everyone, and now he could tell that his father had a new one. That morning he'd wakened to see Daddy standing in the bedroom doorway, watching him.

He'd looked to Johnny as if he'd had a surprise for him but had forgotten what it was. When Margaret had come out of her room to say hello, their father had given her a quick hug and plodded downstairs as though he hadn't quite known where he was going. They'd heard him switching on the television and had followed him in time to see the forecast. Johnny was sure that his father had known it was coming—that it was part of the secret he had in store for them.

Did his mother know? Johnny didn't think so; when she had come downstairs she'd seemed to wonder why Daddy was looking so pleased with himself. "Mummy," Johnny had told her, "there's going to be snow everywhere for Christmas."

"That should please some of us. How soon, Ben? How heavy?"

"As heavy as you'll ever see."

Johnny hadn't thought the forecast had been quite so extreme, but Daddy often used words to make things bigger. "Not for a few days, though," Mummy had said as if she were making a wish. "I can do without going into Leeds on a Saturday so close to Christmas."

"You won't have to."

They were referring to a secret the children weren't supposed to know, about Christmas presents which needed to be bought in Leeds. "We'd better start building up our strength for the winter," Mummy had said, heading for the kitchen. "Come and talk to me if you like."

Above the boisterousness of the children's programs which he and Margaret agreed between themselves to watch, Johnny had heard his mother saying "Were you as lonely as I was? I felt as if a piece of me was missing." He'd squirmed with embarrassment and tried not to listen, until his mother had asked "Where did you get to last night after you came home? Couldn't you bear waiting?"

"I don't mind when I know it's worth waiting for."

When the aroma of breakfast had enticed Johnny to the kitchen, he'd found his parents holding hands. They'd kept touching each other throughout the meal as if to make sure the other was still there. Rather than giggle, Johnny had gazed at the sky above the swollen forest. "I don't think you'll be seeing it yet," Mummy said eventually, "not out of a clear sky."

He didn't quite know how to describe the sky above the forest. "It isn't clear," he said.

"Neither is your head," Margaret informed him.

"No arguing for the sake of arguing," Mummy told them, "or there'll be no more late nights."

"Only earlier ones," Daddy said.

"You might try to help."

"I'll take them out, shall I?" he said, and asked the children, "Where shall we go?"

"Leeds."

"Richmond," Margaret said, "to see what my next year's school looks like."

"Maybe your father would rather not drive after he came so far last night."

Certainly something had just bothered him, and Johnny didn't see how it could have been the mention of next year. "How about a walk somewhere?" Daddy said.

"In the woods," Johnny shouted.

"Margaret?"

"If you like."

"How about you, Ellen? You'd like to see how the forest is now."

"I would, but not today. Too much work. Speaking of which, I scribbled down a few thoughts about our book. They're on the desk."

"Couldn't you find any paper?" He got up at once, as if he couldn't bear to be in the same room with the joke. "Let me see what I think."

Mummy cleared away his plate, having given Johnny the bacon his father hadn't touched. As soon as she heard the workroom door close, she said "Go easy on your father today, both of you. I think yesterday took quite a lot out of him."

When they'd helped her clear up after breakfast and their father hadn't reappeared, Johnny wondered if he'd fallen asleep at the desk. Perhaps he had only been taking in what he'd found there, because after a few minutes which made Johnny feel shivery with impatience he came downstairs, so quietly that nobody noticed until he was in the room. "You've far more sense of the book than me," he said. "I've no life to give it, but you have."

Mummy took his hand again, looking so girlish that Johnny made a face at Margaret, who frowned reprovingly at him. "You haven't finished it," Mummy said.

"I already had before I went away. It's your turn now. Keep my name with yours on the story if you want to."

"Of course I want to. But Ben, you're the writer here."

"What do you two think? Should your mother tell her story while she can?"

"Yes," they cried.

"Don't let your imagination go back to sleep," he told her, and gazed at her until she nodded. "Get ready for the cold, you two, and we'll be on our way."

"Bathroom first," Mummy said.

"No need to rush," he called as Johnny raced upstairs. "We've all the time in the world."

Johnny tried to be patient while his sister took ages to brush her hair. He zipped up his fat anorak and dashed out of the house. The sky above the moors was frustratingly clear, and the bright blur above the forest had to be a kind of mist, something to do with all the snow which had stayed on the trees. Johnny squinted at it as he marched ahead of his father and Margaret. It could hide something as big as the forest, he thought, and imagined a huge flock of birds or insects, millions of them with just enough space between their bodies to let them hover. He imagined them exploding out of the mist like a blizzard, and stopped short of imagining what they would look like—not like birds or insects at all. He stumbled on the track and touched the icy skull of a figure as tall as himself, which jolted him out of the daydream.

He must have been like that while he was sleepwalking, he thought, and that was why he couldn't remember doing so. His mother was smiling through the kitchen window, Margaret was ducking in case he meant to fling snow at her; neither of them appeared to have noticed anything unusual above the trees. His father had overtaken him and was striding towards the forest, above which was only a misty blur. Johnny avoided looking at it as he tramped across the crunchy grass to the trees.

The hovering mist steeped the forest in a twilight in which the tree trunks, which resembled scaly bones, appeared to glow. As soon as Johnny set foot on the path between them he saw his breath. He ran along the path, searching for trees he could shake to dislodge snow from them, trying to run far enough to be out of sight of his family and lie in wait for them. But the trees wouldn't shake; when he threw his weight against a trunk, that didn't bring down even so much as a snowflake. For a moment he thought the others had sneaked behind him, and then he saw them approaching on the path, his father's eyes gleaming in the twilight, Margaret rubbing her arms with her mittened hands. She looked ready to suggest going home out of the cold, and so Johnny shouted "Let's play hide-and-seek. Daddy can be It."

Their father went to the nearest marker post, which was painted with a blue arrow, and stared brightly at them before closing his eyes. "You'll be found, I promise," he said in a voice like a wind through the trees. "Off you go."

When Johnny saw that his sister was staying near the post he raced on tiptoe into the forest. By the time his father had counted thirty aloud, Johnny had run far enough for the path and his family to be invisible for tree trunks. He darted behind two trees which grew very close together, and crouched to peer between them. He heard his father shout "Fifty" to announce that he'd finished counting, a shout which sounded tiny in the silence. Johnny crouched lower, waiting to catch sight of his father. He was still watching, and listening for movements in the hush which felt as if it were pinned down by all the trees, when he sensed that his father or Margaret had crept behind him.

No, not them. Their breath on his neck wouldn't be so cold, and even if both of them were standing there, their presence wouldn't feel so large. He swung round, sprawling on fallen needles. There was nobody to be seen, only trees like an enormous cage, but for an instant he felt as if whatever he'd sensed at his back had just hidden behind all of them at once. It had to have been the twilight, and the breath on his neck must have been a stray breeze. All the same, he was glad when he heard his father shout "I see you, Gretel" and Margaret's squeak of dismay, because then he was able to dash back to the marker post without fear of being made It.

When Margaret began to count, he ran off the path. Though she was almost shouting, her voice immediately sounded even smaller than his father's had. Johnny dodged away from his father, who was also heading deeper into the forest, and hid in the midst of a circle of five close trees. He saw his father vanish among the trees to his left, and could just hear Margaret still counting, and so surely he was wrong to feel as if he weren't alone in his hiding place. He glanced all around him, and then up. Of course, the mist was as close as the treetops to him. The pale blur above the branches laden with snow made him think of a patch of a face—a face so huge that he was seeing too little of it to distinguish any features. The thought of a face as wide as the forest and hovering just above it sent him fleeing towards the marker post as soon as he heard Margaret stop counting.

"I see Johnny," she called almost at once, and beat him to the marker, though without much enthusiasm. When he skidded onto the path, kicking needles across it, she said "I don't want to play any more."

Now that she'd admitted it, he didn't need to. When he shrugged so as not to seem too eager she called "Dad, we've finished playing."

Perhaps Daddy thought she was trying to trick him, because he made no sound. Was he stealing towards them or standing as still as the forest? "We aren't playing any more," they shouted more or less in chorus, but the silence seemed to cut off their shouts as soon as the sound reached the first trees. "He's going to scare us," Margaret wailed.

Johnny couldn't tell if he shivered then or if the forest did. For a moment he thought the trees had somehow drawn together, then that something had inched towards him and Margaret between far too many trees. He could hardly see beyond the nearest trees because of the fog of his breath. When a figure appeared to his right, between trees so distant they resembled a solid scaly wall, he wasn't sure that he wanted to see what it looked like.

He sucked in a breath which tasted like a stream of ice, and saw that it was his father. It must have been the cold which had made him look different—the blurring of the air—but as he advanced deliberately towards the children, his face was so blank and pale that Johnny felt anxious for him. Then his father saw that Margaret was shivering, and an expression of concern developed on his face. "Is the cold getting to you?" he said. "We'd better speed up our progress."

"Can't we go home now?" Margaret said.

"Why, we haven't got anywhere yet. We've hours before it's dark." He turned along the path, walking so fast that the children had to trot in order to keep up with him. Johnny supposed that was meant to keep Margaret warm, or was his father in a hurry to be somewhere? His father's face had become expressionless yet purposeful, and Johnny wondered if it was possible to sleepwalk while you were awake.

Now they were almost at the point where the path began to curve out of the forest. Daddy left the path without breaking his stride and headed deeper into the forest, into the maze of pines which reminded Johnny of giants or insects, thin scaly bodies rising to bunches of legs with claws of ice beneath their blank white heads. Their stillness made the entire forest seem about to pounce. He would have followed his father if Margaret hadn't stopped on the path, protesting "Daddy, you'll get us lost."

"No need to be afraid." He twisted round and beckoned, his feet moving in an odd little dance as if he was unable to keep still. "This is the last place on earth I'd lose you. Quite the opposite."

"Mummy wouldn't want us to go where there aren't any paths."

"There are paths, believe me. You'll see." But her mentioning Mummy had affected him. At first he looked angry and then, as he glanced at the poised silent forest, his face cleared. "She ought to be here," he murmured. "It should be all of us."

He returned to the path so abruptly he might have been pushing himself away from something. He looked bewildered, and on the way to renewed blankness. "We'll go back for your mother."

"She'll be busy," Margaret told him.

His eyes gleamed a warning; then he smiled, so vaguely that he mightn't have known why. "Perfect," he said. "If we wait there'll be more to see."

As he led them along the path towards the moors he kept glancing behind him into the pines, though he appeared to have forgotten what he was looking for. Johnny didn't like to speak until they were well along the path. "What are we going to see if we wait?" he said at last. "More snow?"

His father beamed at him as if Johnny had solved a problem. "Snow like you've never seen," he said. "The winter to end all."

THIRTY-FOUR

It didn't start snowing for almost a week, and then only on television. Johnny saw it on the children's news, and shouted for them all to come and see. There were blizzards in the north of Scotland. Queues of sluggish vehicles turned even whiter in the seconds they were on the screen, their yellow headlights dimming; people masked with scarves leaned into the white wind so as to stay on their feet; a flock of sheep would have been indistinguishable from the blizzard except for their eyes. When a pine forest filled the screen, Margaret thought for a dreamlike moment that it was Sterling Forest, all its colors swallowed up by white. "It's coming," Johnny cried.

"It won't be as bad as that here, will it, Mummy?"

"What's bad about it?" Johnny complained as if her saying so would keep it away, baby that he was. "It looks good. I thought you liked snow."

"Not that much."

"Let's wait and see what the forecast says," Mummy said.

That wouldn't be on for almost an hour. Margaret went up to her room. The floor above was dark; her father must have switched off the workroom light to help him imagine his story. She left her bedroom door open so as to have the rest of the house for company, and took down from the shelves in the corner by her overloaded wardrobe the big Grimm Brothers book.

She sat on the edge of the bed and opened the book on her lap. When she was Johnny's age she'd read it so often that if she held it any other way the pages sagged forward on the strip like a bandage to which they were glued. It fell open at the story of Hansel and Gretel, and she remembered the name her father had called her in the forest as some kind of joke. Perhaps she was too old for the story; the burning of the old woman seemed pointlessly violent and cruel. She tried the Hans Andersen book instead, but that seemed even bleaker; the thought of the Snow Queen made her shiver. She left the books in Johnny's room and put on her headphones to listen to one of Ramona's tapes of Pile of Cows, the rock group from Leeds, until Mummy called "Dinner in five minutes."

Margaret was down in time to see the long-range forecast, and so was her father. The forecaster, an owlish man whose expression suggested that he was keeping a joke to himself, stood with his back to a map of Europe across which whiteness was crawling. The map turned into one of Britain, and it looked to Margaret as if a white claw were closing around the island. Blizzards were expected in the south of England by the weekend. "Why can't they be here?" Johnny complained.

"Suppose it's like that for weeks here, Mummy? How will we live?"

Her father gave Margaret a dazzling smile. "You'd be surprised."

"I'll go into Leeds tomorrow to stock up on provisions. We've plenty of room in the freezer."

"Had enough pictures of snow?" Daddy said, and switched the television off. "They won't bring it any sooner."

Johnny thought they might, Margaret knew, though his expression only admitted that when he thought nobody was watching. As they took their places at the dining table she said "I put my old fairy-tale books in your room. They're yours now."

He thanked her and cheered up at once. "The old stories never die," Daddy said.

After dinner Johnny kept parting the curtains to look for a snowfall until even his mother lost patience with him. He was making the house feel surrounded, Margaret thought—making the night outside feel almost solid, and pregnant with snow. It reminded her of last Saturday in the forest, when she had become acutely aware of the weight of snow on the branches and afraid it would give way, burying her and Johnny and her father. No longer liking snow as much as she used to must be part of growing up.

So many unfamiliar things were. At least Ramona had been through them too: feeling lonely when you didn't expect to, and wanting to cry for no reason, and finding your brother becoming more and more of a pain. The idea that as Margaret grew up, her feelings might keep growing bigger too, dismayed her. She could talk to her mother about the way her body would soon be changing, but she didn't like to mention her feelings, because they seemed somehow disloyal to the family. And now there was something else she couldn't tell her mother—that she was afraid the snow might catch her on the way back from Leeds.

She lay in bed that night feeling helpless and childish. She was being sillier than Johnny; she'd heard what the forecast had said. When she wakened in the morning she felt as if she hadn't slept. She stumbled to the window, her feet tangled in the duvet. Towards the horizon the moors were white as if the snow were waiting there; but the whiteness was mist like a huge lingering breath. She had a quick wash and ran downstairs to watch the forecast. Snow had closed over the southern tip of England and was inching northwards across Scotland. The map showed cold suns multiplying over the rest of the country, displaying their rays like wings. They made Margaret think of angels, new lights in the sky, Christmas, though they would be gone by then. All that mattered was that the forecast showed her mother would be safe.

Except that forecasts were sometimes wrong, she thought as she walked to school. She didn't know what to say. Johnny reached the school gates and turned to wait, and Margaret blurted "Will you come and meet us?"

Her mother looked puzzled. "Why, would you rather I did?"

"Not instead of Daddy. Can't you both come?"

"We'll try. If I'm home. I'm not going to the end of the earth, love, only Leeds. Maybe I'll get your father to help carry. That way I should be quicker." Her mother kissed her and Johnny and then Margaret again. "Don't worry, this will be my last trek."

Once he and Margaret were in the schoolyard, Johnny said "Why was Mummy saying not to worry?"

"In case it's so crowded in Leeds that she isn't back in time to meet us," Margaret said, feeling as if he had stolen the reassurance she'd gained from sharing her anxiety with her mother, feeling the responsibility of being a big sister weigh her down. Johnny ran off to play with his friends, and she watched her mother becoming smaller and smaller as she walked downhill beneath a sky which was growing paler, frosting over.

Margaret had been looking forward to rehearsing the nativity play, but it wasn't as much fun as usual. She and Sarah and Rachel were people at the inn—the teacher's pet, Allie, having been chosen to play Mary despite groans of protest from all the other girls—and the children in Johnny's year were animals who came to the crib at the end. Ordinarily Margaret enjoyed remembering to speak up while she complained about the wine which Sarah had served her and which was really black currant juice, but now she couldn't even take much pleasure in watching Johnny and his friends run squeaking into the school hall. When Mrs. Hoggart asked her what was wrong, she could only say "Nothing, miss" for Johnny's sake.

At lunchtime she played with Sarah and Rachel to distract herself, but she kept thinking that the schoolyard hubbub wasn't loud enough, as if it somehow concealed a silence. The bell rang at last, sending her class back to the hall to continue rehearsals. Margaret didn't have to sing a solo in any of the carols, but until Mrs. Hoggart singled her out she thought she was losing herself in the choruses. "Try and keep up, Margaret," the teacher said. "We want your parents to be proud of you on the night, don't we?"

Margaret had the sudden terrible notion that unless she sang with all her soul she would be acting as though she didn't expect to see them again. For the rest of the afternoon she sang as if only the carols were able to delay the snow. "That was much better. You sounded like you had something to sing about," Mrs. Hoggart said.

The final bell shrilled, and Margaret ran to the classroom ahead of the rest of her class. She grabbed her lunchbox and her coat from the corridor and struggled through the crowd of children from the other classes. She hadn't yet been able to see the school gates, but at least the sky beyond the windows was clearing. "'Scuse me. 'Scuse me," she said, and dodged out of the school, into the shadow of the forest. Then she felt her heart stumble. All along the railings parents were waiting for their children, but neither of her parents was there.

At least one of them would be here by now unless something had gone wrong. She found herself wishing that she were either as young and unaware as Johnny or much older; it seemed horribly unfair that she should have to prepare him for the worst at her age. She felt as if the clear sky overhead had suddenly turned black. Children who seemed hardly present to her pushed past her towards the gates, and then she heard Johnny run into the yard.

"There's my sister," he was complaining to his friends. "I've got to go now." For a moment Margaret was certain that she would burst into tears, but she managed to stiffen her face as she turned to him. She was trying to think what to tell him when he walked straight past her.

Rage flared in her, so violently that it frightened her. She swung round, trying to restrain herself from grabbing him, because she would only hurt him and make the situation worse, if it could be worse—and then she saw why he was walking so confidently towards the gates. Daddy was coming up Church Road.

She felt dizzy with relief, and yet the sight of him wasn't quite as reassuring as she would have expected. Why wasn't Mummy with him? Margaret closed her eyes and swallowed and sidled between two prams out of the gates, and raced Johnny downhill to their father, who gave her a vague smile. "Where's Mummy?" she said as neutrally as she could.

"She'll be at the freezer. We're only just home."

That ought to have rid Margaret of her fear, but perhaps there was more to it than she'd realized, unless it was only the shadow of the forest which was making her so shivery. She held onto the jagged top of a garden wall until Johnny and her father looked back to see why she wasn't following. "Come on if you want to see your mother," Daddy said.

Margaret trudged after them, past the information center where Sally Quick had hung Mummy's paintings on the walls, alongside the dead railway and up the rough track. Though the shadow of the forest had reached the house, none of the visible windows was lit. The snow figures were glowing; mustn't that mean the kitchen light was on? She ran past the house, though the chill of the forest seemed to leap at her; ringing the doorbell and waiting would take too long. Her mother was in the kitchen, and waved to her through the window.

Margaret felt as if she had to give everyone a hug. She sprinted up the garden path and embraced Johnny, who protested "Get off," and her father, who looked bewildered. As soon as he unlocked the front door she raced to the kitchen and clasped her mother tight. "I love you too," Mummy said, and returned the hug. Margaret was tempted to blurt out her fears, but there was no need; they no longer mattered— the family was together and safe. She wasn't going to take any more notice of her imagination, of any feelings she might have about the winter. She squeezed her mother again and held onto her. "We'll never forget this Christmas, will we?" she said like a promise.

THIRTY-FIVE

As Ellen stirred the soup she remembered meeting Ben on the heights. She remembered the smell of the sunlit grass, the rounded mountains like the flanks of animals too huge to waken, bright ripples spreading leisurely behind a boat on a lake until they were almost as wide as the shore, the hush which seemed to slow down the song of a bird and set it like a jewel in the air, and it occurred to her that these were precisely the impressions she needed to convey in the last scene of the book she was rewriting. Was this how writing felt to Ben, the story either demanding to be written or struggling to take shape even when he wasn't at the desk? He'd often said it was the nearest he came to being pregnant, but it didn't feel much like pregnancy: there was nothing physical about the newness growing inside her, and perhaps that was why she felt compelled to set it down before it vanished. She called the family to dinner and ladled out the soup. "Don't say very much to me," she said. "I've an idea I want to write."

The children were almost too good. Even when Johnny forgot he was supposed to avoid distracting her, he remembered at once and put his hand over his mouth. The idea of requiring the family to be so muted just to let her work dismayed her. "I wasn't asking you to stop breathing," she said, and he nodded as if the silence had filled his mouth. The silence wasn't helping her at all, it was simply isolating the dinner table sounds until Ellen had to start a conversation herself, no easy task while Ben was sitting like silence made flesh.

As soon as dinner was over, Margaret said "Me and Johnny will help Daddy wash up."

"You get my vote," Ellen told Ben, and was rewarded with a vague smile for kissing his cold forehead. If the midnight sun idea was trying to take shape inside him, no wonder he was preoccupied. "I'll try not to be too long," she said, and went up to the workroom, composing her first sentence on the way. "It was nearly midsummer," she wrote on the sketchpad, and suddenly she didn't need to think what to write; her impressions of the day above the lakes were bringing the characters alive as if they had been starved of sunlight. Before long she was writing almost in a trance, and almost unaware of her surroundings until she had finished.

She'd heard Ben putting the children to bed. She read through what she'd written, then gazed out of the window. She thought she'd managed to convey everything she had set out to express, but the dimly luminous forest made both her achievement and herself feel suddenly insignificant, less than a spark in the darkness. Perhaps writing had exhausted her, for she was shivering. She hurried down to Ben, who was watching the weather forecast as if it were a coded message he'd forgotten how to read. "Is this any good?" she said, handing him the sketchpad.

"Of course it is." He seemed to feel it wasn't necessary for him to read her work. When he'd done so he gave her a smile whose wistfulness took her aback. "It's better than good."

"Do you remember?"

"Remember what?" Almost as soon as he saw her disappointment he said "Where you got it from, you mean? Why wouldn't I?" He leafed through the pages as if he might have missed a point, then returned the pad to her. "It's your book now."

"Ours."

"If you like. I'm glad we had the chance to write one."

"I was thinking about your Father Christmas idea. I thought his dreams could be where all the presents come from. Maybe one year someone wakens him too early and he can't get back to sleep. I don't know what happens then, but I thought we might find out together."

"If there's time."

Of course there wouldn't be before Christmas. In the morning the first cards were on the doormat—two identical puddings from Norwich, Father Christmas climbing scaffolding to reach a chimney in front of a printed message from Stan Elgin and his firm—and she began to experience the usual pre-Christmas panic. There was just a fortnight to Christmas Day, and she still had to buy cards and the food she hadn't thought worth carting home from Leeds, still had to choose last-minute presents. "I'll be organized next Christmas," she told Ben as usual, thinking that he needn't look so unconvinced. She wasn't that disorganized; at least she had thought to stock up on petrol on the way back from Leeds, filling several cans as well as the tank.

She and the children spent the morning at the market, where everyone kept saying "All the best" while their breath smoked like the chestnut stall, and staggered back laden with decorations, presents, crackers, cards. It took the family most of the afternoon to put up the decorations, especially since Johnny climbed the ladder at the flimsiest excuse, but by nightfall every downstairs room except the kitchen was crisscrossed with streamers, holly dangled from picture rails, mistletoe hung in doorways. "Is everything as it should be, do you think?" she asked Ben.

He'd seemed uninvolved, though busy, and she wondered if he was remembering his Christmases here. He turned to the children as if they knew more about the season than he did. "Have we forgotten anything?"

"A tree."

"We've a forest of them, Johnny. Go and see them whenever you like."

"I mean one we can have in the house." When his father looked as if he were about to refuse, Johnny cried "We always have one. It won't be like Christmas."

"It won't," Ben said flatly, and seemed to relent. "I don't suppose one tree will make any difference."

Ellen switched off the lights as they left the house. Above the roof the sky was so clear that she could see a sprinkling of galaxies in the black depths beyond the stars. She followed Ben and the children past the crowd of shrunken figures staking out the house until the snow came. "We won't need to go far, will we?"

"How far do you think we should?" Ben said.

Above the whitened treetops the mist glowed sullenly like clouds above a snowscape. Rank after rank of trees emerged from the dimness, forming a darkly luminous pattern which fastened on her vision. If she ventured into the secret twilight she was sure there would be more to see, but how could she even consider wandering into the forest at night with the children? One day Ben could show her the depths of the forest, but not now. "Just far enough to dig up a little tree," she said."

"No distance at all." He shrugged and stepped off the marked paths, though surely he could have chosen a shrub from the very edge of the forest. She had to keep blinking her eyes as she watched him, otherwise the trees appeared to step forwards almost imperceptibly as he passed between them. She was about to call out to ask him how much farther he meant to go when he halted. "This is for us," he announced.

He'd found a shrub not quite as tall as himself. He fell to his knees and began to dig at the roots with a trowel. "Come here," he said in a voice which seemed more breath than words, and sat back on his heels. "Everyone should have a dig."

For a moment the sight of him, a dark shape crouching among the trees with a glint of metal in its hand, seemed to Ellen to suggest a fairy tale or a childhood nightmare which it had provoked. It was just Ben waiting there, she told herself, and led the children off the path.

She took the trowel from him and poked among the scrawny roots while a cold smell of growth and decay filled the air. As she freed the roots, their spidery tendrils brushed the backs of her hands, scattering earth and fallen needles and glistening insects which scuttled into the dark. She dug halfway around the tree and passed the tool to Margaret, who probed the ground and recoiled when a root sprang up through the needles as if impatient to be free. Johnny dug like a terrier until his father stopped him. "It'll come now," Ben said.

235

Ellen trowelled the soil away from the roots as he lifted the tree, and then she stood up. Perhaps she moved too quickly, for just as the tree emerged from the soil the air seemed to darken overhead. It felt to her as if the open sky had suddenly appeared—as if the trees had been pushed apart. She wavered dizzily and glanced up, and saw the white belly of the mist lowering itself onto the treetops. She grabbed the children's hands and started away from the pit where the tree had been, only to discover she had lost the path. Ben seemed to know where he was going, and so she followed him.

She'd darkened the house so as not to be dazzled on the way back, but now she realized that the lights would have allowed her to orient herself. Still, the forest was thinning ahead of Ben, until she could distinguish beyond the trees a dark bulk which dwarfed a host of pale shapes—the house and the snow crowd. "Let's run and get everything ready," she said.

She conducted Margaret and Johnny down the track while Ben followed with measured steps, the thin silhouette of the tree craning over his shoulder and waving insect limbs behind his back. By the time he came into the house she had produced the tub and decorations from the cupboard under the stairs. He stood the tree in the tub and packed earth around the roots, and the children helped drape the branches with streamers and skeins of bulbs. Ellen switched on the bulbs and turned off the living room light, and the family sat in front of the shining tree.

For her the tree had always had a special magic, but this year the magic was darker. The lights nestling in the depths of the tree made her think of stars; the sight of them hovering in the dark seemed almost to bring the black sky down through the house and into the room. As the winter nights grew longer and colder, she thought later as she lay in bed, primitive folk must have thought the sky was coming to earth. She slept and dreamed that the stars were cold, covered with ice which kept them shining as they fell towards her, until she realized that there was no light for them to reflect and they went out, leaving her struggling to waken from the dark.

She must have dreamed that because she was waiting for the snow.

In the morning it hadn't arrived, nor the next day, nor the day after. Despite the absence of clouds, the air felt weighed down by the massing of snow, an impression which made the bright sky seem unreal. Her classes in Leeds were finished now until the new year, but at least there were plenty of seasonal preparations to keep her busy, since Ben insisted on typing the new book. In three days he transcribed exactly what she'd written, though she had been hoping he would put something of himself into it, and posted the typescript to Ember.

Waiting for the publishers to respond made her unexpectedly nervous. Perhaps she had always believed that they were bound to like Ben's tales as much as she did and that her illustrations were only a bonus, unnecessary to their success. Thank heaven for the time of year, she thought, for an evening of carol singing with Hattie Soulsby to subsidize the playgroup. Without that she would have been in danger of brooding on her nervousness, which had begun to feel so large and vague that it could hardly be explained by anxiety about the book.

Hattie brought her husband, a large shy man whose duffel coat gave him the appearance of a monk. Margaret and Johnny shared the music Stefan and Ramona were reading with the aid of a flashlight. The waits started from the town square, where frost glinted on the pavement like reflections of the stars. Half a carol brought Mr. Westminster to his front door, to clear his throat ferociously and drop several pound coins in Hattie's plastic bucket. Sally Quick had mince pies waiting for everyone. Tom, the bus driver who lived opposite, seemed abashed that he only had money to offer, and joined the procession as it climbed Church Road. Les Barns was so delighted to see him—"So that's what it takes to get you out at night, you daft bugger"—that he too joined the waits.

This was how Christmas should be, Ellen thought: the air so cold it made the dark between the streetlamps glitter, the cottages displaying trees and open fires, the community rediscovering itself. She squeezed Ben's hand, but he was gazing above the town at the cloud rooted to the earth. Terry West led "The Holly and the Ivy" in a high strong voice, and Ellen found herself thinking how many ancient customs had been taken over by Christmas: the pagan holly and mistletoe, the fairy on the tree, the tree itself, even the date, which had originally been the winter solstice, the shortest day. . . . On the way home up the track she saw the shining tree and felt as if stars had got into the house. When she opened the front door she heard the tree creak, and long shadows reached out of the living room and scuttled over the carpet. "The tree's saying hello to us," she said.

All the walking must have tired her, because she overslept on the morning of the nativity play, of all mornings. Surely Ben could have wakened her and the children before heading for the workroom. She hurried Margaret and Johnny to school and shopped on her way back. As she let herself into the house she heard Ben's voice upstairs. "She's here now," he was saying.

"Who's that?"

Silence met her, and she wondered if he had been talking to himself. She had almost reached the workroom when he responded, "It's for you. The publishers."

He was holding the receiver away from his face as if he resented its presence. "Alice Carroll?" she mouthed.

"Nobody else."

Ellen lifted the receiver from his hand and perched on one corner of the desk. "Hello, Alice."

"Ellen. Glad I could get you. Half the calls I've tried to make this morning, the lines have been down with the snow." She paused. "Do you happen to know if I've offended your husband in some way?"

"Not that he's told me," Ellen said, hoping that would make Ben look at her. He continued to gaze at the forest, so intently that his eyes appeared unfocused; he hadn't moved except to lay the hand from which she'd taken the receiver palm down on the desk, fingers splayed, so like his other hand that she could imagine the two were symmetrical. "Why do you ask?" she said.

"Just that he didn't seem interested in discussing the new book."

He didn't regard it as his, Ellen thought, but couldn't he see that even if she had written every word of it, it would be his too? "I think you may have called while he was trying to bring something else to life," she said, and suppressed the panic which made her nervous of saying "Tell me about the book."

"I was supposed to go to a party last night, but the snow put paid to that, so I read what you sent me. I thought I'd call rather than write you a letter so near Christmas. I wanted you both to know that the rewrites are exactly what the book needed. As a matter of fact, as far as the text goes, I think it may be your best book."

Ellen was dumbfounded. "I mean," the editor said, "once you've illustrated it."

"Thanks for saying so. Thank you," Ellen said, still unsure how she felt. "Have a good Christmas."

"Many of them."

Ellen said good-bye awkwardly and leaned her back against the window so as to look into Ben's eyes. "She likes the book now."

"I'm pleased for you."

"For us, Ben, us."

He grasped his chin and turning his head, met her eyes. "It'll always be us, I promise."

She had the disconcerting impression that even now his thoughts and his vision were somewhere else. She mustn't pester him if he was trying to work. "I'm here if you want me," she told him, and went downstairs, wondering why Alice Carroll's praise hadn't assuaged her nervousness. Perhaps her nerves needed time to recover.

She listened to the radio while she wrapped presents, wrote cards in response to some of the morning's mail, copied changes of address into her address book, iced the Christmas cake, made beefburgers for dinner. She had to keep searching the stations for programs of carols. Between the stations, and sometimes between the carols, the radio would fall so silent that she could imagine it was stuffed with snow. The news reports were about little else but snow: several motorways rendered impassable, towns and villages cut off, worse to come. Whenever she heard how the snow was advancing she glanced out of the window, but the sky and the horizon were clear.

Ben didn't want coffee or lunch. Surely he wouldn't disappoint the children by not going to the play. "Will you be ready in a few minutes?" she called as she reached for her coat.

"For anything," he called in a windy voice which seemed to fill the house. Almost at once he ran downstairs and grabbed her by the hand, and would have pulled her out of the house immediately if she hadn't reminded him to put on a coat. As he urged her along the path beside the allotments and sneaked through a gap in the churchyard hedge near the school, he seemed close to dancing. "Nearly there now. Not long now," he told her, so unnecessarily that she laughed, as they ran through the shadow of the forest. Given his mood, she couldn't resist asking, "Has it been a productive day?"

He smiled so widely that her own face ached in sympathy. "Wait and see."

A makeshift stage stretched across the school assembly hall, two sets of tables and chairs representing an inn beside a cardboard stable scattered with hay in front of a tall length of plywood painted with palm trees and a night sky. The plywood masked the classrooms where the performers were audibly hiding. Heads kept poking around it, searching for their parents. Margaret leaned out and flashed Ellen a smile which was trying to appear unconcerned, Johnny grinned as if his face might stay like that throughout the performance, and Ellen crossed her fingers for them. At least now she had a reason to be nervous.

By the time the play commenced, it was dark outside. Stars gleamed through the high windows behind the audience as Johnny's teacher dimmed the lights. Mrs. Hoggart struck up "Silent Night" at the piano, and the voices of the unseen children began to sing.

In the first scene Margaret acted her role of a difficult customer at the inn with such vehemence that Ellen came close to tears. She wasn't the only mother whose voice wasn't quite steady as they joined in "Once in Royal David's City." Joseph was holding his tablecloth robe so high above his ankles that he must have tripped during rehearsal. Mary rocked the baby Jesus ferociously throughout the inn scene, and at one suspenseful moment appeared to be about to drop him, though he looked as if he would bounce. The innkeeper forgot most of his lines and was prompted so loudly that his parents in the audience kept echoing the prompter. By now Ellen was suppressing both laughter and tears, and several of her neighbors on the bench were having the same problem. It was a relief when the onstage cast and the choir invisible began to sing "We Three Kings of Orien' Tar" and the parents could join in. She wondered if the heating had broken down; though the children might be too busy to notice, their breaths were faintly visible.

The kings brought in their treasures, a box piled with chains painted gold followed by two jars which Ellen suspected had contained bath salts, and then Johnny and the rest of his year scurried squeaking around the hall before subsiding somewhat reluctantly in front of the hay. Everyone sang "O Come All Ye Faithful," and the lights came up so that parents could photograph the players. As Ellen took half a dozen photographs Ben smiled oddly at her, as if he thought her actions were somehow redundant, though the pictures would bring back memories in years to come. "Be quick changing," she called after Johnny and Margaret, and rubbed her arms through her coat to keep warm.

Mrs. Venable was apologizing for the chill, which had obviously caught her and the heating unprepared, when the children began to reappear from behind the night sky. One of Johnny's friends pointed up at the windows, and a chatter of excitement multiplied as children crowded into the hall, buttoning their coats and clutching their costumes in plastic bags. "Well, that seems to be the explanation," Mrs. Venable said, following their gaze. "The snow's here at last. Don't catch cold on the way home. I'll have the heating seen to for tomorrow."

Johnny ran to his parents, squeaking "Come on" at his sister, who was chatting importantly with some of her friends. His voice was so high that it sounded as if he hadn't stopped playing the mouse. Ellen wiped away traces of the whiskers which had been drawn around his mouth, and let herself be tugged along the corridor. But the families already in the schoolyard had halted there, blocking the doorway, and the buzz of excitement had become a growing mumble of bewilderment. Frost sparkled on the concrete of the schoolyard and the bricks of the school walls, but that was all. Of the whiteness which had loomed at all the windows facing the forest, there was no sign.

THIRTY-SIX

On the way home Johnny kept protesting "It *was* snowing. I could see it."

"I thought it looked as if it was," Margaret said.

Her attempt to placate him only aggravated his frustration. "It *was*," he declared, as if repeating it and glaring at the sky would make it so. "Jim and David who are in my class saw it. Melanie Burton who took me to Mrs. Venable when I cut my leg in the playground did, and she's older than you."

"Melanie's sister is in my class, little boy, and she says Melanie's a scaredy cat who has to have a light on in her room at night or she can't sleep."

"So? Maybe you did when you were little."

"That's a really sensible answer, Johnny, a really intelligent thing to say. And just in case you're wondering, I've never had a light on when I go to sleep. It isn't me who wanders about at night when he's supposed to be asleep because he can't wait for it to snow."

"I seem to remember a toddler who nearly cried her eyes out when her china cottage with a light in it got broken," Ellen murmured.

"That was because I liked seeing the little cottage when I was going to sleep, Mummy. I was never afraid of the dark."

"I'm glad neither of you are, because it's nothing to be afraid of, so let that be the end of the argument," Ellen said. "As for the snow, Johnny, we must have been expecting it for so long that we saw it, that's all. Don't you think so, Ben?"

Ben had been gazing at the stars above the forest as he walked, watching the forest grow almost imperceptibly brighter and feeling as though he was about to understand what he was seeing, truly understand for the first time in his life. "Maybe it was a dream," he said.

Margaret raised her eyes heavenwards and sighed. "We weren't asleep."

His smile seemed to rise from deep inside him, and made his teeth ache with the cold. "Not our dream."

Johnny giggled and saw he wasn't meant to do so. "Whose was it, then?"

"What do you think would dream of snow? Maybe something that needs it to be even colder so that it can wake up."

"It's just a story, Johnny," Margaret said. "Don't be telling him stuff like that, you'll be giving him nightmares."

A surge of love for her passed through Ben like an icy wave. He felt as if he were observing the family and himself from somewhere high and cold and still. The darkness all around them was a huge insubstantial embrace whose stillness he was sharing. "Think for a moment, Johnny," he said. "What exactly did you see?"

The boy stared stubbornly at his own feet. "I told you, snow."

"What was it doing?"

"Falling, of course." Johnny looked up. "Not falling, exactly. More like it was a sort of curtain hanging there with a kind of pattern on it."

"You saw a pattern? What kind?"

Johnny closed his eyes and held onto his mother's hand to guide him along the main road. Eventually Margaret said "There wasn't a pattern, but Johnny's right, it was just standing still in the air."

"So you see, Johnny, it couldn't have been snow," Ellen said. "I expect it was frost on the windows and light reflecting off the forest. Never mind."

Ben smiled behind them in the dark. At least they had all had a glimpse of what he'd seen. The swarm of whiteness which had appeared at the windows like moths drawn to the light or to the children and their parents had been shifting stealthily, restless to settle into a pattern, to show them its face. The waiting which his life had been was almost over. His stories had kept his instincts alive until it was time for those instincts to grow clear. His aunt had been unable to destroy them, and she had been too late in selling the Sterling house to prevent it from passing to him. He could see his life, and it was irrelevant except as a thread leading here through the dark.

Now he understood the panic which had brought him racing home from promoting the book. It hadn't meant that he would never see Ellen and the children again; deep down he'd been afraid that he might not recognize them. But the change he'd sensed gathering was taking its time, though his life seemed full of signs of it—the fragments of ritual scattered through his Stargrave childhood, the midsummer day when snow had kissed his hand in the churchyard like a promise, his books which were by-products of the rediscovery of ancient truths. It would be here soon, and he mustn't be afraid. "Just as long as we're together," he sang and taking Johnny's free hand, danced with the family up the track to the house. Tomorrow would be the shortest day of the year.

THIRTY-SEVEN

Thank heaven for Christmas, Ellen thought—for the way the season had revived Ben. Now that he'd returned to the family, the old enthusiastic Ben who liked nothing better than to make her eyes and the children's light up, she could admit to herself that one reason for her nervousness had been a secret fear in case his introversion wasn't only a side effect of his work. Now she was able to laugh at herself and at him as he sketched an elaborate sign in the air with the key before unlocking the front door and flinging it wide as if he were ushering the family into somewhere much larger than a house. The tree in the living room creaked, long fingers of shadow rearranged the traces of colored light which lay on the hall carpet as though a rainbow were dying there, and all of Ellen's senses seemed to waken: she smelled the pine and listened to the whisper of falling needles, which sounded for a long moment as if it weren't contained by the room, as if the tree had brought the edge of the forest into the house, a forest as large as the dark. For a moment, as she shivered, she thought she could see her breath. "Here we are," Ben said as though he was announcing their arrival, and switched on the light in the hall.

Ellen let out a sigh, which she couldn't see after all. "That was strange. Maybe it comes of helping tell your story. I was imagining the kind of thing you must imagine sometimes. Can it be a bit unnerving until you see how it can be turned into a book?"

"A bit unnerving?" He gave her a smile so encouraging it looked manic. "However it feels, I'll be here. It can only bring us together."

"Good for it, then," Ellen called after him as he followed the children into the living room, saying, "Leave the television off, Johnny. Open up your mind to something bigger."

"I want to see what the weatherman says."

"We don't need him to tell us what's coming. Can't you feel it out there?" When Johnny darted to the curtains and peered between them, only to turn away in disappointment, his father said, "We'll have to wake your imagination up."

"Go on then."

"Let's see what we can bring alive between us. Remember the idea I had about the midnight sun? Let's each try to imagine what the sun kept dormant and tell one another over dinner."

When Ellen reached into her imagination while she grilled the burgers she'd made earlier, she found she was fixated on the cold which felt like a presence beyond the window blind, ready to invade the kitchen whenever the heat wavered. She could imagine the snow figures crowding towards the window, mounting one another until they stood outside the glass like a faceless totem pole, waiting for her to raise the blind and see them. She caught herself thinking that the blind appeared whiter than usual, as if something paler than the strips of plastic were at the window. She turned away and felt the cold like a prolonged chill breath on the nape of her neck. "Take some plates, you two," she called.

"You interrupted me while I was having inspirations," Margaret complained as Johnny marched into the kitchen, looking too preoccupied to have heard the call. Ellen finished preparing a salad and sent it through with Johnny while she followed with the burgers in their buns. "Well," Ben said at once, "what do you think was under the midnight sun?"

"You go first, Johnny," Margaret said.

"A bit of the cold that'll come when the sun goes out."

"No," Margaret said, "a bit of the cold there used to be before there were any stars."

"Maybe just a single crystal." Ben's eyes were brightening. "Where's the rest of it, do you think?"

"It went away when everything got made."

"Or it's out where there's nothing but dark," Margaret said.

Johnny bit into his burger and chewed fast. "What's it doing, then?"

Ellen felt as if the three of them were waiting for her to speak. More disconcertingly, she felt that they were waiting for her to say what they had already thought themselves, because all that she'd heard so far were ideas which had occurred fleetingly to her when she was in the kitchen. She'd taken part in plenty of brainstorming sessions while she was working in advertising, but never one in which all the participants seemed to speak with the same voice. "It's dreaming," she said.

"Of what?"

"Of us," Ellen said, and sought an answer to Ben's question which the children might find less disconcerting. "Of everyone. The midnight sun stops it from wakening, and the world is what it dreams until it does."

"Not quite. Not only that," Ben said. "It must dream of perfection, of re-creating everything in ways we can't begin to imagine."

"It's only a story, remember," Ellen told the children, "for our next book."

Ben was obviously delighted by their having shared their fancies. Throughout the meal he kept smiling as if to encourage the family to continue imagining or even to ask him some question. After dinner he followed her and the children into the kitchen and loitered, gazing at the blind as if he could see through it, while they helped her with the washing up. "How shall we pass the time now?" he said.

"Play a game," Margaret told him.

"Ludo," Johnny cried.

"That's an old word," Ben said, and brought the battered game from in the cupboard under the stairs. He seemed fascinated by the patterns the counters made on the board as the play progressed, and Ellen couldn't recall ever having seen a game bring them so frequently close to symmetry. When Johnny's eyelids began to droop she announced that the game in progress would be the last, and was taken aback when it was his father who protested. "No rush to break up the party, is there? It's going to be a long night."

"With Christmas on the other side of it, and we don't want people being too tired to enjoy that."

For a moment Ellen thought he was about to disagree, but what was there to contradict? When at last the game was over, Margaret said "I'm going up now, Johnny."

As soon as Ellen headed for the bedrooms to say good night to the children, Ben came after her. Of course he wanted to bid them good night too, yet his behavior seemed indefinably childlike; surely he wasn't trying to avoid being left by himself. She kissed Margaret and Johnny, snuggled their duvets under their chins, turned out the lights in their rooms. Ben murmured, "Get some sleep now" with an urgency he ought to realize would be counterproductive, and lingered in the dark with them until Ellen was downstairs. "Another game?" he said as he came down.

"I'd just like to sit and look at the tree for a while."

"We both will." He switched off the overhead light and sat on the edge of a chair. Shadows of branches patterned his face, reflections glinted in his eyes like shards of ice. He was gazing so intently into the depths of the tree that he made her feel as if she were over-looking something there. "Do you want to talk?" she said.

"No need."

It must be a trick of the light which caused the needles on the branches to appear identical wherever the bulbs illuminated them. The pattern drew her gaze into the unlit depths, and she felt as if the branches were reaching for her until she closed her eyes. That was more peaceful, almost enough to send her to sleep, except that whenever she began to drowse the silence lurched towards her, stopping her breath. She felt suspended between sleeping and consciousness by the silence which was displaying her heartbeat, making it seem both to be growing louder and quicker and to have detached itself from her. Then she realized that not all the soft dull sounds were her heartbeats. Some of them were at the window.

Her eyes sprang open. For a few seconds she was dazzled by the tree; then she saw Ben watching her awaken. His smile widened, glistening as if his mouth were full of ice. "It's here," he said.

Angered by the shiver which his words sent through her, she pushed herself out of her chair and stumbled to the window. She wasn't fully awake yet; she had to grope among the folds of the heavy curtains in order to locate the gap. The patting at the window sounded as impatient as she was. Chilly velvet snagged her fingernails, and then she found the opening. She parted the curtains and stuck her head between them.

The night flocked to meet her. It was snowing so heavily that the lights of the town appeared doused. Flakes almost as large as the palm of her hand sailed out of the whiteness and shattered on the window. She had never seen snowflakes so crystalline; in the instant before each of them broke and slithered down the glass, they looked like florid translucent stars. She peered past them, wiping her breaths from the window, and managed to distinguish a glimmer of the lights of Stargrave drowning in white. Beyond the town and the railway line, a mass like veils as tall as the sky was dancing on the moors. She was gazing entranced at the snow, feeling her breaths becoming slower and more regular as the colorless onrush appeared to do so, when a dim figure rose out of the snow and came towards her.

It was Ben's reflection. His face was a featureless pale mask which seemed to be trying to swarm into a new shape. She turned to him so as to dispel the illusion, and found he was closer to her than she'd realized. His eyes and his smile looked illuminated by the snow. "Shall we get them?" he said.

"What?"

"You mean who."

"It can wait until the morning, Ben, surely. If we wake them now they'll never go back to sleep."

"Maybe they're still awake. At least we can go and see."

As soon as she let the curtains drop, he padded through the

shadows which rooted the tree to the floor. She caught up with him on the stairs, but the snow was ahead of them, thumping softly and insistently at the windows of the children's unlit rooms. The breathing beyond the ajar doors told her that Margaret and Johnny were asleep. "They can have a surprise tomorrow," she whispered.

"That's true," he said with an odd shaky smile. "Let's go and watch."

When he ran upstairs she made to quiet him, but he must be tiptoeing. Apart from the sounds at all the windows, the house seemed hushed as a snowscape; even her own footfalls sounded muffled to her, and she felt as if she were in a dream. She joined Ben as he opened the workroom door.

The night was beyond it, swooping luminously towards the house. When he took her hand and led her to the window, Ellen felt as if she were walking into darkness much larger than the room. The snow must be rushing down from the moors above Stargrave, but it looked as if it were rising from the forest in a ceaseless wave and homing in on the house. She was hardly aware that her hands were grasping the far edge of the desk so as to have something to hold onto. There were so many patterns in the air that she felt dizzy, almost disembodied—so many patterns moving in so many different directions that they seemed to be taking the world apart before her eyes. The whiteness streamed out of the forest like the seeds of an unimaginable growth; the sky seemed to sink towards her, an endlessly prolonged fall. She felt as though everything, herself included, were slowing down. Stars of ice exploded on the windows, and she thought that soon she might be able to distinguish the shapes of the flakes in the air.

She was distantly aware of her breathing and of Ben, resting his chin on her shoulder as if she had acquired a second head. When he commenced stroking her, his hands moving down her body with exquisite slowness, those sensations felt distant too. She thought he was describing patterns on her skin, patterns which seemed part of the dance of the snow; he might almost have been using her body to sketch what he was seeing. As his fingertips moved down her thighs she opened like a flower. Her flesh had never felt so elaborate, so capable of growing unfamiliar.

She wanted to reach for his hand and lead him to their bedroom, but the flood of snow was blotting out her thoughts, and she couldn't let go of the desk. She pressed her spine against him as he lifted her skirt and slipped her panties down. When they fell to her ankles, her distant feet moved automatically to kick away the garment, and then his penis reared up into her.

It was so cold that she gasped and began to shiver uncontrollably with shock or pleasure or the all-embracing chill. Patterns surged out of the night, his fingers roamed intricately over her as he rose higher and higher within her, waves of shivering spread to the limits of her body and seemed to pass beyond them. When he came, it felt like ice blossoming. She pressed her lips together for fear that the cry she was battling to suppress would bring Margaret and Johnny to see what the matter was.

Her shivering abated somewhat as he dwindled gradually within her. Her skin was tingling so much it felt unstable as a bubble, and her legs continued to shake. When she closed her eyes and leaned back against him, the onrush of patterns lingered on her eyes. "Let's go to bed. I'm cold," she said.

"Yes, that's enough for now." He took hold of her so firmly that she felt safe in keeping her eyes closed as he guided her away from the window. "It's going to be colder," he said.

THIRTY-EIGHT

At first Ellen knew only that she couldn't move. The weight which had gathered on her torso was so massive that it was forcing her arms and legs wider, as if her limbs were straining to become symmetrical. She felt as though she were turning into a sign—of what, she didn't know. In a moment she realized that the mound which was weighing her down was herself.

If she was pregnant, so was everything around her. Stargrave and the trees and crags and moors were swollen with a new life which was taking shape in utter silence, the silence of the life it was supplanting. If she succeeded in moving or even in making a sound, might that at least slow down the change?

She became aware that Ben and the children were somewhere close to her, though she couldn't hear them breathing. She had to rouse them. She drew a breath which shuddered through her, and the convulsion of her body went some way towards releasing her from her paralysis. She was able to raise her head shakily, despite the burden which was sprouting from her face.

It took her some time to see that the white glow was emanating not only from her surroundings and from the sun in the black sky but also from herself. Then her dazzled eyes adjusted, or reverted to a state sufficiently familiar to let her see with them, and if the sight which met them couldn't make her cry out, nothing could: the sight of Ben and the children and herself.

Though the cry stuck in her throat, it wakened her. She was lying in bed, arms and legs splayed, a mound which must be of the quilt looming over her. There were no sounds at the window; the silence seemed as profound as it had been in her dream. Despite the stillness or because of it, she felt as if something immense were surrounding the house. "What is it?" she wanted to know.

She wasn't aware of speaking aloud, but Ben answered from beside her, sounding fully awake. "The last day," he said.

His response made so little sense to her except in terms of her dream that she felt as if she hadn't wakened after all. Now that she knew he was there she wasn't afraid to go back to sleep, so long as the dream wasn't waiting. Sleep claimed her almost at once, and then there was only stillness until Johnny and sunlight came into the room. "It's snowed lots," he said excitedly. "Come and look."

"I know it has, Johnny. Just let me wake up." She was trying to decide to her own satisfaction what had happened last night. She and Ben had made love in front of an uncurtained window and a blizzard; no wonder she'd felt so cold and so odd. She heard Ben on the floor below, telling Margaret to come to her bedroom window. It was a day for the family to be together, Ellen thought, not for her to muse in bed. "Let's see what the night's brought," she said, and Johnny ran the curtains back.

For a moment she could see only whiteness beneath the sky, and she felt as if she were back in her dream. Then she saw the simplified outlines of the moors, barely distinguishable beneath the frozen sea of white which stretched to a parade of clouds at the horizon, clouds which looked as if the snow were beginning to ornament itself and reach for the blue sky. To Ellen the landscape appeared incomplete, waiting for its details to be filled in. If it seemed somehow ominous, that was the fault of her dream, and she mustn't spoil the day for the children. "Looks like a good start to the holidays," she said, and chased Johnny down to the bathroom.

She was in the shower, having ensured that Johnny didn't just pretend to wash his face and brush his teeth because of his eagerness to play, when she heard his voice through the downpour. "Pardon?" she called.

This time Margaret shouted it with him. "We're going to have a snowfight."

For no reason she could bring to mind, Ellen was suddenly nervous. She turned off the shower and pushed back the clinging plastic curtain. "How deep is it out there? Better not go too near the woods."

"They can't do any harm. I'll be seeing they don't go far," Ben said outside the door. "They may as well make the most of the day."

She heard the children racing downstairs and Ben's tread following them. She stepped dripping out of the bath, fumbled with the slippery doorknob and hurried onto the landing, towelling herself to keep warm. "Ben, come here a minute."

He looked up over his shoulder, then his body turned towards her. Below him in the hall the children were stuffing themselves into their anoraks. He put his finger to his lips as they ran to the front door and slammed it behind them. "Thought of something?" he said.

"Did you talk to me during the night, or did I dream it?"

"Depends what you think you heard."

"Something about the last day."

"Sounds more like a vision than a dream if you heard a voice saying that. Maybe painting and taking my story over have opened up your mind."

All this seemed so irrelevant it only made her more nervous. "But was it you I heard?"

"Would you like it to be?"

She lost patience with him. "I thought you were going to keep an eye on the children."

"I won't leave them alone." His expression flickered as he turned away. "Don't let's drift apart now," he said, and strode out of the house.

She heard his footsteps engulfed by snow as he pulled the door shut, and then the children shrieked. She would have smiled, imagining him pelting them with snow, except that she was trying to

255

determine what expression she'd glimpsed on his face. Really, it was unfair of him to talk about drifting apart as if she should blame herself; he was the one who was playing word games. Still, she could be joining in the fun instead of brooding. She pulled on a sweater and jeans and ran down to find her boots in the cupboard under the stairs.

She was shrugging on her anorak as she dragged the front door open and stepped outside. "Where are you?" she called.

Beyond the doorstep, the snow was up to her ankles. She could see how the children had had to pull their feet out of their footprints, whose outlines were crumbling. Quite a few of the prints had been trodden down by their father. Except for their trail, the snow was as unbroken as the silence between the squeaks of snow crushed under Ellen's boots. Ben and the children must be lying in wait for her, she thought, and prepared to dodge as she followed the trail around the outside of the garden wall, up the track towards the crowd of white figures which had grown fatter and more featureless overnight. The figures moved apart as she approached, and just as she passed the corner of the garden, snow flew at her. She ducked, more out of nervousness than to avoid the snowballs, and scooped up a handful to shy at the children as they dashed away from crouching behind the wall. "Don't hide from me, all right?" she said.

She meant that for Ben too, and when he rose from among the swollen figures she flung as much snow as she could pick up in one hand at him. He seemed content to watch while she and the children played; even when the children scored hits on him he responded only with a smile so untroubled it looked secretive. Before long Ellen's feet began to ache with cold. "You play with the children for a while, Ben," she said. "I'm going to make something to warm us all up."

She sat on the stairs and pulled off her boots, one of which proved to be leaking. She changed her sodden sock and made for the kitchen. She was expecting to see Ben and the children outside the window when she raised the blind, but they were under the trees. The forest crouched over them, a mass of white poised to draw them into its bony depths, where the tree trunks appeared to shift as whiteness glimmered between them. Ben and the children were each rolling a snowball towards the house, and she turned from the window, telling herself not to be so ridiculously nervous.

When she went to the window to announce breakfast she saw that Ben had piled up the three giant snowballs like a totem pole. He'd rolled the largest against a group of the smaller figures so that they propped up the construction, and Ellen thought they looked as though they were worshipping it. "It hasn't got a face," Johnny said to his father.

"It will have," Ben said. "I think we're being summoned."

Ellen enjoyed the sight of color returning to the children's faces while she ate breakfast. "Will you play with us again after?" Johnny asked her.

"I'd like to get some new boots first. Did I just make a joke?"

Ben looked mysteriously amused again, and oddly wistful. He reached across the table and laid his icy hand on her wrist. "I was thinking how trivia becomes part of us all and how easy it should be to slough it off."

"Is anyone coming with me while the others wash the dishes?"

"Me," the children chorused.

"I don't mind. You won't be going anywhere," Ben said.

She shooed the children to the bathroom, and was ready with anoraks and scarves and gloves and a deaf ear to protests when they ran downstairs. From the front doorstep she saw Ben at the sink, the snow figure towering over him. "Shall I bring you anything back?" she called.

He raised his head but didn't turn it. "Only what you have to."

The white silence seemed to mute the slam of the front door. A bird flew away across the moors, its song chipping at the stillness, and then there was only the frustrated revving of a car engine somewhere in Stargrave. "What did he mean?" Margaret said.

"Ourselves, I suppose."

"Why is he being like that?"

"Because he's a writer, sweetheart. He gets on my nerves sometimes too. He wasn't saying he didn't want us. I'm sure he meant anything but."

"I think he's all right," Johnny said, and Ellen didn't know if he was expressing loyalty or reassurance or a hope. "Race you to the road," he said, nudging Margaret, and skidded away down the track.

"Mind you don't twist your ankles," Ellen called after them, and trudged in pursuit, slowed down by her climbing boots. As she led the children along the muffled dazzling road towards the hushed town, the hard surface under the snow cracked, sinking her heel into a frozen puddle. She imagined the whole of the road being as precarious, undermined by the cold, ready to give way. She was beginning to wish she had left the children with Ben; she might have made more headway on her own. Because the snow was silencing their footsteps, she had to keep glancing back to confirm they were behind her, a tic which only aggravated her reawakened nervousness.

It took her a quarter of an hour, more than twice as long as usual, to reach the first pavement. All the houses were top-heavy with snow. Despite the screech of spades on flagstones as shopkeepers cleared snow from in front of their premises, the town seemed laden with silence. Above the streets full of parked cars sheeted with snow, Ellen heard children playing on the common, their distant voices thin as birdcalls. From the foot of Church Road she saw them, tiny figures dressed in bright colors which kept being obscured by explosions of white. The forest reared above them like a wave about to break, but why should that make her uneasy? "Come on, let's get your poor old aging mother something to keep off the shivers," she said.

She was sitting on the only chair the cluttered shop in the station building was able to accommodate, and pulling on wellingtons which tied at the knees, when Sally Quick found her. "For once we could use a few more walkie-talkies," Sally said.

"Surely there can't be anyone out on the moors in this."

"Only the farmers, I hope. I was meaning the phones. The lines must be down somewhere with the snow. We can't even phone across town at the moment. Don't say you were expecting your publishers to call."

That wasn't why Ellen had experienced a twinge of panic. She must be thinking of her parents: if communications weren't restored, she and the family wouldn't be able to call them on Christmas Day as usual. "Can anything be done?"

"We'll have to wait for Leeds to fix it, though heaven knows what they can do in this. When Eric from the dairy went to fetch his load this morning he couldn't get more than a few hundred yards past the bridge. The snow was over his wheels out there. We're going to be living off whatever's in our shops and houses until conditions improve."

"I may have something surplus in the freezer if anyone gets desperate."

"Let's hope things don't come to that, but bless you for offering." She picked up Ellen's old boots and followed her to the counter with them. "It'll take more than a bit of snow to spoil Christmas in Stargrave, and I can see it's making Christmas for the kids."

As Ellen came out of the station she heard the children on the common, their cries so tiny they sounded in danger of being wiped out by the silence, but all she could see beyond the roofs was the forest poised above the town. Around her, as her ankles began to ache with the chill of the snow in which she was standing, everyone looked unconcerned: people were depleting the food shops and even the video library, but otherwise the snow seemed hardly to have affected the town. Not yet, she thought, and told herself to stop being so gloomy: was she going to be the only member of the family not to enjoy the season to the full? She was picking her way across the icy ruts on the road when Kate West emerged from the computer shop. "Cheer up, Ellen," she called. "It may never happen."

Ellen gave her an embarrassed smile. "I don't even know what it is."

"If you're wondering how to keep these two occupied you know they're always welcome. I've just bought a new computer game for when boredom sets in. You and I are lucky to have children who are readers and can make their own entertainment, but I suppose even they'll feel robbed."

"Of what?"

"I take it nobody watches daytime television in your house."

"Not as a rule."

"You'll see nothing but snow if you do—interference, I mean. And the radio seems to have lost its voice as well."

Johnny was watching his toes burrowing in a pile of cleared snow. "Kate, when can we come and play with the new game?"

"Now, if you like," Kate said, winking at Ellen to forestall any rebuke. "We ought to make sure it's popular before the shop shuts for Christmas. I'll have them until whenever you want to collect them after lunch, Ellen."

"You're a life saver, Kate. Stefan and Ramona must come for lunch soon. Both of you be good until your father or I come for you," Ellen said.

No sooner had she tramped past the shops than she was met by a silence which seemed to extend to the edge of the world. The children on the common were building snow images now. The shadow of the forest crept towards them as the shrouded treetops reached for the low sun. She marched up the track, retracing the trail of her footprints, and let herself into the house.

After the glare of the snow, the hall was as dark as the forest must be. She heard the tree creak, and then light streamed down from the top of the house. Ben had opened the workroom door. "Only me," she announced.

Wood creaked above her, disorienting her until she realized he was leaning on the banister. "Where are they?" he demanded.

"At Kate's. I thought we might like to be on our own for a while."

"How long for?"

"They're having lunch there," Ellen said, trying to blink her eyes clear. Of course it was the stairwell that made his voice sound as large as a wind. "Come down. Whatever it is, you can tell me."

"Whatever what is?"

"Whatever's been making you so secretive lately."

She waited, but he didn't stir. She couldn't tell if he was arrested by her words or if his thoughts were somewhere else, but he seemed unlikely to come to her, and so she started up the stairs. "I don't know why, Ben, but it's making me nervous."

"I was too. It won't be for long now, I promise."

She felt as though she were dreaming the conversation, it was so difficult to grasp and so isolated by the silence. She didn't speak again until she was on the stairs leading to the top floor. "What won't?"

"Ellen . . ." It sounded like a plea. He clenched his fists, and she saw him shudder from head to foot. She was running to hold him when he swung towards her, his face blank. "If you need me to talk, I will when the children are here. Better collect them before it's dark," he said, and went into the workroom, closing the door behind him.

THIRTY-NINE

"Better collect them before it's dark . . ." He couldn't have meant anything by that, Ellen told herself, yet it had left her feeling more on edge than ever. She felt as if he'd trapped her in the dimness with her doubts, and she might have pursued him into the workroom if she hadn't been overcome by a fit of shivering as she noticed how cold the house was. Ben must have let the central heating lapse. Breathing hard into her clasped hands, she ran down to the kitchen.

The timer on the boiler had switched off the heating shortly after breakfast. Had he been too preoccupied to turn it on again, or could he have gone out of the house? She thought he might have been molding a face on the snow giant beyond the window, except that the marks on the spherical head didn't add up to anything she would have called a face; she wasn't sure what the pattern, which appeared to have emerged from the way the ball of snow was formed, reminded her of. She spun the wheel to override the timer and listened to the twangs of metal as heat coursed through the house. She stood by the boiler until she felt unfrozen enough to move away, then she went into the living room.

The tree was dark. She switched on the bulbs and tried the television. The transmitter must be snowbound; the screen showed an endless fall of white. She was hoping Kate had been mistaken about the radio, but all it emitted was a stream of static which sounded constantly about to shape itself into a voice. She gave up and sat listening to the silence and her thoughts.

At least now she felt certain that she knew why she was on edge, and perhaps she could persuade herself that she had no reason to be: whatever Ben's secret was, it surely couldn't be anything bad if he insisted on telling the children at the same time he told her—but why must he be secretive at all? She had only to ask him, except that might spoil the surprise; she was almost sure that underlying his mysteriousness was a boyish eagerness to astonish. In that case, why was she still nervous? Her thoughts and feelings chased one another until she had to close her eyes and rest her head on the upholstery of the chair. She didn't know what made her open her eyes and glance past the tree to the doorway.

Ben was watching her from the foot of the stairs. She couldn't see his face for the dazzle of the tree, only a pale blur. "I didn't mean to wake you," he said at once. "I was just seeing where you were. You sleep while you have the chance. I can get the children."

"I wasn't sleeping, just resting my eyes," Ellen said, but he was already retreating upstairs. "You needn't leave me alone unless you want to. We can always talk."

He faltered and then came to her, so slowly that he reminded her of a child trying to frame an excuse. "We don't have to," she said, almost laughing at his reluctance but not quite able to do so. "We can do whatever you want to do."

"Nothing much we can do now except wait."

He walked past her and stood at the window, gazing towards the blanched town. His face was so expressionless that she thought he was hiding impatience. "Let them have a few hours with their friends," she said.

He stretched out his arms and pressed his hands against the panes. "They may as well."

What on earth was there in his response to make her shiver? Just one reassurance, she promised herself. "It's going to be a pleasant surprise, isn't it?" she said.

"What is?"

"Whatever you're keeping from us."

"Keeping from you . . ." he said oddly, and pushed himself away from the windows. The patterns which his hands had left there shrank and faded from the glass. They didn't much resemble the marks of hands, but she was concentrating on his face, which looked pleading. "Trust me," he said.

"I do, Ben, you know that." Surely he meant it as an affirmative response to her question; what else could he mean? All the same, she was shivering. "I'm cold," she said.

"It's the shadow of the forest. It's reached the house."

The explanation wasn't especially comforting. His sitting with her and holding her would have been, but she oughtn't to have to ask. "I'm going up," he said.

"To do what, Ben? What's keeping you up there?"

He halted in the doorway with his back to her. He was so still, and paused for so long before he spoke, that she held her breath. At last he said "How did telling that story feel to you?"

"Our book?" Presumably his question had been an answer of sorts, or a stage on the way to one. "Like remembering things I'd forgotten I knew. Like letting the story use me to tell itself."

"That's it. The children will be fine with us to guide them." He paused again as he set foot on the stairs. "Be sure to let me know if you're going out."

"Why do you ask that?"

"So I won't need to start wondering who's in the house."

His demand had angered her, but she couldn't sustain anger in the face of his response; it was just another feeling to add to her confusion. She listened to his footsteps climbing the silence, the occasional muffled creak of a stair, the distant thud of the workroom door, the isolated sound of her own sigh. If he was going to play the solitary artist, so could she. She shoved herself out of her chair and sprinting to the top floor, pushed the workroom door open. "I'm just getting my sketchpad."

Ben was at the desk. Beyond him a sun like a mirror of ice was lowering itself through the white sky towards the forest. His hands were upturned on the desk as if they were reaching for something he saw, unless he was gazing at them. In the pale light they looked drained of color. "Work in here if you like," he said.

Even though the skylight under which her drawing board stood had acquired a thick lid of snow, she would have stayed if there had been so much as a hint of invitation in his voice, but she felt he was barely aware of her. He seemed more interested in the white blur which was hovering above the forest and which, she told herself, couldn't possibly be the reflection of his face. "There's more room downstairs. I'll make lunch soon," she said.

"Not for me."

"Dieting to get ready for Christmas?"

He didn't answer. The room felt as though it was filling with a stillness which she lacked the energy to break. She grabbed her sketchpad and some pencils and retreated to the dining room, where she switched on the chandelier above the table and sat facing the window. The shadow of the forest was oozing down through Stargrave; some of the windows on Church Road were already lit, and the covering of snow had begun to shine dully in the gloom. She flipped the pad open at the first unmarked sheet and picked up a pencil without knowing what she meant to draw. It seemed not to matter so long as she marked the snowy blankness of the page.

Perhaps she could draw an image which would help bring Ben's story alive. She drew a disc a third of the way down the page to represent the midnight sun, taking her time to describe as nearly perfect a circle as she could, then she sketched a forest of pines and spruce low on the page. The picture didn't amount to much as far as she could see, and so she began to raise trees above and behind the first trees, drawing the branches in increasingly intricate detail, until they looked more like shapes of frost than trees and then, as she elaborated the next rank, like neither. She found the image disconcerting, and its appearance when she hadn't realized it was in her mind was more so. She turned over the page, having thought of a new subject: the crystal from before the beginning of time.

Of course it was Ben's idea, not hers, and she found that she didn't know how to give it life. She let the point of the pencil rest on the center of the page, until the very blankness of her mind seemed to start it moving. It drew a minute line and crossed it with another, then divided the angles between them and separated the end of each line into halves which flowered like frost, then it returned to the center and divided the angles again . . . Long before it finished she lost count of the number of tiny precise movements it described, but when at last it faltered she saw that she'd drawn a crystal or a symbol of one, a shape so small and pale it was well-nigh invisible yet so complex it hinted at patterns beyond imagining. She gazed at it until she thought she understood how it might grow, and then she recommenced drawing.

She didn't know how long it took. At first she kept glancing at the window as the shadow of the forest seemed to loom at it, until she grew engrossed in her task. The more she drew, the more she felt that the pattern was already there before her, waiting to be deciphered. The shape of the page frustrated her, but what else could she use? She felt as if she would be unable to let go of the pencil until every inch of the paper was taken up. At last she finished, and put one hand over her aching eyes for a good few minutes before she examined her work.

It was exquisitely detailed and yet by no means clear. All the lines were as faint as her first drawing of the crystal. The pattern made her think of ripples frozen in the instant they reached out of sight, but what kind of ripples, in what medium? It made her think of the center of a spider's web so wide it might be infinite. She gazed into it, trying to grasp what it should mean to her, until she had to squeeze her eyes shut to rid herself of a sense that it had fastened on her vision. It was behind her eyelids too. She turned her eyes towards the window in the hope that doing so would clear them, and realized with a start how long she had been at the table. Outside it was nearly dark.

Was Ben collecting the children from Kate's? Could Ellen have been so engrossed that he'd left the house without her noticing? She stood up quickly, almost tripping herself with the legs of the chair, and ran into the hall. "Ben, are you up there?"

There was silence, but it didn't feel as though she was alone in the house. "Are you still there, Ben?"

She was lifting her coat from the post at the foot of the banisters when the floor at the top of the house creaked, and she heard his voice. It sounded distant, and either she misheard his words or he meant them as a joke, but at least she knew where he was. "Are you coming with me to fetch the children?" she called.

"You'll come straight back, won't you?"

"I expect so."

"Then I'll wait here."

Perhaps he'd fallen asleep at the desk; he seemed to be struggling to control his voice. "Will you be all right by yourself until we get back?" she shouted.

"I'll make sure I am."

He sounded more determined; his voice was larger and stronger. "We won't be long," she promised. She wriggled her hands through the sleeves of her coat and zipped it up as she opened the front door. She took one step into the twilight, and her teeth began to chatter.

FORTY

Except for the misty blur above the trees, the sky was clear. The night was closing around Stargrave, darkness spreading over the horizon beyond the railway to meet the shadow of the forest. Both of the lonely farmhouses she could see on the moors were lit. Their yellow windows were brighter and steadier than the star which flickered in the depths of the rising night, but it was the darkness which Ellen felt coming into its own—the darkness, and the lurid glow of the snowscape, and above all the cold. The temperature must have fallen several degrees since she had last been out of the house. She felt as if a claw of ice had seized her face. She thrust her hands into her gloves and hurried down to the main road, stumbling over footprints.

By the time she reached the shops, the cold was close to overcoming her ability to think. Each breath stung her nostrils, each step struck chill through her boots. The snow on the pavements was trodden down, and walking was treacherous with frozen slush. Most of the shops were open, their windows gray with condensation, but they had few customers. A family with a terrier on a leash crossed the square, their footfalls sounding compressed, their heads hanging low as if they'd been defeated by the cold. "Watch you don't fall," the woman with the terrier said, and Ellen saw that they were only attending to their steps.

As she turned along Hill Lane, she faltered. The mass of white above the streets—the common and the forest which was almost indistinguishable from it except for the hinted shapes of trees—was glowing. It put her in mind of an enormous crumpled page which was illuminated from within, and it appeared not to be entirely blank: she thought she saw patterns extending from the dimness beneath the trees onto the edge of the common. She made herself concentrate on the street she was climbing. Poring over her drawing must have affected her eyes, but she had to ignore that for the children's sake.

Soon she couldn't see beyond the town for the streetlamps, which seemed to huddle together as they approached the common. Nearly all the houses had at least one downstairs window lit. Their illumination shone through curtains and Christmas wreaths and lay on the pavement or in gardens, exhibiting snow. A door opened ahead of Ellen, and a woman hurried across the street to deliver a saucepan covered with a steaming cloth to an aging neighbor. "Don't leave it open, we'll catch our deaths," a man protested as the woman dashed back into her house. The door slammed, and then the street was deserted apart from Ellen and several figures poking their white heads over garden walls.

By the time she reached Kate's and Terry's house her face felt like a frozen mask. As she stepped onto the short path, the roses on the trellis over the gate shed snow on her. She heard Johnny and Margaret laughing as she picked her way along the icy path beside a snowman surrounded by footprints. She dragged one hand out of her pocket and prodded the doorbell, and Kate ran to let her in. "You look as if you could do with something to warm you up."

"Don't open any Christmas spirit just for me."

"Christmas has already started in our house." Kate led her into the main room, where symmetrical angels had been unfolded and hung from the cornice, and slid the double doors open to the dining room. "Scotch is the answer to this kind of weather."

"I'm glad something is."

"Don't go imagining this is the kind of winter you've got to look forward to for the rest of your life. It can be cold here, but it's never been like this."

Ellen's face and ungloved hands were already aching with warmth. Kate poured out single malts and clinked glasses with her. "Here's to coping with the winter. We always have."

"How's Terry managing with the van?"

"With the van, not at all. He's been out all day with one of Elgin's wheelbarrows, delivering books to the old folk. You can't keep a good librarian down."

"Here's to him."

"And to whatever keeps us all going. Children, and people in general. And pictures and stories that need you and Ben to put them on paper." Kate squinted at their empty glasses. "Well, that saw that off. Better have one for the road, or not for the road if you want to stay longer."

She was heading for the cabinet when the doorbell rang. "Would you see who that is, Ellen? It must be important if they're out on a night like this."

Was it Ben? Perhaps a drink or two would help him relax. Ellen opened the front door, hoping to see him. But it was Terry, about to prod the button again with the key which his gloved fist had proved too cumbersome to wield. "Another minute out there and you'd have had to defrost me in the microwave," he said, shouldering the door closed. "How are your pipes?"

"Pretty healthy as far as I'm aware. How about yours?"

"I don't mean your innards, I mean at your house." He fumbled his gloves off and winced as he wriggled his fingers. "I met Stan Elgin by the church, Kate. Some of the houses on the top road are already frozen up. He's going round to tell folk to keep their heating on overnight. I said I'd tell our street once I get warm."

"I'll do it if you like, love. You've been out enough."

"I'd much rather you stayed in, at least until we see how tomorrow is. And Ellen, if I were you I wouldn't wait much longer before you take the children home, unless you're planning to stay over, which you're certainly welcome to do. Right, Kate?"

"Any time."

"It wasn't that bad when I came," Ellen said.

Terry clasped his hands together and raised a glass of the malt to his lips. "I'd say the temperature has dropped several degrees in the last half hour."

Ellen downed her scotch and went to the foot of the stairs. "Say good-bye, you two. Time we were going."

She was sorting out their boots from the chaos under the stairs when all four children stampeded down. Margaret was glittering like a fairy on a tree. "Look, Mummy, Ramona says I can have her party dress now it doesn't fit her."

"You're lucky to have such a good friend. Better not wear it on the way home. You can dazzle your father with it when we're safely shut in."

Margaret ran upstairs in a whirl of spangles which reminded Ellen of snow dancing in the wind, and Kate went to the kitchen to fetch a bag for the dress. Stefan and Ramona were playing pat-a-cake, clapping at each other's hands in a pattern so complicated they lost the rhythm and collapsed with laughter. "You try it, Johnny," Stefan said, and when they'd had enough: "I'm sorry I forgot to sort out my monster cards for you. I'll give you all the spares next time, cross my heart and hope to die."

Kate reappeared as Margaret came downstairs, and folded up the dress for her before slipping it into the bag. "Ellen, if you want to borrow any extra clothes to keep the cold off you and the children, just say."

"We'll survive, don't worry. You look after yourselves," Ellen said. Once the children were as insulated as she could make them she urged them out onto the path. "I'll be in touch," she told the Wests, smiling at the sight of the four of them crammed together in the hall, and shut the door quickly to keep in the warmth.

Even before the strip of light on which she was standing vanished, Ellen felt the night close in. It felt as if there were nothing behind her but darkness and a cold so profound that the air itself seemed to ache. "Off we go, Sherpa Peg and Sherpa Johnny," she said.

Margaret stayed close as Ellen skidded downhill, one hand poised to support herself on the encrusted garden walls. Johnny would have skated down to Market Street if Ellen hadn't stopped him; though there was no traffic, she preferred to keep him with her in the dark. Eventually they reached the level road, where marble replicas of cars were parked beneath the streetlamps. More of the shops were closed, their decorations gleaming from the unlit interiors as though frost were developing on them, and the windows of the few lit shops were opaque with trapped breaths. The only sign of life was the confusion of footprints preserved by ice on the pavements. As Ellen led the way into the road, Johnny began to sing:

"Snow in your ears

And snow up your nose,

Snow in your eyes

And snow for your toes . . ."

"Shut up, Johnny, I'm cold enough as it is," Margaret complained. "What sort of stupid song is that?"

"About a snowman. It just came into my head."

"We'd never have known."

"Don't you listen to her, Johnny. I expect she's wishing she'd made it up herself." Nevertheless Ellen was glad that he'd fallen silent, whether from pique or because he'd run out of ideas; the song had reminded her of the snowmen she'd passed on the way down the hill. She'd been too busy keeping her footing to spare them more than a glance, but she had the impression that there had been something odd about their rudimentary faces—as if, she thought now, they had all been sketches of the same image, trying to make it look more like a face. "What do you want to sing, Margaret?" she said to quiet her nonsensical thoughts.

"I don't feel like it. I'm too cold."

"What's your favorite carol?"

"'Silent Night,' I suppose."

"Mine too," Ellen said, and began to sing it, raising her voice to encourage the children to participate. Johnny did so halfway through the first chorus, and Margaret picked up the next line. By then, however, Ellen was finding phrases in the carol uncomfortably appropriate. It was increasing her awareness of her surroundings, of the calm which didn't seem as holy as she would have liked, the brightness where the snow reflected the glare of the lamps leading into the outer darkness, the sense of being surrounded by sleep as if she and the children were part of a dream. If their singing had brought someone out of a house or even to a window she would have felt less isolated, but every door stayed closed, and not a curtain moved. Once she thought she heard a fourth voice joining in, but surely it was an echo; it sounded too close to be inside a house—too close for her to be unable to see where it was coming from. Perhaps it was Stan Elgin, though if he was nearby she wondered why she hadn't heard him going from door to door.

The carol took the family as far as the last streetlamp. They were singing "Slee-eep in heavenly peace" as they left the light behind. To their left the snowbound landscape stretched to the edge of the silenced world, to their right it swept upwards to the vast snowy efflorescence which was the forest, up further to the icebergs of the crags. The sky was black except for the random patterns of stars—so black that she could imagine that the stars were flickering because the dark was overtaking them. She felt the heat draining out of her body into the sky and the landscape.

As they trudged past the outlying cottages, Margaret broke into song. Ordinarily "The Holly and the Ivy" would have been a good choice for a walking song, Ellen thought, but just now she would have preferred not to be reminded how the song took ancient traditions and tried to disguise them as Christian, traditions whose age was no more than a moment of the ancient darkness overhead. Besides, not only did the carol emphasize the stillness rather than relieving it, but Ellen's impression that there were more than three voices had returned. She blamed her imagination until Margaret's singing faltered and the girl began to peer at the swollen hedges which glowed like a moon in a cloud on both sides of the road. Didn't her behavior suggest what the icy whisper must be? "It's just wind in the hedges," Ellen said.

"I thought there were birds moving about in there," Johnny said.

When had she last seen birds around Stargrave? But she couldn't feel a wind either. Presumably she was too cold. She stumbled past another cottage and began to sing:

"God rest ye merry gentlemen,
Let nothing you dismay.
Remember Christ our savior
Was born on Christmas Day . . ."

Of course, she thought, the echo was under the railway bridge, even if it seemed to be behind them and around them, more like a stealthy chorus, a whispering which seemed enormous and yet on the edge of inaudibility. It must be the bridge which turned the echo of her last words into a sound like muffled icy laughter. She peered along the road at the lightless mouth and the hint of whiteness at the far end of the tunnel, and looked away quickly. Her eyes were misbehaving again; the whiteness had appeared to lurch forwards into the tunnel. "Nearly there now," she said firmly, and stepped off the road onto the track past the lit and curtained cottage. Then she sucked in a breath to suppress whatever comment she might have blurted out. As far as she could see, their house was dark.

"It looks as if your father's gone out looking for us," she said. She fumbled in her pocket and managed to extract her keys without dropping them as she picked her way along the track. She would feel better once she was home, she promised herself. She could only assume it was the way her vision was struggling to grasp the obscured shape of the forest which had caused the patterns to reappear in the snow, stretching across the common and up to the ridge. She hurried the children towards the house, gripping the key to the front door so hard between her finger and thumb that she could feel the chill of the metal through her glove. But she hadn't reached the front step when the door of the dark house swung open. "I was just coming to get you," Ben said.

FORTY-ONE

For the moment all that mattered was to get the children and herself inside and shut the cold out. Ellen pushed Margaret and Johnny into the hall with her clumsy magnified hands and stamped her feet on the doorstep. She could hear snow scattering around her boots more clearly than she could feel her soles thumping the step. She swayed into the house and fell against the door to close it, and found that she could see nothing but the glimmer of Ben's face. "Someone switch on the light, for heaven's sake," she said.

Ben didn't move. She couldn't distinguish his expression or even his features, just the pale blur which the icy glow through the panes of the front door made of his face. She closed her eyes, because the dim glow was causing his face to appear to shift restlessly. The switch clicked, and the light turned her eyelids orange. She forced them open at once.

He was at the foot of the stairs, between her and the children, one of whom had switched on the light. His face was blank except for an ambiguous gleam in his eyes. "There you are," he said.

She didn't know if he was greeting them or alluding to the light, but she assumed his tonelessness was intended as a rebuke. "I meant to come home earlier," she said, "but I couldn't face the walk without some fuel inside me. Take your wet things off, you two, and jump into a hot bath. You could be making us a hot drink, Ben, while I persuade my fingers to work."

"Whatever keeps you happy," he said, turning away so quickly that he sent a cold draft through the hall. Surely whatever surprise he had in store for the family could wait a little longer—he needn't act like a disappointed child because they'd kept him waiting. She would go to him in a few minutes to make friends with him.

The children piled their outer clothing by the front door and raced upstairs as the kettle on the cooker began to creak with heat. Ellen sat on the stairs and levered one of her boots off with the other, tugged off the latter with her cumbersome hands and then trapped the gloves in her armpits so as to pull her hands free. She flexed her fingers and unzipped her anorak as they began to tingle painfully, and staggered on her shivery legs to lean against the hall radiator. The next moment she recoiled from it, for it was even colder than she was.

The thought of going out again to find Stan Elgin, or waiting while Ben did so, almost made her weep. She hobbled to the kitchen, trying to wriggle her fingers and toes. When she stepped off the carpet onto the linoleum it felt like stepping barefoot onto ice. She tiptoed rapidly to the boiler, only just keeping her balance. Then she wavered, and her heels struck the linoleum. The heating hadn't failed; it was switched off.

She spun the timer wheel and heard the warmth surge through the house, then she stumbled backwards and lowered herself onto the nearest bench. "When did you turn off the heating, Ben? What were you thinking of?"

He was at the window, his palms flat on the metal of the sink. The shape towering outside the window seemed to be in the process of merging with the smaller figures, whose positions looked more symmetrical than they previously had. "Us and the children," he said.

Had he been so preoccupied by their absence that he'd switched off the boiler without thinking? "We're here now," she said to placate him. Hearing water in the bath overhead, she braved the linoleum so as to reach the hall. "Is the water hot?" she called.

"Yes," Johnny and then Margaret said.

"What do you want to drink? Hot fruit juice or hot chocolate?"

"Hot black currant," they responded virtually in chorus.

"That's what I was going to make for them," Ben murmured. "We don't want them going to sleep."

"Coffee for me," Ellen said, and padded into the living room to find her slippers. She eased her feet into them with a sigh of anticipation and held onto the radiator to feel the warmth spreading through it and through her, then she turned and sat against it until the heat was deliciously unbearable. She dug the keys out of her pocket and dropped them into her handbag beside her chair, and marched back to the kitchen, where Ben was pouring hot water into the children's mugs. "I'll take them their drinks," she said.

"I'll bring yours up to you."

"Don't you want to let us out of your sight?" Ellen said smiling.

"Nothing wrong with that, is there?"

"I should say not." She would have stayed with him to prove he had no reason to sound so defensive if the children hadn't been waiting for their drinks. She squeezed his waist and carried the mugs to the bathroom.

Only Margaret's head was visible above the white mound. At the other end of the bath Johnny was brandishing the fingerless wads of white his hands had become. "No need to use quite so much foam in the bath," Ellen said, blowing the foam off his right hand and kissing his fingers before giving him and Margaret their mugs. "Careful, it's hot," she said.

At least the bathroom had heated up, but the landing must be taking longer, because as Ben came in with her mug the room immediately grew colder. He closed the door and leaned against it, which kept the heat in but also made the room feel unusually claustrophobic. "We aren't going anywhere," Ellen said, which prompted him to smile, though he was gazing at the unrecognizable blur of his face in the steamed-up mirror rather than at her. He looked capable of standing there until the children climbed out of the bath. She drank her coffee unhurriedly and collected the children's mugs. "I'll take these down. Don't stay in the water too long or you might find yourselves stuck in the ice," she said.

She thought she was going to have to ask Ben to move away from the door. She wasn't even sure that he would hear her, his gaze was so bright and blank. When he reached behind him and closed his hand over the doorknob, she had to tell herself not to be ridiculous: of course he didn't mean to prevent her from opening the door. There, he'd pulled it open and was sidling around it to wait for her on the landing, which was unlit once more. "Aren't you going to put on the light for me?" she said.

"Do we need lights on a night like this?"

"If we want to make sure I don't fall downstairs."

"I don't want that to happen to you."

"Or anything else bad, I hope."

"Nothing bad, I promise," he said, switching on the light above the hall. "Only wonderful."

She smiled at him, but his gaze was somewhere else. As she went downstairs he stayed outside the bathroom. She glanced up from the hall and saw him watching her over the banisters. He looked nervous and eager. "Try and contain yourself for just a few more minutes," she said.

All the way along the hall she saw the figure towering outside the kitchen window. She switched on the fluorescent tube as soon as she could. The glare made the figure appear to step forwards, and she closed the blinds. They turned the kitchen even whiter, white as the inside of an iceberg. She didn't know why she should be troubled by that, nor by the liquid whisper which had started outside the drawn blinds, growing louder: it was only the sound of the bath emptying into the drain. "Nobody wants dinner for a while, do they?" she shouted along the hall. "You two have been kept supplied with sweets this afternoon, if I know Kate and her mob."

She heard the bathroom door open. "Your mother says you've had enough to eat," Ben said. "There are more important things than eating."

"Close the door, Daddy," Margaret protested. "You're making us cold."

"Hurry up and get dressed, then. Don't keep us waiting."

He really oughtn't to imply that Ellen shared his impatience, but who else could he have meant? At least she was about to learn what they had been waiting for, and that should put an end to this wretched nervousness. She heard Johnny thundering to his room, crying "Eeeyowww" like a jet plane, and then there was silence until Margaret said "Daddy, you don't need to keep standing there. I'll be down as soon as I'm dressed."

"Daddy looks like the guard in that prison film we saw."

"Except I'm here to unlock you," Ben said, and Ellen wondered what he could mean. "Don't fuss at them, Ben," she shouted. "Let the poor girl take her time."

"I'm just putting on my slippers," Margaret announced, and moments later she and Johnny ran downstairs. Whenever Ellen saw their scrubbed pink faces after they'd had a bath she thought they looked heartbreakingly vulnerable, almost newborn. They must be racing down because they wanted to hear what Ben had to tell them, but as Ellen saw him switch off the lights upstairs and follow them quickly and silently she could have imagined they were running away from him. "Anybody for another drink?" she said.

Ben sighed like a wind through a distant forest. "No thanks," Johnny said, and Margaret shook her head.

Ben reached the foot of the stairs and stood between it and the front door. "We'll go by the tree," he said.

He didn't move until Ellen had followed the children into the living room, but then he was in the room almost before she knew it, and closing the door behind him. As she sat with the children on the sofa and put her arms around them, he turned off the overhead light and strode past the lit tree to the window. He'd pulled back one curtain before she realized what he was doing. "Leave those shut, Ben, for heaven's sake. You'll be letting all the heat out of the room."

He hesitated, staring at the reflection of his face, which looked as if it were emerging from the snow, a blurred face half the size of Stargrave. "I thought you'd be able to watch while I talk."

"We'll use our imaginations. Close the curtain, Ben, please."

By the time he did so, the room felt significantly colder. Ellen pushed herself off the sofa and turned on the gas fire, which began to whisper and creak and brighten as Ben went to the chair facing the sofa. He sat back, his hands flat on the arms, his face caged by shadows, his eyes gleaming. He was silent for so long that Johnny started giggling. "Tell us, Daddy," he spluttered.

"I was just thinking how to lead you into it."

Johnny's giggles trailed off, crushed by his father's unexpected seriousness. "If I ask you a question, Johnny, will you trust me?"

"Yes," Johnny said with just a hint of dubiousness.

"Do you still believe in Father Christmas?"

Johnny giggled. When his father stared at him, eyes gleaming, he mumbled "I don't know."

"What do you think?"

Ellen felt the boy snuggle against her as if he was trying to hide. "Ben," she said.

"It's part of growing up." His eyes turned towards her like shifting fragments of the night sky. "What about you, Margaret? What have you got to say?"

"I think you should leave him alone."

"Too late for that. I meant, do you still believe?"

"You know."

Of course she had seen through the myth years ago, and had been pretending ever since for Johnny's sake. If Ellen sympathized with her, did that mean Ellen didn't want him to grow up? "Ben, if this is your idea of a Christmas surprise . . ."

"It's just a way of getting there. I'm trying to make it easier for everyone."

She indicated Johnny. "Then what's happened to your imagination, Ben?"

He sat forwards, and she felt as if the dark had also moved towards her. She was wondering why her question should have provoked him to react so ominously when Johnny said "We were talking at playtime and some of my mates were saying Father Christmas is just your parents buying presents and hiding them."

Either he was bracing himself for the next question or Ellen was so nervous that she fancied he shared her apprehension. "What did you say to that?" Ben said.

"I said I thought I saw you once, at the end of my bed last Christmas."

"Your mother and I thought we might have wakened you, but we decided you were still asleep." Ben sat back like a king on a throne. "Time to wake up, Johnny. You'll be glad you did."

Ellen felt as if she were hearing his words in a dream, they seemed so unlike him. She hugged Johnny, and was about to intervene again when his father said "I remember how I felt when I found out. I was disappointed too, but at the same time I saw that I'd known the truth for a while and hadn't been letting myself realize. That's how people are."

Johnny had to learn sometime, and he wasn't unduly upset as far as Ellen could judge. Ben's next words seemed so poised, so secretly eager, that she couldn't help growing tense. "Why are people, do you think?"

"Like that?" Margaret said. "Because they want to think nice things."

"Rather than the truth, you mean? Do you think we should be afraid of the truth?"

Johnny wriggled, and Ellen loosened her hold on him. "No," he said loudly.

"That's it, Johnny. I'm proud of you. However frightening the truth may seem we have to face it, because being afraid of it won't make it go away. Being afraid only shrinks our minds and makes people invent myths small enough for them to cope with."

Ellen's instinct was to keep quiet, but she felt as though the dark was forcing her to speak. "I don't see what this has to do with Father Christmas."

"I wasn't talking about him." Ben crouched forwards. "I told you that was only the first step. I'm talking about Christmas itself."

Ellen thought she must have misunderstood him, until his unwavering stare made it plain that he'd meant what she feared he had. "Let's discuss your ideas another time, Ben. The children don't want to hear them."

"I do," Johnny protested, and Margaret said "You would."

"Don't stop me now, Ellen, when we're so close. I was just about Johnny's age when I nearly saw the truth, and it's taken me all this time to get back to it. I suppressed what I knew because I was afraid it would kill my aunt, but you aren't like her. You love danger and the heights."

"Not danger that involves the children."

"Call it adventure, then. Try not to interrupt me unless you absolutely have to, all right? It's time to look beyond the myths."

He was watching Johnny as if to prompt him to respond, and Johnny did. "What did you think when you were my age?"

"I'll tell you what I might have thought if I'd been brave enough—I might have thought that the idea of God coming to earth in the form of a man was about as likely as some fat old character being able to climb down chimneys."

This time Johnny's giggle was nervous. Ellen was opening her mouth to put a stop to the subject when Margaret said "You don't have to believe it literally happened. A priest said so on the radio."

"Exactly," Ben said, clapping his hands. "It's a symbol. And symbols are ways of disguising what people can't bear to see clearly."

"I wouldn't say it was that simple," Ellen said, but Margaret interrupted her. "What's Christmas supposed to disguise?"

"I believe it's a symbol of how God came to earth in the form of everything on it."

"Why should anyone be frightened to think that?"

Ben didn't answer immediately, and Ellen found she was holding her breath. The hiss of the fire seemed to intensify, though it wasn't quite keeping the cold at bay. Ben's head turned slowly, scanning the three of them, before he spoke. "What do you think God is?"

"How should we know?" Margaret said. "Nobody really knows."

"Do you think he's an old man with a beard who can be in all sorts of places at once, like Father Christmas?"

The children laughed, and Ellen would have liked to do so. "That's how painters used to picture him, isn't it, Ellen?" he said.

"I suppose so."

"So what is he like if he isn't like that? Could he be a bit like a person whose mind is so superior to ours that we can't begin to imagine his thoughts?"

"Maybe," Margaret admitted.

"Something that was there before the universe was made?"

"Yes," Johnny cried, and Ellen felt him start to raise his hand as if he were in school. "The Bible says."

"That's what it says. But people never seem to wonder what it avoids saying."

"Ben, I think it's time—"

"Just listen," he said urgently, and paused. Of course he wasn't telling them to listen to the hiss of the fire in the midst of his silence, and it was Ellen's nervousness which made her seem to hear another sound, a whisper in the surrounding dark. "If something lived in the dark before there were any stars or worlds, let alone any living creatures," he said, "it couldn't have been even remotely like us."

"I didn't mean he would look like a person," Margaret said.

"But dozens of religions imagine God that way. Why do you think they need to?"

"Why do you?"

Ellen thought Margaret had intended that as a retort rather than as a question, but Ben answered at once. "To help us not to remember what we're afraid of, what the human race has invented whole religions to conceal. All religions are like stories people told by the fire when there was nothing but the fire and stories to keep off the cold and the dark, because people couldn't bear to know what was out there beyond the light."

Both children nestled uneasily against Ellen. "Ben, that's enough," she said.

"No, it isn't. It can't be now." He moved so close to the edge of his chair that he appeared to be squatting, and stretched out his hands as if he were offering his audience the dark. "Ever since then we've believed we've progressed beyond our ancestors because they thought the darkness hid something so alien that they peopled it with gods and monsters and demons, but they were right to think so, don't you see? What lived all by itself in the dark was so unlike us and everything we know that it *couldn't* have created us and the rest of the universe, not consciously, at any rate. I believe we're its dreams, us and everything around us, and you know how unlike reality dreams are. But sooner or later it had to waken, and then—"

Ellen felt Johnny writhe in her hug. He struggled free of her and fled past the tree, which swayed and creaked and seemed to be doing its best to trip him up with its shadows. "Wait, Johnny," his father called in a voice like a gale as the boy fumbled the door open and ran upstairs. "I haven't finished."

"Yes you have," Ellen said as Margaret hurried out of the room, calling to Johnny. Ellen's anger must be constricting her voice, for she could barely hear herself. "What's got into you, Ben? What do you mean by telling them a story like that at Christmas, or any other time for that matter? I think in future you'd better tell me your ideas first so I can be sure they're suitable."

He was still at the edge of his chair, squatting just within the glow of the fire. He looked bewildered by the reaction he'd provoked, and his bewilderment disturbed her more than anything he'd said. She turned away, shivering with rage and grief and undefined fear. She was at the door when he stood up with an odd movement of his whole body, which made her think of a mime of sudden growth. "Leave us alone, Ben," she said wearily. "Give me a chance to patch up the damage you've done."

"I need to—"

"Whatever it is, it can wait," Ellen said, and strode out of the room. The sight of the unlit hall dismayed and enraged her. What sort of game was he playing, darkening the house and then upsetting everyone? When she switched on the light above the stairs, it seemed to emphasize the dark beyond its reach. She was tempted to switch on all the lights, particularly at the top of the house, where she sensed the cold and the silence weighing on the roof as if the night had closed wings over the house. She'd no time for such thoughts now; imagination had done the family quite enough harm for one day. She pulled the door shut behind her and ran up to Johnny's bedroom.

Johnny was sitting next to Margaret on his bed, fists clenched, knuckles digging into the mattress. As soon as his mother appeared, he jumped up and went to stare at the ranks of plastic soldiers on the dressing table, and dabbed furiously at his eyes once his back was to her. "Daddy was just being silly," Margaret told him again.

"Exactly, Johnny. It was just another of his stories, one he shouldn't even have told you," Ellen said. "You believe whatever you want to believe that means you'll have a lovely Christmas."

He emitted a loud sniff and swung round, grinning lopsidedly. "I knew it was really you and Dad who buy our presents," he said.

For a moment Ellen was able to think that nothing else was wrong—that the past half hour had been simply an unusually problematical episode of family life, the sort of confrontation which would prove to have left them with a better understanding of one another. Then Johnny's face stiffened, and the way his gaze edged reluctantly towards the door jolted her heart. She could hear what he was hearing: slow footsteps ascending the stairs.

FORTY-TWO

"It's only your father," she said. Perhaps Ben's footsteps were deliberate because he was taking time to frame an apology, or perhaps he was having to force himself to approach now that he realized how thoughtless he had been. He must be trying to muffle his footsteps so as not to unsettle the children further, but his tread only sounded ominous, soft and ponderous, somehow enlarged. Ellen saw the children shiver, and felt suddenly colder herself. Keep going, she willed him, go up to the workroom. But his footsteps halted outside the bedroom door, and there was silence except for a sound she couldn't bear to hear—the tiny chattering of Johnny's teeth. "What do you want, Ben?" she said.

"To talk."

The children glanced imploringly at her. "What about?" she demanded.

There came a soft thump at the panels of the door, and the children flinched. Ben must be pressing himself against the door, because his response caused the panel which was level with his face to buzz like an insect struggling out of a nest. "Can you hear me, Johnny?" his blurred voice said.

"Yes," Johnny admitted, and obviously felt compelled by the silence to raise his voice. "Yes," he called.

"I didn't mean we'd disappear when it wakes up, if that's what you were afraid of. I only meant we'll change."

For a moment Ellen couldn't believe what she was hearing. She stalked to the door, keeping her fury concealed so as not to alarm the children further. She snatched the door open, slipped through the gap and closed it in a single movement made deft by rage. "Have you no sense, Ben?" she said, too low for the children to hear. "Don't you care what you're doing to them? What kind of Christmas do you want them to have?"

He raised his hands as if he meant to seize her out of frustration. His face was blank. "The kind I'm looking forward to," he said.

She felt as if the air were turning colder, as if he were somehow towering over her though his face was level with hers, but she wasn't to be intimidated. "If that has anything to do with what you were saying downstairs, I suggest you go and write it and get rid of it that way. But keep it away from the children, I'm warning you."

A flicker of bewilderment passed over his face, and he stretched out his hands to her. "I'm here when you need me."

He looked as if he was trying to appear reassuring but couldn't quite remember how. Ellen wanted to hold his hands and not relinquish them until she'd discovered what was wrong with him, but she couldn't let him win her over so easily when she was standing between him and the children. "We need you as you've always been," she said.

"And ever shall be, amen."

He gave her an unsteady smile in which she thought she saw a plea, and she was just able to take the frail joke as an indication that he hadn't really changed deep down. "That may do for me, Ben, but what are you going to tell the children?"

"What they still have to be told."

A shiver so violent it felt like a spasm carried her out of his reach, shaking her head, slashing the air with her nails to prevent him from following. "Don't you dare come near them when you're like this. If you do I'll take them out of the house, I swear it."

287

"Where do you imagine you'll go?"

She wasn't going to argue with him. "Enough, Ben. More than enough, if you want us to stay together. Just leave the children alone until you're sure you can keep those ideas to yourself."

When she grasped the knob of Johnny's bedroom door and held onto it, he shrugged and headed for the dark at the top of the house. "Should be prepared," he was muttering. He sounded grotesquely like a Boy Scout, and she wanted to believe that a kind of reversion to boyishness was at the root of his behavior, that inhabiting his imagination for the sake of his writing had rendered him temporarily unable to appreciate that some of his fancies should be kept from the children until they were older. When she heard the workroom door close softly, she looked into Johnny's room. "Let's go downstairs. It's too cold up here for sitting around," she said.

As the children hurried past her, both of them glanced nervously towards the workroom. He'd better stay up there until the family could trust him, Ellen thought in a fury of dismay at the change which had overtaken their life. She shepherded Johnny and Margaret down to the living room, where the gas fire was cooling, its porcelain creaking as if it were settling into a new shape. She switched on the overhead light, and the tree withdrew its shadows into itself. "Say if you're hungry, you two," she said.

"I'm not," Johnny said untypically.

"Sorry, Mummy, neither am I."

"So long as you regain your appetites in time for Christmas dinner," Ellen said with a jokey fierceness which was intended to conceal her grief. Since it didn't quite work, she grabbed the nearest source of distraction, the remote control for the television. "Let's see if the world's still out there," she said.

She rather wished she hadn't said so. Every channel was swarming with white particles which appeared to be settling into patterns that drew her vision into them. She tried the radio, only to find that it was emitting a sound which sounded like exactly the same hiss of static and which made her think of an oppressively amplified snowfall. When she'd switched off both sets, the silence seemed to blanket her thoughts. She took a deep breath. "Well, what shall we play?"

"That game where we have to draw bits of a drawing and not see what it looks like till the end," Johnny said.

"All right," Margaret said as if she was indulging him.

Ellen went along the hall for paper. As soon as she opened her pad on the dining table, the patterns she'd drawn earlier fastened on her vision. She blinked hard and slowly, and leafed onwards to the blank sheets, two of which she tore out and brought to the living room. "You can start, Johnny, since it's your game."

Johnny found one of his annuals on which to rest the page. He sketched a head and folded that strip of the paper before passing the sheet to Margaret for her to add a neck and shoulders. Ellen was appending an upper torso to the hidden features when she remembered what the surrealists had called this game: "the exquisite corpse." It was surely much older than the surrealists, she thought, but that didn't strike her as particularly reassuring. At least the game was cheering Johnny up. She folded the page and gave it to him so that he could giggle over drawing a stomach. Eventually the page returned to him for the feet to be added, and then he unfolded the drawing.

He was expecting it to make him laugh, and so it did, but not much. "It's good," Margaret said, sounding more dutiful than pleased. While the figures revealed at the end of a game were in the main satisfyingly absurd, this one seemed wrong in a different way. It was unexpectedly regular, as if they had all been trying to describe the same form. In its roughness Ellen thought it resembled a cave drawing, a primitive attempt to depict . . . what? If it had really been primitive art, she would have interpreted it as an image in the process of manifesting itself or of undergoing some transformation. Its stature conveyed an impression of hugeness; the hints of patterns within its outline suggested the beginnings of further growth. Most disconcertingly, the more she examined the face Johnny had given it, the more that face resembled a caricature of his father's, such a caricature that it seemed to be on the point of turning into something else entirely. She was gazing at it when she heard the workroom door open and footsteps descending the stairs.

She hadn't quite closed the door to the hall, and making a point of closing it now would only aggravate the children's nervousness.

Instead she picked up the next blank sheet and began to sketch a face as Ben's slow soft footsteps reached the middle landing. She meant to seem unconcerned so that the children would be. The trouble was that the face she was drawing reminded her too much of Ben's, and when she tried to alter it, it began to look nothing like a face. She felt as if she were calling Ben down by drawing him.

His footsteps reached the hall and paced to the kitchen, and she heard the rattle of the window blind. Her pencil was covering the face with patterns like a tattooist's nightmare as the measured footsteps passed the door again and reascended the stairs. Too much time seemed to elapse before she heard the workroom door shut, and the children relaxed so obviously that she had to ask the question which had been forming in her mind. "Has Daddy been doing anything else to frighten you?"

"No," Johnny said at once with a mixture of loyalty and bravado.

"I was scared he was going to get us lost in the woods when we were playing hide-and-seek."

"He wouldn't have."

"I didn't say he would. Mummy asked if he ever made us scared, if you were listening."

"That isn't what she said."

Even an argument might be welcome now, Ellen thought, if it let them talk out their tension, even if their squabbling chafed her nerves. But the argument trailed off, leaving the silence to mass in the room as the cold had seemed to gather while Ben was approaching. "Shall we have another game?" Ellen said, and tore off the strip of paper on which she'd drawn. "It's Peg's turn to start."

Margaret accepted the page and the pencil balanced on the annual, and stared at the blank sheet as if she could already see an image there. She picked up the pencil reluctantly and drew a head, shading it from view with her free hand. She had been drawing for some time—long enough, Ellen thought, to have drawn more than a face—when her eyes widened as if she was emerging from a trance, and she crumpled the page.

"Don't waste paper, darling," Ellen said, holding out a hand for it. Margaret shrank back in her chair, and Ellen wasn't sure if she was doing so in order to avoid revealing what she'd drawn or because she'd heard the sound which had caused Ellen's voice to waver: the opening of the workroom door.

Ben was coming down again. How could his footfalls sound so large and vague? If he meant to unnerve her, he was succeeding; it must be her nerves which were making the room feel progressively colder. She couldn't take much more of this, and the children had suffered more than enough. His footsteps came into the hall, to the door, and she felt her breaths shake. He paced to the far end of the hall and back again like a jailer, and then the stairs began to creak beneath his soft deliberate tread. As soon as Ellen heard him pass the middle landing she murmured "Would you like to go and stay at Kate's tonight?"

The children gasped with delight, and managed not to clap their hands. "Yes please," they whispered.

Ellen put her finger to her lips and listened until she heard the thump of the workroom door. "Come on then," she said, and tiptoed to the cupboard under the stairs to hand the children their outdoor clothes. She wasn't afraid to have Ben realize they were leaving, she told herself, but she wanted to avoid any argument, which the children were bound to find distressing. By the time they were dressed she had pulled on her boots and was zipping up her quilted anorak with her gloved left hand. "Quietly," she murmured, dismayed to have to do so, and hurried the children to the front door, trying not to let them see that she was alert for any sounds from above. She pushed the strap of her handbag over her shoulder as Margaret turned the latch and tugged at the door, then tugged again. The door was mortise-locked.

"Quick," Johnny pleaded, and clutched his mouth to keep his loud shrill voice under control.

"It's all right," Ellen said, pulling her purse out of her bag and opening it with the other hand—but it wasn't all right, not at all. Her keys were no longer in the bag, where she had dropped them when she'd brought the children home. Ben must have taken them while she was in Johnny's room.

She was struggling not to betray her feelings to the children while her thoughts chased one another—the kitchen door was locked, the windows were, the phone wasn't working and even if communications had been restored it was in the workroom—when she heard a creak behind her, on the stairs. Ben was on the lowest flight, having somehow reached them without her hearing a sound. He was holding up his left hand, displaying her keys beside his pale expressionless face.

All the rage she was suppressing cramped her voice, which came out thin and clear. "Thank you, Ben," she said, and stuck out her hand.

She thought she would have to go up to him. Surely then he would be forced to hand over the keys, unless he wanted to forfeit the children's trust forever. When an expression too swift to read crossed his face, and he came towards her with increasing speed, she braced herself. Whatever she was expecting, it wasn't that he would place the keys in her hand. She almost dropped them, for they were so cold that her hand jerked.

As she turned towards the door, hating herself for dreading that he would change his mind and grab the keys, he spoke. "We'll all go out," he said. "I won't talk unless you ask me to. You'll see."

FORTY-THREE

"We don't want you with us after you locked us in the house. I'm taking the children to Kate's and then you and I are going to have a long talk. I think you need treatment, Ben. Maybe you've been working too hard, but I think you'd better stay away from the children until you've seen someone who can help . . ."

Ellen heard herself say all of this, as though the silence had intensified to a point where her thoughts were audible; she could even hear the sob which she mightn't be able to smother. But she mustn't risk starting an argument now, when she was so close to letting the children out of the house. If she had to pretend that nothing was wrong in order to deliver them safely to Kate's, then she would. She hugged them swiftly and murmured "Not a word" and slipped her key into the mortise lock.

The key hadn't finished turning when she hauled at it to move the door while her gloved hand grappled with the latch. Metal scraped metal, and the door swung inwards. Even the iciness which immediately reached for her felt like a release. When Johnny faltered, staring past her into the hall, she could have hit him; there was no reason to hesitate, nothing outside except snow. "Don't dawdle now, Johnny," she said low and urgently.

Margaret had already stepped over the threshold onto the footmarked marble path. He joined her, but looked back at once. "Daddy hasn't got his coat or boots on."

Ellen gestured Margaret to open the gate. "That's Daddy's problem."

Margaret's face stiffened as if her emotions were too violent or too confused to express. "He'll catch pneumonia if he comes out like that," she said.

Ellen felt grief swelling in her throat and behind her eyes, but she forced it back. "Then he'd better stay at home."

"I'll get dressed if it'll keep you all happy," Ben said in a voice which filled the hall like a parody of Christmas cheerfulness. "I'll catch up with you."

Ellen's grief withered as soon as he began to speak. Did he really believe he could keep them happy when it was his fault that they were the opposite? She marched down the treacherous path as if she were trying to break through the mist of her breath. She was at the gate when he called "We'll go along the common."

Ellen glanced back. He was leaning out of the doorway, his hands gripping the lintel. He looked poised to chase after her. Initially the route along the common would take her and the children away from the houses, but it was marginally the shorter route to Kate's. "Best foot forward," she told the children, and turned uphill.

The house and the snow image swollen by its huddle of worshippers went by, and then there was only an expanse of snow between her and the trees. The forest looked as if it were crouching, poised to move and change; it looked like an explosion of whiteness frozen in the moment before it engulfed everything around it. She had to turn her eyes away, because the depths of the forest drew her gaze, showing her rank upon rank of trees forming from the darkness as if they were advancing to meet her, disclosing shapes which must surely be tricks of her imagination. Now she'd glimpsed them she seemed unable not to see them; if she let her gaze rest on the common she couldn't fend off the impression that the forest was bordered by patterns on the snow, patterns which developed the shapes she thought she had distinguished in the forest. She tried concentrating on the sky, but its blackness was ominously close, not so much relieved by the unsteady stars as emphasized by them. "Doesn't matter, can't matter," she heard herself think, and squeezed the children's hands. Their gloves and hers made them feel more distant than she would have liked, but their trusting grasp helped her ignore everything except the need to see the children to Kate's. She didn't let go until she reached the corner of the allotments and turned along the narrow path above the town.

The view of the streets was less reassuring than she had hoped. The streetlamps and the lit windows seemed dimmer than they should be, and yet there was no sign of mist except for her breath and the children's. "Not now, Johnny," she snapped as he prepared to scoop a handful of snow from the top of an allotment fence. "Just keep your mind on where you're going. We don't want you wandering off the path."

She only meant that the longer grass beside the obscured path would slow him down, but Margaret glanced uneasily at the forest. Her glance seemed to bring it more alive, and Ellen felt as though an unseen presence were pacing them, keeping to the dark beneath the trees. Had Ben sneaked up there? But the presence seemed larger, not pacing them so much as staying abreast of them without moving. It was the forest itself, of course, because now she could tell that the presence was at least that large, and if it seemed vaster and yet somehow contained by the forest, she had to blame her overwrought imagination. Thank God, she and the children were nearly at the end of the allotments, in which the mounds and intricate spires of snow had assumed shapes almost impossible to relate to the growth they presumably hid. Just a few hundred yards and the family would be alongside Church Road, and she would be able to assure herself that the lights weren't as dim as they looked.

Johnny was picking up speed. She squeezed Margaret's shoulders and murmured "Don't slow me down." She didn't want the children straying out of arm's reach, though at least they weren't out of sight behind her. She was about to glance back to see if Ben was following when she realized fully what she was seeing ahead.

The allotments gave way to the back gardens of Church Road, most of which were crisscrossed with deep footprints, carvings in marble.

295

Icicles turned clotheslines into spiny half-translucent insect shapes; toothed slabs of snow overhung the roofs as if they might fall on anyone who strayed too close. That much was normal, but wherever she looked Stargrave appeared to be embalmed in snow and ice. Icicles had massed around each streetlamp, turning them into crystal fruit, and every window was thickened by frost. Where the rooms were lit, the muffled light showed the frost as a glass tapestry of patterns very similar to those she had tried not to see in the snow.

The appearance of the town mustn't matter, nor the silence. She was suddenly more afraid that unless the family kept moving, they would be unable to move for the cold, which was rendering her almost senseless. "Go on, Johnny," Margaret complained. "You're holding us up."

He was shading his eyes with one gloved hand like a boy explorer. "What is it, Johnny?" Ellen said, wincing as the cold twinged her teeth.

"Something funny at the church."

Before she could tell him to move or focus her eyes on it, Ben said "Go and see what it is. We could all do with a laugh."

Ellen swung round and almost went sprawling. He was only a few paces behind her. As soon as their eyes met, he gave her an apologetic smile whose tentativeness made it into a plea, but how could she respond to that when the trail of his footprints indicated that he had been dancing behind her, weaving a pattern of steps in the snow? She was furious with herself for having failed to be aware of his approach. "I didn't mean that kind of funny," Johnny told him.

"You want to see though, don't you?"

"Yes," Johnny said as if he was almost sure he did.

"We'll race there," Ben declared, and was past Ellen so quickly and effortlessly that she didn't realize his intention until he grabbed Johnny's hand and ran with him towards the churchyard, Johnny squeaking and nervously giggling as he skidded along the path beside his father's trail of footprints, which were extravagantly large and oddly shaped. Ellen felt as if panic had kicked her in the stomach. She had to restrain herself from shoving Margaret aside and sprinting after Johnny to drag him away from his father. She would catch up with them at the church, and meanwhile she couldn't think of anywhere

Johnny would be safer. "Let's go and see what the fuss is about," she said in Margaret's ear, and urged her past the school.

Was the pattern of the children's footprints in the schoolyard really as symmetrical as it looked? She couldn't spare it more than a glance, because Ben was already pushing Johnny through the gap in the churchyard hedge and following him through it. She dodged around Margaret, through snow and long grass which felt to her numb feet like a single hindering medium, and ran along the path, shattering Johnny's footprints. She flung herself through the gap in the hedge, dislodging a whispering trickle of snow—less of it than she would have expected, as if it were frozen fast to the twigs—and skated to a halt when she saw Johnny and his father.

They were standing hand in hand among the graves and gazing at the church, which was dark. At first she wondered why the stained-glass window with its image of St. Christopher appeared to be glowing, and then she saw that the window was covered with frost, transformed by it. The boy perched on the saint's massive shoulder and supported there by his great hand was cocooned in whiteness; the girl who was holding his other hand was almost invisible except for the upper part of her face, in which her eyes gleamed with no light behind them. The saint's own face was hidden by a circular excrescence composed of icy filaments, a mask which resembled both a fungus and a parody of radiance and which appeared to be using his arms to reach for the children, and it made Ellen shudder. As soon as Margaret sidled through the gap in the hedge, Ellen hurried her towards the gates which led onto Church Road. "Too cold for standing, Johnny," she called, striding towards him and his father.

It wasn't only the sight of the inhumanly transformed saint which was making her anxious to be out of the churchyard. All the memorials were changed too: the stone crosses had become huge spiky jewels of marble and ice, no longer remotely like crosses; the statues of angels looked as if they were struggling to emerge from snowy chrysalids and reveal quite another form. She found one statue especially disturbing, a figure which seemed frozen in the act of fleeing or helplessly trudging towards the gap in the hedge. Beneath the frost its body was black as a priest's uniform, though its head and its outstretched supplicating hands were wads of white. She had no time to examine it more closely, not when Johnny and his father were heading for the open door of the church. "Don't go in there," she cried.

"Can't I just see if the crib's lit up?"

"It won't be, Johnny." She would have said anything to prevent him from stepping into the lightless interior, because now she was close enough to the doorway to sense how cold it was in there: colder than death, she thought, colder than any church should be. She wanted to believe that she was only imagining movements beyond the stained glass, pale movements at least as large as the window, but she couldn't deny the sight of footprints leading from the church door to the unfamiliar life-size figure near the hedge. She was close to a panic which would either blot out her thoughts or render them unbearably clearer—so close that she had no idea what she would say if Ben wanted to know where she was taking the children in such a hurry. But as she wrenched at the gate to break it loose from the ice which had glued it shut he reached past her and heaved it open for her, causing it to scream.

Church Road curved downhill on both sides of her. It used to look as if it was embracing the haphazard streets, gathering them into an untidy bundle, but now she had the unpleasant notion that it was imprisoning the houses within its perimeter while the cold overtook them. How could the Christmassy prospect of the snowbound lamplit streets affect her that way? Perhaps she was reacting to the stillness which reminded her of a held breath larger than the snowscape, or to the streetlamps which resembled vegetation from another world, or to the sight of all the windows blinded by cataracts of ice. She felt as though the cold were about to overwhelm her, freezing her where she stood, but she mustn't let it do so. She clutched the children's hands with hands so numb they were indistinguishable from her gloves, and ushered the children across the road. "Nearly there," she would have murmured if she hadn't feared that even a whisper would be audible to Ben as he closed the gate.

As soon as she ventured into Hill Lane, the narrow street closed in. The houses seemed to lean towards her and the children beneath the weight of snow on the roofs. Since the buildings at the top of the lane had no gardens, she was close enough to see into any of the downstairs front rooms whose curtains weren't shut tight. Even where the rooms were lit and, in two instances, where the curtains were fully open as well, she could distinguish very little through the carapaces of frost except Christmas decorations hanging immobile against the glass. At least there were people in the rooms, for she glimpsed movements, however slow and pale they seemed—so slow that they reminded her of larvae stirring in their sleep. It was Ben's fault that she was thinking such things, his fault that the further she advanced down the lane, the more she felt as if the presence she had seemed to sense in the forest was behind the houses too.

She quickened her pace as much as she dared once she reached the curve in the lane and saw Kate's house a few hundred yards ahead, where the draped front gardens began. Even the sight of the house made her nervous. Of course, she was anticipating how Ben might react when he realized she was leaving the children with the Wests. She forced herself not to run down the slope with them, because they might fall on the frozen snow. Let Ben think he had no reason to give chase.

As she passed the curve she glanced back. He was halfway down the first stretch of the lane, strolling between the crystallized lamps and smiling to himself as he surveyed the vista of iced houses. Before he could catch her eye she steered the children out of sight, though she faltered for a moment as she noticed a figure at a bedroom window just ahead of her. The blanched face and hands were pressed against the whitened glass as if they were glued to it, and they seemed swollen out of proportion to the dim shape of the body. "Hurry," she said, tugging at the children, and ran with them to the Wests' gate.

She was first beneath the arch of roses, which had sprouted new translucent thorns. She stumbled along the path, her feet aching as if she were hammering them with ice, her nostrils stinging painfully with every breath, and leaned on the doorbell as the children waited by the arch. Their faces were so blue with cold that she pressed the bell again at once. She heard the ringing shrill through the rooms, but there was no other sound from the house.

She was hauling at the door knocker when she realized it was frozen to its metal plate. The edge of the door was glittering dully, outlined by ice. Could the door be frozen shut? Even if it was, surely Terry would be able to open it if only he would come to it, and where else could the Wests be except in the house? "Keep ringing the bell, Johnny," she said, glancing nervously at the shadow which was swelling downhill towards the curve in the lane, and ran to the front window.

Between the orange curtains was a gap as wide as her hand. Through the luxuriant frost on the window she could just distinguish a group of figures beneath the light in the center of the room. They could only be some or all of the Wests; why weren't they responding to the bell? She rubbed at the frost with her gloved palms, she scratched at it with her padded fingernails, but neither action cleared the glass. As Ben's shadow came dancing over the snow, she dragged her keys clumsily out of her pocket to scrape away the frost.

The screech of metal on glass formed a discord with the shrilling of the doorbell, which Johnny hadn't ceased for a moment to press. She had to grit her teeth until they ached while she continued with her task. Her wrist was tiring before she'd managed to clear a crosshatching on the glass, still whitish enough to blur the room. She rubbed the patch of glass vigorously with her knuckles. She was desperate to see, and then desperate not to believe what she was seeing. But now the ragged patch in the midst of the frost was too clear, and she could only stand where she was, paralyzed by the sight beyond the window.

The room she had visited that afternoon was practically unrecognizable. A thick pelt of frost covered the furniture, the carpet, the books on the shelves. Under the light, whose lampshade icicles had transformed into a chandelier, Kate and Terry and the children were kneeling in the space between the chairs. Whether they had done so to pray or to huddle together more closely, she couldn't tell; she had a horrible impression that they had been trying to form some kind of structure with their bodies, or that something had arranged their bodies into a grotesque symmetry. She wanted to believe they weren't her friends and their children at all, or even human. Though their clothes were just identifiable beneath the coating of frost, she couldn't see their faces. Their bunched heads were visible only as a blur within the object which surmounted their shoulders—a globe composed of countless spines of ice.

Ellen might have stood there until the sight and the cold froze her mind entirely if Johnny hadn't tired of ringing the doorbell. The abrupt silence sounded like a shrill echo. "Is anyone coming?" he demanded.

She'd been convinced that nothing could be more terrible than the spectacle beyond the window, but now she realized there was a worse possibility: that he and Margaret might see it. With an effort which made her feel so sick and dizzy she had to grasp the icy windowsill, she turned and smiled unsteadily at him. "Nobody's there. Never mind."

"But you said we could stay with them. Can't we wait a bit and see if they come back?"

The thought of the occupants of the room rising up to greet Ellen and the children, shambling crabwise under the weight of their new translucent head, almost choked off her words. "It's too cold for waiting," she said, and her voice jerked louder as she saw Ben in the shadow of the arch. "Let's get home."

When she pushed Johnny he moved away from the house, dolefully but readily enough. For a moment she thought Margaret was going to be more reluctant—an expression which showed she knew something was wrong had tweaked her mouth—but then, bless her, she walked ahead of Ellen without speaking. Ben had stepped forwards. While the children sidled round him, he stared hard at Ellen. Had he overheard Johnny's plea? He seemed only to be scrutinizing her emotions, discovering the horror she was fighting to conceal. What he read in her eyes sent him striding to the house to peer through the peephole she'd created.

If he let the children suspect the truth . . . She no longer knew what he was capable of. She was taking hold of the children to hurry them away when he turned from the window. He looked apologetic but not even slightly distressed. "Ready to come home?" he said.

She wanted to believe he was controlling himself as she was, for the children's sake, but wasn't he too convincingly unconcerned? What had his expression been when he saw the contents of the room? Her mind felt as if it were shrinking, refusing to accept anything further, contracting around the only plan of action it was able to produce— that she should go back to the Sterling house, because the car was there. "Do as your father says," she said for Ben to hear, and was pushing them under the arch, towards the slope to Church Road, when she saw the figure she had noticed earlier at the upstairs window. Its face and hands were huge now, and she could see that they were frozen to the pane.

Though her hands wanted to clench, she managed to steer the children away from the sight. "We'll go along Market Street," she said in a voice as tightened as her mind. If she kept quiet and did her best to seem as unconcerned as Ben appeared to be, if she managed not to wonder what they might be passing as they walked between the silent blinded houses, perhaps her fears would remain formless, a darkness surrounding the spark of her consciousness.

The family was on the slope which wandered down to the main road, Johnny holding hands with her and Ben while Margaret held tight to Ellen's other hand, when Johnny cried out. "Hey!" he shouted.

Ellen thought his father had caused him to cry out until she saw Ben's puzzled glance at him. Margaret was the first to realize that he was shouting at the stillness of the town. She gripped Ellen's hand as though she was securing herself, and launched her own cry. "Wake up!" she yelled.

Her shout seemed to disappear as swiftly as her white breath. There was no response, no sound or movement within the intricate icy shells which covered every window. "Don't," Ellen whispered, jerking the children's hands, feeling too much like a terrified child herself. The stillness appalled her, the sense that the four of them were alone in Stargrave, but even worse was the possibility that the shouts might awaken some other response. "Save your breath," she said, though the words made her inexplicably nervous. At least now they were at the main road—the route to the car.

It showed her more of the deadened landscape, the deserted square, the darkened shops sealed by ice, the tangles of footprints like a memorial to the townsfolk, preserving the pattern of a dance in which they had participated unaware. But the road led to the bridge and out onto the moors, out to the world beyond. She mustn't let herself start wondering if there was life beyond the moors, which were pale as the moon. Whatever had happened to Stargrave and its people, surely it couldn't have overtaken the world. There would be time for her to attempt to comprehend what had happened when she had taken the family somewhere safe.

She wouldn't leave Ben behind if she could persuade him into the car. Surely he wouldn't stay in the dead town, and surely even in his present mental state he wouldn't try to prevent her from taking the children away from Stargrave. Nothing could, she told herself— certainly not the stillness, even if it felt like an icy presence towering at her back, a presence which seemed to lean closer as she and Ben led the children past the first of the outlying cottages. It felt as if the dead town were rising up and looming over her, waiting for her to look up and see its vast new face. There was nothing to see, and she wouldn't be forced to look, though not looking made her feel as though the enormous silent presence were herding her and the family towards the track to the forest. She needn't be afraid of the forest when they would reach the car first. She forced her numb indeterminate hands to grasp the children's hands more firmly as she came to the beginning of the track.

The car looked like a shell dwarfed by the forest—like a snow sculpture less convincing than the figures behind the house. It would take minutes to clear the windscreen and the windows. She would never be able to conceal her intentions from Ben, and she had to believe that there was no need, that however calm he was managing to seem, they were united in distress. "We've got to start the car," she said.

He was gazing up the track, and his face remained blank as he spoke. "Give it a try," he said in a tone which could mean anything.

"You and the children clear the glass while I start the engine." She relinquished Johnny's hand so as to grope in her pocket for her keys. Her finger and thumb felt impossibly distant from each other and from her as she used them to lift out the keys. She couldn't help remembering how Ben had taken the keys from her handbag, but that mustn't matter now; only driving mattered. She ran to the car and scraped the lock of the driver's door clear of snow, and succeeded in fumbling the key into the slot. Her gloved hand was so clumsy that she twisted the key too hard, then let go of it for fear it would snap. She could feel that the lock was frozen. "Come in the house while I fetch some hot water," she said, quickly enough to keep her shivering out of her voice.

She was talking to Ben as well as to the children, but he stayed by the car. She ran up the slippery path to the front door, where the key skittered over the lock until she managed to control her panic. She pinched the key between her finger and thumb, which felt like a rag doll's, and slid it shakily into the lock.

The dark hall met her with a feeble surge of heat which reminded her unpleasantly of a dying breath. She slapped the light switch and sprinted along the hall, trying to ignore the dark which towered overhead. The faceless guardian appeared at the kitchen window as the fluorescent tube fluttered alight. There was a kettle of water waiting to be heated on the stove, and at least her gloved hand was capable of turning the control. "Don't take anything off," she told the children, "we'll be out again any minute." She couldn't tell if she was hot or cold or if the house was, she wasn't even sure if she was seeing her breath. "Didn't anyone close the door?" she cried, and ran back along the hall, trying to identify the soft flat thuds beyond the door. Ben was punching the windscreen to crack the snow. "Don't do it too hard," she called to him, and heard him say "Don't worry" as she closed the door. She raced to the kitchen again, but the kettle wasn't yet steaming. "Walk about to keep your circulation going," she said, and led the children round and round the kitchen until she felt trapped in a ritual dance. When the kettle began to spout mist, she seized the handle with her fattened hand and urged the children out of the house. Ben had almost cleared the windscreen and the other windows of the car, except for faint patterns which she preferred not to examine too closely but which she prayed wouldn't interfere with her vision while she was driving. She poured a little of the boiling water on the lock and around the edge of the door, and placed the kettle on the snow, which shrank back from it, cracking. She aimed the key at the lock and found the aperture at once, an achievement which seemed like a promise. She turned the key and pulled at the handle, and the door opened with a creaking of dislodged ice. Bending her legs in order to sit behind the wheel was agony, but she had to bear it, telling herself that it would lessen once she was driving, once the vehicle heated up. She poked the ignition key into its slot and turned it, turned it again, turned it while treading on the accelerator, turned it when she'd pulled out the choke. The engine remained silent as the snowscape.

She tugged at the bonnet release and climbed out of the car, biting her frozen lip. The bonnet hadn't lifted as it should, but that was because of the snow weighing it down. She swept the bulk of the snow off and heaved it open, and stared into the exposed machinery. She felt her eyes prickling with tears which felt as if they were turning into shards of ice. Even if she succeeded in unfreezing the electrical components, the vehicle was useless. The radiator had burst, and icicles hung out of it like teeth in a spitefully grinning mouth.

Of course the town was full of cars, but there was no reason to suppose they weren't in at least as bad a state. She was standing helplessly, feeling as if she had somehow let the family down and wondering what she could possibly say, when she felt a cold arm hug her and turn her towards the house. "We're here to stay. There never was anywhere else for us," Ben said.

FORTY-FOUR

It was nearly time, Ben thought. The winter had finally emerged from the forest, and soon it would come for them. Everything around them was a sign of it. The world had been awaiting it without knowing, disguising it as myths to suppress the terror of it, but you had to give yourself up to the terror before you could experience the awesomeness. He'd done his best to guide the family through the process, but Johnny had made Ellen stop him. Now she and the children weren't ready, and it was nearly time.

He mustn't blame them. They hadn't had his upbringing. At least they had responded to his stories, which had been symptoms of the imminent awakening in the forest and of his buried awareness of it—responded so enthusiastically that he was sure their minds were capable of being opened further. He must be patient with them, as patient as he had time to be. Surely now, after seeing so much in the town, Ellen had to accept that he knew best. He moved closer to her and put his arm around her. "We're here to stay. There never was anywhere else for us."

He had to feel sorry for her—she was staring at the damaged engine as though she had been robbed of her last hope—but he thought that, disillusioned as she was, she might be more receptive to the message he had to finish communicating. When he turned her towards the house she didn't resist, which was encouraging. "Come in with us, you two," he said. "I hope you enjoyed your walk."

Ellen grew tense at that. He hadn't intended to sound as if he were dismissing what she'd seen; after all, the children hadn't encountered anything they couldn't handle. He ought to be able to choose his words more carefully—he'd had enough practice—though he found the task burdensome now that he was brimming with the imminence of an experience beyond words, older than the hindrance of words. "We want to talk to you," he said.

Ellen glanced at him, too briefly for him to meet her eyes. He was unexpectedly relieved not to have to meet them, because he had realized he wasn't referring to her. "We're together," he said loudly, and snatching Ellen's keys from the ignition, strode to the house. "We'll go up," he said.

"Do you think the phone may be working now?" she whispered.

So the car hadn't been her last hope. Perhaps there was always one more so long as you were alive. He had forgotten the phone, but he was willing to pretend he'd had it in mind if the pretence would lure them to the workroom, where he could keep an eye on them and on whatever might emerge from the forest. "We'll have to see," he said.

The reawakening of hope seemed to restore her to herself. As he prepared to unlock the front door she took her keys from him, gently but resolutely. He found her determination both touching and frustrating; couldn't she understand that it was irrelevant? She was clinging to fragments of life as she had always lived it, as if they contained some magic which would revive normality when this winter came to an end, but they were only a refusal to accept that it never would. At least she was opening the door, and it was up to him to ensure that was a first step towards acceptance.

"Quick, you two, into the warm," she said tightly, flapping her hands at them as if she were trying to limber her quilted fingers, and pushed the children into the house as soon as they were within reach. Once she was over the threshold she faltered, blinking at the lit hall. She must be wondering belatedly why their house hadn't yet been overtaken by the winter. Wasn't that his cue to explain that whatever happened, she and the children would be safe with him? If she understood that, he could begin to persuade her that they were being saved for last, to complete the awakening as they experienced it and became part of it—but her concern for the children had already preoccupied her. "Don't stand there like statues, take some things off and keep moving," she urged them.

There really wasn't time for this, Ben thought, especially when it would make no difference, but if he told her so the argument would delay them further. He watched her and the children drag off their outer clothes, hanging them on the coatstand and piling their boots around it like some kind of sacrifice to the night beyond the door. It was only when they stared at him that he remembered he was wearing a coat and boots himself. "You could have been trying to phone," Ellen said, her voice uneven and accusing, as he hung his coat on the single bare hook.

"We don't want to be separated now."

Her eyes grew suddenly moist, and he sensed that she wanted to run to him. He wondered what she could be thinking: was she remembering the new shape the Wests had formed? He felt as though whatever was dreaming him was using his words to convey more meaning than he had intended. He'd worked with words for so long that they wouldn't let go of him, but he'd had enough of wordplay; it was time to be clear. "Ready now," he said.

As he climbed the stairs she followed him and shepherded the children after him. He couldn't help smiling to himself as she switched on the landing lights; they wouldn't need those for much longer. He opened the workroom door and stood aside for the family to precede him.

Ellen hesitated once she had switched on the light and stepped into the room. For a moment he thought she'd seen what he had seen: a vast swift movement beyond the window, as if the frozen forest had betrayed its stillness for an instant, though he knew it was rather that the disguise of the forest had slipped momentarily as it or its denizen watched her. But she was only bracing herself to pick up the telephone, praying silently that it would work. Never mind: she had brought the children into the room, and he closed the door and leaned against the inside. "See what you can raise," he said.

He watched her approach the desk, the children trailing after her. From where he stood, the room and the desk and her drawing board and the rest of the contents looked like an entrance to the forest, a last symbolic clutter to be left behind on the route to the truth. He saw that the forest was beginning very gradually to shine, ranks of trees in its depths growing dimly visible as if they or what they hid were inching towards the house. Wasn't there the faintest pallor of frost on the interior wall around the window? Ellen gained the desk and stood staring at the phone, visibly keeping a final prayer unspoken so that it wouldn't dismay the children, and then she thrust out her stiff hand and fumbled the receiver up to her face.

She dropped the receiver at once. It clattered like a bone across the desk until its cord jerked at it, swinging it round with a screech of plastic on wood. Margaret cried out as it fell, and Johnny did when it struck the desk. It was the loudness of the sound which it was emitting that had caused Ellen to lose her grip on it, and at first even Ben thought the sound was only static. Then, as Ellen reached shakily to cut it off, he heard that there was more to it. "Ellen," he shouted.

She had already depressed the receiver rest, but it didn't matter; the sound returned unchanged. It was a mass of whispering, so many whispers that it seemed to fill the room—a sound like wind through a forest, except that it was more elaborate and more purposeful. "Listen, all of you," Ben said in a voice which he heard merging with it. "Hear what it's saying."

Ellen stared uncomprehendingly at him, then her expression became one of loathing. She was trying to pick up the receiver to silence it, her fingers growing clumsier with rage, when Johnny cried "I can hear something."

He'd learned the secret, and Ben was proud of him, though it didn't take much effort to decipher the message—it was rather a matter of relaxing and allowing the sound to make itself clear. "It's calling us," Johnny said, clutching at his mother's arm.

That was why it sounded so elaborate: it was pronouncing all their names at once with its voices like an endless snowfall. Ben saw Margaret begin to hear them, her eyes widening and trembling. Then Ellen managed to seize the receiver and slammed it onto its rest. "What are you trying to do?" she whispered, glaring at him.

He had to speak plainly, he reminded himself. "Give you an idea what's on the way," he said, "so that it won't be so much of a shock."

She looked capable of creating trouble when there was no more time for it. He ought to remember that she hadn't had his advantages —that she'd been confronted unexpectedly with part of the truth when he had been anticipating it all his life—but he mustn't allow her to deny it, even if, given more time, that might have been her first step towards comprehending it. The forest, or the entity it symbolized, stirred again restlessly beyond her and the children, and he felt himself losing patience. "You've already seen more than they have," he told her, lowering his voice to show her this wasn't meant for the children to hear. "Won't you help me get them ready for it? We only saw a tiny hint of what's in store for us, and I know they were your friends, but even so, didn't you think it was beautiful?"

He seemed to have overestimated her. Her face pinched tight around her mouth as if she didn't trust herself to answer him. She glanced past him, so fleetingly that he knew she was considering a bid to sneak the children out of the room. He leaned hard against the door, his body stiffening with impatience. "I'm not saying we'll end up like that," he said. "I don't know how we'll end up, but I'm eager to find out. Aren't you, just a little? You know we'll all be together—they were, you saw." A sudden idea brought a smile to his lips. "If you ask me, I think we just now heard them and the rest of them letting us know they're waiting for us."

He kept the smile up for as long as he could, but when even putting an appeal into it didn't win him a response he felt his mouth droop clownishly. He could sympathize with her for being confused earlier, but how could he express himself any more clearly? Was she deliberately resisting the truth? Observing her and the children, all of whom had turned so pink with the heat of the house that they looked unshelled, he was positive she couldn't ignore it; these raw soft shapes weren't how life was meant to be. She'd had her chance, and he couldn't afford to waste any more time on her when he still had to reach the children. At least up here she wouldn't find it so easy to prevent him from talking to them, and surely at their ages they must be more open to newness than she was. "Have either of you any idea what your mother and I are talking about?"

"Of course they haven't," Ellen cried.

His impatience was suddenly almost uncontrollable, and seemed to twist his body into a new shape under the skin. "Let them speak."

Margaret was visibly struggling to do so, and he produced a smile to help her. But all she said was "Stop it, Daddy, you're frightening us."

"You aren't frightened, Johnny, are you," Ben said, so certain of the answer that he didn't bother to make his words sound like a question. The boy shook his head and moved closer to his mother, looking shamefaced. He hadn't grabbed her arm before in order to stop her replacing the receiver; he had been afraid to hear. All at once Ben was disgusted with the three of them, and with his own efforts on their behalf. "I'm not trying to frighten you, I'm trying not to," he said through his teeth.

The children huddled against their mother. The three of them stared at him. At least he had succeeded in holding their attention, and perhaps they would keep quiet now; they appeared to have run out of words. Behind them the forest stirred again like a spider sensing movement in its web, though of course it wasn't really like that; his mind was simply clinging to old metaphors. "You can't just go on being frightened," he said urgently. "Unless you look at what you're afraid of, you'll never see how much more is there until it's too late for you to appreciate it. I want us to share it, don't you understand? You don't want to be alone with it, do you?"

They were staring at him as though they couldn't believe what they saw or heard. What was wrong with them? "Your mother has an idea what I'm talking about even if she won't admit it," he said, hearing his voice grow thin and cold. "It isn't so hard to understand if you let yourself dream it instead of trying to force your mind to work. Think of it as a story that's truer than anything you thought was true. What's happened to Stargrave is only a sign of what's coming, an image that's simple enough for us to grasp, like a picture in a baby's first book."

He thought they might laugh at that and by laughing realize how accurate it was, but it didn't seem to appeal to them. "If you're wondering why Stargrave has begun to change and yet we haven't," he said, doing his best to put some warmth into his voice because surely this was the moment which would bring the four of them together, "I think it's because the Sterlings have been part of what's happening ever since Edward Sterling came out of the midnight sun. I think we've been left until last because we were already closer to it. Come on now, that must make you feel happier, knowing we've been chosen because of who we are."

"Chosen for what?"

"Shut up, Johnny," Margaret wailed, lashing out at him. "I don't want to hear."

"You won't have to," Ellen promised fiercely, hugging them both and glaring a challenge at Ben, and abruptly Ben had had enough. He was trying to think why the spectacle of the children cowering into the protection of their mother's refusal to use her mind should seem familiar, and then he knew: the three of them were exactly like the brainless woman and her brainless children who'd hindered his return to the family grave and the forest, the day he'd run away from Norwich. He stared at their eyes moist as a cow's and their sniffling raw nostrils in their stubbornly stupid faces, and disgust overwhelmed him. "If you won't listen, you can look," he snarled, and punched the light switch so hard that the plastic cracked.

The forest surged towards the house while standing absolutely still, and its glow reached into the room. He hoped that would draw their attention to the window, because there was certainly something to see: a pale shape which could only be a face, though it was broad as several trees and composed of swarming filaments, had appeared in the midst of the forest. Although he couldn't see its eyes, he knew it was staring into the room.

It was there for the family to see, a sight whose existence even they couldn't deny, but they wouldn't see it until they stopped gazing aghast at him. He wasn't threatening them with violence; it had been frustration which had caused him to break the light switch. Words were useless. He raised one hand and pointed at the face behind them.

312

He stayed like that as a shiver passed slowly through him. The figure which had risen from the forest had lifted a pale hand and was pointing at him. He let his hand sink, and its hand disappeared into the snow, then reappeared as he made to touch his face. The children were sobbing, and Ellen was hanging onto them as though she weren't sure whether she was protecting them or herself. His hand faltered short of his chin, because he'd understood they were seeing what he was seeing: the face breaking out in patterns like frost, like music rendered visible in ice—his own face, which he could see reflected in the window.

It was just another metaphor, another sign of the imminent transformation, but he couldn't quite bring himself to touch his face and discover what exactly what exactly was there. Ellen and the children were to blame, shrinking away from the sight of him in such terror that he was beginning to lose his nerve. He couldn't stand them any longer. They screamed as he lurched towards them, and he thought they might topple across the desk and through the window. He no longer cared what happened to them. He'd moved away from the door so as to open it, to get away from them. He turned his back on them and seized the doorknob, frost flowering across the panels of the door as he did so, and strode out of the room.

He heard the children snivelling as he went downstairs, and Ellen murmuring to them. Let her say what she liked about him if it improved her mood. Soon she and the children would be beyond such reassurances, ready or not. He flung open the front door and stepped into the embrace of the night.

He was stepping onto the track when he heard Ellen turn the key in the mortise lock. He would have expected to hear the bolts, but they must be frozen open. He smiled sadly—apparently his face still could. Try as she might to keep him out, she was only wasting time in being afraid of him.

He slowed his pace as he continued along the track. Though he felt like running to find whatever was awaiting him, he wanted to see everything there was to see, every stage of the metamorphosis of Stargrave. Nothing moved except him, but he sensed that the frozen stillness was aware of him. He went forward deliberately, relishing his

313

anticipation, watching the forest begin to reveal its glimmering depths. Then a tiny sound from behind and above him distracted him, and he looked back.

Ellen and the children were at the workroom window, gazing down at him. The sight of the family, so distant and yet so clear within the rectangle of brightness, took him off guard. Despite their fear of him, he could see that they were still concerned for him. The thought reawakened memories: Ellen saving him on the mountain, Margaret and Johnny appearing from within her in the delivery room, sleepless nights he and Ellen had spent worrying about childhood diseases, the years they'd struggled to make ends meet, the times they'd laughed together because at least they had one another . . . There was no going back to all that, nor to the family itself, but he was reluctant to turn away from this last view of them; he found himself willing them to step back out of sight so that he could move on. Then he sucked in a breath which made his lungs ache, because the cold was spreading swiftly up the outside of the house like flames of ice. He'd taken one inadvertent step towards the building when the whiteness blotted out the windows. The workroom window turned opaque, and the only sign of Ellen and the children was a muffled short-lived scream.

FORTY-FIVE

"Don't be afraid," Ben shouted. "Stay together so you'll always be together. It won't hurt. It won't take long." His voice was dwarfed by the sky, where the stars looked like crystallized loneliness. The house gleamed, a sepulcher whose marble was proliferating, merging with the snowscape. Surely his voice could penetrate the windows, however encysted they were, but there was no response from within. Perhaps the family was too afraid of him to respond, but he didn't even know who'd screamed, how many of them had, or why. "You'll be fine, you'll come through it so long as you look after one another," he shouted, and the stillness displayed his words to him. For all he knew, he might be talking nonsense. He wanted to believe that he was trying to reassure the family when in fact he was trying to reassure himself.

He stared at the workroom window as if the burning of his eyes could melt the whiteness. He'd seen the kind of transformation which would overtake Ellen and the children; the Wests had shown him. He'd found it awesomely beautiful, but what else could he say about it? Only that the Wests were dead, killed by a visitation which appeared to have used their living bodies to construct a symbol of its presence, and that Ellen and the children soon would be—their bodies would,

315

at any rate. It was inevitable, he tried to think, but that didn't absolve him. They were dying because he'd brought them to Stargrave—because of who he was. They would die because his return had somehow brought about the awakening.

He hadn't known it would. Perhaps it had been the trace within him of whatever Edward Sterling had brought beyond the restraint of the midnight sun which had compelled Ben to return in the first place. Perhaps the compulsion of that buried trace to return to its origins had used his yearning for his parents and grandparents to bring him back, to set about sketching the basis of the patterns which allowed the presence in the forest to take hold of the world. The presence was pitiless, devoid of emotion, with no other purpose than to reproduce itself. Now it had Ellen and the children, and they meant nothing to it except as material it could use. The death of Stargrave hadn't appalled him—it was too large a concept to be anything other than awesome—but suddenly this did. He drew a breath which felt like a lump of ice in his chest. "Ellen," he shouted so loudly that he must have been audible on the far side of Stargrave if there was anyone to hear him, "tell me you're still there."

Silence. Stars flickered as if the dark had snatched at them, but that was the only movement above him. He sensed a vast stirring behind him, in or of the forest. "Stay away," he muttered, wondering if Ellen could be refusing to answer him because he'd terrorized the children. "Let me hear you, Ellen, or I'll break into the house," he shouted, dismayed to think that the threat might work.

Dead silence. All at once his words seemed less of a threat, more like the family's last hope. He sprinted towards the house, falling and bruising his forearms, bruises which felt as if he were pressing ice to them. He shoved himself to his feet and ran to the kitchen window. He thumped the glass with his bare fists, not caring if he cut himself so long as the window gave. But the encrusted glass scarcely even vibrated; the sole visible effect of his blows was to disturb the patterns of frost, which flooded back immediately, elaborating themselves further wherever they were disturbed.

He glanced about wildly in search of something he could use to break the window. There was the kettle, an icicle dangling from its spout. He grabbed it from the hollow it had thawed and ran back to the window. He was several feet away when he slipped and fell towards the house, the kettle striking the window with all his weight behind it. Even that had no effect beyond another restructuring of the translucent patterns. The house was impregnable as an iceberg and, he thought, as devoid of life.

The thought came close to paralyzing his mind. He found himself staring at the kettle in his hand as though the dull gray object could inspire him. He flung it away from him, and it landed near the car with a sound like a tinny knell.

He stared in meaningless hatred at the gaping car, the useless kettle, the dent it had thawed in the snow its only achievement. He remembered Ellen using it on the car, refusing to despair, the children staying near her as though her hope could keep them warm. He lunged at the kettle, intending to kick it further away from him, a futile expression of his rage and helplessness—and then he saw why it had seemed to suggest the possibility of action. Even if he was too late to save Ellen and the children, perhaps he had the means to destroy what had destroyed them.

He'd forgotten that the lock of the car boot would be frozen. When he thrust in the key and turned it, it snapped. This further triumph of the ice enraged him. He kicked savagely at the boot until the lid buckled sufficiently to afford him a handhold, then he dug his fingers under the lid and wrenched at it, growling through his gritted teeth. By the time it gave, the metal to the right of the lock bending back all at once with a screech, his fingers were raw and throbbing. They could still close around the handles of the two five-liter containers of petrol and lift them out of the car.

Ten liters might seem infinitesimal compared to the presence in the forest, but he felt instinctively that he needed only to destroy its center, just as the kettle had destroyed the snow. "Only"! He had to try—he had to prove to himself that he wasn't just part of the invasion which had consumed the life of Stargrave. He gave the house a final glance, feeling as unreasonably hopeful as Ellen had been, but it was utterly still. Closing his grasp more firmly around the handles, ignoring the ache which felt like agonizing frostbite, he started along the track.

The forest appeared to be ready for him. As he left the buried allotments behind, the spaces between the trees at the edge seemed to widen, the ranks beyond them retreated stealthily. It felt as if the reality underlying the snowscape were growing more aware of him. He could see layers on layers of crystalline patterns through the crust of snow underfoot—extending, he suspected, into the soil beneath it. He felt as if he were walking on the surface of a mind, each of his footsteps setting off some unimaginable thought of him. How far and how deep might the transformation have reached? He thought of the farmhouses beyond the railway, and glanced back.

The two buildings were so distant they looked shapeless, no more than dark blotches on the snow, but he could just distinguish a lit window in each. The sight felt like companionship. He was gazing at it so as to fix it in his mind when he saw that he must have been mistaken; the window of the nearer farmhouse wasn't lit, it was white as a cataract in an eye. How could it have appeared as yellow as the farther window? He squinted at it, trying to convince himself that his vision had been at fault, and then the window of the other farmhouse, almost at the horizon, dulled and iced over.

The transformation was spreading like negative fire across the moors. Every moment more of it surrounded him. Yet he didn't move immediately. From where he stood he could see the faintest glow through the ice on the workroom window, a glow which wasn't visible in the other windows on that side of the house. He felt as though the winter hadn't quite triumphed there, as though while there was light in the window there would be life in the room. Perhaps the idea was simply the product of desperation, but it sent him marching across the common, clinging to the idea as he clung to the plastic handles. He reached the trees and sensed their awareness of him.

It felt as if the entire forest had turned towards him while remaining utterly still. A shiver passed through him, and then he was calm as death. Nothing could touch him now that he no longer had Ellen and the children. He stepped over the threshold of the forest, and felt the trees close in behind him.

The paths had been erased by snow, the marker posts had grown into saplings of ice. The awareness of him which surrounded him would lead him to its center so long as he didn't lose his nerve. He wished the petrol wouldn't slosh about inside the containers with every step he took—the sound was dismayingly loud, and he thought it was unmistakable—but there was nothing he could do to hush it. "Just a little present I'm bringing you," he said through his teeth, and strode along the invisible path.

The Christmas firs gathered around him, the pines stepped back to wait for him. The trees were almost unrecognizable as such; they were taking on shapes of which their wood was the merest skeleton, translucent filigrees embroidering the cracks of the bark, encasing the slender trunks and rising to the marble efflorescences overhead. He could distinguish so much because the forest was shining with its own light, each crystal of frost separate and distinct. Was he really proposing to spoil all this? "Yes," he whispered. The only light he wanted to see now, too late, was the light in Ellen's and the children's eyes.

Perhaps he shouldn't have declared his intentions so fiercely. At once he felt as if he were surrounded by a multitude of watching shapes poised to seize him. Every tree seemed to conceal a shape which was about to step from behind it or emerge from within it. Panic swelled like ice in his guts, and he couldn't move for shivering. Was this the best that Ellen and the children, or the memory of them, could expect of him? He ground his teeth until his jaws throbbed, until the ache gave him back some sense of himself, and then he staggered forwards as though the weight of the petrol were dragging him. "Do your worst," he snarled, but his bravado didn't reassure him, it only demonstrated how effortlessly the silence extinguished his voice. Now the forest had taken on the aspect of countless legs reaching down from the black sky, or of the fingers of a member unimaginably like a hand, which the infinite dark was using to trap him. He could only head deeper into the forest at a stumbling run. He was across the threshold of the pines now, and felt as if he'd tricked himself into going on. Whichever way he headed, terror would be crowding at his back.

For the moment the forest, or its true nature, seemed content to lie in wait for him. By its pallid light he was able to see the layers of patterns beneath the snow. They were swarming, he saw— transforming as they crept towards the edge of the forest and out into the world. Otherwise there was no movement except the guttering of stars in the infrequent dark gaps overhead.

He no longer knew how cold he was or how much he was shivering. His hands and arms and shoulders ached so badly that they felt locked into position, but he didn't dare put down the containers when that would entail halting. His stumbling body had taken over from his mind. He sensed a gathering behind him, as if the shapes the trees hid were emerging, but he wouldn't look. If it was only his fear which was driving him onwards, that no longer seemed to matter. He could see from the shapes of the trees ahead that he hadn't far to go. Each tree was crowned with an identical sphere like a moon composed of glassy filaments which had engulfed the foliage, and beneath each sphere a white form as large as himself was nesting.

He was stumbling forwards so fast that he was under the first of them before he was sure what the white forms were. They were faces, magnified human faces composed of ice and encased in a shell of it—faces of the townsfolk, displayed like trophies, like decorations in a cathedral where the worshippers had become part of the fabric. There was old Mr. Westminster's face, there was Edna Dainty's. All of them looked frozen in a parody of calm, and Ben knew instinctively that their metamorphosis was only beginning. As he crossed the boundary they marked, another one formed on a tree to his left with a whisper of ice like a thin muffled scream. The process looked as if a swarming of the snow had rushed, or been chased, up the crystallized tree and been caught by it. The face was a child's face.

He couldn't put a name to her, though he might have seen her at the school. The spectacle of her face trapped in ice like amber and transformed into it appalled him. Were Ellen and the children among the trophies of the forest? He stared about him until his eyes trembled and stung, but he couldn't see them. He had to believe they weren't yet there. He was so intent on distinguishing who had been caught by the trees that he didn't realize how close to the center he was until the sky gaped like an inverted pit ahead of him.

A violent shudder halted him. If one foot hadn't been planted in front of the other, the shakiness which seized his legs now that he was stationary would have thrown him headlong, a worshipper compelled to prostrate himself. The glade was deserted, glowing like a moon trapped just beneath the surface of the earth, and he had never seen anything so terrifying. He thought he knew why its emptiness intimidated him: because the glade no longer harbored the presence which had drawn the forest about it to conceal itself. The presence was all around him, wider than the horizon—how much wider, he dared not think.

But that wasn't the whole of his fear. However empty the glade appeared to be, he sensed that it was waiting for him.

Even if he couldn't stop shivering, he was able to think. If he didn't go to find whatever was there, it would come to find him. Any moment now the weight of the containers of petrol would cause him to drop them, and with them would go the last of his resolve. He stared across the glade at the ranks of iced faces, and suddenly they felt like a single mute accusation directed at him. "I'm sorry," he whispered and then shouted, but there seemed to be no difference between the two in the midst of the silence. He couldn't expect a response. He was alone with what he had helped to awaken—alone with that, and with the memories of how he'd terrified Ellen and the children, of the ice overwhelming the house around them, of the dying light in the window. Disgust with himself, with the way he'd treated them and with his present cowardice, blazed through him. "I'm still here," he declared, and tottered forwards, the plastic containers thumping him at every step.

He couldn't help faltering at the edge of the glade. He'd thought the open space was covered in snow, but now he saw that the grass was hidden by a sheet of ice several inches thick. Translucent patterns teemed from the center and out through the forest, layer upon layer of waves like a blossoming of frost, a transformation whose hunger

321

wouldn't be satisfied until it had consumed the world. The remains of the oaks crouched towards the glade like spiny giants whose skeletons were collapsing beneath the weight of their transparent flesh, the pines with their huge new faces crowded around it, worshippers neither human nor vegetable but something new and terrible, and Ben felt the center drawing more of the world into itself with every moment he wavered. Did he really imagine that he could challenge such power? If he achieved nothing more than to declare himself separate from it, at least that would prove he was still human, still the person who would have defended Ellen and the children from it if he hadn't been blind to their plight. If that was all, it would have to be enough. He could see the center, he could walk straight to it if he didn't lose his footing on the ice; what was there to stop him? Only the waves of terror he was suffering, and hadn't he ranted about going beyond terror? He'd expected that of the children, and now he couldn't do it himself. The thought was a fire in his guts. His shakiness couldn't stop him walking. He lifted one foot as if he were stepping into an abyss, and trod on the ice of the glade.

A shudder passed through him and made his scalp crawl. He could feel the patterns moving underfoot, an incessant vibration whose complexity threatened to fill his mind, leaving no room for thoughts. The movement felt as if he'd set foot on the surface of an appallingly alien world. He clutched one container of petrol between his shaky ankles while he struggled to unscrew the cap of the other, then he flung the cap across the glade. It skittered over the ice and came to rest against an oak.

He wasn't sure what he'd thought might happen to it, but it seemed to have demonstrated that he would be safe. He gripped the open container between his ankles and skated the other plastic cap across the glade. The surface was ice, whatever it felt like. He wished he could avoid seeing the patterns racing past him, because they made him feel as if the ice of the glade were drawing him in; they infected him with a dizziness like the beginning of an interminable helpless fall. He closed his aching hands around the plastic handles, the smell of petrol reminding him that the forest no longer smelled of pine or of anything else, and stepped across the last threshold.

The darkness overhead seemed to lower itself towards him. Somehow the glade felt more open than a mountaintop, and much closer to the infinite dark. The glade focused the dark, he thought, which was why he felt as though he were shrinking with every step he took. He was shivering with cold and with a terror he was battling to keep vague, but he mustn't let his feelings daunt him. Another few steps would bring him to the center, and he'd do his best to make the inhuman stillness flinch.

He took one more step on the hectic ice, planting his foot as stably as he could on the surface which he could hardly bear to look at or to feel, and then he knew what he was doing—what he had once again allowed himself to be lured into doing. No wonder he felt as if he were dwindling. He'd let himself believe that he could affect the transformation, but that was only a final illusion. He was returning to the spot where he'd awakened the patterns, so that he could be fitted into them.

The thought shattered the last of his defenses. He clutched at the plastic handles as if they were his only hold on the reality he knew, and shrank into himself, desperate to hide. He had felt himself dwindling because of the immensity which he'd sensed watching him.

He felt as though layers of protection were being peeled away from his consciousness—as though an aspect of his mind of which his imagination had been merely the seed were flowering uncontrollably. He was being watched by something capable of swallowing the stars. More than the glade was the focus it used to perceive, more than the forest which felt for an instant like a single organ, emotionlessly aware of him; the transformation spreading out into the world was itself a medium which the inhabitant of the dark beyond the stars was using to perceive the world. The world and the stars had been less than a dream, nothing more than a momentary lapse in its consciousness, and the metamorphosis which was reaching for the world was infinitesimal by its standards, simply a stirring in its sleep, a transient dream of the awful perfection which would overtake infinity when the presence beyond the darkness was fully awake.

It would have reached for the world eventually, whether or not he had helped it take hold. Even if he could have saved Ellen and the children and too many others for him to bear thinking of them, just by resisting the pull back to Stargrave, in a sense it didn't matter; the vast other was lying in wait for the universe. Perhaps it already occupied the same space in some way—perhaps the existence of the universe was all that prevented its awakening. He couldn't hope to oppose it. The containers of petrol were dragging him forwards to stumble his last few mindless steps, and then he would let fall the containers and himself.

Then a thought, like a spark which was almost too dim to see but which wouldn't quite go out, occurred to him. If he was unable to affect what was happening, why had he been enticed back to the glade?

He'd told the children that they had been chosen because of who he was. In retrospect his presumption seemed worse than grotesque, it seemed unforgivable, but might it have touched on the truth? Even if he was no more than a fragment of the pattern, that seemed to mean that the transformation needed him. He was bearing the last trace of Edward Sterling's legacy back to its kind. No wonder he seemed less than an atom to the watcher in the dark—but all at once that perception of himself was liberating, because it no longer seemed to matter what he did to himself. He was more than a fragment if he could choose not to be one.

He staggered to a halt a few paces short of the center of the glade. Dropping the right-hand container, which struck the ice with a dull flat thump that the silence instantly erased, he dug in his pocket for the book of matches on which Howard Bellamy had scribbled his address and closed his throbbing fist around them.

As soon as he halted, the dark grew more aware of him. The sky seemed to lower itself spiderlike, the entire forest turned inwards to him. He felt like an insect which had roused a carnivorous plant. He'd worried it, he thought wildly, but he hadn't even started. He tipped the open container of petrol towards himself, thrusting his fist underneath it as his grip on the handle wavered, and the liquid spilled with a gulping sound over his legs. When the container was lightened enough for his shaking arms to lift it higher, he poured petrol over his chest and then, closing his eyes and holding his breath, over his head.

Nothing seemed about to stop him. The smell of petrol, and his sense of what he meant to do, were threatening to make him sick. He couldn't stop now, he'd committed himself. He shied the empty container into the trees and managed not to lose his balance as he stooped to heave up the full one from the teeming ice. As he straightened up, the container began to empty itself over his stomach with a gulping which sounded dismayingly eager. He raised it further as soon as he could, and forced himself to hold his arms high until the last drops of petrol had trickled over his scalp. He dropped the container and kicked it away blindly, and opened his stinging eyes to find a match.

His fist had kept the book dry. One match would do the trick. He lifted the cover with a glistening wet finger and tore off the nearest match. He struck it, thinking of the time he'd spent away from Ellen and the children, when he'd sped home to protect them, never realizing that he was being lured to do the opposite. The surge of guilt which overwhelmed him wasn't quite equal to the panic he experienced as the match flared. He shook it and flicked it away from him, and it landed with a hiss.

It sounded as though the ice were mocking him. "Don't be so sure," he snarled, and ripping out another match, set fire to the book.

He knew what he was doing—knew that there was no taking it back. Both his hands caught fire as the matches burst into flame, and he dropped the book between his feet. At once flames raced up his body and reached his face before he could draw breath to scream.

The forest seemed to emit the cry for him. The snow between the trees rose up and flocked towards him with a screech of ice on ice. In the moments before the fire which was himself blinded and deafened him, he saw the swarming patterns reverse their direction and rush towards him as though to extinguish him. He felt the flames boiling his eyes and entering his skull through every orifice, and he thought he would go mad with agony before he died, an agony which felt as if it might never end.

And then the agony fell away from him, although he was still conscious. He seemed to be borne away by the icy flock, lifted into the endless dark. He felt he was merging with the blizzard, but it was more than that: he was expanding like a galaxy. Perhaps his consciousness was doing so at last; perhaps his terror of the presence he'd glimpsed in the forest had been a symptom of his failure to grasp the awesomeness of it. Perhaps this insight was all he could expect, the nearest to a resolution of a lifetime of expectancy he could hope for, or perhaps it was only the beginning.

EPILOGUE

Though the restaurant near Covent Garden was new, it tried to seem older. Beneath the half shell of the pediment, the front door was of stout oak and sported a heavy brass knocker, the face of a jovial chef with a ring between his teeth. Beyond the latticed windows whose panes resembled flat transparent breasts set in glass, a few blurred shapes of diners were silhouetted against a fire. On the pavement by the doorway, one of a pair of blackboards supporting each other and staggering a little whenever the wind found them announced that for the duration of the Christmas holidays, a magician would be performing at lunchtimes and in the early evenings. "We can go somewhere else if you'd rather," Kerys said. "I only booked us in here because I thought you'd have the children with you."

"Why, do you think I'm too old for magic?"

"You better hadn't be. The food's meant to be good," Kerys added, and grinned wryly. "Don't you dare say what you're thinking."

"I was thinking it might be an adventure."

"I've known writers I'm afraid to open my mouth near because anything they hear you say, they'll worry it to death. Not that I want writers who don't care about words," Kerys said, and turning the heavy doorknob, let them in.

The low ceiling of the long dim stone-floored room was supported by new oak beams. Benches composed of back-to-back pews which faced bare tables protruded from the walls. Beyond the ranks of booths a log fire blazed in an open hearth on which the flames made a set of gleaming fire irons appear to dance. On the plaster walls between the pews, most of which were noisily crowded, holly wreaths hung. Everything about the restaurant, including the vaguely Dickensian uniforms worn by the staff, was intended to appeal to a generalized nostalgia, but Kerys obviously hadn't expected the decor to be so concerned to invoke an old-fashioned Christmas. Once they were seated in their booth and the waitress had cleared the places the children would have used, Ellen was silent until the champagne arrived, and then she clinked glasses with Kerys. "To *Christmas Dreams,*" she said.

"And all the other books I hope we're going to do together."

"I hope so too."

Just as the pause grew awkward, Kerys said "Will you want to help promote it, do you think?"

"Try and stop me. I'd be out promoting it now if I'd delivered it in time for you to have it in the shops this Christmas."

"You had to take all the time you needed," Kerys said as if she didn't suspect Ellen of bravado. "Did Alice Carroll have much to say about your coming to us?"

"There wasn't much she could say once I told her how much you were offering."

"No more than you're worth. And remember I said that if you ever feel Ember aren't doing right by your—by the earlier books, you know where they'll find a home."

"I'll remember. Now, Kerys, listen—"

But a mobcapped waitress had stopped at their table, asking "Ready to order?" Ellen and Kerys selected their meals from the schoolroom slates which served as menus. As soon as the waitress moved away Ellen said "Kerys, you needn't be so careful what you say to me. It's been a year."

"I won't if I'm making it harder for you. I didn't know if you wanted to talk about it, to me anyway."

"Why not to you? You're a friend," Ellen said, smiling wryly at the way the roles of counsellor and counselled were switching back and forth. "Besides, talking may help me remember."

"You don't think you're having problems with that because . . ."

"Because I can't bear to think I've lost Ben?" The aching hollow opened up within her before the words were past her lips. "I don't think so. I know I've lost him, I won't ever stop knowing, but I'm beginning to get over it, I'm even beginning not to feel guilty because I am. The children and I, we look after each other. They're growing up."

All the same, they would have liked to see the magician, a young man in a top hat and tails who was performing for three children in a booth by the fire. As Ellen watched he lit a piece of paper on which the eldest had written his own name and then, having reduced it to ashes in the ashtray, produced the signed paper from them. The sight of the children's absorbed faces illuminated by the flames affected her with a yearning so intense that she winced. As the children applauded, Kerys turned away from watching. "How are they taking it, your two?"

"They got over the worst of it sooner. Their friends helped, the ones who were left. Children can bear a lot if they have to. Sometimes I think that's a tragedy and sometimes a miracle. But they don't remember any more than I do."

"Do you want to talk about what you remember?"

"I thought you'd never ask," Ellen said so that Kerys wouldn't blame herself for doing so. She drained her glass slowly, trying to reach into the gap which interrupted her memories, but all she could find there was an image of endless unmarked snow. "I remember it being so cold we thought we were all going to die," she said.

"Everyone thought they had it bad, but where you live is supposed to have been colder than anywhere else in the country, so cold the weather people don't know why."

"So cold that I think it affected our minds up there. Nobody remembers what happened on what's supposed to have been the worst day."

"When the town fell asleep, it said on the radio."

"Radio, television, newspapers . . . The world's forgotten about us by now, thank God, except for the counselling service that came in.

331

Some people still use it, but it didn't seem to do much for me. I'm not complaining." She waited while Kerys refilled the glasses. "As you say, the cold put the town to sleep, but nobody remembers that. I remember waking on the floor at the top of the house with no idea of when the children and I had gone up there or why. We must have been trying to keep one another warm. I don't know how long it took us to disentangle ourselves so we could go to the window. It was frosted thick and frozen shut—it took the three of us to shift it. You might think opening a window on a night like that wasn't such a brilliant idea. The children did," she said, and paused, but the flicker of another memory was already extinguished. "We got it open, and there was the snow, nothing but snow. And yet somehow I knew the worst was over."

She had never understood what she had been afraid to see which had made the sight of the forest huddled under snow beyond the blank common so reassuring. She'd craned out of the window until she had been certain that the air, icy though it was, was growing warmer. "You must have felt . . ." Kerys said, and trailed off.

"I felt as if I was still waking up, because it was only then I realized Ben was missing. So we went down through the house calling for him, and we found the front door was locked. I think he locked us in so that we couldn't follow him if we regained consciousness. It shows how desperate he must have been, to have forgotten I had a key too."

"You think he went for help."

"Nothing else makes sense. He'd left our car when he found the radiator burst, but he'd taken the petrol out of the boot. He must have gone into Stargrave hoping to find a car that would run, only there weren't any. We went out of the house and shouted for him, but I didn't dare go far with the children while it was still so cold and dark. I'll always wonder whether if I'd left them in the house and gone on by myself I might have been able to bring him back."

"You couldn't have left them alone on a night like that."

"That's what I keep reminding myself. Sometimes it helps." Ellen sighed and managed to smile, and squeezed Kerys' hand to cheer them both up. "So the children and I got into my bed and piled all the quilts on top of us, and it wasn't long before we had to push most of them off. We didn't sleep much. As soon as it was daylight we put on all the clothes we could and went into the town."

"What was it like?"

"Not as quiet as I was afraid it would be. There were already people in the streets, trying to find out if their neighbors were all right, having to break in where they couldn't get an answer. Well, you heard about it in the news. Almost two hundred dead, and most of the rest needed medical help. At least that was already on its way because the meteorologists had realized how cold it must have been. The woman who ran the playgroup was looking after all the toddlers, and I left Johnny and Margaret helping while I looked for Ben. That's really all there is to tell."

Kerys' eyes were brimming. "Has it helped?" she said hopefully.

"I'm sure it must have, Kerys, and seeing you certainly has. Now here comes lunch to give my mouth something else to do and let you have a chance to talk."

Over lunch Kerys enthused about *Christmas Dreams* and proposed that Ellen should illustrate a book by a children's writer Kerys had discovered. So that was the purpose behind their meeting. Once Ellen had read the opening pages and learned how much Salamander Books would pay her to illustrate the story, the offer seemed irresistible, particularly since it would give her more time to compose her next book, the story about the man who lit a torch from a star and fended off the next ice age. She and Kerys celebrated with another bottle of champagne. "Next time bring the kids," Kerys said. "You know they're always welcome."

"They'd be here now, but they're going to a pantomime with one of Margaret's friends from her new school."

It was almost dark by the time the women left the restaurant. Taxis packed with shoppers and with festively wrapped packages dodged through the side streets. As the women said good-bye on New Oxford Street, outside a store where mistletoe dangled above the window dummies and a taped choir sounded as if it would never tire of wishing its audience a merry Christmas, Kerys took hold of Ellen's shoulders and kissed her on the mouth. "Give that to the kids for me and tell them I've sent them books for Christmas."

Ellen walked to Kings Cross. Bare trees gleamed metallically in the squares; between the streetlamps the pavement glittered like coal. She felt lonely yet befriended, robbed of the part of herself which was Ben and yet discovering aspects of herself which, while they would never replace him, would at least prevent her from failing. "Happy Christmas, wherever you are," she whispered. The streets were dark enough to let her weep.

She dabbed at her eyes as the tearful lights of the station appeared ahead. She found a window seat on the Leeds train and waited while the carriage filled up. The brakes kept emitting a loud sigh as if the train were impatient with being held back. A minute or so after it was due to leave, it crawled out of the station. Soon it was racing past streets which made Ellen think of glaciers composed of headlights. These streets gave way to suburbs where deserted streets looked scoured by the streetlamps, and then there was only the night and the glow of an occasional distant house like the ember of a fallen star.

She ought to have known she would miss the children when this was the first time she'd left them in Stargrave. The experts said there was no evidence to suggest that the area would ever be so cold again, but she wished she weren't recalling memories she had refrained from telling Kerys: her walking the frozen streets of Stargrave and promising herself that Ben would be around the next corner, that she had only to catch up with him; her asking the ambulancemen from Leeds if they had seen him on the road and then having to wait an endless hour for the team from Richmond to arrive; the numbness which had spread through her mind as she'd seen draped corpse after draped corpse borne out of the houses on the upper slopes of the town, a numbness which had felt like muffled fear and then like knowing Ben was gone for ever . . . She tried to concentrate on the book Kerys had given her to illustrate, and nodded halfway through it and fell asleep.

A voice as large as a cavern wakened her. It was announcing the arrival of the train in Leeds. She jumped down to the platform, the impact jarring her fully awake, and hurried to the car park. The car engine was cold; it kept stalling whenever she had to stop for traffic lights. Night separated the villages beyond Leeds, and then scattered the houses, and stones like houses blurred by ice loomed out of the dark. She didn't know when she had last seen the stars as clear—so clear they seemed to tremble on the edge of a new meaning while they emphasized the night. Of course this was the shortest day of the year.

The railway bridge clenched her headlight beams, dazzling her as she drove beneath the arch. The car swung into the open and up around the curve, and Stargrave appeared by stages: the crags on the high moor, the forest hovering like a spiky earthbound cloud miles long, her tall lightless house, the town itself. Skeins of streetlamps and bright windows led like candles to the multicolored glow of the church. She drove up Church Road to Margaret's friend's house.

As she parked just beyond the cottage opposite the playground, she saw the front door swing inwards. What had happened in her absence that someone was waiting for the sound of her car? She'd thought she might see the children in the playground, but only a wind through the forest moved the swings. She switched off the engine, a muddle of suppressed fears making her clumsy, and struggled out of the vehicle so that she could see past Janet's parents' van.

She shoved herself around her car to the pavement, and saw Margaret and Johnny running to meet her, Margaret in her party dress and new big heavy coat with huge lapels, the hood of Johnny's anorak flapping at his tousled hair. "Are you glad to see me?" she said, hugging them. "Did you have a good time?"

"It was brill, Mummy. The Snow Queen's palace was all made of ice, all sparkly . . ."

"And when the girl tried to save the boy there were terrolls that looked like snowmen that chased her . . ."

"They're called trolls, Johnny, not terrolls."

"You call them what you like, Johnny. Don't you think terrolls is a good word for them, Margaret? Worth putting in a book." She thanked Janet's parents for having the children, and promised to give Janet and her younger brother a treat before they all went back to school. "If you'll excuse me, I'm almost ready for bed."

"I'm not."

"You never are, Johnny." She handed him and Margaret into the car. "Home we go," she said, and drove carefully downhill.

There weren't many For Sale signs, and almost none on the occupied houses. The community was determined to re-create itself as far as it could. She found the sight of so many decorated windows, holly or colored lights or paper angels facing the night, oddly suggestive, but whatever it almost recalled seemed as remote and unlikely as a scrap of a dream. She swung the car up the track and parked by the house, stretching so vigorously as she climbed out that she shivered. She was opening the gate when Johnny cried "Look, a star's moving."

A gleaming speck which appeared momentarily bright as a star was descending from the sky, sailing past the roof of the house. It was a snowflake, one of a number falling lazily to the earth. "Let's catch them," Johnny shouted, and ran to be ready for the one he'd first spotted. "Mummy, I've caught it," he cried.

Ellen saw it land on his palm. When she went to him she was astonished by how clear it looked, a feathery star composed of glass, and how it seemed to be lingering. Margaret had caught one too, but rubbed her hands together quickly to make it vanish. Now Johnny's was a large drop of water which he let fall to the ground. "I'm the boy who caught the snowflake."

"It's just a story, Johnny," Ellen said told him, not knowing why she felt she needed to, and ruffled his hair when she saw his disappointment. "A lovely story, though, and it's ours to keep. But the rest of our lives will be our best story of all."

A wind like a whisper of agreement passed through Sterling Forest as she ushered the children towards the house, and a few more snowflakes fell. They hadn't really taken longer to melt on the children's hands than they should have, she told herself. She unlocked the front door and switched on the hall light, and thought how to cheer Johnny up. "Next year if you like we'll see about making a path all the way through the woods," she said, and followed the children into the house, where the tree from the forest was waiting. She breathed in the warmth and the scent of pine, and murmured something like a prayer, too low for the children to hear. "Let this be the Christmas we missed," she said.